# I Surrender All

'Lissa,
Hope you enjoy?!
Love you!
Ch—

Lissa,
I got you an inlay!

# I Surrender All

*Your Destiny Has Always Been Your Own, Surrender All
And Seize Your Moment to Shine*

CHANDA TOLBERT

iUniverse, Inc.
Bloomington

**I SURRENDER ALL**
Your Destiny Has Always Been Your Own, Surrender
All And Seize Your Moment to Shine

Copyright © 2012 by Chanda Tolbert.

All rights reserved. No part of this book may be used or reproduced by any means, graphic, electronic, or mechanical, including photocopying, recording, taping or by any information storage retrieval system without the written permission of the publisher except in the case of brief quotations embodied in critical articles and reviews.

This is a work of fiction. All of the characters, names, incidents, organizations, and dialogue in this novel are either the products of the author's imagination or are used fictitiously.

iUniverse books may be ordered through booksellers or by contacting:

iUniverse
1663 Liberty Drive
Bloomington, IN 47403
www.iuniverse.com
1-800-Authors (1-800-288-4677)

Because of the dynamic nature of the Internet, any web addresses or links contained in this book may have changed since publication and may no longer be valid. The views expressed in this work are solely those of the author and do not necessarily reflect the views of the publisher, and the publisher hereby disclaims any responsibility for them.

Any people depicted in stock imagery provided by Thinkstock are models, and such images are being used for illustrative purposes only.
Certain stock imagery © Thinkstock.

ISBN: 978-1-4620-5741-2 (sc)
ISBN: 978-1-4620-5742-9 (ebk)

Printed in the United States of America

iUniverse rev. date: 01/19/2012

To my precious daughter, Jaila Amani—
My definition of a perfect love . . . Thank you for giving me life.

My Special Dedication: For the Real Men, Real Fathers in my life— thank you for our very special and personal relationship . . . may you all rest in peace.

Elder Edgar White, Kenneth E. White, Marcus S. White, and Kristopher C. Miller

# Acknowledgements

FIRST, I'D LIKE TO THANK Judy Arginteanu for her tireless work and dedication to this project. As a first time novelist, her patience with the editing and corrections of this novel were truly a Godsend. *"What a Trooper!"* Thank you Judy, for making my dream, a reality.

I would also like to thank Tracy Jones for his incredible work on the cover art. Your phenomenal artwork embodied exactly what I was feeling when I came up with the cover concept. Thank you Tracy, you are a wonderfully gifted artist.

To Michele Spaise, my personal photographer. Your work is awesome! Thank you for your time, your love and your *amazing* grace. I love you!

To my family, friends, and loved ones; I can honestly say that I am blessed to have all of you in my life; you have given me love, understanding, and patience. Thank You!

A special thank you to my baby brother, Raydell Reid. You have always been there for me, as my confidant, my protector, my friend, I love you more than you know.

To my mom and dad, thank you for raising us with love, and providing us with the best life possible. I am so grateful.

To my grandmother, Lavada White, thank you for teaching me about the love of Christ. "Train up a child in the way he should go: and when he is old, he will not depart from it." Proverbs 22:6 I love you grandma.

To Pastors Ralph and Alika Galloway, and the entire Kwanzaa family, you have no idea how your love and prayers kept me sane during the most trying time in my life. Thank you, I love you all.

Special thanks to Pastor Alika for taking the time to write the forward for this book, I am so grateful as well as honored. You have meant so much to me as my Pastor, my mentor, and my friend. There are no words great enough to express what I feel about you.

Lastly, and certainly most importantly, I'd like to thank God for his constant presence in my life, for the messages, the blessings and the undying love. Thank you Lord, most of all for the gift of life, and my ability to share it with all of you.

> "In all thy ways acknowledge him, and he shall direct thy path."
>
> Proverbs 3:6

# Forword

> *The summit of happiness is reached when a person is ready to be what she is....*
>
> *Erasmus*

CHANDA ... IS READY TO BE who and what she is! In her compelling, thoughtful God inspired book Chanda tells the world who and what she is, and who and what God has called her to be. She is bold and honest and transparent, all adjectives used to describe someone who is filled with Gods Spirit, and driven to a place of Spirit filled transformation. When one is willing to tell the truth to oneself and to the world, then one is ready to be free. Scripture is clear ... It is the truth that sets a person free. Chanda is free indeed. Just listen to her as she states:

> *"I want the freedom to be exactly who God created me to be, the freedom to live this life without prejudice or guilt. But most of all I want the courage to stand up and have all of that."*

Once in an interview Maya Angelou was asked "What is the greatest virtue?" Without hesitation Dr. Angelou replied courage. She went on to say that without courage one cannot love, hope, nor dream nor accomplish anything with nobility and honor. Chanda has courage! She captures the reader's attention with her courageous story of redemption and struggle and failure and recovery. This is a story not for the faint-hearted if you are looking for what true courage is—you will find it here. If you are afraid to look at your own life you will find the courage to do so within these pages—if you know someone who needs to but is looking for the way—God has provided the perfect tool.

> *"I believe true happiness comes from a place of absolute peace and contentment with one's present situation. A place where life may not be perfect, but you live perfectly in the moment"....*
>
> Chanda

All the way through the New Testament Jesus speaks peace—not as the world brings it, but beyond the worlds capacity to do so. Chanda Tolbert is a woman filled with peace, a peace that passes all understanding. The peace that sees possibility in failure and the peace that has brought her hope and a fearless determination to use all that God has given her to transform her own life and others.

I for one am grateful to my sister for her gifts of wisdom, creativity, thoughtfulness, kindness, compassion and truthfulness. Her story is the story of someone allowing God to pick up the broken pieces of one's life and make them over. God has given Chanda a testimony for her tears and power for her pain. And she in turn has given them to us through her life, her story and her testimony. *Thanks be unto God!*

*Pastor Alika Galloway,*
*co-pastor Kwanzaa Community Church,*
*Minneapolis, MN*

# Chapter 1

"Shit." Jasmine squinted and thought. "*Them damn curtains.*"

The iridescent gold and brown silk curtains she had bought from Ralph Lauren last summer always closed completely, thanks to the custom stitching and weighted bottoms. But the awkward crease the cleaners had left allowed the sun to just slip through the small opening, enough to awaken her three times last week. And she was so tired.

*Not again.*

She threw back the covers and swung her feet to the floor.

"Ooooh, I hate mornings." And even though she had one of the worst hangovers ever, she knew she better get up and get to church. It was six forty-five a.m. and church started at nine.

"*Damn, I got to make moves.*"

This was a difficult morning for Jasmine; different from any other Sunday morning she had after a night out with her girlfriends. The pounding in her head was getting stronger, and the blurred memories of the previous night's escapades were beginning to resurface, but Jasmine did everything in her power to keep them down. She had only gotten home at two-thirty, so with four hours of sleep, it was hard to focus. But she knew she couldn't miss church.

# Chapter 2

WHEN MY GRANDFATHER, ELDER EDMOND Wallace was ordained as a pastor, the strength of his character, and the power of his oratory made him a magnificent speaker as well as a compassionate servant of the lord. He was a generous man who shared his graciousness with everyone he met. He started our church, New Jericho, Our Church of God, on the south side in Minneapolis, to save souls and solidify his place in heaven.

My grandmother, missionary Vera Wallace, was small in stature but a gigantic force in the eyes of God; she was the mastermind behind the dynamics of the church, who made most of the decisions about direction and growth. After all, she was the *first lady*, a title that carried its own special perks and duties, mainly that of the enforcer.

My mother Bernadette, my uncles, Keith, Cordell, and Darrin and my aunt Denise were the first members of the church—and I, being the oldest grandchild, became the first of the next generation of soldiers in the army of the Lord. Whether I wanted to or not, I was saved, baptized and inducted into life as a child of God.

When my mother and father divorced I was five years old; my brother was two. My mother kept us through the week, and my father picked us up on the weekends. My father, Wes, worked as a driver for UPS, and my mother worked for L.E.A.P., a small nonprofit organization affiliated with the Urban League. They both instilled in us the importance of hard work, but because my mother's job often kept her late, my brother and I ended up at our Grandma Vera's way later than we expected. And it was those nights that we got a real taste of heaven, literally. The church was our second home, and we hated it.

My grandparents were Christians. Pentecostal Christian to be exact; a Christian so Christian that wearing makeup, or even fingernail polish, was a no-no; pants or open-toed shoes without nylons (regardless of the outside temperature) got you a harsh stare, and blouses that allowed any amount of cleavage were out of the question. Try it, and you'd be sent to your room immediately to change. If you talked back or disrespected anyone older than you, you might as well have picked up your ticket to Hell, do not pass go, do not get to see the Savior.

These minor infractions were just small things that "saints" (the holier than thou members of the church) talked about, and over time they were usually forgotten. But sometimes there were sins that were considered so bad that you had to do a different kind of penance to get yourself off the hook, a more formal one in front of the congregation to show you were truly, deeply sorry.

It was a Sunday like any other, except that my entire family was visiting another church—for whatever reason, we visited other churches quite often. The pastor called on one of the young ladies in the congregation to come up front to present herself before us. I remember the young girl, about fifteen, saying she didn't know what to say, and she refused to move from her seat. We watched. The pastor persisted; she resisted. But she finally approached the pulpit after her mother encouraged her, telling her she'd help her get through it. The girl still didn't know what to say, she finally mumbled an apology to everyone who sat waiting and watching.

None of us really knew what was going on until she headed back to her seat and I noticed she was pregnant.

Oh my God, they forced her to repent in front of everyone, like she was on trial, like something from the witch-hunt in Salem. Damn . . . how embarrassing.

For the rest of my teenage years, I never strayed, and made damn sure I didn't do anything that would cause that sort of reprimand. To this day, that experience haunts me, and what that young girl endured, conflicted me about going to church and being close to God.

That was the way I was brought up. Back in the day, no one's family was excluded—or immune—from church life. Churches were run like businesses, all a part of a large religious conglomerate. Even our church; we were one of many that reported not only to God, but also to a sect more prominent than our own.

Reigning over all the churches were bishops, statewide and nationally, who ordained the pastors and reverends under their jurisdiction to run the churches. The pastors or reverends appointed members of the church to carry out specific duties. There were ministers, deacons, missionaries, elders, and a host of other titled people who helped run the church and helped the members of their congregation. Of course, us PKs (preacher's kids) were forced into taking positions.

I was in the choir, which practiced Thursday nights and Saturdays. I was an usher—we had meetings every Sunday after church—and I also taught Sunday school, which meant I had to be at church every Sunday by nine a.m. That's what my grandmother wanted me to do, so I did it, I did it all, and there was no way I would or could refuse.

My mother's job was an important one; she was the secretary/treasurer, so she also had to be there every Sunday to collect the money, count it, and make sure it got recorded and deposited. She never missed a Sunday and never complained.

But my uncle Darrin had the best job of all by far. He was the piano/organ player and the self-proclaimed "church pimp." Our church didn't have very many members, but the few we did have were mostly women—single women, who unintentionally gave uncle Darrin his second job, which over time became his main job. Uncle Darrin had a way with women, his charismatic style, and his infectious laugh made women flock to him. Not to mention he was handsome and cool.

The women at the church, as well as the women he met outside the church, would pretty much do anything to get next to him, even if it meant giving him money to do it. They would constantly call him; I knew that because he lived with us for a while and he forced me to answer the phone. "Uncle Darrin, are you here?" "No I ain't here." "He said he ain't here." And for whatever reason they fell for that. They chased him and vied for his attention at all costs; sometimes literally paying the price (he accepted check or cash). Either way he got what he wanted, and so did they.

It was funny—all Uncle Darrin had to do was play. He was like the Pied Piper or something; the music had all of us sprung. When we heard the music that flowed from his fingertips, no doubt a gift from God, it was hard to believe everything he played, he played by matching up the keys of the piano with the key of the voice he was listening to. He didn't know how to read a note, but with the anointing from God he could control the whole church.

Looking back, I think he used this gift to mesmerize the entire congregation; a lot of the time he was bored and he would purposely play "shouting music" just to see the congregation get happy and shout. (Shouting was a quick-footed dance step that the members of the church did when the Holy Ghost entered the sanctuary. This dance truly mastered only by the elderly ladies of the church, it was a way to praise the Lord and give thanks for all your blessings.) Uncle Darrin had the power; he even had family members jumping and shouting up and down the aisles—and we knew his game. I would just look at him and laugh; he would smile, give me a quick wink, and just keep playing.

\* \* \*

The whole experience was really funny as I thought about it now, but as a kid it felt like torture. We were supposed to go to church all the time, and like it. Service would last all day long and there was nothing you could do about it, just sit there and be quiet—oh, and you better not fall asleep that might have gotten you a pinch or a flick in the head. (I never really got any of those, but my brother and cousins did.) The all-day service never ever bothered the saints; it was what they called tarrying, when you sat with God and just chilled, I guess.

My other uncles and aunt escaped by growing up; they hardly ever came anymore after they were grown and out of the house. Back then, that was the only way to get out of the church, grow up and move out. And sometimes that still wasn't good enough. They'd still get phone calls from my Grandma chastising them for not being in the church

As I got older and moved to my college campus, being away from home, even though it wasn't very far, changed the dynamics of my church life as well. Between classes, partying, and more classes, I figured going to church could wait. Going to church was a chore, and one I could now choose to no longer do—after all I was studying to be a lawyer and what was more important than that?

So I never went and neither did any of my other family members, everyone quit going.

Except for uncle Darrin, who went every Sunday. It was almost blasphemous—he always bragged about never missing a Sunday, and continued to show up and play, but we all knew the real reason: He was getting paid, and nothing was going to keep him from that paycheck.

My grandparents were very proud people, so when their entire family rebelled against the church it made for an uncomfortable situation whenever we got together. My grandmother always let it be known that she was disappointed in all of us. Sometimes she was subtle about it, but most of the time she didn't hesitate to tell us how unhappy it made her and how unsaved it made us.

Grandma Vera had so successfully mastered the art of guilt transfer it was almost unbearable. We tried our best to do and say things to calm or appease her. If one of us missed a service or planned an evening out for New Year's Eve, she reminded us of the wrong were doing and left us to wallow in a pool of guilt and shame. When we tried to explain, she sent us on a ride that never ended, convincing us that everything in our life that wasn't quite right was because you were not in the church. So when we approached her, we usually kept the explanation to ourselves, and presented her with gifts—cash was usually her preferred method of restitution. I think in spite of all the grief we suffered, she was deeply hurt to live to see that none of her children, or even her grandchildren, ended up being a missionary, or a pastor, or something prophetic.

And we felt the grief, believe me. I always felt I had let my grandparents down because I didn't immerse myself in the church, but I tried to get involved at least on Sundays to try to give them a little joy. It was sad. We were slowly killing them spiritually, but even though all their children turned out to be less than what they expected in Christ, they never stopped loving us and praying for us.

Sometimes, I hoped my career as a successful lawyer could somehow replace my grandmother's need for me to be a missionary, and I knew that at times she was very proud of my accomplishments.

But I still felt that my grandmother would have loved nothing more than to see me on the pulpit swaying back and forth, preaching the word of God. After all, she had groomed me for it, and she hoped—expected—me to come around, her own little evangelist.

I was eight when I first got saved; I remember how my grandmother made a point to keep me close. By twelve, I had become my grandmother's little evangelist protégé and the family's savior. I remember when I read a paper in front of the congregation about the chapters we had studied for the week; my grandmother told everyone about the message and bragged about how good it was; she actually believed that that one paper meant I was going to be a preacher, and that someday her little grandbaby would stand before the masses, teaching and preaching the word of God. But I chose college and law school, so those wishes for me were forever buried under a rising tide of textbooks and student loans.

\* \* \*

In those days, there were no visible millionaire preachers, like the incredible Bishop T.D. Jakes and the anointed Dr. Creflo

Dollar, these two preachers had changed the game as well as that notion of the lowly, impoverished Christian pastor like my grandfather, who struggled to make ends meet while battling to win souls for Christ. These new-age preachers spoke of prosperity and sustainability, which they themselves had achieved, as was apparent by their mega-churches and nationally televised ministries. But that was long after I had made my choice, and I knew there was no way I was going to make the kind of money and live the kind of lifestyle I was determined to live by being a preacher.

Sitting on the edge of the bed that Sunday morning, I wondered: What if I made a colossal mistake? Was I supposed to be preaching? My life right now is so far away from what God wanted, was I too far gone to come home?

After last night, I thought maybe I was.

# Chapter 3

Every weekend the girls and I partied, and it wasn't an ordinary party. We made it a never-ending, bona fide "all-out party over here, y'all." I did appreciate what my grandparents had taught me, but I still had to work out that flesh thing—what would Jesus do over what my body wanted to do; hadn't quite worked that part out yet.

But even with the excessiveness of our weekend antics, I made a promise to myself after I graduated from college, no matter what: That I would be bound to the promise of remaining close to God and the church.

Maybe I made that promise because I felt like I was blessed and protected by the prayers of my grandparents and wished to one day make them proud. I knew they were proud of me for being a good attorney, but I wanted them to be proud of me for my walk with Christ. So if I attended church at least on Sunday mornings, it would be like a form of restitution; maybe if I set foot in the holy house on occasion, some of the partying I did through the week could be left at the altar.

Still. Shit, some of the things my girlfriends and I did on Friday and Saturday nights—there was no telling how I was going to make it to that glorious place everyone in the church was literally dying to go to. As a young girl, I remembered at funerals everyone always talked about this heavenly place of rest where there was no crying, no dying, no war, no pain. I just never understood why you had to die to get there.

\* \* \*

Church back then always started at eleven a.m., and lasted almost until 3, because of the several offerings taken and the long-winded preacher who, at the end of his sermon, always had an altar call. But as times changed and churches became more relaxed the old ways were set aside. The dress code eased up and the hours spent worshipping together changed as well. Churches began to start services at nine a.m. for those who wanted to get out earlier. I was one of the ones who opted for the earlier time. It was supposed to just lighten up the afternoon services so the sanctuary would not be so packed, but it ended up just filling up the first service: Everyone wanted to get out early, the men so they could get home to watch whatever sport was in season, and the women for down time at home. It didn't empty the eleven o'clock service; it just provided seats for everyone.

The nine a.m. service had to be done by ten-thirty, so the regular eleven o'clock service could start on time. I loved getting home from church by ten-thirty because it gave me enough time to unwind; I really needed that time, to be ready for my usually crucial Monday mornings, which involved the senior associates meeting, and a debriefing about upcoming cases immediately following. An hour and a half of church instead three and a half hours? Shit, I loved that. I knew it wasn't exactly the way to think, but I didn't care, I wanted to do other things on Sundays. Plus always being hung over made it real hard to sit for too long.

I lay back again and stared at the ceiling. *Pull yourself together and get moving.*

I shook off the cobwebs and tried to stand up; but the nauseous feeling welling up in my stomach was stronger than my will to get up.

*I can't miss church.*

I stood and tried to walk.

I stood up quicker than I realized, making the room spin even faster, and the leftover taste of last night's vodka martinis surged into my mouth and I couldn't hold it. I ran to the bathroom, and wondered if I should go head first, or tail first? I really had to pee, so tails won.

I held my breath and tried not to vomit—I hated to throw up—and quickly sat down, anticipating the relief that was sure to come. *Whew.*

As the smell of urine rose from the bowl, I tried to remember what took place just hours before. But my splitting headache and parched throat made it hard to concentrate on much of anything, much less recall much about our night of insanity, but I knew we had fun.

I sat there a moment and tried to collect myself. *This is crazy.*

I stood up—slowly this time—and took another deep breath.

"Please don't vomit." I spoke to my stomach and throat as if they were human; it seemed as though this time—for a change—they listened.

I walked to the sink to wash my hands and laughed out loud when I saw the four different club markers that decorated both my hands. *Damn!*

I squinted at my reflection. I stared at my face, something I never enjoyed. I always made a point to wash my face in the shower because of all the things I hated about my face and skin. Now I had made the mistake and looked too deeply.

The raccoon mask from smeared mascara I consistently wore, and the bags under my eyes, which were bigger and baggier than usual, always seemed to overshadow the almond-shaped, cocoa brown irises I had been born with. My eyes were my one feature I liked and trusted; all the other parts of my body had betrayed me at one time or another, but my eyes usually stayed truthful. And I always looked deep into other people's eyes to get from them what they were really about. Good or bad, eyes never lied.

But this morning what I saw made me cringe. Things in my eyes didn't look just right, in fact I had never seen that look in my eyes before and it frightened me.

I grabbed a washcloth from the bureau and tried to not only wipe away some of my worst features but some of the guilt that was overwhelming me as well.

I looked in the mirror again, hoping to see something different; it didn't work. What I saw was cynicism and sadness.

Neither the dulled look in my eyes nor the guilt that had settled on my face disappeared; it only made the pain of my guilt-ridden conscious worse.

Man, it hurt. But, shit, what could I do? That was what going to church was all about, right? Renewing your relationship with God, repenting and starting over.

I realized the lie I lived would eventually catch up with me, but I had time, right? I was young; I had my whole life ahead of me. I had always heard that God was a merciful and forgiving god, but sometimes I wondered if he got tired of me coming to the altar *every* Sunday crying, repenting and asking for another chance. I sincerely hoped my luck wouldn't run out. But what if it did? Oh well.

# Chapter 4

GROWING UP, I PRIDED MYSELF on being a quiet, unassuming girl who never caused trouble or interfered in anyone else's trouble. The way it was for me, vanity and arrogance were never practiced openly, and meekness and modesty were praised. It sort of caused me to lose sight of who or what I was capable of being.

Without that confidence, it most affected me in the looks department. I never considered myself beautiful, just average—average face, way average body. Other people sometimes found beauty in me, and when they complimented me, I tried to thank them, but usually I just bowed my head and said, "Yeah, right." I never meant to downplay my sense of self-worth, but the humility—at all costs—that was drilled into me made me gravitate to that self-deprecating mode. It didn't seem to affect my brother—he would flamboyantly talk up his good looks, and so did my uncles Keith and Darrin. But I saw it as bragging, something I couldn't—or should I say, wouldn't do.

Except when I hung out with my Aunt Denise—-she was the coolest. She was the youngest child of my grandparents and we were very close, even though she was twelve years older. I remember the two of us, with our Care Free Curls freshly done, staring at ourselves in the mirror chanting and laughing over and over, death before deformity. We were insane, but it was one time in my life I felt like I looked like something.

\* \* \*

I had problems with so many things about my body. I tried to overlook them most of the time, but sometimes it would get the best of me.

My skin was one problem. It was a nice caramel color, but I was relentlessly plagued with outbreaks of acne that appeared at the most inopportune times. Like the big zit on my forehead right before prom and the whiteheads that would form every time I ate chocolate. To make matters worse, even though I knew it was a bad habit, I would pick and poke at my face, which led to dark spots and scars. Long after most people had grown out of these problems, they still plagued me; I finally went to a dermatologist, who prescribed a special regimen, which eventually worked.

My body was a completely different issue. I was also very self-conscious about it. I had long legs. They were nice, thicker than I ever cared for, but nice, I guess. In high school I won second place for nicest legs contest. It didn't get my picture into the yearbook, but it felt good to know someone had noticed them.

I also had a self-proclaimed problem with my butt. My butt was the family curse—from having a little too much "Indian in the family," a comment I stole from a Native American comedian.

Our butts kind of resembled flattened bicycle tires, not completely flat, but damn close. It poked out a little, giving my backside some shape, but nowhere near what I felt my fair portion should be. Singers like Beyoncé and Jennifer Lopez had way more ass than they needed, I just wanted things to be fair. Worse than that, I had very little in the way of hips. I was sort of shaped like my grandfather—wow, how great was that? And in the wake of this disappointment, a new creature surfaced to put me, and all those like me, to shame.

They were the big-booty girls from the videos. They had come out of nowhere and were here to stay, dashing any chance for attention for us old regular girls. Men—black men especially—loved those big ol' asses and they never once hesitated to let that be known. It was evident in the music videos. They started out with regular slender, cute girls; then, one day, it was nothing but girls who looked like they could carry a glass on their ass while standing straight up.

I knew a few women who had pear shapes—thinner torso, wider hips and thighs—but they had nothing on the video vixens. Those girls were something else. And I, of course was shaped like an apple: Bigger, wider mid-section and torso, longer thinner legs, hips, and thighs. Eww, gross.

Those women with the perfect little perky breasts, the super-thin waistline, and the big banging booty had me and all the other less than perfect women, sweatin', trying to be like them. These girls flaunted their asses as if they had been sculpted out of clay.

Some of them didn't even look real. It wasn't until I went with my brother to a strip club that I saw it with my own eyes; "Damn. Yep, they real."

Who could compete? Not me.

What would any man in his right mind want with an average-looking, flat-assed, awkwardly shaped woman like me? I was at a loss. Usually I tried not to let it bother me. But bad days were really bad. Out with the girls, and you're the only one who gets no play. Devastating.

I wasn't a complete loser, though. I had one major thing going for me: I was nice. I didn't judge, which went a long way, seeing as how most niggas had major problems. You did what you did for you, and that ain't got nothing to do with me. I was the one exception, but everyone else got the benefit of the doubt.

I got a lot respect for treating people kindly. Everyone thought I was sweet and that sometimes translated to cool points, which translated to sexy points. It made me more sexy than beautiful, and the guys who really dug sexy noticed me. The cats that were into the drop-dead, body-banging, gorgeous type of chick never tried to date me; they just thought I was mad cool. Don't get it twisted—they would have slept with me, but I could never be the one.

So all in all, I had mixed feelings about the whole big booty thing. But I started a workout plan, just in case the infomercials I saw every night were true. I noticed after several months that my butt had begun to round and lift a little bit; the one pair of booty jeans I did own didn't look so ridiculous when I drummed up the courage to sport them. But the exercises in no way gave me the results I thought I deserved. I wanted it all—that donkey butt.

The only other thing I liked about myself was my hair. I kept it in a chin-length bob, and I had my hairstylist relax it as soon as I noticed the edges getting nappy. A few years ago I started adding chestnut highlights to accentuate the color in my eyes. Just being able to swing my hair made men stop and take a second look, and I enjoyed that.

\* \* \*

My looks were what they were, and there wasn't much I could do about it. But my career and the way I lived were fully under my control. I loved nice things and needed a position that would get me those things, plus allow me to maintain a particular lifestyle. After I graduated from the University of Minnesota, my degree from William Mitchell Law School got me hired as the lead attorney for one of the top law firms in Minnesota. I worked hard for two years and modestly collected a very high six-figure income. I may not have been super-duper fine, but I had enough money to make it look like I was.

So every week without fail, I got my hair, feet, and nails done—my hair at Hair Freedom, an African-owned shop not far from downtown, and my nails and feet at the Korean shop in the strip mall near my mother's house.

I always took my mother to the Korean shop and paid for a manicure for her, too. But she didn't really like going there. She hated how they always spoke to each other in their native language and busted out in laughter whenever it seemed most inappropriate. It always seemed right when the manicurists were about to scrub the calluses off our feet, they'd have something funny to say. Those outbursts always made my mother smack her lips, something she did when she was displeased or even worse, disgusted. She'd look at me with the evilest of eyes; all I could do was smile and shake my head. My mother couldn't understand why there were no black-owned nail shops we could have gone to. I didn't know, I liked the way my nails were done. My mother was funny though; even though her nails looked nice, she'd head for the door while I paid and I could hear that lip smack as the door shut behind her.

I guess everything in life was a trade-off.

# Chapter 5

**M**Y STOMACH GROWLED, AND I started to feel the nausea from all those vodka martinis settling in. I slowly walked through the large six-paneled French doors that opened up into my newly redesigned kitchen, and begun looking for something to eat.

I designed my kitchen to be elegant but practical. Because it was my favorite room in the house, I purchased and installed only the best. I included the latest model of stainless steel appliances, an island that shared a cast iron grill and gas-burning stove, a wine cooler and every kitchen gadget imaginable.

I loved to cook. I learned how to cook from watching and helping my mother and my grandmother cook years and years of fabulous-tasting food. They spared nothing when it came to cooking out of love for the family. So the kitchen was a wondrous place of pleasant and peaceful memories for me. My whole family could cook; it was like what we were destined to do.

The island I installed also served as a sushi bar, with six bar stools with place settings that looked like they came straight out of a Japanese restaurant surrounding it. Sadie and I loved sushi; everyone else was cool on it. And Angel couldn't mess with it at all. She was allergic to fish, all kinds of fish—shellfish, freshwater and saltwater fish, everything. It made her break out and if she wasn't careful it could kill her. So on sushi nights Sadie and I stayed in the kitchen while the other girls kicked it elsewhere.

The cabinetry that encircled the entire kitchen was custom-made oak with several of the cabinet fronts made of leaded glass in order to show off my large collection of crystal wine glasses. I remarked to Sadie that I wanted the kitchen to be finished last so that she could take her time in selecting just the right ambience.

Sadie LaDuke was one of my best friends. She was an architect and designer for one of the top architectural firms in Minnesota and she had a very impressive resume. Together we designed my kitchen based strictly on my style and the statement I was trying to make.

That morning, I walked over to the cabinet where I kept the fresh coffee beans and placed a half a cup of coffee beans in the stainless steel grinder. As the grinding sound of beans and metal came to a stop I started the coffee pot. I grabbed a banana from off the top of the refrigerator and bread from out of the breadbox and began to think about what I was going to wear to church. I put the bread in the toaster and uncovered the butter. As the aromatic scent of Colombian coffee fields wafted throughout my penthouse apartment I grabbed the Sunday paper from outside the massive oak and bronzed front door. I thumbed past all the depressing news and the stories about the future of the economy, and turned to the Sunday crossword puzzle.

Crossword puzzles were something I had done for years. When I was a little girl, about twelve years old, I did crossword puzzles everyday with Uncle Cordell. We sat quietly and worked together to answer as many clues as we could. We had gotten pretty good at them, until Uncle Cordell's eyes started to give him trouble. Then it turned into me writing and reading all the clues. We still did well, but doing crossword puzzles is a very visual game and not being able to read the smaller numbers was a problem. Monday through Wednesday's puzzles we usually finished, because they were rather easy, but Friday, Saturday and Sunday's puzzles were ridiculous. They were extremely hard so we got all we could and that was that. It truly was one of the things I loved to do to relax, and it also left me with fond memories of time spent with my uncle.

As I looked over some of the questions on the puzzle, the toast popped up and the coffee finished brewing. I grabbed the toast and spread it with the room-temperature butter, and poured myself a cup of coffee. I opened the refrigerator and took out the French vanilla-flavored cream and poured a little in my cup. I reached in the drawer for a spoon and was startled by the telephone ringing. I ran over to the phone.

"Hello?

A sweet melodic voice came from the other end.

"Jasmine? This is your grandmother. Are you going to church this morning?"

"Yes, ma'am, I am."

"Well, baby, my ride canceled on me this morning, could you pick me up?"

"Absolutely, Grandma, I'll be there at about eight-thirty."

"OK, thank you, baby, I'll be ready."

I looked at the clock. It was already seven-fifteen and I hadn't figured out what I was going to wear yet. I rushed into the large walk-in closet and started thumbing through the satin-covered hangers.

*Where is my royal blue dress?* It usually hung right between my olive green and camel brown suits.

I was very meticulous about how I organized my things—meticulous may not be the word for it, I was actually pretty anal about it. All of my clothes and shoes were organized by designer first, then by color. I installed one of those new California Closets to make sure everything was in its place and everything had a place. So not finding my dress where it was supposed to be was a problem.

Had I left my favorite sundress at the cleaners, or worse yet, had someone borrowed and not returned it? I carefully looked through each and every hanger and right before panic set in, I noticed the straps of my royal blue dress between two of my dark blue suits.

Whew. I quickly pulled it out. I removed the plastic and laid the dress on the bed and went to look for my sandals. Even though the church I went to looked down on women who wore sandals without nylons, it was going to be somewhere around 82 degrees today and I was not about to burn up just to please some little old lady on the front pew.

I turned on the shower and began to undress. I really enjoyed taking showers in my apartment, because the hot water always got nice and hot. Not like the rusty, smelly water that I had to deal with while living in the small apartment with Sadie.

Sadie and I shared a very small two-bedroom apartment when we left the dorms after our second year in college. The apartment was located in southeast Minneapolis not far from campus; it was really bad, but it was all we could afford at the time, and we dealt with all sorts of vagrant types, but we endured and vowed to never live like that again.

This pact between best friends proved to be the best thing that ever happened to us. Right out of college, Sadie purchased a four-bedroom, three-bath house in the nicest suburb in Minnesota. Hall and Grabhorn Architecture hired her on the spot, and she made partner within two years. Me, I purchased the penthouse apartment twenty-four floors up in the swank, elegant combination apartment-office building named after one of the top executives in the city, Dr. Jim Pinecliff, the Pinecliff Estates.

I had dreamed of living in a penthouse apartment ever since I visited the senior partner of the law firm's penthouse. His penthouse was in downtown St. Paul and had the most beautiful view of the downtown skyline, and because I admired it so much my dreams of having my own penthouse easily came true.

The doorbell rang just as I was shutting off the water. I grabbed my big black fluffy robe and ran to the door. I looked through the peephole and recognized the distorted face of the concierge, Jonathan.

I opened the door and smiled. "Hi Jonathan, how are you this morning?"

"I'm fine, Ms. Burrell, how are you?"

"I'm great. What brings you up here so early?"

"I have a delivery for you, it came yesterday afternoon, but I'm afraid I missed you."

"Oh. Oh yeah, I had a late night last night so I took the back elevator in order to . . . uh . . . you know."

"Yeah, I know." Jonathan smiled a sheepish smile and handed the package to me.

"Thank you, Jonathan, and here." I reached in my purse and gave him a ten-dollar bill. "Take this, I really appreciate you bringing this package all the way up here. Oh, by the way, could you bring my car around? Let me get the keys."

"Sure thing, Ms. Burrell, I'll have it right down front."

"Please call me Jasmine." I smiled and handed him the keys.

"All right Jasmine, I will." He smiled and walked towards the elevators. I closed the door. "Boy, he's a cutie," I thought.

Seven fifty-five. Oh my God, I better hurry up.

I threw the package on the couch and rushed to the bedroom to finish getting dressed. The outfit looked great and I went to the vanity to put on some makeup—very little though, I always opted for the natural look when I went to church, just to make it a little easier on myself. They were definitely going to remark about my dress so I replaced the heavy lipstick with liner and gloss; hopefully that would save me some of the funny looks and snide remarks.

\* \* \*

Jonathan rang that the car was down front and I grabbed my purse, sunglasses, and Bible, and proceeded to the elevator. When the doors finally opened, Mr. And Mrs. Smith walked off; it looked like they had just finished their morning run. The two of them seemed like the best of friends. It was obvious they had a wonderful relationship; I was so jealous. I secretly wished to have a relationship like theirs again.

"Good morning, Mr. and Mrs. Smith."

"Good morning, Jasmine. Off to church, I see."

"Yes sir, I am."

"Are you two at that running thing again, huh?"

"Yes little lady, that's what, keeps those old fires burning." He smiled and slapped Mrs. Smith on the behind.

"Ahh, stop it dear, not in front of the young lady."

"Oh Marge, relax, I'm sure Jasmine has had her behind slapped many times—ain't that right, Jasmine?"

I felt my face turning red as Mr. Smith burst into a loud laugh. I put my shades on my head and practically bumped into them as I tried to quickly get on the elevator.

"Have a nice day, you two."

"Oh we will, Jasmine, you can bet on that." As the elevator doors closed, I heard Mrs. Smith reprimanding Mr. Smith.

"You shouldn't say things like that, you embarrassed her."

"Oh, she'll be fine sweetheart, she's a big girl."

As the elevator descended to the first floor I couldn't help but smile; wouldn't it be nice to have someone to grow old with like that?

The doors of the oversized elevator open up to the immaculately decorated lobby. Enormous gold and pewter vases filled with large blooms of colorful flowers adorned every corner of the room. All the walls were elegantly covered with artwork dating back to the 18$^{th}$ century, and the marble floors were polished so that you could see yourself in them. At the front desk were two employees, the desk clerk, and the concierge, Jonathan.

"Hi, Ms. Burrell, you look great. Your car is waiting out front and here are the keys."

"Thanks, Jonathan, I really appreciate it."

I was really in a hurry now, but had to remember to walk gingerly across the freshly polished marble lobby floors towards the front revolving doors. Sometimes the floor was pretty slippery. Two summers ago I slipped and fell; I cracked my tailbone and broke the heel on my brand-new Donna Karan shoes. I was pissed; it wasn't the fact that I had to spend a night in the hospital and one week in bed; I was more upset that I broke the heel off my new cocoa brown suede shoes. I was pretty bruised up, but spent the next two days calling around for a shoe repair shop that could make my shoe perfect again.

The owners of the building paid for the repair and sent me the largest and most beautiful arrangement of flowers I had ever seen. I guessed it was just to keep me quiet and to prevent me from suing their rich asses off. I never intended to sue them, but they knew I had them by the balls and I didn't hesitate one bit to let them know my background and what I was capable of. For my trouble they threw in one year's free parking in the best space in the underground garage, right at the lobby doors. I accepted the space and smiled with an unabated gratitude that only a sly fox attorney could give.

I stepped outside. *What a beautiful day, I'm glad I got up.*

I smiled and took my Gucci rimless sunglasses off my head, placed them on my heart-shaped face and walked down the front steps to my convertible Mercedes SL500. I pushed the security alarm.

This car was my dream car when I was in college. One of the basketball players for the school had a black one and I secretly admired it from afar. Even though I knew it was wrong, I tried to date that guy just so I could get a ride in it. We went on two dates and I decided he was too shallow and kind of dumb. I figured he was one of those exceptional ball players that—oops—accidentally got pushed through school just because he could play. I actually felt sorry for him. One career-ending injury and he would be homeless for the rest of his life. But the car was the bomb.

As soon as my graduation tassel moved from one side to the other I was at the car lot buying one. It was metallic blue with a dark blue convertible top that matched the soft leather seats. The dash was wood grain and I purposely chose an automatic so that cruising would be most enjoyable. The silver chrome body kit and the twenty-two-inch rims were immaculate, and I kept it clean.

I opened the car door, got in, and retracted the convertible top. The heat from the sweltering sun beat down on my back.

*Damn, it's hot as hell out here, but damn, it feels good.*

I knew when I got to my grandmother's house, I would have to turn on the air conditioning so I soaked up the sun that beamed down on me so freely. I looked in my rearview mirror, checked for oncoming traffic in the side view mirror and put the car in drive. As I started to pull out, the beating, bumping sound of someone's car coming around the corner. Kinda ticked me off—who the fuck was beating so loud? I grabbed the rearview mirror and focused in on who or what was making the racket? The brand-new black-on-black Cadillac Escalade, with the new twenty-six-inch spinning Sprewells pulled up slowly then abruptly swooped around and pulled up next to driver's side window of my car.

"Figures. It's that trifling nigga, Todd James."

# Chapter 6

Todd James was one of my past acquaintances—way past. He was a professional football player for the Minnesota Vikings and was on the injured reserve list for a torn ligament in his knee. He was a tall milk-chocolate brother with a head full of beautiful dreads, except for the top. The locks in the top were gone; he had snatched his helmet off so many times in a fit of anger on his way to the sidelines or when the sun was way too hot that the dreads that were on top sometimes got caught, and the helmet pulled the locks out. He wore baseball caps to cover his head when he wasn't practicing or playing in a game. The baseball caps never bothered me, and although the missing hair was sort of a turn-off, he was sexy, and fine as hell.

I met Todd two years ago at Charisma, a flashy club in downtown Minneapolis. He was chillin' over in the VIP booth with his homeboys and I was there with the divas. I noticed him his body immediately.

He had the body of a Greek god with brilliantly chiseled arms and legs and an ass to die for. It was so strong and so tight, the first time I saw it, I just wanted to walk up to it and bite it, a big juicy bite. One of the girls at the table remarked about how soft and smooth his skin appeared to be; I took it a step farther, and wondered if that velvety milk-chocolate skin covered his entire body. After a few vodka martinis I was bound and determined to find out.

I watched from a distance, him locked up in VIP with his huge bodyguards and his entourage of homies and hoochies.

I giggled to myself. *He thinks he's the bomb.*

"Sadie, watch me check this ho," I said.

"Jasmine, what you gonna do?"

"Nigga, you know me."

"Girl, I ain't paying to get in VIP."

"Yeah, yeah, I know, just watch me go to work."

"Now you know what's gonna happen if you give him the "evil eye.""

"Uh, duh, we all gonna be in VIP."

She laughed, and nudged the other girls and told them to watch.

The divas and I had actually calculated the value of VIP status versus the money spent to get there and realized we liked our money more. So we never paid to get in VIP, even though we all had enough money and then some. But if someone else was paying, it was all good.

I cased the joint and found that the restrooms were right behind VIP and decided I'd spruce myself up—a little bit. I slowly and calmly sauntered over towards the VIP area staring at Todd the entire distance. He licked his lips as I approached and I winked as I entered the restroom. I stayed for about three and a half minutes, and as soon as I stepped out of the door, he stepped out of VIP and right in my face.

He smiled.

I seductively stared at him, and undressed him with my eyes. He stared back; twenty-seven...twenty-eight...twenty-nine...thirty. Got 'im.

He was mesmerized, physically and emotionally under my spell. I had used the infamous evil-eye technique on Todd, guaranteed to seduce any man who dare stare longer than twenty-nine seconds. This look, only truly mastered by Sadie and myself, was the dagger of death for most men. There were only a few men who were immune to the evil eye, so we figured they were either gay or they exclusively dated white girls. Either way, if it didn't affect them, we didn't want them. The other Southside Divas said they couldn't do it, so they rarely even tried. Sadie and I didn't care; it just gave us more guys to choose from.

Over the course of the night I realized Todd had a lot of money and loved to spend it. He bought the most expensive champagne and kept it coming, as well as making sure his boys had whatever it was they liked to drink. This was a definite plus in my book. I hated cheap-ass niggas; there was no use for them in my life. I didn't mind paying sometimes if I was in a long-term relationship, but niggas tried to take advantage after they found out I was an attorney. Playing that "I left my wallet at home card"; oh well, sorry, you don't eat. I intentionally stopped telling new dates and new acquaintances the whole truth about my profession; first of all, it intimidated the hell out of them, and second they all of a sudden would have major issues come up in their lives that would call for them to ask me for money. I helped one guy out by buying groceries for him and his kids because he was a seasonal construction worker and didn't have any work right then. Grown-ass man asking a woman to help feed his kids? What the hell?

But Todd was definitely different. He picked up the tab on everything. He ordered bottle after bottle of Crystal and tried to get me to drink both champagne and more vodka martinis. I knew I couldn't handle any more and started passing the drinks around to my friends who I talked Todd into letting into VIP. He was real cool about it; besides, he had a gang of homeboys in there with him so the divas went to work as well.

Todd was the kind of guy that was full of himself, and I could totally see through his counterfeit façade. All night he bragged about his prized possessions, which included several cars, a phat crib, and a boatload of miscellaneous shit. He also raved about all the women who wanted him and told me about how he aimed to please most. He no doubt in his mind, was a winner all the way around.

Of course, none of his irrelevant chatter impressed me, because I had my own shit, and on most occasions I avoided niggas like him, but Todd was fine.

The night was fantastic, we danced all night, drank all night, and when the club closed, we stood outside and traded numbers.

But the night apparently wasn't over for Todd. He wrapped his massive arms around me and practically begged me to go home with him. I usually didn't go over to their house, they usually ended back at my place, one of my control mechanism. But for some strange reason I trusted Todd and agreed to follow him to his house in Eden Prairie. Besides, he was a professional athlete and I knew he wasn't dumb enough to risk his entire career by trying to fuck over one of the top lawyers in the state.

And to top it all off, the alcohol and the need to see this brother completely naked had my entire body on ten. I wanted to bite into that milk chocolate drop and hold it in my mouth until it melted. I was also for some reason feeling particularly lonely and wanted to be held. So the decision was made. I said bye to the girls and reassured them I would be OK. They made me promise to call when I got home just to make sure I made it.

Todd and I both drove drunk, twenty minutes away, and one right behind the other straight into the garage at Todd's house. It was a blessing we both made it safely. We parked side-by-side, got out and went at it. We teased, touched, and kissed all the way into the house. I knew from the way he kissed I was in for spectacular night.

I entered the house, and between all the kissing and touching I noticed how insanely elegant his house was. It was a newly constructed urban contemporary house, beautifully maintained and decorated immaculately. The four bedrooms and three baths seemed to me to be a little over the top since he was the only one living there. But Todd explained that his boys were over all the time because of the game room so after drinking all night some of them decide to crash for the night in order to cut back on the DWIs.

"Oh I see. And how many of you have DWIs and are currently driving, may I ask?"

"You're an attorney, right?"

"Yes I am, Todd. What does that have to do with anything?"

"I'm not telling you anything. I plead the fifth."

I giggled. "All right, I'll let you off the hook this time. Next time I may not be so easy on you."

Todd quickly walked me through the rest of the house. The kitchen was the bomb, the living room and dining room were off the chain, and everything else was a blur. He was walking so fast I felt like I was on a mini tour running behind schedule. We ended up in front of a big red door. He paused for a minute and then slowly, methodically opened the doors.

"Oh my God." I covered my mouth in amazement. Inside the heavy solid wood doors was the most ridiculous game room I had every seen. He had every game imaginable; pinball machines, PS2 hooked up to a flat-screen television bigger than the fifty-two-inch in my apartment, arcade video games. The classics, too: Ms. Pac Man, Donkey Kong, Galaga, and Centipede. I was in heaven. I loved video games, especially the old-school ones. I thought back to how I used to play them all the time at the restaurant I used to work at when I was working my way through college. He also had every high-tech gadget imaginable—wow, a techie—and the sickest thing of all, a stereo system that amazed me to no end. I swooned.

"Todd? All of this, is this really necessary?" Todd being a big video game buff like myself, remarked, "Girl, this is just the tip of the iceberg, I got games for days, real slot machines and a pool table the size of Texas. Come in this room."

I followed Todd to another room and almost fainted. The master bedroom was like a fantasy world. Every sight and sound was reminiscent of an East African safari. From the beautiful pink and yellow fresh flowers to the real leopard rug hanging above the bed, this room was short of spectacular. I whirled around so fast I almost lost my balance, but the liquor and Todd's anxiousness grabbed me. For a moment I thought he grabbed me to hold me up, but soon found out when I landed on his waterbed that he was just assisting me down. I lost my head for an instant; but as the hot smell of liquor from Todd's breath teased, then overwhelmed my nostrils, I realized my position.

"Uh, hey Todd, hold up a minute."

The California king-size waterbed posed a problem. I couldn't move. Those massive muscles I admired earlier at the club pinned down my arms, and the waves in the bed made it hard for me to get any leverage to push him off.

"TODD! I said hold up a minute."

"What is it, baby? Is there a problem?" Todd looked into my eyes and sensed my fear. He backed away. "Sorry Jasmine, I thought..."

"Don't worry, Todd, I'm fine, I just need to go to the bathroom. OK?"

"OK. The bathroom is through those doors."

I entered the bathroom and shut the door. I contemplated my next move. I had already crossed the threshold into the uncertain world of one-night stands, and even though I felt comfortable with Todd, I didn't know him. All I knew is that I wanted to taste him and now the moment was upon me.

Should I, could I, go through with it? "Hell yeah," I thought to myself, "I'm a Southside Diva and I'm gonna show this nigga so real good professional pussy."

There was a need for me to rethink my plan. Because of the waterbed and the position I was just in, I had to make sure I had more leverage than he did. First, I took my can of mace out of my purse and turned the notch off safety and carefully placed it in the open outside pocket as a precaution. I had learned from the past not to take chances and I knew how to play it if things got ugly. Second, from law school, I had mastered the three C's: being cool, coy and cute, to cause the opposition to drop their guard. I always hoped that the three C's would be enough. Third, I put the police on speed dial. I was thankful I never had to use these tactics, but knew they would come in handy someday. The mace was backup for any excessive force. I thought about getting a conceal-and-carry license, but never went through with it.

When I stepped out of the bathroom, he was already in the bed. I assumed he was naked so I began to slowly and seductively undress, and I heard the faint sounds of Tyrese's "Sweet Lady" playing in the background. He had also lit a few candles. The fireplace in his bedroom was glowing brightly and the smell of

African musk incense was lightly floating through the air. It was actually kind of romantic.

"Wow, this big oaf is sweet after all."

Then I found out what he had to offer....

Todd was one of those talkative brothers who ranted and raved about what they intended to do to you while they were so-called doing it. He was a sensationalist with minimal skills and even less in the package department.

By that time, though, I was committed. I lay down hoping for the best, but considering the lack of girth in his manhood, I wasn't exactly expecting fireworks. Good thing.

He smiled and kissed me. Nice at first, but it was only a matter of time before the soft, gentle, sensual kisses turned into a wild, insane rotating tongue-fest—where I felt like if I didn't have my own, I could have easily kept his. And on top of that, he added a soundtrack that sounded like cats in heat. A debacle unfolding before my eyes—that is, if I hadn't already shut them.

By the time he entered me, I no longer wanted to be a part of this fiasco, but what could I do? I shook inside, while he bounced up and down on me, grabbed, rubbed, and sucked my breast too hard, all while he screamed and yelled profanities at the top of his lungs. He had totally and completely lost his mind.

"Come on, girl, ooh shit, you know you like it, ah damn, don't you, fuck, come on give it to daddy."

I lay there stunned; what was I supposed to say? I really felt embarrassed for him.

"Ooh, aah, give it to me?" I said.

"Yeah, yeah, I'm fucking this pussy, ain't I, girl. Ooh shit!"

"Oh yeah daddy, you sure are," I said, stifling a yawn.

After my third or fourth "ooh," "aah," and yawn, his voice cracked and he screamed. His head fell on my chest and I realized he was finished. I didn't know if I should have been happy or mad. Todd looked up and kissed me on the cheek,

"Oh, girl, you got the bomb pussy."

As he returned his sweaty forehead to my chest and had me smothered with the rest of his body, I had no choice but to reply positively.

"Oh yeah, Todd, you're the real deal. Wow, you really know how to treat a woman."

I really didn't know why I lied. Maybe it was the fact that I knew he was drunk and I didn't want to get anything ugly started. He had home-court advantage and I never messed with that. Besides, he would be asleep in a few moments and if I didn't cause a stir, I could sneak out while he snored.

"Well, you know, Jasmine, I just got it like that."

Staring at the ceiling, I rolled my eyes.

Oh my God, for real? What the hell am I doing?

This tired-ass nigga; damn, I wished I had just carried my ass home, lonely would have been a whole lot better than this bullshit.

# Chapter 7

"What's up, girl?" I slowly turned my head towards him, as he yelled again.

"Hey, Jasmine, what's up?"

"Look, nigga, turn that loud-ass music down, you disturbing the whole neighborhood, this ain't no ghetto you done rolled up in."

"Oh, I'm sorry, Jaz."

As the loud beating sound from the four sixteen-inch speakers posted up in the back of his trunk slowly faded out, I yelled to him, "Hey, don't call me Jaz. You of all people have not earned that right."

Jaz was short for Jasmine, but the nickname given to me by my father when I was only seven years old was because I had developed such a love for jazz music that I couldn't sleep unless it was playing in the background. Growing up, my father always played jazz music when we came to visit him. I grew to love artists like Grover Washington Jr., Kenny G and Najee'. Only my family and closest friends were allowed to call me that.

"So how've you been?"

"I've been fine, Todd. And yourself?"

"I've been great, I just bought a house out in Lakeville, girl, it's the bomb, you have to come out and see it. Do you think we could get together some time? I really miss hanging out with you."

"Well, Todd, I don't think that that would be too cool. You remember what happened the last time we were supposed to hook up."

I had always tried to hide, better yet forget, those incidents in my past that included men, particularly those times that caused me great pain.

A couple of winters ago, two weeks before Christmas, I decided to give Todd another chance. He had been calling and wanting to get together but I had refused because of my first, second, and third sexual encounters with him. I really didn't want to go back there and I knew I shouldn't have, but what the hell; free meal, free liquor, and maybe he would eat me out?

We decided to stay in because it was so cold, about three degrees below zero, and planned a nice romantic evening at Todd's place. I didn't mind the drive out to his crib, because he had such a nice place, especially the game room.

At about seven in the evening, I arrived at Todd's place dressed to the hilt in a very expensive black and gold suede pantsuit. I was pretty excited, because I decided to shock Todd by wearing nothing underneath my outfit.

I carefully climbed out of the car but noticed as I walked up the driveway a black and white convertible Mustang sitting right behind Todd's truck. I didn't think anything of it because Todd always had his football buddies stopping by; I walked up to the front steps adjusted my goodies and rang the doorbell. When the door opened, I was taken aback. A tall slender, fair-skinned woman dressed in only a bathrobe peeked her head out the door.

"May I help you?"

"Umm, is Todd here?"

"Yeah, sure. Can I tell him who stopped by?"

"Umm it's . . . ummm . . . . you know what? Never mind, I'll just call him later."

"OK," she said, grinning wolfishly, and shut the door. I could hear her giggling softly as she walked away, into the house.

This lying motherfucker; I was floored. I ran to my car and sped off.

Later on that night Todd called and asked what had happened.

"Jasmine, where are you? I thought we were supposed to meet at eight-thirty?"

"Oh Todd, I wasn't feeling well so I couldn't make it. And by the way we were supposed to meet at seven-thirty."

"Are you all right? Do you want me to come over?"

"No, no, I'm fine. I'll call you later." I hung up, seething, but damned if I was going to let him know it. I watched some bad TV—I don't even remember what—and finally fell asleep.

I woke up to Todd yelling my name.

"Todd, what can I do for you?"

"I'm just trying to find out why you're so short with me?"

"Look, when you make plans with someone you need to take better note of the time."

"Are you talking about the date we were supposed to have? Yeah, now that I think about it you never called me back. I had the place laid out for you and you were too sick to show or even call me?"

"Yeah? You got the nerves to wonder why?" I couldn't believe that he was the one acting all offended.

"Yes, tell me why, what happened? Jasmine, why are you acting like this?"

"Negro, you had some light-skinned female up in there butt-ass-naked and you want to question me??"

"What are you talking about?"

"You know exactly what I'm talking about, you like to play games and I certainly don't have time for that or you."

"But Jasmine... wait a minute..."

"Todd, why don't we just say goodbye before this gets ugly? Look, I have to pick up my grandmother for church, how 'bout I talk to you some other time?"

"Jasmine, let me explain."

"No need, Todd, I totally understand."

I checked my mirrors and sped off, but I could practically hear him thinking, "Damn, what the hell is up with her?"

It didn't matter what he thought, though; he was history.

\* \* \*

Over the years, I found that men were pretty gullible when it came to women who were good and catered to their egos. I had hooked up with a lot of guys and had given up a lot of booty—some good, some bad, and, some just downright disgraceful. I realized the more I tried to turn those maybes into a permanent fixture, I immediately got bored. Don't get it wrong—there were some relations that turned into relationships where emotions got involved and I had to check myself and revert back to diva status.

Sometimes the men fell hard and wanted to be apart of every aspect of my life; that wasn't going to happen. On several other occasions, men fell in love. So as diplomatically as I could, I explained to them that falling in love with me after one night was impossible. Take it for granted those poor chaps were never to be seen again. Most of the men I dealt with understood the situation and we usually parted ways peacefully and amicably.

Todd was special—borderline slow. And I mean that in the nicest way possible.

# Chapter 8

I T WAS EIGHT THIRTY-FIVE IN the morning; my grandmother didn't live far, but I didn't want to hear her mouth if I made her late. I sped down Park Avenue towards my grandmother's house, parked in front and pushed the button to close the convertible top. I turned on the air conditioner and waited as the hot air started to blow cool. It took a while for the humid air to turn to that ice-cold chill I knew my grandma liked. As I waited, I stared at my grandma's house, the house I grew up in.

It was a great house, a big blue and white two-story colonial. But now it looked like it could use a new coat of paint—the parts that weren't covered in vines. Since my grandpa had passed, my grandma just hadn't seemed to be able to keep the house up. It was starting to look like it belonged in the swamp somewhere.

"Damn, I need to have someone come out and remove that crap before it covers everything."

My grandfather bought the house we grew up in just a few months after he and my grandma moved here from Chicago, in 1966. My mom used to talk about how they had to live with aunt Millie and their cousins for the first few months until Grandpa had everything all tied up.

Minnesota was supposed to give us a new life, and in some ways it did. It was a far cry nicer than the streets of Chicago, where Mama was known as a fighter. Mama was really tall, and rail-thin as a kid. The other kids thought they could tease her and get away with it; but that wasn't the case. Mama had beat up several kids, including boys. In one particular incident she went up in a girl's house, dragged her outside and beat her up her in front of the girl's mama and her brothers. When my grandfather found out, he really didn't do or say anything. He just told her to stay out of other folks' houses and went back to work. I guess back in those days settling fights with your fists in Chicago was acceptable.

You would think that moving to a nicer place would chill Mama out, but it was only a matter of time before Mama was beating up her cousins too. They wouldn't leave her records alone, her forty-fives. So they had to get it as well. I believe my mother fought every single one of her cousins and that number was well over five. Even though my grandfather was still in Chicago, it seemed as though Mama had free rein on beating up people; she never once told me she got in trouble for it.

I laughed, thinking about Mama beating someone up. That was sure one trait I didn't inherit.

The yard hadn't changed much. The old tall pine tree still stood in the yard, with pinecones now the size of my hands. I remembered how we tried to climb it when we were kids, clinging to branches big enough to hold us. We always got in trouble, because the large pools of sap that stuck to our clothes and hands never seemed to wash away.

The wildly misshapen bushes were still there, too, and the big pink and white flowers that grew every spring looked particularly stunning today, what with the warm weather and all the rain we had had. I never knew what those flowers were called, until Mrs. Smith pointed them out in our rooftop garden. They were peonies, and I loved the way they smelled. My grandmother never let us pick them, so the ones I got to play with were the ones that shed and fell to the ground.

The yard hadn't changed much. The old tall pine tree still stood in the yard, with pinecones now the size of my hands. I remembered how we tried to climb it when we were kids, clinging to branches big enough to hold us. We always got in trouble, because the large pools of sap that stuck to our clothes and hands never seemed to wash away.

The walkway was the same and the gate that we ran through to the back yard was still in tact. The only thing I didn't have fond memories of was the strange sinkhole that sat right at the front of the yard next to the sidewalk. Damn; it was still there.

It was a really weird hole in the ground that no one could explain. I remembered for years, my grandfather filling it up with dirt, mulch, and leaves—whatever he could find. And every year after the winter thaw, that hole reappeared. I remembered my brother Raymond and I tripped and fell into it several times per year.

Once, when he was running away from me after he'd punched me in the nose, his foot slipped so deep down in the hole that he almost broke his ankle. My grandma called the paramedics but they said that it was only a severe sprain. I felt bad for my brother because he had to wear a splint for four weeks. But he deserved it—shouldn't have hit me.

I smiled to myself as I passed the hole and the tree. I walked up the front stairs and rang the doorbell.

Of course, my grandmother was ready; she handed me her bag and her Bible and I escorted her down the stairs and toward the car.

Grandma Vera was a stout, short little lady. She had been a dancer in her younger days, and you could still see how strong her calf muscles were. In fact, she had kept a lot of the tone she had developed as a younger woman. She had a medium-dark skin tone, like a perfectly roasted chestnut, and she usually wore wigs because her hair was thinning; but underneath, it was now pure white. She had dyed it for years but just recently decided to let it all go natural.

She came out the door in an off-white suit covered in hundreds of pearl-blue sequins. Her four-inch snakeskin heels, also pearl-blue, matched her hat, which was covered in feathers and patches of snakeskin leather.

"My goodness, Grandma, you look great."

"Thank you, baby, you look good too, but I hope you brought a sweater or something to cover up those arms."

"Yes, ma'am, I did. It's in the car." Here we go, I thought to myself.

"Can I help you down the stairs?" I asked cautiously. She was already commenting on my bare shoulders and I didn't need anymore reprimands if she felt like "today" she didn't need help down the stairs.

"Sure, baby, your ol' grandma is getting up in age. I could use a little help from time to time."

"Here, Grandma, take my arm." I put out my arm and waited as she slowly walked down the stairs.

"I got it now, child, go on ahead and get that door open; it sure is hot out here, I hope you got the air conditioner on?"

"Yes, ma'am, I do." I raced to the other side of the car and opened the door.

"Girl, I sho' wish you would get a car that doesn't sit on the ground."

"I know, Grandma. Maybe next time I will buy something a little bigger."

"Whew," she blew the breath out of her cheeks. "It sure is cooler in here. I like that, this hat sho' got me burning up."

"Don't worry, Grandma, we'll be to church very soon and then you can relax."

I checked my mirrors, mostly to look at myself because I felt like I was melting; and proceeded to pull into traffic. I always changed the way I drove whenever my Grandma was in the car—no music and no speeding.

I had a great deal of respect for my Grandma and didn't want to do anything to offend her. She didn't like most secular music—anything that wasn't gospel. I had forgotten to include at least one gospel CD, so that meant silence. Besides, she couldn't stand when the music was turned up too loud. "Turn that music down so I can see!" she'd always say—and she wasn't even the one driving. But that didn't matter, whoever was driving turned the music down instantly.

"So, Jasmine, who's the lucky man in your life?"

Wow, where did this line of questioning come from? "Uhh, there's no one right now, Grandma. I'm single and loving it."

"Ahh, come on, child, you can't be single forever, you have to find yourself a good man and settle down."

I know, Grandma, I'm working on it."

"Oh, you are, huh? Whatever happened to the real cute, successful boy you were dating for a while. Uhh, what's his name?"

"Marcus?"

"Yeah, Marcus, where is he?"

"Grandma, you know he's in Europe."

"Well, why don't you and him get together? I sho' liked him; he was a gentleman and very pleasant to be around."

"Yes I know, Grandma, but he's gone and that is all I can say."

"Well, you gon' mess around and some white girl gonna snatch him up, and then you'll be sorry."

"Look, Grandma, I would prefer not to talk about this anymore."

"OK, child, I was just saying, you really need to think about your future."

"Grandma, that's what I thought I was doing, graduating with a law degree and being a defense attorney for one of the top law firms in Minnesota—as a matter of fact the country."

"You right, baby, you're doing really well for yourself and I'm proud of you. But you know all that money ain't gonna keep you warm at night, and it sho' ain't gonna make you happy if you ain't got no one to share it with."

"I understand, Grandma. I'll work on it."

Dang, Grandma always trying to get me married off, I thought—though I wouldn't dare say it out loud. And why did she have to bring up Marcus? Now my whole day was ruined.

I was still at the wheel, but I was on automatic, thinking about Marcus and all the what-ifs; I came to when Grandma screamed, "Jasmine, girl, you done drove right past the church."

"Oh sorry, Grandma, let me make the block and I'll let you out at the front door."

"Girl, I don't know what has gotten in to you lately."

"Yeah, I know, Grandma. Save me a seat I'll be right in."

I drove slowly to the parking lot and searched for a spot, of course the lot was full we were a little late. Fucking Todd. I pulled around to the near side of the lot and was just about to leave when I saw a small spot next to a BMW with the word "PASTOR" on the license plate. I pulled in carefully and sat there for a minute with the car idling.

Why did she have to mention his name? God, life is so unfair.

I could feel the tears welling up in my eyes; I shut off the car. Man, buck up; pull it together! I scolded myself. I checked the rearview mirror to make sure my mascara had not run. I was cool; I set my car alarm and walked slowly to the church front doors.

When I opened the doors to the church, the usher immediately quieted me because the church was in prayer. In the Pentecostal church you had to remain very still and very quiet during prayer; all movement had to cease until the whole congregation said "Amen."

I stood there and waited for the deacon to finish the prayer, but my thoughts were nowhere near what he was saying. I spent the whole prayer thinking about Marcus and what he was doing. I even missed the "amen," and only figured out it was over when the people who had entered next to me spoke it aloud.

Oh no—where was Grandma? I looked around for her, and of course she was seated way up near the front row. Dang, she always be running up front.

The ushers finally motioned for me and the other late people to enter and I tiptoed to the front of the church and sat next to my Grandma.

"Hey, baby."

"Hi, Grandma." As I took my seat and looked around, I noticed the same four little ladies seated on the front row;

sometimes they kept so still they reminded me of the statues I'd seen at a wax museum, until they hollered or moved their heads to the music.

They looked so cute—almost like little kids, but I knew better. One false move from a member of the congregation and those sweet little ladies turned into seething demons—ironic huh? One little lady had on all yellow; from the bright sunburst yellow hat all the way down to the bright yellow suede shoes, she was sharp. I giggled, thinking about if the divas could have seen her.

As the service warmed up it was time for the choir. Faith of Our Lord Tabernacle was known for their choir, the choir could blow. But there was one girl in particular always caught my attention. She was so delicate and seemed really young but I found out weeks before that she was actually in her early twenties. It was scary, she reminded me of myself when I sang in the choir, strong and posed when singing, but timid and shy as soon as the last note was sung.

The choir director motioned for the choir to stand and in one fell swoop the choir seats were emptied. The choir always looked sharp; they were dressed in royal blue and black robes with lapels that nearly reached the floor.

"They look real good, don't they, Grandma?"

"Yes, they do," Grandma smiled. "You need to be up there."

I cringed. She had to go and say that.

The music in the church rang out like a direct phone call to heaven. "Jesus Will Work It Out," the lead singer belted out with all her heart.

"That girl can *sang*," shouted my grandma, as the whole congregation stood up and burst into laughter, clapping in rhythm to the song. The choir sang for about ten minutes. When they finished, the congregation standing in sweat-filled pews felt uplifted and free. The choir director motioned the choir to sit, and the band kept playing just as loud and as strong as when they started until the MC came back to the podium and motioned for them to bring it down.

"Praise God, that was wonderful," the MC shouted, "Jesus will work it out!"

"It's time for the best part of the service, the time of giving, so everyone reach deep and bless this church and our Pastor as God has directed you."

When a basket finally got to Grandma and me, I put my offering in, thanking God for blessing me with the money to be able to give. I had been taught at a very young age that it was better to give than to receive and that you received your blessing according to your giving. So I always give a generous offering on top of my tithe, my ten percent; because of the blessings I had already received.

The sermon began at nine-thirty sharp. Pastor Robert Taylor was a hefty, dark-skinned man eyes the size of saucers that seemed to pierce right through my soul whenever he looked my way. His huge, booming voice filled the whole church, and sometimes you could hear him bellowing all the way down the street.

He began to pray; the whole church bowed their heads and listened as the Lord's eloquence streamed from the mouth of this chosen vessel.

"Amen, saints," the whole church said. "Amen."

"Today's topic, saints, is 'Trusting God,'" he said. I twitched. Here he goes, all up in my backyard; I better take notes. As I searched for a pen I could feel the corners of my mouth turn up in irritation. Wow, it never fails. Can't I have one Sunday when the preacher ain't talking to me?

The sermon was excellent and after church I went right up to the pastor and told him so, even though everything he said hit me like a ton of bricks. Trusting God was one thing I had a problem with—I just couldn't easily "live by faith and not by sight," even though that scripture had been drummed in me I'm sure since childbirth. I was one who needed immediate gratification, and learning to wait on the Lord was something I ignored many times over. I figured if He wasn't going to do it when I needed Him to, then what's the use; I'll do it myself.

"Great sermon, sir, I really enjoyed it."

"Good, young lady. Now you take those words to heart and do as the Good Book says."

"Yes sir, I will."

After I shook a couple of hands and hugged a few people, I turned around to look for Grandma and found her talking to the little lady in the yellow hat. I walked over and introduced myself and told the little lady how much I adored her dress. The lady smiled and gave me a huge hug.

"Thank you, darling."

"Are you ready to go, Grandma?"

"Yes, baby, I'm ready."

"Sister Mimi, I'll talk to you later on, all right?"

"Yes, Sister Wallace, see you next week. Bye now."

I felt pretty good after service and I held Grandma's hand as we walked to the car. The sun was shining brightly and I thought about how good it felt on my face. I was truly blessed.

I helped my grandma get into the car and we waved at all the saints as we drove down the two-way street towards home.

# Chapter 9

When I arrived at home I couldn't believe the day I had just had, from running into stupid-ass Todd to my grandmother badgering me about Marcus. I felt blindsided by events.

Even though it was Sunday and I had just left church, I really had to have something to calm me down; a shot of something would put me in the right frame of mind. I rummaged around in the liquor cabinet and pulled out the last little hit of Jameson. I swallowed it straight from the bottle, and then threw it in the recycle bin.

Damn, I hadn't thought about Marcus for months and now I was on collision course with mood swings and depression.

It was about eleven forty-five and the sun was beaming through the windows, illuminating the whole front room. I was kind of in a funk but wasn't going to let this beautiful day pass me by. I decided to take a walk along the new cobblestone boulevard. The city decided downtown needed a facelift. They put in a cobblestone walkway along with a biking trail to beautify the area. I hadn't had a chance to see it yet, but figured there was no better day than today to go and check it out. But first I had to get out of my church clothes.

I went to the closet and pulled out the blue and green walking shorts I bought in Mexico last summer and the light green tank top I borrowed from Sadie. It was very important that everything I wore matched, even if I was just going for a walk. And the only top I had to match my shorts was Sadie's.

"Dang, she's probably looking for this; I've had it for probably six months. Well, I won't say anything; I'll just wait until she asks for it."

Sadie and I always shared clothes and we each knew that if we wanted to, we could go to each other's houses and find our own wardrobes in the closets. But it was cool, we were so close that it really didn't matter who had what item; we both knew if we needed something the other one had it.

I changed clothes, put my tennis shoes on and walked towards the front door when the phone rang. I looked at the caller ID.

It's Sadie. Damn, spoke her up.

"Hey, Sadie," I said, picking up the phone.

"Hey, what's up, girl?"

"Nothing much—just coming in from church with Grandma. What's up with you?"

"Girl, you would not believe what happened to me after we left the club last night."

"What?"

"That nigga Calvin, the one with the moon booty?" We called Calvin 'moon booty' because he had an ass from outta this world—big, round, and flabby. It looked like it should have been on a woman.

"Yeah, what about him?"

"You know I went to his crib last night."

"Yeah, and?"

"That motherfucker is filthy."

"Say what?"

"Well, you know he had that funny-ass, foul-ass smell about him."

"Yeah, I remember you telling me about that."

"OK, peep this; I go to his house, the house is nasty, his mattress is on the floor and there is trash and shit everywhere, right?"

"OK, so what happened?"

"Nigga, I went to the bathroom and started to sit down and a cockroach was staring me dead in the face; like what's up, who are you, we ain't never seen you in here before. I screamed—girl, scared the shit out of me. I got my purse and my shit and said I'll holler. Jasmine the shit was crazy."

I burst into laughter. "Now that's funny."

I couldn't help it even though I knew my continuous laughter was going to make Sadie mad.

"Look, ho, it ain't that funny."

"Oh yes it is, ho, I told you about messin' with those ghetto-ass niggas."

"Damn, girl, I thought he was cool; he was clean, fine and had a good job, just nasty as hell. I should have known."

"Well, where did you think the foul-ass smell came from—something about him had to be funny?"

"I know. That's what I get, nigga's ass bigger than mine. Ugh!

"So how was church?" she asked.

"It was great; you know it always seem like the pastor is talking directly to me. I don't care what sermon it is, it's got my name all over it."

"Yeah, I hear that. I don't go to church as much as you, but when I do, I feel the same way. So what you getting ready to do?"

"I was going for a walk to clear my head, Grandma was trippin' on me about finding a man and settling down, and why did she have to bring up Marcus?"

Sadie gasped. "Oh my God—the forbidden word."

"Oh shut up, girl, you're crazy."

"Jasmine, you're the one that said we couldn't say that word around you."

"Yeah, ho, and you still can't say it."

"Marcus, Marcus, Marcus."

"OK, smart-ass, wait until I see you."

"Whatever, girl, go on and go for your walk, call me when you get back."

"OK, I'll do that."

"Oh by the way, do you still have my light green tank top?"

"Uh no, I gave that back to you long time ago."

"Yeah, right; quit lying, ho, your ass probably got it on right now."

I busted out laughing.

"Bring me my top, ho."

"OK, I'll bring it to you after I wash it."

"You better; I'll talk to you later."

"All right, holler."

Sadie was the bomb. She reminded me of one of those women straight out of a fashion magazine. She had long, soft black hair that she always wore in the tightest ponytail ever created, and her caramel-colored skin was flawless. Her makeup, which she applied herself, was always perfect. She swore up and down she had a problem with raccoon eyes but I never saw that. She looked like a supermodel.

The brothers couldn't resist her long legs slim waist and round ass. When they were out, Sadie got play from all the men that loved big asses and I got play from all the men who loved big-ass tits. We complemented each other in that way. And we loved it.

Sadie was my girl, and I loved and admired her so much that I pretty much let her talk me into anything. Including things that sometimes got us too much attention, but I didn't mind one bit we were best friends and I had her back in whatever.

\* \* \*

Our freshman year in college, the Kappas were having the biggest party of the year. It was homecoming and Sadie and I decided to crash the Kappas' step show. There was almost always alcohol at these parties, and the drinking age was 21, so freshmen weren't allowed.

Sadie was a year and a week older than me; she turned eighteen in January of our senior year in high school, but I wouldn't turn eighteen until January of next year. So we always had to wear those stupid underage wristbands, which pretty much marked us as being too young for anything, including sex. We hated that idea the most.

We found out about the party by dipping in on a conversation between two fine-ass brothers walking down the hall. One of them had the Greek letter for Kappa burned into his right forearm. We looked at them, then we looked at each other. Without even saying it out loud, we knew: We're there.

We had two problems, though. How were we going to get in? And what were we going to wear? That last was he bigger problem of the two.

Both Sadie and I being born in January made us Capricorns—stubborn, bullheaded and determined. So giving up without a fight was never our style.

"A party like this comes around once in a lifetime so we have no choice but to act. And act fast," Sadie said. We figured in order to get in without anyone noticing we were underclassmen, we'd have to wear something that would make a big impression, make us look like we fit in. Something so fly they would forget about carding us or anything and just let us in.

Of course, Sadie saved the day.

It didn't look that way for a while, though. Early afternoon, the night of the party I talked to Sadie; she still hadn't come up with anything for us to wear. We couldn't go in half-steppin or we'd be laughed at, and talked about all over campus.

"Sadie, you better find something for us to wear, or I ain't going."

"I will, chill."

"I'll be home by seven o'clock."

"Yeah, yeah, I know."

Sadie put up the ironing board and grabbed the new pair of jeans she bought from Express. She plugged in the iron and waited for it to heat up; as the hissing sound of steam whistled out from the iron-holes, she laid her jeans flat against the cloth and began to iron. Just as the heat started to press out the wrinkles in her jeans, she had an idea. She set the iron upright on the pants leg and rummaged through the closet looking for her lavender silk top.

About a quarter of the way through, she smelled something burning. She whirled around, realizing she accidentally knocked the iron over onto her jeans. She rushed to the ironing board, and snatched the iron from the jeans, but it was too late; it had burned a sizable hole right above the knee.

"Damn! What am I going to do now?"

She was pissed, but must have had some sort of epiphany—or at least a stroke of genius. Instead of throwing away a perfectly good pair of jeans and looking for something else to wear, she improvised.

She cut holes in the jeans all over, all the way down each leg, front and back. Then she washed them so that the fibers started to fray. Then she tugged and pulled at the strings to make it look authentic. She called me at work and told me she thought she had something for us to wear.

"Sadie, it better not be something wild and out of pocket."

"Hell no, it ain't wild, it's cool and it's what we're wearing to the Kappa party tonight."

"What did you do? I'm not wearing anything crazy again, you remember what happened last time."

She laughed. "I know, I know—this is way better than that; hurry up."

"All right, but it better be good."

I opened the door and couldn't believe my eyes. Sadie was standing there looking sexy as hell, thigh and calf muscles showing through all the slits she had made.

"Oh my God, I love it," I screamed. "Hurry up; do mine like that."

"Go and find some jeans."

I ran to the dresser and started digging around for an old pair of jeans I was willing to cut up. I found a light blue pair buried under my old high school sweatshirt that I hadn't worn in months, so I figured I wouldn't miss them too much. I handed them to Sadie.

"Hold up—I better try these on first. I don't want my fat-ass thighs squeezing through the holes." I was worried I had gained weight over the summer from all the drinking, eating, and partying.

Sadie cracked up.

I undressed and put the jeans on. "Whew, they still fit."

Sadie took my jeans and started cutting them, making slits all along the front and down the back.

"Hurry up and throw them in the washer," she practically ordered me.

I ran down the hall to the laundry room, and just sat there, watching them go around, first in the washer, then the dryer. When I pulled them out, they were perfect. A few fibers to pull but overall they were the bomb.

Sadie suggested we wear the jeans with matching tank tops, leather boots and leather jackets, in different colors. I wore a black tank top with black boots and a black leather jacket and Sadie had on a brown tank top with brown boots and a brown leather jacket. We were exactly what we thought we were, "the shit," as usual.

When we got to the party, we had no trouble getting in—everyone was staring at us trying to see what we had on. We walked in like we owned the place; no one had time to card us or even ask us any questions. We partied hard that night and danced until we couldn't dance any more. We left feeling pretty good about ourselves.

The next thing we knew, every female on campus was wearing holey jeans. Every time we saw some girl, running around like that, we smiled to ourselves; we knew we had started the whole fad.

Well, at least we thought we did. Sadie and I had done some crazy things while in college, but it felt good and that was all that mattered.

# Chapter 10

I gathered up my iPod, put on my tennis shoes and headed for the front door. As I stepped across the threshold, I glanced over my shoulder and noticed the package that I had thrown on the couch. I turned, shut the door, and hurried over to open it.

I looked for a return address but there wasn't one. So I looked at the postmark; it was sent two days ago from Hawaii. I was mystified; who would have sent me a package from Hawaii? I opened up the box and foraged through the tissue paper until I uncovered the most beautiful coral and turquoise pendant.

Oh my God.

I dug around in the box but I couldn't find a card until I lifted up a small piece of tissue paper and noticed some really strange writing on a small piece of lined paper, like it was from a small notebook. It almost looked as if whoever sent it had purposely written in block letters to keep me in suspense. It read, "To the most wonderful woman in the world." It was signed "a dear friend."

The hairs on my neck stood straight up. Who could this be from? It was gorgeous and it must have cost a fortune. I took the note and the pendant, carried them into my bedroom, and placed them gently on the dresser.

Who could be in Hawaii right now? I stood there, going over all my friends, family and even acquaintances.

Then it hit me.

Marcus; maybe it was Marcus. He knew I loved jewelry—but what was he doing in Hawaii?

# I Surrender All

As I cradled the pendant in my hand, memories came flooding back to me of a special night not too long ago.

* * *

Marcus had been the love of my life. He was the proverbial tall, dark and handsome man. His skin was the color of a cup of hot mocha, and his smooth-as-silk bald head was always shining. Women flocked to him whenever they could get close.

He had lustrous dark brown eyes and the most perfect lips ever created: They were round and full, and his lower lip had a sensual touch of pink right in the center.

The fullness of his lips captivated me, especially when we kissed. He was an aggressive kisser. I loved to tease him; I would pretend to give in, then pull back. He would get so excited that he would grab me and thrust his tongue deep into my mouth so that I would know deep in every part of me the intensity of his need to feel me. Of course I loved kissing him. The control he had over me aroused me, and I gave him more of me than I ever intended.

His years playing college basketball had left him with chiseled arms and legs, and his hands and feet were soft, like a woman's. I used to tease him about it, but I truly loved massaging his hands and feet—and I didn't really like touching feet like that.

But for all that, it was the person inside I loved the most. He was the most humorous, calm spirit I had ever encountered. Funny but down to earth, he was interested in so many things; he could adapt to every situation, whether we were at the ballpark, a fancy restaurant, a museum, or a loud nightclub.

Still, at heart he was really a homebody. That's where he liked to be the most, at home drinking coffee and listening to music. He had developed a fixation on different types of coffees, carefully selecting the best beans and grinding different flavors together to craft wonderfully smooth creations, which he called his little piece of coffee heaven.

So that's what we usually did, sat and drank coffee. I shared many nights at Marcus' place; we would sit together by the fireplace, looking deeply into each other eyes and drinking the best cup of coffee ever brewed. I loved coffee, but had to have it lots of cream and sugar. Marcus hated that; he would almost scold me, telling me that all that extra stuff ruined the true flavor. I didn't care though. I drank my coffee the way I liked it, extra sweet with cream.

# Chapter 11

It was a warm June night and Marcus had invited me over for dinner and a little playtime, so he called it. I could hardly wait; I was so excited I had to apologize to everyone in my office for acting so strange all day. Marcus made me crazy; he had a spell over me that I didn't quite know how to control. He was good to me and loved me and I knew it. I loved to please him and he me. I knew it would be a special evening, and I wanted it to be perfect. This meant the works; I started making appointments.

I had just had a manicure and pedicure the week before, but that didn't matter. I called the little Korean shop and spoke with Tram. She was happy to hear from me and told me she'd be ready whenever I could come in. I figured if I could get to her as soon as they opened at eleven, I could be done and over to Andrea at the hair salon by one.

I had one major problem though—getting Andrea to fit me in. I knew I could sweet-talk her into giving me a spot, but time was of the essence.

I had just had my hair done the week before so when I called Andrea to make the appointment she was surprised.

"Girl, you were just here a couple of days ago, what's going on?"

"I have a very special night planned and I have to look perfect."

"You must have a date with Marcus."

"You know I do, girl, he's made all these plans and I have to be right. I'm probably gonna sweat it out anyway, but it has to be done. Do you have any time for me? Please, please say you do."

Andrea burst out in a hearty laugh. "Yeah, girl, you know I have a spot for you. Can you come in at one-thirty?"

"Yes that's perfect. I'll be there."

I arrived at the salon at one-thirty sharp, straight from the Korean shop. My nails and feet were perfect and getting my hair done would be the last thing before I was completely ready for the evening.

The receptionist always knew I saw Andrea. She asked me to have a seat and went to get Andrea.

Andrea came right out, smiling broadly.

"Ready to get this party started?" She hugged me so hard she practically squeezed the breath out of me.

I smiled. "Yes I am. Thank you so much for getting me in, Andrea. I really needed this."

"I know, girl, you've been coming to me for so long, you know I'm going to take care of you. So tell me what's going on tonight."

"I really don't know, Andrea. He called and told me to meet him at his house at six-thirty tonight. He said he had a big surprise and not to bother about bringing anything but my beautiful smile."

"Damn, girl," Andrea screamed, "where did you find him?"

"Girl, I don't know, he found me."

"Come on, Jasmine, let's go to the shampoo bowl."

I settled into the chair and leaned back, letting Andrea run the water until it got to the right temperature, as I daydreamed about Marcus. I couldn't believe it; just months before I was alone and going through a mid-life crisis at twenty-four.

As Andrea washed my hair I loosened up even more, with the kind of relaxation only a good scalp massage and shampoo could give, and it erased all the anxiety from earlier that morning.

I loved the salon—not just for Andrea, but the whole ambiance. It was called Hair Freedom. The owner was a petite woman from Mozambique named Niarobi Fuusa. She had long thick dreadlocks, thicker than most locks I had seen, and a dark round face, with eyes the color of burnt gold, and she walked around the salon as if she were the Queen of the Nile.

The salon itself was an African dream. Every painting, sculpture, and knick-knack had come directly from Niarobi's brother's store in Africa, and each item was meticulously placed to show off its strength and character and play off the rest of the decor.

Victor was a world traveler who bought items from all over the world, but he had a special place in his heart for the traditional art from the small village where he and his sister grew up. He had set up his original shop when he was nineteen, on the border of Mozambique and Zimbabwe, and hired the village children to help him run it. Now his three sons ran it while he was gone.

Even though he was rarely seen at the salon, the time he spent in Minneapolis was generally used to network his business; he sat on several boards and helped to start a nonprofit organization to wage war against child labor. The one-of-a-kind pieces he brought back were handcrafted items that had no trouble fetching his asking price. He believed in helping out the smaller, more impoverished countries of Africa and sometimes would negotiate the sale of an entire collection in order to get the best prices. He knew selling the pieces individually would net more money, but if he sold an entire collection he wouldn't be left with straggling items in his storage garage.

While Andrea finished me up at the shampoo bowls, a nice-looking brother came in and sat down at the bowl next to mine.
"Hello."
"Hey, how you doing?" I smiled.
"Oh, I'm fine, thank you."
"You sure are," Andrea burst out.
We couldn't stop grinning, she eyeballing me and me her.
She whispered, "Damn, he fine as hell."
"I know, huh?"
"So Mr. Fine, do you have a name?" Andrea asked him.
I glared at her. She was always so bold.
Just as he was about to respond, Bryce, the flamboyantly gay hairdresser from the other side of the salon appeared out of nowhere, switching and waving his hand.

"All right, ladies, stop ogling my clients. Y'all know better, you better get you some business."

"Oh Bryce, sorry—we didn't know he was with you."

"Yes he is, and a fine specimen he is, isn't he?"

"Yes ma'am, he is, girl," exclaimed Andrea. "We will definitely be on our way."

"Yeah, y'all make it back to your seats."

I held my towel on my head and close to my neck so it wouldn't drip, while Andrea followed me back to her chair.

"Damn, girl, what's up with that?" I giggled.

"Girl, that fine-ass man be coming in here all the time, he just don't know how much it hurts to see another brother gone by the wayside."

"What you mean, wayside?" chimed in Gabriele, a stylist stationed next to Andrea. "Don't you mean the backside?"

Everyone in earshot broke out laughing.

I usually tried to contain my laughter when I was at the salon, because so much trash was talked about folks that I didn't want anybody to start on me because I was laughing at them. I was a brainiac nerd all through high school and most of college and didn't know how to *cap,* like when you played the dozens. So I just sat quietly and held my breath during all the laughter and tried not to let on that I was cracking up inside. But this time even I had to laugh.

Andrea began blow-drying my hair, making conversation impossible, and my thoughts returned to Marcus. I tried hard not to get all riled up, because getting my hair done was supposed to be relaxing, but the thought of an evening alone with Marcus had me all crazy inside.

I asked Andrea to pass me a magazine to get my mind off him, and of course Andrea handed me the latest issue of Essence with Will and Jada on the cover. Oh my God, what a beautiful couple. Damn, they almost look like brother and sister. I turned to the article about them and began to read. I started to feel inspired as I read about their relationship and how they treated and respected each other. I felt like I was developing that type of relationship with Marcus and to see a couple actually making it made me happy.

In the article, Will and Jada stressed their shared values of teamwork, honesty, and pure, unconditional love. They explained that's how they had survived Hollywood and all its crazy problems—no privacy, temptation everywhere, inflated egos. By remembering their commitment they were able to keep their family together and strong.

Wow, how cool, I thought. If things go right I hoped maybe someday Marcus and I could get to feel the way they do.

Andrea finished up the last curl and told me she was done.

"OK, Andrea, thank you." I handed her a fifty-dollar bill and told her I would call her with the details.

Andrea smiled. "I know you will, girl."

"Thanks again, Andrea, and I'll talk to you soon."

"OK, Jaz, I'll see you next week. Thank you, too."

I walked to the car, hair dancing in the soft breeze, which now commanded my attention. What a beautiful day. If I can just make it through this day I know my life will be better.

There was one more thing I needed to do before I was completely satisfied with my preparations.

I needed new lingerie; I knew the perfect shop. After I left the salon, I drove over to Uptown and pulled up in front of the most elegant lingerie boutique in Minnesota. It was in a converted Victorian house, like so many of the stores in the neighborhood, one of the city's most chic addresses. Most of these boutiques only sold specialty items, many of them imported, and catered to a wealthy clientele; the shop owners usually had a specific list of clients they called when new shipments came in. I wasn't on this list—yet.

I walked through the stained-glass front door and was greeted by a tall, very thin blond woman in a skimpy sundress. She had a perfect size-six body; she reminded me of one of the old Barbie dolls I used to collect as a child.

"Good afternoon. Is there something I can help you find, ma'am?" she asked. A cloud of perfume followed her around the store. I couldn't identify it, but I enjoyed the spice and sensuality of the scent.

"Well, yes, I'm looking for something really special. I have a very important evening planned with my boyfriend and I want to look my best. I'm looking for bra and panty sets as well as a nice negligee, preferably something that comes to here," I said, and motioned to the middle of my thigh—"the shorter the better."

"Well, let me show you to our newest line. They just arrived today and they're gorgeous."

I followed the Barbie doll look-alike to a special room designed for private showings and sank into the chair upholstered in velvet. The young lady disappeared into a back room and returned with a selection of items.

"Now, Ms. . . . uh, I'm sorry I didn't get your name. My name is Kirsten."

"My name is Jasmine Burrell."

"Why yes, Ms. Burrell, take a look at this line. First of all, the bra and panties in this line are one-of-a-kind pieces handmade from the purest raw silk. They only sent one in each size, and color, so you have first dibs." She smiled as she handed me the first set. "Also the colors are hand-dyed and each garment is pre-washed and conditioned so you feel nothing but the smoothest touch against your skin. Here, feel this."

I reached out and touched the panties. Shit, she was right; the silk was so soft that I couldn't pull my fingers away.

"This material makes it a little more expensive but I believe you and your boyfriend will really enjoy them. Don't you?"

"Yes I do, Kristen. How much are the sets?"

"This set goes for a hundred and fifty dollars, but I guarantee you won't be sorry. Plus, I think you're worth it."

I touched the bra and panties one more time. She was right. I'm worth it, and so was Marcus.

She showed me a few other sets in different colors and styles, and some really sexy negligees that fell right at my thigh; I liked them all. My favorite was that first set she'd shown me—it was kind of a metallic color that seemed to shimmer, going from navy blue to green as the light caught it. I also liked the white and silver embroidered negligee. It was so elegant, and I really wanted Marcus to see me in that one.

I asked for the items I selected in a size seven panties and a 38C bra. She went right to the back and found the sizes I needed. I bought the blue set, the black set, and a white and gold set in those same two sizes but in a different line. I also bought several camisoles and negligees. Might as well stock up, I figured.

As Kirsten rang up my items, I realized I also needed some perfume—maybe something like what Kirsten was wearing.

"Kirsten, do you sell the fragrance you're wearing? I love it."

"Yes we do—it's called Eternal Love; it's actually a blend of essential oils, but it's one of our best sellers."

I smiled, "I can see why. It smells wonderful."

"Here, try a little on. It starts strong in the beginning, but then it matches scents with your body chemistry, and the endorphins they put in this fragrance are guaranteed to drive any man absolutely crazy."

I smiled. "Then I'll take two bottles."

Kirsten laughed. "Is there anything else you need, Jasmine?"

"Actually, yes. Do you sell candles?"

"Sure, but I you might do better at a store like Candelabra—they have a wider variety and their prices are better. Or you could try the store right next door—it's kind of like that, so you could probably find what you want."

"OK, thank you. I'll do that."

I paid and went next door. It was one of those New Agey shops full of soaps, sprays and lotions, candles and bath beads. As I walked through the doors a mix of scents, softly enveloped me like a cloud of serenity. The first candle I picked up, part of an entry display, was an aromatherapy candle created more for relaxation than for fragrance. This is exactly what I need, I thought.

Then I went over to the candle section; it seemed like they had every scent known to man (including some I had never heard of), but they seemed to specialize in jasmine, mint, rosemary and vanilla. I wasn't a real fan of the scent of vanilla—I didn't want to smell like a cake—but I actually liked the combination of vanilla and jasmine. The jasmine added a spicier edge to the scent, and it seemed to balance the sweetness of the vanilla.

I chose five candles—that seemed like it would be enough to keep the room at just the right, soft light, but not so many that the fragrance would be overpowering. Then I carefully selected five holders to match the candles.

I walked out the door with a sense of accomplishment and growing anticipation. Then I glanced at my watch. It was already four-thirty.

"Oh shit, I have a ton of things to do." I sprinted to the car, placed the bags carefully in the trunk, and gently shut it. Then I jumped in the car.

The ride home was exhilarating; the anticipation of seeing Marcus was all I could think about. It usually took me twenty minutes to get home from the Uptown area, but when I woke up from my fantasy I realized I had done it in twelve.

Wow. I knew I had driven way too fast, but Marcus—damn.

I grabbed the bags from the trunk and ran up the front steps to my apartment building. I could tell by the smirk on the doorman's face that the silly grin that had seemed permanently plastered on my face all day was a bit ridiculous, but I couldn't control it. Besides, I didn't care.

"Good afternoon, Ms. Burrell. You sure are in a good mood."

"Hello, Mr. Bradley, yes I am. Thanks for getting the door for me."

"It's my pleasure Ms. Burrell. You have a nice day."

"You too. Mr. Bradley."

I walked over to Jonathan and asked if I could leave the car out front for a moment; I was only going to be a minute. Yes, he said, but he needed the car keys in case he had to move it. I took the key off the ring, thanked Jonathan, and ran over to the elevator and triple-pressed the button, as if that would make it come quicker. As I waited, my thoughts inevitably returned to Marcus.

# Chapter 12

NO ONE EVER REALLY UNDERSTOOD how our relationship developed so quickly. It was like we already knew each other—in another life, maybe, and through some cosmic miracle we were reunited in this dimension. Not a day went by that we weren't together and there wasn't a moment of wasted energy. Our relationship was built on love, respect, and open communication.

I remember one Saturday afternoon. I was in the living room watching a cooking show when Marcus and his best friends Charles and Devon barged in from playing basketball and decided they wanted to watch the NBA playoffs.

The fact that they came busting in on my show was not really the problem. I knew Marcus was going to want to watch it when he got home and in all actuality, I wanted to watch it too. I loved sports, which always gave me brownie points when it came to meeting men. I actually knew a little more than a little bit about the three key sports, basketball, football, and baseball. But I watched everything, anything that had to do with someone hitting, throwing or smacking around a little ball. And boxing was my favorite. Big, burly, beautiful, men, sweaty and throwing that testosterone around really turned me on.

So when Marcus and the guys came in and started talking about watching the playoffs, I immediately changed the channel, and I asked them if they wanted a beer. Everyone replied yes, so I got up and headed to the kitchen. As I was leaving I heard Marcus holler out "my nigga."

I brought them the beers and sat quietly in the corner while they watched. But I was pissed. I was in no way shape or form "his nigga." It was not my style to front him off in front of his friends, though. I had seen Carla, another one of the Southside Divas, do it to her man on several occasions. I felt you always left your man with his dignity when he was with his boys. But after they were gone his temporarily inflated ego was yours.

After the first half was over, I called Marcus to the bedroom. I looked him dead in the eye and told him that I didn't *ever* want to be *called "his nigga"* again.

"Have you grabbed Devon's ass, or ever kissed Charles in the mouth?" I demanded, to make my point perfectly clear "Shit, they were your nigga's too; you doing all of them?"

Of course he wasn't, he said, with a half-smile. I could tell he did not find my comparison too amusing. But he got the picture and promised never to do it again.

Then he grabbed me in a bear hug and whispered in my ear, *"you still my nigga."*

I laughed and swatted him away. That was one reason I loved him so much—he always knew how to make me smile.

# Chapter 13

When I finally got to my apartment I searched the closet for just the right outfit. I pulled out the tight fitted floral peach and white dress. The dress was a little wrinkled, so I turned on the hanging steamer and headed for the shower while it heated up. As the hot water streamed over my body I felt that warm, liquid sensation when I thought about Marcus's touch began to rise, starting from between my legs, then into my belly and my chest. I gasped and clutched my breasts, rubbing them gently; as a single tear ran down my face, I softly, mouthed the words

"Thank you"—to God.

I stepped out of the shower feeling refreshed. I dried off, put on a smoothing lotion that made my skin soft to the touch, and proceeded to get dressed. The bra and panties set fit perfectly; I couldn't help but admire my figure as I checked myself out in the mirror. That didn't happen very often, but since I had been with Marcus, I could stand to look at myself again. He made me feel so perfect, so beautiful.

I put on the dress, which felt soft and silky against my skin; and it was warm and cozy on top of that, thanks to the steam iron. It felt so good; I began to caress my body and realized I was rubbing myself a little too hard. I was starting to get all worked up again; then I glanced at the clock—damn, I have got to get my shit together. It was already five-thirty and I really wanted to be on time.

I slipped into the matching peach and white sandals then raced to the mirror. A little foundation, blush, mascara, eyeliner—whew,

I was done—for now at least; I always waited to put on my lipstick in the car on the way. I needed it to be as fresh as possible. I grabbed the perfumed oil out of the shopping bag and carefully put a drop on what I felt were the most sensual spots, starting with the area along both sides of my neck from behind my ear down to my collarbone, the small indentation right below my Adam's apple, the creases of my elbows, and the insides of my wrists. For extra emphasis I lightly oiled my cleavage. I knew where this evening was headed and I wanted him to know I knew.

*Now* I was ready. I ran to the phone and called Jonathan to let him know I was on my way down; the car was waiting. I grabbed the shopping bags and a bottle of wine and stepped out of my apartment, closing the door behind me. Just as the door clicked shut, the elevator doors opened, and I entered, smiling and glowing, inside and out.

When I stepped out of the elevator into the lobby, Jonathan looked up from his magazine. I blushed deeply; his eyes almost popped right out of his head.

"Wow, Ms. Burrell, you look beautiful. Here are your keys."

I smiled. "Thank you. Bye, Jonathan."

"Bye, Ms. Burrell, have a wonderful night."

"Call me Jasmine."

# Chapter 14

By now it was quarter to six, and the drive to Marcus's house was about a 20-minute ride. He lived in a very affluent area of Edina that was mostly seven-figure professionals. His father had bought him a house when he turned eighteen, but made sure Marcus was a part of the whole process. After the purchase was completed, Marcus was to pay all of the utilities and costs of upkeep while he was in school. And he would take over the mortgage payments as soon as he graduated from college. I guess Mr. Damon was trying to teach Marcus the importance of home ownership, and it worked. Marcus never missed a payment, and kept the house in tip-top shape.

Marcus's parents were both doctors, so they made sure Marcus and his five sisters knew the value of a good education and hard work. They taught them at a very young age what it meant to be an African-American in America: Always be better than the best, and never forget where you came from.

Everett and Lolita Damon were the most successful couple in their quiet neighborhood of Edina. They both attended Ivy League colleges, his father at Yale and his mother at Harvard; he was a pediatrician and she was a clinical psychologist; they both specialized in the health and mental welfare of children. And since they had had six children themselves, they were the living embodiment of the importance of family.

Marcus' house was a two-bedroom, two-bath Victorian-style home on a yard the size of two football fields. It had an in-ground pool and four-season porches that looked out over a tiny stream in the backyard. Marcus and I spent hours sitting out on the porch drinking coffee, planning our future, and making love on the settee.

As I drove towards Marcus' I decided to stop at the corner store for lemons and a bag of ice. I had thought of something that would drive Marcus mad. I pulled into the parking lot and got out, tugging my dress down a little bit because driving made it rise up above mid-thigh. I was already showing enough cleavage to stop traffic, so going into the store with my ass hanging out would have been too much.

I asked the clerk where the ice was kept; he pointed to the back freezer and mumbled something under his breath as I walked away. I knew he must have been staring at my ass, because when I returned he had a slick-ass grin on his face. I smirked back and plucked two lemons from the tiny produce section.

"Will this be all, ma'am?"

"Yes, sir."

"It will be two dollars and thirty-seven cents."

I pulled out a five-dollar bill, collected my change, and sped towards Marcus's house, pulling into his driveway. The digital clock on the dashboard flashed six twenty-nine.

I looked up toward the front door, and there was Marcus, giving me a look with those brown eyes of his. He was obviously as anxious as I was.

He poked his head out the door. "Hey, I see you need some help, let me get those bags."

I beamed as I reached over and opened up the passenger door to let Marcus get the bags.

"Ice? Why did you buy ice? You know I have plenty of ice."

"Dang, I know. God, you're so nosy, mind your own business."

"OK, OK, I will. Come here and give me a kiss."

I walked over to Marcus and kissed him softly on the lips. I felt the blood coursing, and my body warm up a few degrees as I gently placed my tongue in his open mouth. We stood there for few minutes kissing and smiling and kissing again.

"Wait," I blushed. "This is almost too much. Let me get the door." I grabbed the knob and held the door open for him to carry the bags in.

We walked through the immaculate foyer into the kitchen, which was a treat in itself. The house was decorated in a contemporary yet masculine fashion—bold colors, accented with muted purples and grays. There were oversized couches and chairs, stone and marble tables, smoked glass lamps, and a excessively manly entertainment center. All the fixtures and décor were well ahead of 21st-century trends, like the concepts had come from a futuristic magazine or something. The designer had come all the way from Europe to perfectly match every aspect of the house, down to the covers on the electrical sockets.

Marcus had been studying to become an investment banker but really enjoyed home decorating as a hobby. So the decorating along with the coffee thing made him seem a tad bit domesticated, which his boys razzed him about, but I loved it.

I followed him into the kitchen and started helping him empty the bags.

"Uh wait, I'll do that; is that smoke I smell?" I said.

"Yeah, why? I was grilling."

"Well, you better go check on it, I think something is burning."

"Girl, you're crazy—ain't nothing burning, because I've already taken everything off."

"Oh, well, go find something else to do."

"Oh, I get it. There's something in those bags you don't want me to see." He laughed.

"Whatever, just go."

He poured himself a cup of coffee and walked out to the porch.

Once he was out, I took out the bottle of wine and opened it. Rosemount shiraz was best when it had a chance to breathe. It usually took about ten minutes and I wanted it to be just right. Then I put the ice in a metal bowl, cut up the lemons and squeezed the juice all over the ice, placed the lemons and rinds on top of the ice mound, and put the bowl in the freezer.

Marcus loved lemons—sliced, no sugar, just straight-up lemon out of the rind. As a kid, he said, after his mother made lemon pies and he stood right next to her and waited for the rest of the lemon. His mother was a sweetheart, and on top of that made the best lemon pies I had ever tasted—next to my mother's, of course.

Now I wanted to sneak up to the bedroom to put up all the candles. As I tiptoed towards the upstairs, I passed the dining room and glanced in. I was completely stunned by what I saw.

Dinner was already on the table, plated on one of his mother's favorite china sets. His mother had gotten it from her mother; Marcus' mother had given the set to him, being that he was the only boy they had had. Of course this made his sisters mad but he didn't care. Months ago one of his sisters had told me how spoiled he was, but I never thought he acted like it.

The dishes—he had cooked them all himself—were waiting to be served from crystal and stainless steel serving bowls. The candles seemed like they were six feet tall, sparkling and reflecting off the Victorian mirror on the wall. The floral centerpiece was stunning, with four different-color roses and lilies, and some other beautiful blue flowers I didn't even know the name of.

I began to cry. As I turned to go upstairs, Marcus startled me. He had been standing behind me for some time.

"I really wanted to grab you and hold you tight, baby," he said softly. "But first I wanted you to see what I had planned..."

I set the bags down and flung my arms around his neck and cried softly in his arms.

"Come on, Jaz, don't cry. This is supposed to be a happy occasion."

He reached over and delicately removed a single red rose from the centerpiece. Then he wiped away my tears with the petals. I thought I was going to faint with joy.

"I don't understand. Why so much?"

"Don't you think you're worth all of this, Jaz?"

"I don't know Marcus. I'm scared."

"You have nothing to be afraid of, I just want you to be with me; let me love you."

With my cheeks still wet with tears, we gazed deep into each other's eyes and I kissed him so hard that this time, *he* almost fainted.

\* \* \*

# Chapter 15

THE TIME HAD FLOWN BY so fast; I realized dusk was setting in. I still wanted to get my walk in, so instead of going down to the street, I decided to go to the walking track at the top of my building, which had a full-fledged gym and spa, complete with state-of-the-art equipment, a pool, sauna, and massage table. The owners had also added a patio area for tenants, which was mostly used for reading, relaxing, and sunbathing.

I closed and locked the front door and took the one flight of stairs up from my condo's floor, coming out on the rooftop patio. It was a botanist's dream, with flowers and trees everywhere—roses, daisies, lilies, hibiscus, which were my favorite—and rows and rows of annuals that lined the picnic area and the walking path. Everything was scaled down, but it practically shimmered with color. The forest-green smell reminded me of the trees I grew up with in my grandmother's backyard. I put in my earphones and hit play on my iPod and began to briskly walk around the track. As I got half way around, I saw someone in the gym using the Stairmaster. It looked like Nathan.

The stocky, almost comically cute middle-aged man waved vigorously; it must be him. I smiled broadly and waved back. Nathan was a really good friend of mine, but lately we were both so busy that we really didn't have time to hang out like we used too.

Nathan was a CPA; he was a partner in the company his father started some fifty years ago. He was short, with balding blond hair that he still highlighted even though there wasn't much left to color. Nathan was one of the few men I jibed with well. He was fun and funny, and always had sidesplitting stories to tell. He also drove a brand-new Jaguar every several years, which I assumed were leased. My mom had always wanted a Jag from as far back as I can remember, and when she met and saw his, she fell in love with it. So on her fifty-fifth birthday, he asked his dealer to help me purchase one for her.

Nathan was a card and I loved to be with him. At times I had thought about a relationship with him but I couldn't commit—one because when we first met, he was going through a terrible divorce, and two, because of the difference in race. I didn't feel I had a racial complex, and I did like him very much; but I felt like I would be betraying my race if I became involved with him. It was just that in Minnesota you didn't see a whole lot of professional black women who dated and represented strong black men; we bashed too much. So as a strong black woman, dating a white man in an exclusive relationship would send the wrong message.

Nathan stepped off the Stairmaster and approached me with a smile the size of Texas.

"Hey, Jasmine, how are you?" He walked up and gave me a huge hug.

"Oh, I'm fine, Nathan, how are you?"

"Great. It's really good to see you."

"You too."

"How are your mother and that new Jag of hers?"

"She absolutely loves it. Thanks again for your help."

"It was no trouble; you know I love your mother."

"Yeah, I know."

There was a moment of uncomfortable silence. "I really miss you, Jasmine," Nathan said. "Do you think you have time to go out with me for dinner or a drink sometime soon?"

"Of course I do."

"OK, I'll call you later this week."

"Great, that'll be fine. Have a nice evening, Nathan."

Nathan kissed me on the cheek and slowly walked towards the elevators.

I finished my walk around the track and wiped the sweat from my forehead and neck. As I entered my apartment, I flung the towel over my shoulder and took out my headphones. I put my things on the table and headed towards the bathroom. I turned on the shower, undressed and got in. As the hot water streamed over my body, I could once again feel that warmth, but this time I began to cry. I hadn't realized how much I missed Marcus; he had been gone now for four years and I had not really found anyone I related to like him. He was everything I wanted and having been with him had pretty much ruined any chances for anyone else.

I got out and put on my nightgown and house shoes. I picked up the book I was reading from my nightstand and crawled into bed. The bookstore clerk had recommended it; it was about two married couples who had been best friends since high school and both couples began having marital problems. They decided to experiment by swapping spouses to see what would happen to their relationships. It was a really kind of crazy and I didn't understand the concept at first.

That night I read through chapter ten and part of eleven, and things in the book started to make sense. The book made the point that two people who had been together for a long time could be together for all the wrong reasons, and that being with someone who really clicked with who you were made the most sense.

I thought about it for a while, then checked the clock. It was already after ten.

"Wow, I better get some sleep. I have a big day tomorrow."

I set the alarm clock for five-thirty, turned off the light and scooted down far enough for the firmly tucked bed sheets to cover me just above my shoulders. As I lay in bed, I thought, I wonder if he ever thinks about me. I closed my eyes and fell into a deep dream-filled sleep.

# Chapter 16

THE ANNOYING SOUND OF THE alarm clock rang insistently in my ears at five-thirty. As much as I tried to ignore it, I couldn't. I threw back the covers and shuffled towards the dresser in the far corner of my room to shut off the alarm. I didn't even have to be at work until eight, but I had it stationed so far away from the bed because of the lesson I learned as a freshman in college.

After spending a long night studying for our psychology final, eating pizza, drinking beer, and shooting tequila, Sadie and I set our alarm clocks for seven o'clock, two hours before the most important test of our freshman year. Then we passed out.

As I woke up, I vaguely remembered pushing the snooze button several times before totally cutting it off. Then I popped straight up in bed and looked at the clock. It was nine fifty-five, and class was at least a fifteen-minute speed-walk.

"Oh my God, Sadie get up!"

Sadie looked up at me from the bottom bunk, dazed.

"Girl, we late!"

She jumped up and ran to the bathroom first, while I packed our bags and put everything by the door; then it was my turn to hit the shower. By the time we got to class we were forty-five minutes late, and we could only get about a third of it done in the remaining thirty minutes

Luckily, I was the teacher's pet, so when class ended, I talked the professor into letting us finish the final that afternoon. But at a cost: Sadie and I had to do a week of after-school tutoring for some local high school students. And we had to do it along with all of our own studying, classes, partying, and work. It was one crazy week. But we never forgot about it; and we were never late to class—or anything else really important—again.

This morning, I jumped in the shower for a few moments. As the steam began to rise and settle on the mirrors and floor I thought about the day ahead. The case I was working on was really sad—two brothers who had been charged with aggravated armed robbery and second-degree murder.

I knew their father from the old neighborhood. He lived right behind my grandmother's house across the alley and would always toss the ball back when it would land in his yard. He was a young guy then who married early but waited to have children because he wanted to able to provide the very best for them, which he did.

He was a hard-working upper middle-class white man with a heart as big as Texas. He ran his own lawn care and snow removal business, which eventually grew to be very successful. He and his wife were high school sweethearts and had been together for about fifteen years before deciding to have children—and wouldn't you know it, the first time out the gate, they end up with twins. Isn't life grand?

I turned off the water and quickly began to dress. My favorite suit was a suede cocoa-brown skirt and jacket with a tan raw-silk blouse. It always looked and made me feel extra-special and confident. Which is exactly what I needed today.

The preliminary hearing was scheduled for nine. I had spent several hours with the gentlemen and their parents. I really adored the parents of these two boys—they were only nineteen years old—and I felt so sorry for them. According to the parents, the boys were really good kids, but they got caught up with the wrong crowd. They said their sons wouldn't hurt a fly, let alone murder someone, and I believed them. But the fact remained that they were at the convenience store at the time of the robbery and the clerk on duty ended up dead. I questioned the circumstances under which the boys were arrested, but was assured by the district attorney that the evidence they had against them was indisputable.

This was going to be tough, so I spent all morning refining my opening argument and what I was going to say to convince the judge to allow bail. While I sipped my coffee and waited for the bread to toast, the phone rang. Who could be calling me this early?

"Hello?"

"Hey Jaz, it's Carla."

"Hey, girl, how are you?"

"Girl, I'm good. I was just calling because I'm going to be near the courthouse today finishing up the corporate buyout of our partner company. I was wondering if you had time for lunch?"

"I sure do, how's twelve-thirty?"

"That would work for me."

"OK, I'll call Verducci's and make the reservation."

"Great, Jaz, I'll see you there."

"All right Carla. If plans change give me a call on my cell phone."

Carla was another one of my best friends; we met years ago at one of Sadie's architectural firm's design showcases for an entire shopping mall. She negotiated corporate buyouts and was considered the best in her field. Shit, she could sell a suit to a tailor, and convince him to buy one for his wife. She was good and she knew it.

Carla was also gorgeous. She had always been beautiful, with a complexion like heavy cream, but she had recently lost a good thirty pounds, so now she was even more of a force to be reckoned with. She was smiling and happy, but she was tough, too: She would not hesitate to put you in your place if she felt that you crossed her. She was never really as wild as Sadie and me, but she ran a close third in the Southside Divas' quest for manly booty.

I had finished my breakfast when I remembered I was supposed to call Sadie back after my walk. I picked up the phone and dialed her office. Sadie was at work bright and early every morning, so I knew she'd be there.

"Hey, Julie, this is Jasmine, is Sadie in?"
"Yes ma'am, she is, let me buzz her office."
"OK, thanks, Julie."
"Hello, this is Sadie."
"Hey, girl, it's Jasmine."
"Oh you finally decided to call me back, huh?"
"Girl, you know I was all messed up yesterday."
"Yeah, I know. How are you?"
"I'm better. I was calling to see if you could do lunch with Carla and me today."
"Oh, I would love to but I have a very important meeting with the head of a new computer corporation. We're in the running to design their new building—thirty-five stories."
"Damn, girl, you be working it, don't you."
"Yeah, got to make that money, baby."
"I hear you, girl, so we'll be at the spot this weekend for sure, right?"
"For sure! You know I'm ready for our weekly mall run."
Yeah, I know, me too; OK, sweetie, I'll call you later."
"All right, Jaz. I'll talk to you."

I hung up and finished getting ready for work. I rinsed off the dishes from the night before and put all the dishes in the dishwasher, something I did every morning. It just made it easy for me to keep the kitchen in order. I had learned from Mama how to clean the kitchen "while" you cooked instead of waiting until after you were done. It always made it easier to keep my most favorite space in the world nice and clean.

When I looked at the clock on the stove, it was already eight-fifteen. I didn't have to worry too much about traffic since I already lived downtown, but I did have to worry about the wait on the elevators at the condo and at the office, so I usually left an extra twenty minutes early just to compensate.

I grabbed my suit jacket and briefcase. Everything was in order and I was ready to conquer the world . . . once again.

I headed for the elevator; there were already three people waiting: Mr. Daniels, who lived two doors down on the right, and Ms. Jamison and her little girl, Anna.

Anna was nine and as cute as button. She was tall and thin and had dark brown, curly hair. Her mom had her hair in ponytails that hung right around her shoulders and she was dressed neatly in her school uniform: white buttoned-down shirt and plaid skirt, bobby socks and sweater that matched the school colors. Anna went to Breck, a private school in the suburbs, and, one of the top schools in the country.

Now, as a third-grader, she had already learned to speak pretty good Spanish. She knew words I didn't learn until college. I walked up behind the three of them and said hello.

They turned around, and in unison said, "Hi Jasmine, how are you today?"

"I'm good, and how are all of you?"

Everyone said well, except for Anna.

"Anna, what's wrong?" I asked.

"I'm not feeling good!" she exclaimed. "My stomach hurts and my mom won't let me stay home from school."

I smiled at Ms. Jamison; "Not feeling well, huh?"

"*No*—Jasmine she's fine. There's a big test today and Anna here is a little scared."

"Anna, did you study?"

"Yes I did, very hard, but I'm still nervous."

I bent down to look Anna face to face. "Well, my mom used to tell me to remember the Three C's: courage, confidence, and concentration. If you practice them all and believe in yourself, then you will do just fine."

"I know, Ms. Jasmine. But I'm still a little frightened."

"It'll be OK," I assured her. "Just believe in yourself.

"OK, I will," she said solemnly.

"Thanks, Jasmine," said Ms. Jamison, smiling at me. "We'll see if we can get that to work."

The elevator ding'ed, signaling it had finally reached our floor. The doors opened and little old Mrs. Jenkins was standing there, smiling and beckoning everyone on.

Mrs. Jenkins was a short blue-haired woman who was on her fifth husband; no one really knew what had happened to husbands three and four, who had passed away under cloudy circumstances; she was considered the shopping queen of the known universe. Her skin was deeply wrinkled, with the consistency of saddle leather—the result of too much sun when she was young—but despite this, she was a stylish lady who was always turned out in high-end name brand clothes.

And she obviously had no sense of smell, because she always wore too much perfume. I always played the "cover my nose, I have to sneeze" role whenever I got into the elevator when she was there; and usually by the time we reached the lower floors, someone really did have to sneeze. It wouldn't have been so bad if Mrs. Jenkins had been taller, but she stood right below the average person's nose level, so if you were behind her you caught the whiff in an updraft. Always, as soon as the doors opened on the lobby everyone exhaled and took long deep breaths; it sounded like a birthing class.

"Good morning," we all said in muffled, nasal voices, as we breathed as little as possible.

"Good day, all," she said, which is what she always replied.

Because she lived in the penthouse she always ended up on the elevator first, which meant the stench would ride down the entire twenty-five floors. But no one had the guts to say anything to her. She was the sole heir to the fortune of a family member who invented some revolutionary item that made some other revolutionary item obsolete. By the time she was twenty-five she controlled half of the commercial property in Minneapolis, but she had never had to actually work a day in her life.

When the doors finally opened to the lobby, I headed to the parking garage, where my car was sitting right by the door, on the main level. I really wasn't supposed to park there over night, because those spots were usually reserved for the more elderly tenants, but because of all that was going on I forgot to move it, and obviously Jonathan had my back because he didn't write me up for it. I waved to Jonathan, thanking him with a thumbs-up, and pushed the alarm button on my remote. The loud chirp from my car alarm echoed in the garage, startling Mr. Chapman, one of the other residents. He was so shaken; I went over to apologize to him. I felt bad. I should have warned him of my presence.

Mr. Chapman was seventy-something, and had suffered shell shock after World War II—what they now call post-traumatic syndrome disorder. He was very thin, with skin a dull eggshell color; it reminded me of the paint I had in my bedroom as a kid. I assumed the freckly red and blue blotches on his skin were age spots, but a lot of the older folks in the building said they were from a chemical bomb that exploded near his camp. The army had to send him home right afterwards, because he had already started showing signs of shock, threatening his fellow soldiers.

"I'm so sorry, Mr. Chapman, I didn't see you there. Are you OK?"

"Aaaaah, yes, Ms. Burrell, I'm fine—just a little jumpy this morning, thanks."

"If there's anything I can do, Mr. Chapman, just let me know."

"Yes, yes Jasmine, I'll let you know."

"Have a good day, Mr. Chapman."

"You too, Jasmine."

I jumped in my car and pulled out of the garage on to the busy streets of downtown Minneapolis. I drove fast but carefully, and I thought about my cases along the way.

Damn, how am I going to convince the judge to give these boys bail? They're so young; I hate to see them go down for this—and what was this indisputable evidence? I knew the DA thought they were guilty, but in the law, it's not what you think, it's what you can prove. I always had full conversations in my head about important matters, and this case was no different.

I pulled into one of the reserved spots for company employees. Any of the lawyers in our firm could use them, first come, first serve. They were located right up front near security and even closer to the elevator. After I worked all day in three-inch pumps, getting to my car to take off my shoes was the first thing I wanted to do.

The elevator watch at work was just as bad as it was at home, so I checked and double-checked to be sure I had everything before I headed for those doors. Lateness was not tolerated. If I had forgotten one thing in the car, the time it took to get back downstairs could mean the difference between winning and losing a case. As I pushed through the entrance double doors, I heard the familiar ding.

I ran towards the elevator doors. I had learned over the years that the ding was the key. You had to stay on your toes and be ready for anything, or you'd lose your spot on the elevator.

Dang. The doors opened and there were already about ten people in the elevator. The couple at the doors before I got there hopped on; I just barely made it, but the lady running through the swinging doors behind me wasn't quite as lucky. I smugly congratulated myself, and pushed eighteen—but sixteen, fifteen, twelve, ten, and seven were also lit up. Damn, that's what I get for laughing at that lady.

I rode up the elevator, dancing the waltz between every ding that marked another floor we stopped on. I finally got to my floor and shuffled off the elevator, while two very tall white men got on. They looked like FBI agents.

Something was strange. One of the men especially stuck out; he was bald as an eagle with a beard trimmed like Ice Cube, so of course he caught my eye, since I was secretly in love with Cube.

(Not that Ice Cube probably would not like being compared to a tall, white, bald FBI agent. Shoot, to really tell the truth, I just fucked up any chance of getting in Ice Cube's pants. Damn, I need my ghetto card revoked.)

I walked into my firm's lobby, then down the hall to the biggest corner office on the floor. There were actually three very large offices on that floor but mine was the only one with a view of downtown on three sides. I walked in and picked up the note my secretary Wendy left for me, letting me know she was making copies of all of today's files. She was a godsend.

I settled in, and saw my phone message light was blinking. That was a little strange; all the important people who needed to contact me had my cell phone number.

I entered my code and grabbed my notebook to take notes. The first message was left at five-thirty in the morning. It was from the father of the two boys.

"Good morning, Ms. Burrell, this is Mr. Johnson. Could you please call me as soon as you get this message?"

I fretted a bit, because I could hear he was choking back tears. I hoped that one of the boys hadn't done something foolish—or worse—that could hurt the case.

Thomas and Timothy were fraternal twins. Thomas was the slightly shorter and stockier of the two, but they were both very athletic and played basketball and football. I had figured Thomas to be the football star because of his size, and Timothy to be the hoopster, but it turned out to be the exact opposite. Thomas was the coldest point guard in the game and was headed to the college of his choice, and Timothy was a Division One wide receiver, with commitment letters from four out of the five top football colleges in the country. So much for stereotypes, I thought. I made a note to call him as soon as I was finished checking the other messages.

The second message was left at six thirty-five.

*"Hey, Jasmine, this is Marcus, Marcus Damon. I'll be in Minnesota on Monday at around noon and was wondering if you had time to get together. I'm just finishing up in Hawaii and will be laying over in Minnesota for about four or five days before I head back to Europe. I can be reached on my cell phone, the number has not changed. Take care, sweetie, and hope to hear from you soon."*

Hell no! Please, not right now, I thought, and slammed down in my seat. I counted to ten, ten times; once was usually enough, but this, this was too much.

Whew, can't go there. Not now. I have work to do, I said, trying to calm myself

I was the consummate Capricorn, it was all about status quo and maximum gain, while at the same time keeping your composure and staying cool. "Never let them see you sweat" was my lifelong motto, which I wore like a badge of honor.

A vein in my head started to throb. Fuck this, I'm not going there!

I shook off the Marcus juju and called my clients.

The phone rang five times before Mrs. Johnson answered with a very quiet hello.

"Good morning, Mrs. Johnson, this is Jasmine Burrell."

"Oh Jasmine, we have been waiting for your call, let me get my husband."

I could hear Mrs. Johnson screaming his name in the background. I listened closely and could hear Mr. Johnson walking briskly on the hardwood floors.

"Good morning, Jasmine, how are you?" Mr. Johnson's tired, groggy voice on the other end startled me momentarily.

"So what happened?"

"Well, Jasmine, the boys confessed."

"What do you mean, they confessed?"

"They told us they were going to take the plea."

"What, why?" I gasped.

"They admitted to being involved with the murder."

## Chapter 17

"How do you know this? Were they talking over the jail phone?" I asked, still in shock.

"No, Jasmine, they didn't say it in that way. When the boys were little we always taught them to tell the truth and if they did so we would never punish them. Well, in so many words, they confessed in a conversation we had last night. They just reminded us of when they were small and if they always trusted and told their parents the truth then they would not be punished no matter what.

"You see, Jasmine, the boys are just as upset about disappointing me than any crime they may have committed. So they decided that if they admitted their part in the incident, then my wife and I would forgive them and they could live with any amount of time given to them by the justice system."

"Are you sure?" I asked

"Yes, Jasmine, we are sure we would like to take the plea. The boys realized what they have done and are prepared to take responsibility for their actions. It's something I taught them a long time ago. I know they did not mean to kill the young man. But that's something they're going to have to live with, along with finding a way to pay restitution to that man's family—which I'll start up, and they'll have to maintain when they get out. So could you please file a motion as soon as possible to have their plea changed to guilty?"

"Are you sure, Mr. Johnson, this is what you want to do?" I asked him again. "I just need some time to look at all the facts and go over their stories again, and I believe we can do better."

"*No*, Jasmine," Mr. Johnson said emphatically. "We are sure. Please call the judge and get the process started. We want this to be over."

"OK, Mr. Johnson, I'll make the call and see if he can recall your case as soon as possible. I'll have my secretary call you when we know something. In the meantime I'm going to see Timothy and Thomas to get their statements. Don't worry—I'll protect them and make sure they get what is fair."

"Thank you, Jasmine, thank you," he said, his voice choking up for the first time in the conversation. Then he hung up.

I rubbed my face and eyes. Then I buzzed Wendy.

"Could you get Judge McVale on the line for me? It's kind of urgent."

"OK, Jasmine, I'll do it right away."

"Thank you, Wendy."

I knew "secretary" was no longer an acceptable term so I always tried to be politically correct and say "executive assistant" when I talked about Wendy.

But really, in my eyes, we were all at one time secretaries in one form or another, doing whatever it took to get the job done you did. That's exactly what a secretary does; making sure the job gets done. The most important person on the team, they're the one who keeps everything and everyone together. And if they're really good the company will profit.

Wendy was a graduate student from the University of Minnesota and had only one semester to complete before receiving her master's when she applied for the position. She had completed undergrad in a record two and a half years; now, at twenty-two, she was ready to take on the entire world by herself. She was smart, funny and very charming; with her big brown eyes and her vibrant smile, she commanded attention any time she walked into the room, and it was obvious she was headed for stardom.

She also had a knack for names and faces. Her mom said it was some type of crazy talent she had since she was a child; in the field of law, it was a gift. She could definitely use it to her advantage and she knew it.

So it hadn't surprised me that after about two weeks on the job, she knew who all the senior lawyers and partners were, along with all their assistants, the custodial team and the lunch ladies. On any given day, Wendy would greet all the clients and lawyers by name and would secretly smile to me in smug admiration of herself.

In fact, it hadn't taken me long in the hiring process to know she was the one; this just confirmed it.

When her application and resume reached human resources, they had read it and interviewed her so quickly that within a week the info was in my e-mail inbox, with high priority.

When we met I was very impressed with Wendy's appearance and professionalism, something that could make or break you in this field. Really, it was a little strange: I felt as though I were talking to a reflection in a mirror. It wasn't that we looked much like each other; it was the way she spoke of her dreams and ambitions that had me excited. She talked about writing, poetry, and music, things I was interested in but hadn't had the chance to do.

"Wendy, you have so many other wonderful talents, why do you want to study law?" I had asked her.

"When I entered college, I never intended to study law," she replied. I was a little puzzled, maybe even a little hurt—after all, who couldn't be in love with the law, like I was?

"Then why are studying it now, and why work for a law firm if this is not your passion? I need an assistant who is going to eat, sleep, and dream the basis and principles of law."

Wendy sat up straight and spoke the most eloquent words. It was a poem she had written, which summed up her life and love for brothers, especially her own.

She and her brother grew up in a middle-class neighborhood. Their parents had divorced when they were young, and they lived most of the time with their mother, but both parents were very much present; their father picked them up every weekend and spent as much time as he could with them. He took them shopping, fishing, swimming, and had them for the summers, when he took them to Virginia where his family was. Their mother, a strong woman, allowed him every moment he desired to continue to raise and nurture his children.

Her brother had been like many the black teenage males in society: basically a good kid—bright, talented, and on his way to a positive productive future—who got caught up in the messed-up world of selling drugs for the easy money, status, and so-called glamour. So she was devastated as she watched her little brother, at seventeen, driven off in a police car, and later, plead guilty to a charge of low-level drug trafficking and fleeing police.

Luckily, because he had no record and was in school, he only had to do four months in the workhouse; but he still had seven years on paper. He got out two years ago, she explained, and hasn't been in any trouble since.

So that's why she wanted to work for a criminal attorney, and why specifically she wanted to work for me. She hoped to some day be a criminal psychologist, focusing on repeat offenders; her brother had managed to stay clean, but in her neighborhood, a lot of those "career criminals" looked like her brother. She had followed my career; she was admired by everything I had done for African-American defendants and was determined to help in the fight to reclaim young black men from the streets. But first she felt she had to understand the legal process before she could begin to make a change.

I hired her on the spot. I was supposed to take the initial findings about any applicant to the senior lawyers, but I knew there was no need to interview anyone else. I made a judgment call and stuck to my guns; the senior lawyers finally agreed, and she had been with me since.

I gazed out the windows and remembered with a little involuntary jump that Marcus had called. I contemplated calling him right then but decided to wait until after lunch so I wouldn't seem so desperate. I also needed to bounce this whole phone-call-to-Marcus thing off Sadie and Carla just to be sure I was doing the right thing. Calling Marcus would change everything, and I didn't know if I was ready for the upheaval talking to him would bring.

In mid-daydream my intercom buzzed; Judge McVale was on line one.

"Good morning, Judge, how are you?"

"I'm fine, Ms. Burrell, how are you?"

"Just fine, your honor, but I've run into a bit of a problem. My case is being called this morning at ten-thirty—the State of Minnesota vs. Timothy and Thomas Johnson. Well, your honor, the defendants have decided they do not want to go to trial. They have confessed and would like to expedite the sentencing procedures. I have spoken to the parents and everyone is in agreement. I have yet to meet with the boys to have them sign a formal statement, but I believe I can get that done within the hour."

"OK, Ms. Burrell, I'll hear your statement at the scheduled time."

"Thank you, your honor. I'll have my assistant call the prosecutor and let them know."

"Well, then, I'll see you and your clients at ten-thirty sharp."

"Yes sir, we'll be there."

I hung up and buzzed Wendy to tell her about the changes and to call the prosecuting attorney Wendell Adams and let him know. Then I called Mr. and Mrs. Johnson to let them know what happened and to be at the courthouse at the scheduled time. It was now nine forty-five and I needed to get to the jail in order to take the twins' statements. I grabbed my briefcase and headed for the dreadful elevators.

I pushed the button to go down. The jail was on the tenth floor, and it occurred to me it would take a little more time to get the boys if the correctional officers weren't expecting me, so counting on the elevators to take their usual sweet time getting there, I ran back to Wendy and told her to call the sheriffs and have them bring the boys out. By the time I got back to the elevators, breathless and a little flustered, the doors had opened. I went to check in with the guards.

I asked the guard up front to call for Timothy and Thomas Johnson and to bring them both to the same interrogation room. They took my briefcase and purse and put them on the conveyor belt to scan them. I walked slowly through the metal detector and collected my things on the other side. I entered Interrogation Room A and waited.

Timothy and Thomas entered the room with hands and feet shackled like they were runaway slaves. I looked at them.

"Hey, guys, is there something you want to tell me?"

They looked at each other in the only way two people born out of the same womb at the same time could look.

"Yes, we do," said Thomas.

As he explained what happened the night of the shooting, he cried. He and Timothy went into the store only intending to scare the clerk into giving them the money from the cash register. The gun was hidden in Thomas' pocket and he never planned on pulling it out. But when the clerk unexpectedly reached for the panic button, Thomas grabbed for the gun in his pocket, and it went off, shooting through his jacket pocket and hitting the clerk in the chest. As I listened, I could feel the hairs on the back of my neck stand up. I looked over at Timothy as he nodded quietly, confirming what his brother had just told me.

When he was finished, I had them sign the statement, hugged them both, and told them not to worry.

"I'll see you in the courtroom in half an hour. Your parents will be there, waiting to see you."

"Thanks, Ms. Burrell," said Timothy said for the both of them. Thomas was still sniffling softly.

"You're welcome, Timothy and Thomas. Take care and try not to worry."

"Yes, ma'am," they both said.

The sheriff escorted the boys back to the holding tank where they would be transferred to another room to get dressed for the hearing. I had always recommended that my clients wear a suit and tie to all court appearances to at least show the judge that the defendants respected the court, and had families and people in their lives who cared about them. It usually helped, but now that the boys had confessed, I wasn't sure of anything anymore.

I headed back to my office to collect my thoughts and make sure I had all the paperwork I needed for the hearing. Then I called Wendy and told her to cancel all my afternoon appointments because I already was so drained that I decided I wasn't coming back after lunch.

# Chapter 18

As I waited for the elevator I thought about my phone call from Marcus with dread. I didn't know how I was going to make the call, but something in the back of my mind said, "Just call him, expect nothing, and don't give up anything." I had learned how to shut down my feelings after Marcus left, and this was one time I intended to be strong and resist the temptation of falling for him all over again.

The elevators opened, I entered the courtroom, and took my seat at the defense table next to Thomas and Timothy. Everyone was very still until the bailiff announced, "All rise" as the judge entered the room.

As the gavel fell, I could see Mr. Johnson slumped in his seat, quietly weeping on his wife's shoulder; it was if the life had drained out of him. Thomas pleaded guilty to second-degree unintentional manslaughter while Timothy pleaded guilty to second-degree aggravated assault. The sentencing was scheduled for exactly one month later.

As I turned to speak to Mr. and Mrs. Johnson, I caught Thomas' eye; it was obvious by the way he stared at me that he was disturbed by what he had done. He had let their father down and now he was going to have to deal with that, along with seeing the face of the innocent person he killed over and over in his dreams.

A tear ran down my face. I couldn't believe I was crying. "This is just another case," I said to myself. "I'm not supposed to have such ties to my clients." I sat down.

"What is wrong with me?" I felt the hairs on my neck stand up. "Damn, I have got to get out of here." I grabbed my briefcase and quickly walked over to Mr. and Mrs. Johnson, hugged them, and told them I would call them first thing in the morning.

Walking even quicker, I practically ran out of the courtroom and slipped into a mercifully open and empty elevator headed to the lower level. Shit. I pressed the button for the garage and waited for my bell. When the doors opened, this time I actually did run to the car. I switched off the security system, got in and sat down, feeling a bead of sweat drip down to the small of my back.

"Damn!" I inhaled deeply and blew several times, remembering the relaxation techniques I'd learned in my college yoga classes. I sat there for twenty minutes concentrating on letting go and just breathing. I felt the tightness in my shoulders and chest beginning to release and I started to calm down. A few more breaths and I would be better.

# Chapter 19

W**HAT A DAY.**
     I called Carla and asked if we could meet at the restaurant earlier. She was just finishing up her meeting and agreed to meet me at Verducci's Italian Bistro.

Verducci's was the best Italian restaurant in the city. It was known for its signature hand-made pastas and hand-pressed rolls, and the lettuce for the salads was some perfectly grown genetic breakthrough that gave Verducci's its reputation. But the best part for us was that their bartenders made the best lemon-drop martinis any of us ever had, and it didn't matter which bartender made them, they were always perfect.

The valet tapped on the window of my car. "Oh sorry," I said, looking up.

"Here's your ticket, ma'am."

"Thank you."

I handed him the keys, got out of the car, and as I walked towards the door, I noticed "Black Magic" rolling down the street. Carla was a car freak and wanted the biggest and best truck made, so without hesitation when the new Hummer came out, she ran to the dealership and bought a cold black-on-black Hummer H2. It was her dream car and she bragged about it on a regular basis.

Carla pulled up in front of the valet desk and got of the truck before the valet could get to her.

She gave the valet the keys and rushed over to me and gave me a firm but brief hug so as to not wrinkle her suit. There was nothing more irritating to Carla than looking anything but perfect. She prided herself on being the sharpest tack in the box. And I didn't fault her for that.

"Damn, girl, you look good."
"No, girl, it is you."
"No Carla, you're wearing that suit."
She smiled. "Yes I am, ain't I?"

Carla was a mess. She really enjoyed herself. Her attitude about life was very pronounced, meaning she pronounced it every time she could. She never let anything stop her and she usually got her way.

A wonderful couple adopted Carla when she was just a baby. And as she grew up she realized she was different from her sisters and brothers.

Being adopted by a well-to-do white family made life for Carla a breeze. Her parents loved her very much and saw to it that she had the best of everything. Carla really appreciated her parents and showed them on a daily basis. She had just recently sent them on a second honeymoon to Hawaii for two weeks and was proud to be able to do it.

Carla grabbed her cell phone and made one last call while she walked arm-in-arm with me into the restaurant. We were seated immediately because of our reservation.

"OK, I'm shutting my phone off now, so I will call you when I'm done. Bye, sweetie, I love you."

I smiled. "That must have been Brandon?"

"Now why would you think that?"

"Well, who else would you be telling I love you?"

"Nigga, you don't know all my business, I might have a little chippy on the side . . . you don't know?"

"Yeah, nigga tell your son I said hi and I miss him. I want to take him to the ball game next week."

She laughed. "Sure, I'll tell him."

Carla had a son, Brandon; he was seven.

David, her ex-husband, was from Africa and fine as hell. Carla scoped him out early and claimed him; she didn't know at the time he was African. They met and had a whirlwind affair until she became pregnant. He was pissed but asked her to marry him anyway (something he probably never intended to do). Things didn't work out.

But Carla didn't let his leaving stop her. After her son was born she parlayed a temporary accounts management position into a permanent top-level executive sales position. Carla knew how to work her mouthpiece and in a matter of months had everyone in her office eating out of her hand. She had access to all the corporate amenities and she didn't hesitate to use them. The company jet, the company suites, any and everything that was floating around the office, and had corporate written on it—Carla was involved. She lived life to the fullest and I secretly envied her for that.

"Damn, Jaz, you look a little flushed. What's going on?"

"Carla, I've had the day from hell. This morning's hearing was so hard, I was nervous, edgy, and overly emotional. You know I don't get like that, I don't know what got into me. Never let them see you sweat, right, you know me. Well, I *sweated* today."

Carla screamed, "Oh my God, girl, what are you going to do?" while holding in a gut-wrenching laugh.

"Carla, it's not funny."

"I know. I know, I'm sorry, girl, tell me what's going on."

I paused; one tear rolled down my face. "Marcus called."

Carla's eyes grew big and she cupped her mouth with her hand. I looked up and said, without speaking, "What am I going to do?" Carla knew exactly what I was saying.

"Don't worry, girl, we won't let you do this alone."

Carla wiped the tears away just as the waiter, in a starched white shirt and black pants appeared from out of nowhere and offered us a glass of water. It was perfectly timed, as if we were being watched. I grabbed the glass and took a swallow.

"Relax, Jasmine, it's going to be cool. Check it out; let's order a drink." Carla turned to the waiter and ordered two lemon drop martinis.

"OK, Jasmine, let's bring this all the way down, baby."

"Yeah, girl, I know I'm trippin'. I'm going to the bathroom for a moment, be right back."

"All right, sweetie, I'll be in there if you're not out in ten minutes."

"I'm cool, Carla; I'll be right back."

I knew my shit was all out of whack. I had to get back on my square.

I entered the bathroom just as a blond woman with unusually large breasts stormed out and almost knocked me over.

"Excuse me, miss."

"Oh, I'm so sorry," the overly tanned blond bombshell said, in a giggly little girl's voice.

"Oh wait," I asked her. "Is your name Molly Spencer?" I'd recognize that voice anywhere, even though she looked nothing like the, girl, I went to school with.

"Uh, yeah. Who are you?"

"It's Jasmine, Jasmine Burrell."

"Oh my God, Jaz. I haven't seen you since college."

The five-foot-nine, one-hundred-twelve-pound college mate squeezed me so tightly I thought, a football linebacker was hugging me.

"Molly, it's great to see you too. How have you been?"

"As you can see, I have been fabulous," she said as she puffed up, and stuck out her chest, flaunting an obvious increase in her frontal view.

"Wow, girl, you sure have grown." I snickered a bit.

"Yes, I know. My husband just bought these for me." She smiled broadly and pointed to a fifty-something gentleman at the bar. I was shocked. "Oh my, he's a little old, don't you think?"

"That's right, girl."

Molly sidled up next to me and whispered in my ear, "He's loaded. After few too many so-called love affairs gone bad, I decided I was no longer looking to fall in love. I was looking for the cash cow.

"Men freak out when you try to do right and love them. So I decided I was going to be and do whatever I wanted, and if a man had a problem with it then fuck him, he can move around."

I thought to myself, Hell, yeah. "Well, do your thang, girl, I ain't mad at you."

I hugged Molly and smiled as she bopped away to never-never land.

"Damn, why can't I be like that? I chose to be ambitious and shit, and what did it get me—long hours at work and cold lonely nights." I looked at my breasts, but the breast thing, I got that covered. I grabbed my boobs and gave them a little squeeze. Perk up babies, we got to make us some money.

I stared in the mirror and smiled at my reflection. You're in control; don't let other people's actions dictate your reaction.

I was serious about staying in control. One missed step and the stone-cold ice princess turned into the waterlogged mess, a crying emotional fool, locked in my room, psychoanalyzing every situation, incidence, and occurrence that wasn't logical to me. Things happen for a reason. But I would always try to figure out the reason instead of just letting it be and living for the moment. It was nothing for me to lose it if things didn't measure up in her mind. So I analyzed and attempted to break down and study any and everyone who I came in contact with; it was my blessing, as well as a curse.

It was a great trait for being an attorney, but it sucked when it came to my relationships with men. After the third or fourth date I usually had the guy already figured out and how I was going to fix him to make him perfect for myself. It obviously never worked, because I was still alone.

I washed my hands and walked slowly back to the table, in a whole new state of mind. Carla sat there in awe. "Damn, girl, what did you go in there and do?"

"Girl, you know when I do my reaffirmations, everything is all good."

"Well, I see that, what the hell you be saying?"

"Don't trip, Carla, it ain't nothing. Just some things that keep me focused. I have a job where I have so many people's lives in my hands I had to find a way to keep everything in perspective. But today got a little out of hand, and I just had to change the formula a little bit in order to get back. So now I'm back."

"Well, damn, girl, work it out."

I laughed, while Carla flagged down the waiter to get more water.

"Guess who I just saw?

"Who?"

"Molly Spencer, from back in the wild days."

"Oh really, what's she up to?"

"Oh, about a 34DD."

"Girl, shut up—she had a boob job?"

"She sure did, and her 'daddy' paid for it."

"What do you mean, her 'daddy' paid for it?"

"Look over there at the bar."

Carla peered over at the bar where she could see the two of them laughing and having a good time.

"Girl, who is that old-ass man?"

"That's her husband."

"SHUT UP!" Carla screamed.

"Yes ma'am, that's Molly's husband. She said she was tired of all the bullshit tied to being in, or falling in, love. She had had several relationships where she tried to do the love thing and it didn't work. So when it was all said and done she decided to go for the money."

"Shiiit, that's what I'm talking about, let me find me a sugar daddy and I'd be cool. In fact, I'll go take hers."

I busted out laughing.

"Carla, you know damn well you ain't gonna let no man control anything you got going on, especially the money.

Carla mean-mugged me. "Nigga, you know I'm right."

I broke out into laughter, while Carla threw up her hand to slap me five. "Giiirl, I know that's right."

She slapped me major five, and like synchronized swimmers we craned our heads around the room, scanning for the waiter and our drinks.

After my second *"Exorcist"* rotation, I saw our waiter coming, drinks in hand. He set the drinks down and asked if we were ready to order.

Carla looked up. "Could you give us a minute?" He nodded, and walked away.

I picked up my martini and slammed it.

"Uh, I thought you had everything under control," said Carla, watching as the drink disappeared down my throat. "What was that all about?"

"My being in control has nothing to do with the martini. Look, I got this."

"Girl, we were just out Saturday night and you polished off five of them."

"And your point?" I glared at Carla and practically dared her to say anything else.

\* \* \*

Back in college Carla and I got into an altercation that almost ended our relationship.

It was Sadie's and my freshman year in college, and we decided to have a little get-together at our apartment. We invited only females who knew each other; they may not have kicked it like the Divas did, but they were cool enough. There were mini-cliques that vibed better than the others, but all in all everyone was cool.

Carla and I had met before but we hadn't gotten the chance to really to get to know each other's personalities. A serious game of Monopoly turned into a serious argument.

"Hey, Carla, you landed on my property with four houses. Shit, pay up, nigga!"

"Whatever, I ain't got it."

"Well, then, you betta mortgage some of yo shit, and get me my money; count it up, count it, bitch."

My competitive nature sometimes got the best of me, and if alcohol was involved my attitude got worse.

"Bitch, I don't have that much money!"

I let the first "bitch" float on by, because I had called her one first. "Then get up from the table."

"I ain't got to do nothing . . . BITCH." "BITCH," a word affectionately used between the sisters—but Carla wasn't my sister yet.

"Look, move around then." And while I mortgaged her property and counted her money, two or three more "BITCHES" floated out of her mouth.

I stood up from the table; "Look, BITCH, I'm not gonna to be too many more of your BITCHES, I'm'a kick yo' ass."

I walked towards Carla, and Sadie grabbed me and stood in between us.

"Look, BITCHES, neither one of y'all fighting up in here!"

We both looked at Sadie, then burst into laughter. Sadie was serious, and we didn't mess with Daddy Diva. We apologized and made things cool again, not knowing that years later we'd be best friends.

\* \* \*

Carla and I been best friends ever since. We, out of all the Divas, had had serious friendship-ending episodes, but in the end, always seemed to work it out. We were friends, and deep down we truly loved each other and weren't afraid to show it.

Carla looked at me. "Chill, girl, it's all right; I'm your girl, direct that aggression somewhere else."

I knew Carla was right, so I immediately apologized and hugged my good, good friend. "Thanks, girl, keep me in check."

I took a sip of water and exhaled.

"OK, Carla, here it is, what am I going to do about Marcus; I don't know if I'm ready to see him."

Carla grabbed my hand, "I totally understand Jaz, yo' girl's gonna hold you down through all of this."

"I know y'all gonna be there for me. But at some point in time I'm going to have to hold myself down."

The waiter returned and waited for our orders. I grabbed the menu and searched for what I wanted to eat. Everything on the menu was a blur; I kept thinking about Marcus and him coming in town.

"I think I'm gonna have the chicken and angel-hair pasta with pesto sauce," Carla said.

"Ooh, Carla, that's a good choice. I've had that before, it was really good. f I get the seafood stuffed shells, can I get some of yours?"

"I'll give you some of mine."

"Hell yeah, you know how it goes down. I've been dying to taste that seafood pasta anyway."

"OK, that's what we'll have. Oh, and two more martinis, please."

"Right away, ma'am." The waiter gingerly walked away towards the kitchen.

After lunch, Carla and I said our goodbyes and reminded each other of our Saturday-afternoon shopping ritual. We kissed and hugged and promised to call each other later. I waited for the valet to bring my car around, while Carla called her son.

I was still a bit stressed out, but I was also tipsy. I was going to go to the gym to relieve a little bit of my stress, but decided against that at the last minute. I'll just run to the grocery store and then home, I thought.

When I got to the grocery store parking lot I heard my phone ringing, but I couldn't find it. I grabbed my purse and found it the side pocket.

"Hello, this is Jasmine."

"Hey, girl, it's Angel. What's up, Jaz?"

"Nothing, girl, what's up with you? Whose number you calling me from? I didn't recognize it."

"Girl, I'm at work, it must be one of our other lines."

"How's the restaurant business?"

"Oh my God, my employees are driving me crazy, they act like they never worked in the restaurant business before. Shit, I'm thinking about firing all of them."

"Oh my God, Angel, calm down, what is going on?"

"I'm trying to get them to understand the importance of customer service. And that you must treat the customer with the utmost respect at all times, no matter what the situation.

"My hostess decided that she would take it upon herself to tell one of my biggest clients that his table was not available at this time because that part of the dining room was closed. But I specifically told her that whenever he came in he got the best table in the house. He had a very important lunch meeting and wanted his usual table and evidently she stressed him out. So he asked for me and I immediately sat him at his table. I took her in back and wore her ass out. I don't think she'll be making that mistake anymore."

"I hear you, girl, the restaurant business is a trip, huh?"

"Yes indeed, but I love it."

Angel was a gourmet chef who at the age of twenty-seven had one of the top restaurants in the city. People would come from miles around just to try her special creations. She was known for her desserts, cakes, and pies that would make you want to slap your mama. She was a chocolate beauty who was as sweet as the desserts she made. When we met we hit off immediately.

"So what's up with you?" she asked.

"I just left Verducci's; Carla and I had lunch today and now I'm a little tipsy. I'm at the grocery store and was going home to relax. I've had a day from hell."

"What happened?"

"First, my clients decided they were going to plead guilty to murder without letting me get a good feel for the case."

"What's that all about?"

"Well, their father said that they confessed to him and that they just wanted everything to be over."

"Damn, Jaz, that's deep."

"Yeah, I know; and that's not the worst of it. Guess who called me today?"

"Who?"

"Marcus."

"SHUT UP! He called you today?"

"Yes, at work, and I've been fucked up every since."

"I should say so, girl. What are you going to do? Did you talk to him?"

"*No.* He left me a message and I'm supposed to call him back."

"Are you going to call him?"

"I don't know Angel, I'm so torn. You know how bad I want to, but I don't know if I can deal with the consequences of making that call."

"I feel you, sweetie. Well, just know I got yo' back"

"I know; that's the same thing Carla said. I'll call you later; I'm about to go into this store, gotta pick up a few things."

"OK, Jaz, I'll talk to you later. Keep your head up, girl."

"I'm trying Angel. Talk to you later. Bye."

I walked slowly to the front doors of the store and grabbed a cart. I put my purse in the child seat and pushed the cart towards the produce department. Before I got to the aisle, I grabbed a coupon book and quickly thumbed through it. Chicken was on sale and so was the Dole salad, two for one. I ripped out the two coupons, and proceeded through the aisles. While I picked through the mound of green peppers, a familiar voice rang out in my ears.

"Jasmine, is that you?"

I turned around and smiled broadly. "Paige, oh my God—how are you?"

Paige and I had been friends since we were three years old. Paige's mother Cheryl was a commercial realtor, so she was always very busy. My mother befriended them when they moved into our apartment building, and allowed Cheryl to leave Paige with us whenever she was out on business, which was quite often.

Paige never really knew her father; he had disappeared right after she was born. But we got really close while she stayed with us.

Paige was gorgeous; she was always dressed to a T, her mother saw to that. She was always an itty-bitty size when we were growing up, while I struggled with my weight and big feet. When we shopped, Paige shopped at all the little-size stores while I had to go to the regular-size teen stores.

Even though I loved Paige very much, I envied her look, her size, and her daring. Paige was not afraid to do or say anything to anybody. Maybe that's why she got into the trouble she was in as a teen. I always thought, though, that Paige not having a father, and the fact that her mother was always gone, and all of the moving was part of the reason for her rebellious ways. But regardless of all the issues she had, anything she needed, I had her back and vice versa.

Up until Paige met Shane, her involvement with the wrong crowds kept her from shining, but after marrying Shane, things mellowed out.

Paige grabbed me around my neck and hugged me tightly, while I tried to squeeze the life out of her.

"Jasmine, girl, I'm fine. How are you?"

"Big pimpin', I'm great. How's the hubby and the kids?"

"Very good, thank you. I just left all of them at home so I could do a little shopping. You know them kids be drivin' me crazy, but Shane is a big help."

"Girl, what is Big Papa up to?"

"Girl, you know he's good; he just took over the bus company and is bringing in a ton of dough."

"Hell, yeah, that's what I'm talking about. He taking good care of you then?"

"Yeah, you know it."

"So what have you been up to, Jaz?"

"Just working, girl, my caseload is out of control and I've been working eighty hours a week trying to catch up."

"Girl, you know we had another baby, right?"

"No—you didn't."

"Yes we did, a little boy who just turned one last Friday; so that makes five."

"Damn, nigga, yo ass is fertile Myrtle fo sho."

"Forget you, you know what up?"

"I guess so, yo' legs." Paige punched me in the arm and burst out laughing.

"Well, damn, you look great," I said.

"Thank you, Jaz, Shane sees to it that I have time to go to the gym. He is truly a wonderful man."

"That's great. What gym do you go to?"

"Oh, we just moved to Maple Grove so it's just a small gym near my house, I take my son to daycare while the other children are at school. Since Shane doesn't want me working, I have all the time in the world to chill and pamper myself."

"Damn, girl, it looks like you're living the life."

"I'm doing really well and I'm finally happy. You know about all the drama I was dealing with my crazy-ass babies' daddies."

"Yeah, I know."

"My husband accepts my other children as his own and we're scheduled to go through the adoption process so that he can adopt them."

"Wow, that's great, Paige. Good luck, sweetheart, after all you have been through, you deserve the best."

"Thank you, Jasmine, I'm hoping for the best." She smiled.

"All right, girl, I'm going to make my way on out of here, I got to get to them kids before they tear the house up."

"OK, Paige, I'll get at you."

"Oh, by the way, are you dating anyone right now?"

"Girl, no, I'm still single."

"Well, my cousin Mario keeps asking about you. You know he's had a crush on you for a long time."

"Yeah, I know. How's he doing?"

"He's doing great. He's just finished school and just got his own place. I think you should call him. He's really nice and I think you two would make a great couple."

"Well, Paige, I'm in no shape to be in a relationship right now, I have so much on my plate."

"I know; just take his number and if you get a chance you should call him."

"OK, I will."

Paige handed me a small piece of paper with Mario's number on it. I stared at the number and smiled. I put the number in my purse and gave Paige a hug and promised to call her to get together.

"Let's get together and go to the spa next week."

"All right, sweetie, that sounds good. I'll check my schedule and let you know when I'm free."

Shane and Paige had the best relationship; they married about three years ago and had two more children, which made me think about my future and how long I was going to be without a man and without the seemingly wonderful comforts of loving one man and having the perfect family. It was painfully obvious that my man problems were out of control, but I tried hard not to sweat it. Whenever my mind tried to play the cruel joke on me about being a lonely spinster for the rest of my life, I justified my loneliness by reminding myself of my six-figure income, my convertible Mercedes, and my immaculate condo in the sky. Those things in my mind kept me sane—for the time being.

At the checkout lane the little old lady who checked my groceries looked a lot like my eleventh-grade math teacher. Short thinning gray hair, wrinkled skin and hands as slow as frozen molasses. It took her over five minutes to find the price for the green peppers. I spoke up and told her they were three for a dollar.

The name on her nametag said Janice and I sat there and wondered what Janice was like in her heyday. It was a shame that she still had had to work. There was no reason in the world for this seventy-something lady to be standing here ringing up groceries. But I knew that these days seniors weren't able to live off Social

Security alone and a great deal of seniors had to get back into the work force to survive.

. Of course, that led me back to my unwanted contemplation of possible spinsterdom, and in spite of myself, I heaved a big sigh. Janice looked up questioningly.

"Oh, I'm just tired," I lied. I certainly wasn't going to get into my life issues with this lady; she had her own problems. Besides, it wasn't a complete lie—I really was tired.

My cell phone rang.

"Hello, this is Jasmine."

"Hey, Jaz, it's Sadie. I got the word about Marcus."

"Damn, you gossippin'-ass bitches don't waste no time spreadin' rumors and shit, do you?"

"Girl, you know we got yo' back. Don't worry about a thing, we'll all be over tonight there is definitely a code blue in effect."

"Code blue? No, Sadie, I'm fine, don't call a code blue on my account."

"Girl, it has already been done. Just relax and let us take care of everything. Got to go, I'll see you at your place tonight. Seven o'clock. Bye."

"Bye, Sadie."

Sadie hung up the phone before I could finish saying goodbye. I don't need a code blue, do I? I thought to myself. I wasn't sure what was going to happen with Marcus coming into town, but I knew my girls were not going to let me go it alone and I held on to some degree of comfort in that. I looked up and saw the checkout lady had finally finished and was patiently waiting for me to pay. I apologized for keeping her waiting, bagged my groceries, and slowly walked to the car.

Then I got in the car and drove towards home.

# Chapter 20

THE DOORBELL RANG AND I knew the night ahead was going to be something to remember. The last time the girls called a code blue, the police were called and the sprinkler system went off. I walked towards the front door, which now seemed to be a mile away, and without looking, swung open the big oak door....

"Hello, Jasmine."

His deep melodic voice seemed to wash over me, swallowing me in a sea of warmth and fear.

"Marcus? Oh my God, what are you doing here?"

"Hey, Jaz, these are for you."

He leaned towards me and handed me a big bouquet of purple, magenta and yellow Hibiscus.

"Hey, Marcus," I stuttered. When our eyes met I remembered. Everything.

"Please, come in, Marcus."

"I was hoping you were going to say that."

The smell of pure masculinity and Sean John cologne made me woozy. I closed the door behind him, and went into panic mode.

I felt like I had been slammed face-first into a wall of emotions I had suppressed for the last four years. This couldn't be happening. It took everything in me to recall my motto, but it wasn't working. I was already soaking wet.

"Hey, Marcus, can I get you something to drink?" I asked, walking into the kitchen.

"No thank you, Jaz, I won't be here long."

"So what brings you to Minnesota?"

"I'm here for a few days on business, and thought if you weren't doing anything you would have dinner with me."

I felt my face turning red. I gasped for air, any air. I fumbled in the cabinet for a vase, trying to compose myself. "These flowers are stunning. Thank you."

"Actually, I had them delivered here from Hawaii, I hand-picked them myself and had them sent when I knew I was going to be here to receive and bring them to you in person."

"So it was *you* who sent me the turquoise pendant. I love it."

"I knew you would." He smiled.

I turned away from him, as a tear rolled down my cheek. He gently placed his hands on my shoulders and turned me around. He looked intently and insistently into my eyes.

"Jasmine, you know me leaving here was out of my control. You and I were embarking on once in a lifetime dreams and I didn't want to be the one to have you, or myself for that matter, missing out on our futures."

"You had just finished law school and I knew if I had stayed around your focus on your career and your dreams would have been second place to our relationship and me. I wanted to give you a chance to succeed without any confusion or complications.

"And you know when I was offered the senior banker's position in Europe it took everything in me to leave."

I looked away.

"Jasmine, talk to me."

I turned back to him, the tears streaming down my face. "Marcus, you hurt me. I thought we had something special and you left like it was nothing. I woke up and you were gone. I was suddenly forced into living my life by myself, fantasizing and hoping for a relationship that wasn't going to be. Praying for another chance. And it never happened. I waited for you to return; I waited for you to come home to say you didn't care about the job or the money or any of that. I waited for you to come and save me. But you never came. How come you never came back for me?"

"Jasmine, please understand. I did this for us."

"Look, Marcus, there is no us. Would you please leave?"

"Jasmine, listen to me. I love you. I have always loved you."

"Marcus" . . . I reached for the door and swung it open. "Marcus, please leave."

Marcus looked deeply into my eyes again, and the rush that flowed through my body was too much for me to bear. I wanted to grab him, hold him, and never let him go.

"I'll go now, but know this: I am not leaving." Then he left.

I shut the door, turned my back to the door for support, then slid to the floor. The tears were in full force now and I knew my girlfriends would be here soon. I was right; less than five minutes later, the doorbell rang, followed by pounding and yelling. I stood up to open the door.

"Jasmine, baby, are you OK?" I could hear Sadie's voice in the hall, but I couldn't seem to open the door.

I guess I didn't need to; Sadie and the girls burst through, almost knocking me down.

"Oh my God," Sadie said. She grabbed me and carried me into the living room; helped by my other friends. They settled me onto the couch.

"We're so sorry we're late, we saw Marcus getting on the elevator. Are you OK?"

The look on my face told them I wasn't OK, "Girl, what happened, what did he say?"

"Look, I don't know." I cupped my face with my hands and tried to disappear into the air molecules.

Sadie looked at Angel. Then she went to the refrigerator, got a bottled water and to the wine cabinet to get the wine.

When the girls called code blue, each one had specific duties to get the situation under control. With each, girl's drama there were a series of steps that were taken to ensure quick recovery, based on our individual personalities. But water and wine were always number one and number two, not necessarily in that order.

I sunk into the couch, crying and mumbling about what Marcus had just told me; I tried to get them to understand but between my sobs and the snot clogging things up, my words were hard to understand. Carla ran to get some Kleenex. They listened.

"He said some mumbo jumbo about why he left," I said, sniffling, "leaving so that I would be successful . . . whatever."

My best friends' voices, distorted and muffled, swirled around in my head. All I could think about were his deep brown eyes. Damn, those eyes.

# Chapter 21

MY ALARM CLOCK WENT OFF and I awoke to the four-year weight that sat heavily on my chest. I struggled to get up. I trudged to the alarm clock, but instead of shutting it off, I ripped it out of the wall. "*Fuck this.*" I had really, finally, had enough.

I looked in the mirror and didn't recognize my face. My swollen, bloodshot eyes were enough to make me feel sick. I called Wendy at home and told her I wasn't feeling well and to forward only very important messages to my e-mail, unless they were calls or messages from my partners or from judges; then she was to call me on my cell phone.

"Of course," Wendy said. "Feel better, OK?"

I said I'd try, but in my mind, I had no idea how I was going to manage. I hung up the phone and got back into bed, something I knew I would regret later.

I fell into a deep sleep and dreamt of Marcus and how things used to be.

There was really no reason for us to meet. He worked at a small bank in the suburbs, while I attended college. We were two totally different people, with not a whole lot in common. But we both loved music and that instantly connected us.

I was working at a little barbecue restaurant in the city. It was a family-owned business run by the father and his three sons.

Mr. Whiting had been a postman; he had three sons who cooked their asses off, all of them. Within one year of opening their restaurant on a busy street near downtown Minneapolis, they were one of the most profitable barbecue restaurants in town. Everyone knew the plan and they all agreed and worked together towards one common goal. They were very modest people and kept everything in the family.

I loved my job because everyone was so nice to me. I worked a few hours after school and half-days on weekends. The pay wasn't so good but the tips were great. It also served as confidence booster because of all the play I would get, even drenched in barbecue sauce.

I was shy as a kid, but I had my grandfather's spirit. He knew how to engage people so they would fall totally and completely in love with him. A simple but stern smile, and his strong and positive hello made people think he was in control of everything. He passed that along to me, but most of the time I didn't use it—only when I felt comfortable in my space was I able to capture my customer's hearts. Mr. Whiting loved me because my spirit fit in with the family and the family trusted me to the utmost.

On Saturdays I was in charge of the day shift, so I started at nine to get ready for our open at eleven. Every other weekend without fail a gentleman named Marcus called in a to-go order to be picked up right when we opened. And every other week he ran in and got his order and ran out.

He was always cordial but he never had extra time to talk; that made me curious. What the hell could he be doing that he would not ever have time for small talk? I thought I might try to strike up a conversation, but three months went by with this guy running in and out of my checkout line, and I never got up the nerve; truth to tell, I had a little crush on him.

It was one of the coldest Saturdays of the year, and the barbecue pit that cooked all the ribs, rib tips, and chicken took a little longer getting up to temperature, so the orders were backed up about twenty minutes. When Marcus called, I took his order and hung up, not realizing I had forgotten to tell him that it was going to be a little bit longer. Maybe this would be a good time to try and talk to him, I thought

When the door opened at eleven on the dot, I felt the thumping in my chest rise up into my throat. He walked in laughing and I realized he had someone with him, another guy. He was nice-looking but not really my type. He was shorter than Marcus and he wasn't fine or anything like that but he was sexy as hell, "silk sheet" sexy.

The two men spoke and laughed as they approached the counter.

"Hello," I almost whispered—a softer, meeker hello than I wanted to give that forced its way up out of my mouth before I could get my courage up.

"Hey, how are you? I have a call-in order I need to pick up and my boy wants to order something."

"OK." The quiver in my voice was too evident; I was giving myself away. I excused myself and went to the back to check on the food—so I said. I ran back to Belinda, one of the other waitresses, and asked her if she could help me with Marcus this time; I'd confessed to her about my crush.

Belinda smiled. "Marcus is here?"

"Yeah, and he has someone with him. So now I'm all flustered."

"I got you, girl, I'll go out front and finish their orders."

"Thank you, girl, I owe you."

Belinda went out through the swinging door and I ran to the back to look through the two-way mirror. I could see Belinda fumbling. "What is she doing?"

"Jasmine, I need you up front," Belinda yelled from the counter.

Oh, hell no! I covered my mouth. I slowly walked up front and asked Belinda what she needed.

"Jasmine this is Marcus; Marcus, meet Jasmine."

Marcus stuck his hand out for me to shake it, but I hesitated.

"Um . . . hi, it's nice to meet you, Marcus." We shook hands; his strong, soft touch made my knees shake. I cut my eyes at Belinda.

Belinda smiled. "And this is his friend from California, Maurice."

"Hello, nice to meet you, Jasmine."

"Yeah, it's nice to me you too."

"So Jasmine, I hear you got a crush on my boy here." My eyes grew big and I felt my face going hot and turning red.

"What, a crush?"

"Yeah, your girlfriend told us you like Marcus."

I turned to Marcus, who was smiling broadly. "Is that true?"

"No, I never . . . um . . ." I couldn't speak.

"See, dude, I told you she wasn't interested in you, she was staring at me." Maurice laughed.

"Order up!" one of the Whiting boys said from the back

I ran to the back and grabbed their orders. I bagged them up and practically shoved them off the counter into their hands, hastily muttering over my shoulder, "Thank you, come again."

I turned and flew through the swinging door, back to the two-way mirror and looked out. Marcus and his friend were leaving and I could finally take a breath.

"Belinda, I'm going to kill you!"

"Girl, quit trippin', he's cute."

"Yeah, but how you gonna front me off like that?"

"Don't worry about it, girl, he was eyeballing you."

"But do you see how I'm looking, barbecue sauce and smoke everywhere? I look crazy."

"That's the best part—so when he finally sees the real you he'll be pleasantly surprised."

"What makes you think I'll see him outside of this place?"

Belinda smiled. "It's called *karma*, baby. If it is meant to be, it will."

I rolled my eyes at her and walked away.

"You're crazy!" Belinda yelled.

"I know but you love me."

I spent the rest of the day thinking about Marcus. Damn, his eyes, there was something about his eyes.

## Chapter 22

The phone rang and woke me from my daytime nightmare.

Who the hell could this be? I looked at the caller id; it was Sadie.

"Hello?"

"Hey, Jaz, how you doing?"

"I'm miserable, Sadie. I can't do this."

"Yes, you can," Her voice, usually upbeat and peppy, had taken on that tone I hated to hear, the voice that checked me and put me in my place.

"Jasmine, listen to me, you're going to be fine. We are not going to let him hurt you again."

"Sadie, do you realize I still have feelings for this man?"

"Yes, Jasmine, I know. But we're going to get through this together. I know how you're feeling and I understand. Always know that whatever decision you make I'll always back you."

The tears were running like open faucets down my face. I tried to stop them without success.

"Sadie, please don't let me make a mistake."

"Hey, baby, don't worry about making a mistake—worry about staying healthy and taking care of yourself; that's all that is important right now."

"OK, Sadie, I'll try."

"Jasmine, are you free for lunch today? I'm meeting with a colleague at the sushi bar. Can you make it?"

"What time are you planning to go down there?"

"It'll be a late lunch, probably about twelve-thirty.

"Yes, I can make that."

"All right. You be there, you hear me?"

"Yes, I hear you, I'll be there."

I cringed. Why did I say I'd go? I just want to sit here in the dark and sulk.

What an idiot, I thought—and of course, that idiot was me. I flung back the covers, put my feet on the floor and headed to the shower.

It didn't have its usual effect. The water felt cold even though the knob was turned as hot as it could go. The fear and frustration built up in my chest felt like a huge boulder trying to break its way through; it was almost too much to bear. I tried to shake it off.

What next, this is insane. I'm not going out like this, I thought. I quickly shifted gears, a self-defense mechanism I learned in college to regain control. After all those exams I had mastered the art of self-preservation—or at least a surface kind of it, anyway—beginning by analyzing everything: every event, every idea, every little quirky aside, and all the important pieces that summed up the puzzle. If I could get back in control of the situation, I could get back control of my life. Marcus turned my world upside-down once and I wasn't going to let it happen again.

The knob on the shower was obviously completely broken. I had called about it before, but called back to cancel when it started working again. It was these little things when I was in this state that sent me over the edge. I stormed out of the shower, and ran to the phone.

"Hello, is this maintenance?"

"Yes, how can we help you?"

"I've been telling you about my shower knob for three weeks now, when are going to get someone up here to fix it?"

"Oh, Ms. Burrell."

"Yes, it's me. Where's the person who's supposed to have my faucet fixed by now?"

"Ms. Burrell, we are very sorry; Jeff has been out sick and we've been short-handed this week."

"But what about last week? Were you short-handed then?" I asked irritably. Then, not waiting for an answer, "Look, Mike, I really don't care about all that, I just want someone to come up here and fix it right away." I slammed the phone down and got dressed.

I pulled out a DKNY jogging suit I had bought when I went to Chicago for a business trip. I rarely got to dress down, so I seized the opportunity—but of course, it was also a chance to wear one of the most expensive outfits I owned. I grabbed my tennis shoes and finished primping. My purse and glasses were sitting in the kitchen and I headed for the car. It was already 10 but I felt like I needed to work off some of my aggression.

I jumped in my car and headed for Aimee's Gym. I liked my gym. It was one of the smaller, more exclusive gyms. Rather than prancing around one of the big corporate types, and Aimee—yes, there was a real Aimee—really did care about her clients. It cost almost twice that of the bigger gyms but I didn't mind; it allowed me freedom to take my time and work out at my own pace without feeling rushed.

Aimee was a Caucasian girl, the daughter of one of my mother's co-workers. She was a petite little thing, and I connected with her the moment I met her. Her presence exuded a special peace that comforted me whenever I saw her. I smiled, thinking about all our workout sessions and how she laughed with me whenever I whined.

The gym was about two miles away, so depending on the roads and traffic my total workout time including travel time was about an hour and a half. I loved that because I learned I could get a lot of things done in a day if I effectively managed my time. A big part of my life was dedicated to planning. I planned everything. Especially when things got out of hand, I could look at the plan and get back on track.

But I had never planned for this. As I walked inside, I saw Aimee behind the counter.

"Hey, Jasmine, odd to see you here this morning; you're off today?"

"Yes. I took the day for some well-deserved me time."

"Great—you of all people need that. Here's a towel; have a good workout."

"Thanks, Aimee, I will."

I was already in my workout clothes, so after I put my things in my locker, I headed straight for the treadmill, jumped on, and began to run.

What was I going to do? The thought of Marcus, my friends and everything that had just happened in the last twenty-four hours were killing me and I needed a way out.

The running really helped to clear my thoughts. I slowly felt the tension drain from my neck and shoulders. Everything was going to be all right; I can handle this. As the stress and confusion began to dissipate I thought about my strategy. I'll just tell him the truth, let him know what he did to me and how it affected my life. He'll understand, I thought. I can do this, I reassured myself, feeling more prepared for another Marcus confrontation. I ran an extra fifteen minutes to set my feelings in stone.

I showered, got dressed, and headed toward my lunch date with Sadie, waving to Aimee as I left.

On the way to the restaurant I felt better. The workout had actually worked—actually, it had been exhilarating. Seems like all those articles about how exercise reduced stress were true after all. Pulling up to the restaurant I took one last look in the mirror and declared my freedom from Marcus. I was ready to close that chapter of my life for good.

# Chapter 23

The sushi bar's Japanese décor, with exquisitely arranged fresh flowers and serene landscape paintings, was exactly what I needed. I took the crystal-white tablecloths and sparkling hardwood floors as a sign of renewed spirit and a fresh start. As I approached the host I saw Sadie in the corner waving.

I told him my party was already here, and he graciously waved me along.

As I got closer I noticed Sadie was sitting with someone. It was a man, a fine man.

What was Sadie doing with him? Then I remembered she had said she was going to lunch with a colleague. Damn, he's gorgeous, I thought.

I greeted Sadie with a hug and a squeeze; she knew exactly what that extra squeeze meant. She smiled broadly.

"Jasmine, this is Kevin Owens, a friend of mine from the firm. He's new to the company and works in the graphic arts department."

I turned to Kevin and put out my hand.

"Hello, it's nice to meet you."

Kevin stood up and I almost fainted. He had soft, curly jet-black hair, and unusually dark features. His eyebrows, lashes, and goatee were like ebony, and it created an amazing contrast against his skin. His eyebrows were perfect arches, like they had been waxed, but I could tell as I looked at him more closely that they weren't. His eyelashes were so long that I felt a breeze when he winked and smiled at me. And for some reason his goatee was driving me crazy—*perfectly* trimmed. He looked like he might have been Puerto Rican or from the islands somewhere because his butterscotch skin was kissed with a hint of mocha.

"Hi Jasmine, nice to meet you too." His soft, caressing tone made me weak.

He held on to my hand a little longer than I was comfortable with. I hesitantly removed my hand from his grasp as gently as I could without seeming rude; then I smiled and winked back. I could tell by the way his smile broadened that he took that as an invitation.

Did I deliberately do that, I wondered to myself. I sat down and turned to Sadie, trying not to stare at him; I just wanted to soak up his presence.

Sadie filled me in on the gossip at her office. Kevin mostly kept silent—he was the new guy—but chimed in from time to time. I told them about the case I'd just finished. They couldn't believe the pressure I was under.

"Dang, Jasmine that's deep, I don't know how you do it."

"I'm so glad I don't have to deal with all those emotions. I got my laptop and I'm in heaven," said Sadie. "No tears, drama, angry clients; wait a minute, I take that back. Mr. Felton was extremely upset with me."

"What happened?"

"Girl, I designed his multi-story office building exactly to his specifications and his costs went over his budget. I told him it was going to happen, but he assured me he knew what he was doing and how much he was spending. He started making major structural changes during construction and that shit adds up quickly. Before he knew it he was out of money. I knew he was going to trip on the firm and me so I called our lawyers and already prepared them for his call."

"What your company gonna do?"

"Handle it. They better, they don't wanna hear me. But enough about my boring life—how was your workout? You still go to Aimee's?"

"Yes, and it was great; I had time to really concentrate on me."

"That's a good thing," Kevin spoke up. "You need to take time for yourself."

I looked at him intently; there was something mysterious about him.

"Yes, it really helped me get focused on what's most important." I looked into Kevin's eyes longer than I intended. A strange feeling came over me.

I looked at Sadie; I knew exactly what she was trying to do—I don't know why it took my so long to figure it out, really. She thought she was so slick. If she could get me focused on something, or someone, new it might help keep those feelings I was having about Marcus in check.

Sadie was only trying to help and I knew that and respected her for her effort. She was my girl, and knew how to play me. And by the looks of this fine-ass brother it was actually beginning to work.

The waiter came but I was a little hesitant to order a drink. I had just worked out, and how would it look if I ruin it with alcohol? Usually when I started drinking, I couldn't have just one.

"I'll have iced tea."

"I'll have a cosmopolitan," Sadie smiled.

"And I'll have a Miller Genuine Draft," Kevin said.

I could tell Kevin was a man's man. He was smooth yet masculine, and extremely cool. He was quiet and patient and seemed to know exactly when to speak so as not to disrupt the flow of the conversation. I could tell he was an observer rather than a talker and I liked that. I began to drop my guard a little bit. But I stayed cool, cool was my middle name; I did *not* want this man to know I was desperate. It had been a long time since I had been out with a guy who was attentive. My last three dates had been arrogant, self-absorbed nobodies; I dated just to get out of the house.

"Well, damn, if I had known it was this type of party I would have ordered something else."

"Girl, with us it's always this type of party. Kevin and I are done for the day so we're drinking."

Damn, I could really use one of those cosmopolitans, I thought.

"So you don't drink?" Kevin asked.

"Drink, me? Ah, yeah, I drink"—drink you under the table, I muttered—but I'm cutting back.

Sadie coughed.

What a lie I'm telling, after all the drinks I had last night and over the weekend. I should be ashamed before God.

"I'm taking a small hiatus," I said, trying to smooth over my lie.

"*Very* small," Sadie whispered.

"OK, so when your small hiatus is over, we should get together and go out for drinks, and you can get what you really want," Kevin said, smiling.

I grinned in spite of myself and kicked Sadie under the table. It took everything in her not to laugh. She looked at me and winked—she knew what I knew. Kevin had touched something. I felt the lock on my heart beginning to loosen, and I kind of liked it.

"Um, excuse me, I'm going to run to the ladies room," Sadie said, kicking me back she gave me the Southside Diva evil eye. I knew exactly what that meant: Put it on him. I winced and quickly turned it into a fake sneeze, trying not to let Kevin know she had kicked me kind of hard. I half-grinned again and gave Sadie the evil eye back as she headed towards the restrooms.

"So Kevin, where are you from, and how'd you get to Minnesota?"

"I'm originally from Staten Island, New York. My father is an air traffic controller, so we were transferred here when I was a teenager."

"Staten Island, huh? What was it like there?"

"It was cool. I was only there until I was ten, then we moved to Houston. But in Staten Island I started modeling when I was really young so I didn't get into much. My parents tried to get me into every print ad in the city."

"Wow, that's cool," I said.

"Yeah, it worked for a while," he said, "but the industry changed and my agents said that the new super-thin white boy look was in. So work for me really slowed down."

"What do you mean, as fine as you are?" Oops, that slipped out. I could feel my face turning red. "I mean, you're so handsome, how could anyone not use you?"

"I guess times and things change, so after high school I got really interested in graphic arts and attended the Minneapolis College of Art and Design to pursue my passion. I've been working at various companies trying to find the right one, so when I met Sadie at an architectural conference we exchanged cards. She told me to come down to the firm and she would see what she could do about getting a position with her company. I did, and have loved every minute of it."

Kevin took a sip of his water and licked off the wetness that remained on his lips. I couldn't take my eyes off his lips. They were perfect. Full, thick and soft—and right at that moment I wanted a piece of him.

I looked up and he was looking directly into my eyes. I could tell he was not interested in just being acquaintances. I started getting a case of nerves—not to mention that my panties were soaking wet. I crossed my legs and began to look around for Sadie. I'm going to kick her ass; she's dead meat, I thought.

Just as I was about to get up, Sadie sauntered back to the table.

"So, how are you and Kevin getting along?" she said, smiling slyly.

"Oh there you are, we missed you," I managed to squeak out. "We're doing just fine."

I grabbed her arm and squeezed it as hard as I could, hoping Kevin wouldn't notice as I tried to practically cut off her circulation. She glared at me, then turned on a smile as she motioned to Kevin. I knew exactly what she was talking about, but was trying not to buy into her little matchmaking game.

# Chapter 24

S ADIE AND I HAVE ALWAYS had this uncanny knack of reading each other's mind. It started in college.

Sadie and I would throw card parties—we liked spades, which was a complicated game with books and trump cards, strategy and bluffing. We invited the girls from our psych class to our apartment to play; these, girls were the coolest. They were in school to get an education, not to find a husband, and we only associated with the girls that had plans for themselves. Those other hoochies thought that they were too good for us and tried to make us believe it. We never did. Sadie and I always thought we were the shit and no one could tell us different.

Everyone had to have a partner, and Sadie was mine. We made sure of that; there was no way anyone could get us to switch so they never tried, even though we would kick butt on a regular basis.

The game of spades would be played to 350, and if a team had a Boston run on them; where one team wins all the books in one deal, then the team that lost had to get up immediately from the table. It always started out as a nice evening, but by the time Sadie and I had beaten the fourth team in a row the girls would start to get mad and say we were cheating.

We weren't cheating. It was like magic when we played. We knew exactly which cards to play and when to play them. We played so well we would get the other teams to make mistakes and end up giving away two or three books. When we counted up the books in our hands to place our bid, we would always add two or three for the ones we expected them to give us.

It was hilarious—you'd think we were playing for millions of dollars. We laughed and talked so much shit that the whole house would be in an uproar except for the two losers at the table.

That telepathy at the card table eventually transferred into other areas, so we got so we could read each other's minds at the drop of a hat. Looking at the same person thinking the same thing, one of us starting the comment and the other one finishing it. It got so bad that before I could get the words out of my mouth Sadie would say, "Jaz, get out of my head." I'd just laugh and shake my head.

So this matchmaking game was Sadie's way of playing the odds. Strategy. Bring more players to the game and see who has the best hand. I looked at Kevin. Damn!

*Marcus who?*

I stared at the little slip of paper with Kevin's number on it. I couldn't get the picture of him out of my mind. I felt my cell phone vibrating on my hip. I had forgotten that I put the phone on vibrate while we were at lunch so that the constant ringing I was used too wouldn't disturb us. I switched the ringer on and looked at the number on the caller ID and smiled. This heifer.

"Hello, hey, girl, it's Sadie."

"I know who it is; what do you want, you sneaky heifer?"

"Soooo, what do you think?" I could hear the excitement in her voice.

"Sadie; you know I'm going to kill you, right?"

"Yeah, I know, but he is fine, ain't he?"

"Yes Sadie, he's gorgeous. How could you put me out there like that?"

"Jaz, you're beautiful, single, successful; Marcus is history, right?"

"Yeah, I guess so."

"What do you mean, you guess so?"

"Sadie, you know Marcus is the only man I have ever loved."

"Yeah, I know sweetie, but it's time for you to move on. I don't want to see you looking like you looked yesterday."

"I know, girl."

"Look, Jasmine, just think about it. You don't have to rush into anything, take your time. Whatever you decide I will always support you. OK?"

"OK. Thank you, Sadie, I really appreciate you. I'll talk to you later."

Sadie was right. I didn't want to go through the hurt I felt when Marcus left ever again I didn't want him back in my life. I was through.

Until the phone rang.

# Chapter 25

STARED AT THE NUMBER; THE ringing in my ears sounded like my high school tardy bell on the first day of school. Three rings, four rings. I heard someone yell, "Answer it!" I looked around but there was no one there. Every bone in my body said *Do not answer the phone.*

I answered it.

The silence was deafening.

"Jasmine?"

I paused. "Yes, this is Jasmine."

"Hey, Jasmine. It's Marcus."

"Hey, Marcus, how are you?"

"I'm fine. I was just calling to see how you were doing and to invite you to dinner tonight."

"You know, Marcus I don't think that that would be a good idea. I had a pretty rough night last night and I don't think I'm ready for another confrontation with you so soon."

"I know, Jasmine, that's why I need to talk to you. I'm not leaving until Sunday now and I just need to explain what I was trying to say last night. Give me just one night. I'm sure you will understand. He paused.

"Look, baby, I'm so nervous right now because I'm in a place that I've never been before and I'm trying to understand these feelings. And after last night, I see you still have some unresolved issues with me and I really want to clear things up. You're the only one that knows the real me, and that's why I'm able to trust you with these emotions. From the first day I laid eyes on you my heart yearned for you. Do you really think I enjoyed barbecue that much? I was in that restaurant every other week."

He laughed, and I could see his perfect smile.

His smile was a reflection of God for me. When he smiled my soul cried out. I never understood what it was about his smile that made me so weak. All I knew was that it felt good. It felt so good.

"Jasmine—will you?"

"Will I what? I'm sorry, Marcus—what did you say?"

"I said: I figure we go out to eat so our feelings can be aired in a neutral space. Meeting at your place or at my hotel room would be torture, don't you think?"

"Yes I agree. Where should we go?"

"I don't know. You're the one that lives here. I haven't been here for four and a half years."

"OK, there's this new Creole restaurant I've been dying to try. What time?"

"How about seven-thirty?"

"Yeah, seven-thirty is fine. I'll call you with the details and meet you there."

I hung up the phone and waited for a sign—any sign. Nothing happened.

As I cruised towards the highway, I thought about Kevin; I wouldn't dare tell Sadie what I had done. She would *not* understand.

When I got home I had three messages on my phone. I was really not trying to listen to any drama from the girls and I knew when the others found out I didn't go to work today they would be calling. They probably figured I stayed in because of all that happened the night before. I was surprised they hadn't called my cell phone. Or maybe they thought I was resting and didn't want to bother me. Or Sadie had already told them the plan and made sure they didn't call; so they left the messages so I would know they were thinking about me. Those stank heifers. I laughed and went to shower.

As the warm water began to wash over my body, I couldn't break free. I kept thinking of Marcus, feeling his hands all over me, like he was standing right there next to me, part of that glorious morning after that incredible dinner years ago.

\* \* \*

The sun was just peeking through the windows of Marcus' bedroom that morning. He touched me and instantly I was awake.
"Yes baby?" I turned to look at him. He was so beautiful. There was nothing but innocence in his eyes; he was looking right through me, studying every part of me. He was the only man that saw my spirit, and he never noticed my flaws.
"Would you like to take a shower with me? I thought we could get up early and go for a walk, maybe pick up some breakfast?"
"Why do you act so white?" I smiled. He put his hands around my shoulders and lightly shook me. I giggled. "Of course—I would love to."
"You're so white," he said, and kissed me.
The soft fullness of his lips touched mine and every dream I had had the night before came true. I took his face in my hands and drew him in deep, and everything around us disappeared. All we had was each other and we liked it that way.
That potent kiss, the taste of his lips, led to the most divine impromptu lovemaking session either of us had ever experienced. We sat basking in each other's presence and spent the next thirty minutes slowly undressing and exploring each other's bodies with the intensity of lost lovers found once again.
The fire between my legs craved his sweet touch. He stopped.
"What's wrong, baby?" I asked.
He placed his finger over my mouth and gently caressed, kissed, and suckled my left breast; he reached out his hand to motion me to the shower, I followed. I was his puppet, and he was my master, I was completely under his command and he had no problems with control. I floated to the bathroom eagerly awaiting his dominance.

He turned on the shower as hot as we could stand, and watched as the steam filled the room, just long enough for it to lightly coat the mirrors and shower door. It was like a low, warm, London fog cocooning us, hiding us from our enemies.

He pulled me close and used a hair clip from my bureau to tie my hair up. He knew getting a black woman's hair wet might cause issues, and he wasn't about to take any chances with me stopping the action to cuss him out. But what he didn't know was that I was so mesmerized by him, he could have dumped a bucket of water on my head and it wouldn't have mattered. I took his hand and slowly walked into the shower with him. He looked deeply into my eyes, and I began to cry. He made me believe again; he truly loved me, and I he.

I was no more, the grand satisfaction of believing in fairytales and the belief that true love did exist was real to me now, and it was all because of Marcus. I swore there would be nothing to separate us, and rose to my appointed place in heaven.

Marcus took the bar of lavender soap and a scrunchie and began to lather it up. I pointed to the body wash in the shower caddy but he liked the feel of the bar of soap against my body. I let him, and ran my hand down the side of his face towards his mouth. He kissed it, twice. I shuddered.

The blanket of suds he made was billowy and soft as he covered my entire body in the foam, starting with my neck and working his way down. My breasts were his first stop. He rubbed and squeezed and caressed both breasts, gently pinching and rolling my nipples between his fingers like he was expertly tuning the channels of a 1970s radio. My nipples became hard, and every inch of my body pulsated. I gasped for air. He smiled.

He turned me around and directed me towards the showerhead; I stood waiting as the stream of hot water showered my body. As the bubbles dissipated he lightly stroked me with both his hands, cleansing me. He watched my reaction closely and decided it was time; with the gentleness of a lamb he began suckling and licking my breasts—first one, then the other—my nipples, the areola and even underneath. I had never realized before how sensitive the lower areas of my breasts were until he lifted them up and licked and sucked me there.

I thought I would scream and tried to compose myself, but I couldn't. I pushed him up against the wall and dropped to my knees. Now, as the water engulfed him, ran down his body, and streamed into my face I took him into my mouth.

His moans and the low growl of his voice as he called my name aroused me even more. I was a pleaser—I got off more on giving rather than receiving. Don't get me wrong—receiving was great, but I always felt more in control of my sexuality when I was causing the screaming.

He rested his head against the wall and moaned louder than I had ever heard him. He took my head in his hands, and gently, tenderly pulled me back and forth by my hair, slowly thrusting deeper and deeper into my mouth. I was treading on new ground and found it to be extremely exhilarating. Then he let out a long, low groan and came. The salty fluid filled my mouth and ran down my chin. I felt so good.

Marcus, now drenched in sweat as much as water, stood me up and cried in my arms, holding me close.

Then he whispered, "Your turn."

Even though Marcus had come he always made sure I was thoroughly pleased. He was so patient and caring, sometimes I couldn't believe he was real.

He spun me around and bent me completely over. My hair, dripping wet, fell out of the clip and lightly lay against the wall and floor. He entered me from the back, steadily at first, but bit-by-bit I could feel the power of his manhood penetrate my hot, wet core. I gasped, grasping the towel rack above my head to keep my balance.

I pressed my pelvis into his to match the intensity of his thrust, catching, holding on to, and returning it with all that I was made of. He responded with elation, his driving force penetrating into my very soul. I felt free; my heart raced and my spirit sang. I began to hallucinate, fantasizing about all things imaginable. I could no longer hold on. I screamed as he grabbed my hair, pulled my neck back and thrust all nine inches into the deepest part of my being. I released a magnificent torrent of tears from every part of my body.

He slowly lowered himself on top of me, exhausted, breathing heavily in my ear. We stayed there for a moment, enjoying the metamorphosis from who we were to who we were meant to be.

We slowly straightened up, and I luxuriously rinsed off and stepped out of the shower and took a towel to start drying off. He came out right behind me and took the towel, gently wiping the water from my body. He opened the African shea butter I had bought for him from a little store in New York when I had gone out there on a business trip a couple months ago, and lightly massaged the cream into my body. I rubbed my naked body against his to spread the cream between us. It was crazy; I could see his manhood begin to firm up. I decided I better stop or else we'd never get to go on our walk.

Most times lovemaking for us was not just sex, and more times than not we were completely entranced. But for some reason this occasion was different. It was like a potent drug, dangerously intoxicating and violently freeing. It was like an exquisitely slow, heartbreakingly beautiful operatic melody, some divine aria, played softly in the background, rising as the intensity of our lovemaking grew, a serene masterpiece of love and acceptance and peace, a glorious gift given by angels, and only heard by those who could truly feel the piercing intensity of physical and spiritual love.

# Chapter 26

Damn, I had stayed in the shower way too long, lost in my memories, and even though I was scared to death, I figured I better hurry up so I wouldn't be late.

I turned off the water and dried off, reaching for a jar of shea butter—what was left of the same shea butter I had used with Marcus so many years ago. It had never been able to part with it, because it reminded me of him and I wanted that reminder sometimes; in fact, sometimes I needed it.

I lightly wrapped myself in my towel and walked over to the bureau to look for the appropriate underwear. I had decided the dress I was wearing wasn't going to need a bra so I just looked for my black lacy thong.

I took the dress off of the satin hanger and held it up in front of me. What was I doing? I was pretty sure that if I wore this dress to meet with Marcus that we would be back at my place screwing like rabbits. I can't wear this.

I started towards the closet to look for something more conservative, but as I passed by the mirror, the Southside Diva in me shouted, Sure you can! Show him what he has been missing. And show him that he's not going to get it again. Ever.

Damn, that's right. He left you; let him know that you're not going through this again and that you're finally and completely ending this, once and for all.

I slid into the slinky black dress and checked myself out in the mirror, adjusting everything until it was perfect. Those extra hours at the gym were surely paying off and I was proud that I was keeping to my promise. I slipped on my black leather high-heeled boots and finished my hair. I decided to wear as little make-up as possible just in case he was wearing something light. I didn't want to smear anyone, which I had been doing a lot lately. I had just smeared my law office partner last week by hugging him for his birthday. I looked for my cell phone and called Marcus.

"Hello Marcus, this is Jasmine."

"Hey, Jaz, I was hoping you were still going to call me." He paused for a minute. "Actually as it got later and later I got a little bit scared. I'm glad you called."

"Uh, Marcus the restaurant is on Gleason and Twenty-first. 2141 Gleason Avenue," I said, ignoring his last remark. "Do you remember where that is?"

"Is that by the library and the police station?"

"Yes Marcus, it's kitty corner from there."

"OK, I'll meet you there at seven-thirty. Drive safely."

"Thank you, I will. You too."

I hung up the phone. Damn, I almost forgot how sweet and considerate he could be. I tried to wipe the silly grin off my face but it wouldn't leave.

I got to my car without anyone in the lobby noticing; they were very nosy when it looked like someone was going out on a date. I checked the rearview again to make sure I was presentable and drove towards the restaurant half smiling and half shaking. This had to be the craziest thing I had done in a long time.

# Chapter 27

You're in big trouble; Sadie, Carla, and Angel are going to kill you, I thought as I pulled up to the restaurant parking lot, got out, and started walking across the street towards the restaurant.

Then I spotted Marcus. Wow, early. He was still early.

He was wearing a dark green suede suit jacket with slightly baggy blue jeans. His crisp white button-down shirt set off the jacket and his beautiful chocolate head was nicely clean-shaven. He hadn't cut his hair that close in the past so I figured he was probably starting to lose his hair, which didn't matter to me either way. I loved the perfect sharpness of his fiercely trimmed mustache and beard; it was driving me crazy, those smooth, perfect lips between those finely groomed hairs.

What was I doing? I wanted to retreat but my feet had other ideas.

His long legs seemed to be stretching towards the sky and I saw that his build—the one I remembered from when we were younger—had changed from a boy's reedier frame to the statuesque silhouette of a grown man. He was strong and sturdy and I felt a little uneasy as I slowed my walk down in order to catch my breath. I paused at the curb and smiled; I couldn't help it.

He walked down the restaurant stairs and took my hand to help me up. When we got to the top step he embraced me.

I melted; it only took a second for the warmth from his body to consume me. A flood of emotion rushed through me, all the things I had planned to say to him were gone. I didn't want him to let me go, so I took a deep breath, relaxed, and embraced him back.

I could tell by his reaction that he was overwhelmed too; his manufactured coolness was a little too obvious, a mask for the strong passionate pulse that surged through his body. As we intertwined, I could feel the tension drain from his body. We didn't stop our embrace, all the while smiling and reacquainting ourselves with each other's touch.

We were no longer hungry—for food, anyway—and decided to go back to my place to talk. That's it, just talk, even though my mind was thinking about other things.

Marcus trailed me in a mid-size rental car, which really wasn't his style; he was more of a sporty dude, but I guess the rental he got was for economical reasons versus style.

It was funny, because he was able to keep up with me, even though Betsy was a speedy little thing, with 125 mph on the dash. I could tell by the way he was driving he had no intentions of losing me; he followed as closely as he could without running into the back of my car.

As I drove toward home, I told myself I was not going to fold, I was going to let him know how I felt and I was going to send him away.

I knew I was going to need a drink to get through this, though, so I had him follow me to the liquor store near my apartment building before we got to my place. I parked and he parked next to me. We entered the store together as if we had done it a thousand times.

He looked at me. "Do you still drink red wine? Shiraz, I think?"

I smiled, "Yes, you remembered."

He winced, but with a twinkle in his eye. "How could I forget? You had me trying a different label every weekend."

I started laughing, "Oh my God, you're right. We did do that."

"No. *You* did that and forced me to drink with you. That sniffing, sipping, and spitting was crazy. I still have nightmares about that one night. I got so sick."

I was cracking up, and Marcus, laughing, grabbed me around my waist and pulled me close. He held his mouth close to my ear, and we laughed until it hurt.

I looked up at him and at that moment realized what the spark was that had been missing from my life the past four years. It was laughter—plain, simple laughter.

# Chapter 28

UNLOCKED THE DOOR TO my apartment and we went inside. I had left incense burning so the room was filled with the aroma of Egyptian musk and frankincense. The air was a little cloudy, but it made the ambience nice and comfortable.

I set the keys and the bottle of wine on the kitchen counter and told Marcus to go find a seat and relax. I excused myself and went to the bedroom; I wanted to make sure everything in my room was neat and clean. I slipped off my boots and changed into a pair of washed-out jeans and a black sweater. I purposely neglected to put a bra on, which was really asking for trouble, but at that moment I didn't care. So much for "I'm not going to fold." I brushed my teeth and touched up my lip-gloss. Marcus was facing away from me when I entered the living room, and I fantasized about walking up behind him and kissing him on the neck.

But I couldn't do it. Something about him being in my apartment stopped me dead in my tracks.

"Marcus?"

"Hey, baby, I was just looking at all the pictures of you and your friends. You really are beautiful. I guess I forgot how looking at you made me feel."

"Baby"—he used "baby" as if we were a couple again.

I put my head down and inhaled deeply. "Marcus, would you like a cup of coffee?"

"Sure, but let me make it."

"Of course, Mr. Coffee—I hope I have everything you need."

Tonight, for some reason coffee seemed the better choice. I put the wine in the cabinet took his hand and walked with him to the kitchen. I showed him where everything was and because I was so flustered, I was glad he was there to help. Luckily I had just been to the coffee shop, where I'd bought several different types of beans and had them all labeled and ready to go. I sat down on the bar stool at the counter and watched as he began to make magic. He selected two types of beans and started grinding them up. He looked up at me and smiled. I smiled back, not realizing it until it was too late. He winked, poured the grounds into the filter and started the coffee. As the hot water trickled through the grounds and the steam began to rise, the sharp, sweet aromas of Sumatra and French roast swirled in the air, the two flavors mixing—something I never would have thought of—gently tickled my nostrils.

I was aroused. Marcus knew I loved the smell of coffee and I think he purposely asked to make it because he knew what it would do to me. And judging from his expression, he figured it was time. He could see my eyes glazing over, and he pulled his stool right up next to mine, facing me, trapping me. I had no room to move—even if I had wanted to.

At that moment, there was nothing more satisfying than having Marcus back in my apartment, in my life. His aura, his gentle presence belonged there and I welcomed the new vibe that was taking over my space. After four years I still had feelings for him and it seemed to me that he was feeling the same way. He took my hand and began to speak. At first the sound, his voice simply mesmerized me, and all the things he said just floated around my head, almost making me dizzy.

But everything came into sudden, sharp focus, when he shifted in his seat and said, "*Jasmine, marry me, I love you. I want you to come back to Europe with me.*"

I drew back on the stool, and my mouth dropped open, my chin practically to my chest.

"What are you talking about?"

"Jasmine, I know you still love me, and you and I both know that this type of love is rare. You and I are different from other people—we believe in the absolute possibilities of love at first sight, we believe there is a chance for soulmates to find each other. I have yearned for you all my life and I was just waiting to grow up so that I could find you. Everything happens for a reason and you are my reason. I need you to be my wife. There is no one else."

I sat there in shock, screaming inside, holding back tears, jumping up and down inside and a whole slew of other things all at once.

"The coffee is ready, Marcus."

He looked at me, confused, his doe eyes caressing my very spirit and an overwhelming peace washing over my body. I looked away and excused myself. He grabbed my arm.

"Jasmine, are you OK? Did you hear what I said?"

"I'm all right Marcus, and yes I heard what you said," I replied softly but firmly. "Just give me a minute, OK?"

I pushed away from the counter and slowly walked into the bathroom, shutting the door behind me I stared in the mirror, but this time the person I saw wasn't me. It was *her* staring me directly in the eyes and not flinching. She was always there during big decision-making moments in my life.

What did she want with me now? She asked me, "Do you still love him?" I could feel a single tear roll down my cheek and I opened my mouth and silently said, "Yes."

Then the floodgates opened. I was in a full-blown sob fest and I could not get it together. I stayed in there for about ten minutes, and I knew Marcus must have been getting antsy. Just as I was about to open the door to yell to him that I was OK, I heard a gentle knock.

"Jasmine, are you all right?"

"Yes, I'm fine, I'll be right out."

"OK, I'll pour you a cup of coffee."

I reached for a face cloth and tried to wipe away some of the tear-stains. I had to listen to the reflection in the mirror, but it still took me another ten minutes to get myself together. I contemplated totally disregarding what Marcus had said—but how could I ignore that? A *marriage proposal*, and leaving the country? This was crazy and I intended tell Marcus that.

When I opened the door Marcus was sitting on the loveseat with his coffee and a cup for me. The fireplace was going and the room seemed dimmer. What was going on?

"Hey, what's up?" I said, pretending to be nonchalant, as if I hadn't just received an earth-shattering proposal.

"Jasmine, come sit with me. I want to show you something."

# Chapter 29

I AWOKE TO THE MAGNIFICENCE of the sun streaming through my room. Its beauty and warmth rejuvenated me, and gave me a strange kind of strength I didn't even know I had. It was like I had been released from a cocoon, freed, and ready to fly. It was a beautiful day.

I sat up in bed and looked at the clock—it was six a.m., and I realized I hadn't even set my alarm. This was the first day in a long time that I had awakened on my own, and it felt really good. Everything in my life at that moment was right and I could feel my spirit changing, growing. I had to pinch myself to make sure I wasn't dreaming.

I raised my left hand against the sun and felt an even brighter force penetrate my soul. The four-carat princess-cut diamond ring that was now sitting on my finger had changed everything. I smiled dreamily, thinking about the night before and the events that led up to this impossible miracle. Then, with a sudden burst of energy, I jumped out of bed and ran to look for Marcus. He had held me in his arms all night—nothing more, but it was all we needed or wanted then.

When I opened the bedroom door, the smell of fresh brewed coffee hit my nostrils and my heart leaped. I wasn't dreaming. I inhaled deeply and realized the aroma was different. It called to me. I imagined myself floating around the room, nose first, following every angle in the room with the change in intensity of the scent.

The smells were so intense it felt like I was sitting in a Colombian field with warm coffee beans being poured all over my body. I looked around for Marcus but there was no sign of him. I walked into the kitchen and saw the note taped to the counter.

*Hey, baby,*

> *Sorry, I had to leave. I have a very important business meeting this morning and I wanted to get a jump-start on the day. I made you some coffee and there is breakfast in the oven. I'll call you later.*
> *I love you,*
>
> *Marcus.*
>
> *P.S. I had a wonderful night. I hope you feel the same.*

This is crazy. I do feel the same.

I held the note in my hand and stared at it, wishing I could make Marcus materialize out of the ink. He didn't, but that was all right. I didn't need the fantasy any longer; I had the real thing.

# Chapter 30

At seven-thirty, I pranced into work like my life couldn't get any better—and really, how could it? Wendy was standing at the copier, and as soon as she saw me, she knew something was up.

"Good morning, Wendy."

"Good morning, Jasmine. How are you feeling?"

"Great! Wendy, how are you?"

Wendy had spent years studying me, my moods, my expressions, my demeanor, and she had learned how to react to my crazy Capricorn mood swings. But this dramatic change in my attitude baffled even her. She put the copier on interrupt; I watched out of the corner of my eye as she sauntered over to me with a gigantic grin and sly-fox look in her eyes.

"Jasmine, how are you?" Then she grabbed me, spun me around and shook me. "Girl, what is going on?" I burst into laughter and fanned the ring in her face. I had never seen anyone's eyes get that big before; she was muffling a scream I could feel down in my bones.

"Is this from Marcus?"

"Yes. He proposed last night and asked me to move to Europe with him."

Wendy's face fell, and suddenly, right then, I realized what I had agreed to.

Wendy tried to force a smile. "That's great, Jasmine, I'm very happy for you." It was clear that leaving the law firm was going to be a problem for her. Damn, a problem for both of us.

The next few hours were spent catching up on paperwork. Then, mid-morning, Wendy buzzed my office and said that I had a delivery. I told her to bring it right in. As she entered, an enormous lilac-colored plastic bag—the color of the area's top florist—completely hid her face and torso. "Oh my God!" I screamed.

"Well, we both know where this came from," she said, and she couldn't conceal the sarcasm from oozing out. It irked me and I asked her to come sit and talk with me.

"Wendy, I know all this seems crazy, and it is. Last night was wild and I can't even tell you what I'm going through right now. I agreed to marry Marcus without even thinking things out. You're the first person I told about this, and after seeing your reaction I realized that I'm not the only one this decision is going to affect."

As the implications of my decision dawned on me, I couldn't believe how thoughtless I had been. I asked Wendy to forgive me for breaking the news to her like that. "I'm sorry for being so selfish, Wendy, can we schedule some time to talk? How about lunch this week? Let me know when you're free. Is that OK with you?"

"Of course, Jasmine," she said, and smiled a little. "Don't mind me, I'm just pouting for my own selfish reasons. You know I'm really happy for you and wish you all the best."

We hugged, and I thanked her, and she got up to leave. I asked her to hold all my calls until eleven-thirty and to e-mail me with the times she would be available. She walked out of my office and closed the door. Over the years, Wendy and I had developed a close sort of relationship that surpassed anything professional. She was like a little sister to me and I loved and respected her. She too, had an uncanny way of breaking through my intentionally set barriers and I welcomed her bright-eyed take on my earth-shattering life issues.

I looked at the clock. Aw shit, ten-thirty already, and I hadn't even told the girls.

I'd been awake more than three hours and I hadn't called them yet, not even Sadie. Boy, was I in trouble. They now had full authority to totally kick the shit out of me.

How was I going to explain a life-changing commitment to the girls without even consulting them first? How could I just say yes to such a major life change?

I walked over to the big purple bag and slowly peeled back the plastic. I peeked inside and the tidal wave of emotion from the night before came slamming down on my chest. This took the cake.

When I was a little girl, my brother and I used to travel to South Carolina to visit my cousins on our father's side of the family. I had told Marcus about a field there that had the most amazing wildflowers, and how I would lay down in them all day watching the birds fly and listening to the crickets sing.

But they didn't grow in Minnesota—in fact, they grew only when the climate and habitat was just right, and their distinct smell and vibrant colors made them very rare and very expensive. I stopped peeling and just ripped the bag open, transported back to the summer days I spent running and playing in that field, remembering how beautiful and peaceful every day was, and how calm and serene every night was.

I opened the card. *Please have dinner with me tonight. Marcus.* Was I really getting married? Was I making the right decision? I looked at the beautiful stone on my finger and the enormous bouquet sitting in my office and nodded yes, yes, I really am getting married.

I took the vase and set it on the glossy maple and lacquer credenza. The gold and blue tones in the vase complemented the kente cloth I had placed on its surface.

Enough messing around. I had to call the girls.

## Chapter 31

PICKED UP THE PHONE to dial Sadie. I had to be careful how I told her because she was going to eat me alive if I wavered the least bit. As the phone rang I took two deep breaths.

I waited patiently for Sadie to answer as I tried to figure out how I could ease into telling her about the proposal. But as soon as she said hello, I blurted it out.

"*I'm getting married.*"

The silence on the other end was not a good sign. I knew Sadie was wondering if she had heard me correctly; there was no way I was getting married—and to who?

"Um . . . Sadie, are you there?"

"To whom am I speaking?" Sadie's voice was cold and I didn't know what to say.

"Sadie, you know who this is. Talk to me."

In a slate stone voice, Sadie said, "You didn't bother talking to me before you obviously made a life-changing decision?" My heart sank. Sadie was one of my best friends and I hated feeling like I let her down.

"Sadie, don't be like this. I need you more than ever right now." I waited for her response. I was even ready to cry if need be; I intended to pull out all the stops so she would at least listen to what I had to say. I heard her draw in a breath. Then, when she spoke, the change was a relief.

"I know, Jasmine, I'm here for you, but you know I got to make you feel the pain."

"I hear you, Sadie, I don't really know what happened. It was so sudden and unexpected that the only reply that I could muster up was yes."

"OK, Jasmine, tell me what happened."

I told her everything, starting with right after her and I had had lunch, and how everything he had said that night sounded and felt so right.

"I love him Sadie, and I don't know how to stop."

I heard Sadie take a deep breath.

"Well, girl, it looks like we have to plan a wedding."

I screamed, and hugged her right through the phone. I knew she could feel it because I could feel her hugging back.

"Thank you, Sadie. Thank you. You don't know what it means to have you back me on this. I've been thinking about you and the girls and how you were going to take the news. Is there any way we can get together for lunch today?"

"I'm busy all afternoon. What about tonight?"

"Yes, tonight would be good," I said, excited that my girls were with me on this, maybe the biggest decision of my life.

Then I saw the card Marcus gave me. "Um .... Sadie, tonight is not a good night. I'm having dinner with Marcus."

"Oh really? Here we go—you're already starting to put us on the back burner."

"Sadie, that's not true. Marcus and I have a lot of things to hash out, plans we need to make. Just let me do this tonight and I promise you got me for the rest of the week."

"I don't know, Jasmine. You know how you get when you meet a man you really like, let alone Marcus. We will never see you again."

"No, Sadie, I promise nothing has changed. Marcus is leaving to go back to Europe Sunday morning and everything will be back to normal."

Sadie's voice was weak. "But for how long?"

I felt a little queasy; I knew she was agonizing over my decision and I tried to empathize with her, but this was my life and I had to live it for me.

I said goodbye, and told her I would call her later.

Sadie was a very strong person and an independent woman, but we had never faced such a major and permanent separation like this. This was new for both of us and would definitely be a real challenge; when I thought about everything as a whole, in spite of my pure elation, even I wasn't sure if I was gonna to be up to it.

It was now past eleven. I couldn't wait to hear Marcus' voice again; I wanted to call him and thank him for the flowers and talk to him about our plans for the night. I picked up the phone and dialed his number. The butterflies swirling around in my stomach were a good feeling this time.

Still, I took a couple deep breaths to clear my head and calm my nerves as I waited for Marcus to pick up. I had known and loved him for forever but I still couldn't get over the uneasiness I felt since he had been back. But when he answered the phone I swore I could feel his warm sensual breath blowing in my ear.

"Hey, Marcus, it's me."

"I know, sweetheart. How are you doing this morning?"

"I'm wonderful. Last night was magnificent and today is even better. I got the flowers you sent and they're nothing short of spectacular. I can't believe you remembered about my aunt's field of flowers."

"Jasmine, I remember everything about you, especially the things that make you happy. That's all I want to do for you—make you happy."

I could feel the tears welling up so I quickly changed the subject.

"Where are we going tonight?"

He laughed, "That is a surprise."

I laughed too. "You've hit me with enough surprises in two days to keep me going for a year."

"I know, but this one I have to keep a secret. Just be ready at seven."

"All right. How should I dress?"

"Anything you wear is fine with me, I know you'll do it up right."

"Sho' you right, Mr. Man. OK, then, I'll see you at seven."

"Oh by the way, don't worry about driving. I'll be sending a car over to pick you up."

"Really? Oh, this is going to be good."

"You bet your sweet-ass it is. Jasmine, I love you."

"I love you too Marcus. I'll see you tonight." I hung up the phone, leaned way back in my chair, and daydreamed of nothing at all.

The time was now. A blank canvas appeared, where before there was just a distorted mask of colors in no clear arrangement or form. I felt like I could draw anything I wanted to. I could finally fill this page with a scene from my own script—not a remake of someone else's.

I was startled out of my reverie as Wendy buzzed me and told me I had a conference call on line one. I was confused; I didn't have it down on my calendar.

I picked up the line, but all I could hear was yelling and screaming, ranting and a bunch of other noise. Then, through the haze of high-pitched screams I could make out Sadie's voice, commanding everyone to *shut up!*

"Hello? Hey, Jasmine it's, Angel, and Carla. I'm here too, Jaz," said Sadie.

"Hey, girls—what's up?"

"Jasmine, stop playing. You know the drill—what's up with you?"

"What do you mean, what's up?" said Carla sternly.

"Hey, nigga it's Carla, stop bullshittin' and tell us what the hell is going on," she said sternly, piercing through Sadie and Angel's background chorus voicing the same sentiment.

I gave up all pretenses and I screamed, "Marcus asked me to marry him last night!" I could hear Sadie in the background—"See, I told you two," and in my mind's eye I saw her smug smile.

"Girl, what is going on?" Angel asked, softly this time; all the screaming had stopped. I calmed down and in a rush, my words tumbling over each other, I explained everything that had happened in the past day in a half. There was another brief silence. Then Carla broke it with "Girl, did you get some booty?"

I laughed.

"Actually, no we didn't want to complicate an already crazy emotional situation by adding sex to it. We talked and cried and held each other all night. And in the morning when I awoke he had prepared breakfast for me, and when I got to work this morning he sent me the most beautiful bouquet of flowers I have ever seen and attached to the card was a note to have dinner with him tonight."

"OK, look, Jasmine." I could tell Carla was reaching for the right words. She didn't want to destroy the moment for me, but she had to know.

"At what point did you decide that you were ready for Marcus to be back in your life? After what you say he did to you. How he hurt you. You've forgiven him already?"

"Carla. I love him, what am I supposed to do?" I said, almost helplessly.

"You know all men are dogs and there is dog in him too. We just don't want you to get hurt again."

"I know, Carla, and I appreciate that. But I'm a big girl, and I know what I want."

"OK, OK, let's calm down." Sadie spoke up. "Jasmine, you're talking about making a life-changing decision in a matter of days. How can you comfortably do that?"

"Sadie, I'm going by what I feel. I have to. I let him go once and I can't let it happen again. And this time I know he feels the same way because of the engagement. You guys, please understand: Marcus and I belong together. We are going to make this work."

"But why do you have to go all the way to Europe, why can't he move here?" This time it was Angel. "What about your partnership with the firm?"

"Angel, you know what? I thought about that and decided I was going to kick back for a little while. Take a break from law, and do some of the other things I enjoy but haven't been able to because of working so damn much. This will give me an opportunity to work on my poetry and writing, my spiritual side."

"Yeah, yeah, whatever," Carla lashed out. "I know what happened; he hit that monkey so good last night you forgot everything you ever learned about being a diva. How could you put us down like that, over some nigga?"

"Carla, I'm not putting y'all down. I love you; you guys are my sisters and I can't make this decision without your blessings. I can't do this alone."

The phone was silent. I could hear someone in the background crying.

"Jasmine, we don't want you to leave us but we understand you have to do what's best for you," I heard Sadie say, sniffling. "So go, and we wish you the best."

"Thank you, Sadie, I really needed that."

"I don't wish her anything good," said Carla, but her anger couldn't mask the tears in her voice. I was surprised; I never knew she cared so much.

"Carla, girl, I'll always be here with y'all. I'm just a phone call away."

"You think I'm going to run up my phone bill trying to talk to you? Forget it."

"Carla, *I'll* call *you*, sweetheart."

"Don't bother."

"Carla, I love you."

"Whatever," she said, and hung up.

But I knew she was just trying to deal with the situation; I couldn't hold it against her. I'd call her later.

We finished up with the plans for Saturday night, almost like everything was normal. I thanked Angel and Sadie, and said goodbye. I almost shed a tear.

Damn, them my girls!

# Chapter 32

I HAD DECIDED TO DRESS a bit more conservatively for this date. The chocolate silk dress said smart and sophisticated, sexy but not too freaky. The dress followed the contours of my body and I relished the feel of the material against my skin.

As I put on my make-up I knew there would be no way I wasn't going to tear up tonight so I decided to lightly powder my face and to wear lip gloss and lip liner. My waterproof mascara usually worked pretty well so I highlighted just the corners of my eyelashes to give them a little length. I gave myself the once-over in the mirror and figured I was as ready as I was going to get. I grabbed my scented oils and dabbed a bit at every pulse point I could think of. The minutes seemed to crawl by, but it was finally six forty-five, and I was ready. I waited for Jonathan to call to let me know when the car Marcus was sending arrived. As I waited, I prayed.

My quick thank-you and request to God for a pleasant evening was interrupted by my impatience. I decided I couldn't wait for Jonathan to call. I knew the elevators could make it a long trip down to the lobby so I grabbed my purse and started to head to the door. I was just about to open the door when the phone rang. I looked at the caller ID and saw it was Mama.

"Hey, Ma, how are you?"

"Hey, baby, I'm fine. How are you doing?"

"I'm good, Mom. On my way out."

"Where you going, girl,?"

"Um . . . I have a date."

"Oh, really? With who?"

I had yet to tell my mother about Marcus, let alone that he had proposed and that I was moving to Europe.

My mom and I were close and I told her everything; she loved Marcus but was upset with him when he left because of how hard I had taken it. She wouldn't understand how I made the decision to go out with him, marry him, and leave the country with him, all in a matter of days without even consulting her; once.

My mom was so cool; everyone loved her. All my friends through high school and college considered her their mother too, and I didn't mind sharing. It was something really rewarding about having a mother that everyone was crazy about. Most of my friends had mothers who were just crazy, with a capital C.

"Uhh . . . just this dude, Mom—nobody special."

"Uhhh, just some dude huh?" she asked skeptically.

"Yes ma'am, I'll fill you in on the details later, but . . . Mom, I gotta go."

"OK, baby. You be careful."

"I will, Mom. I love you."

"I love you too, baby. I'll call you tomorrow."

"OK." I hung up the phone and ran out the door. Sure enough I could hear the phone ringing with Jonathan's call as I ran down the hallway towards the elevators.

When the car pulled up I knew I was in for a special evening. The Lincoln stretch limousine was black and shiny, glistening even, and I couldn't wait to jump in. As I walked toward the car I immediately recognized the driver, who was holding the car door open for me. It was Darryl, a friend of Marcus' who had been away in Thailand for the past five years, working as a mechanical engineer for a large multinational company. There was no mistaking his tall thin frame, his light skin, almost yellow, and the cutest set of dimples I had ever seen on a man. I also remember because he had this really cool, mint 1975 cherry Chevy Impala, fully loaded with whitewalls and everything. I ran up to him and gave a big hug.

"Darryl, oh my God, it's great to see you. What are you doing here?"

"I was in town visiting my sister and ran into Marcus at the gym. He told me what he was planning for you and of course I agreed to help him. I've always loved you for him. He's a great guy and deserves the best. And you certainly are the best."

A tear rolled down my cheek and I kissed Darryl on his.

"Thank you, Darryl. You're a great friend. I'll never be able to thank you enough."

"My pleasure. You're worth every bit of this. Here, let me help you into the car."

He opened the door and as I stepped in, I saw, to my amazement, the whole right side was filled with vases of long-stemmed red roses; there must have been twelve dozen. And in the corner by the backward facing seats was a bar with a glass flutes and a bottle of champagne.

I breathed in as much of the scent as I could, inhaling deeply at every breath, but realized if I didn't control myself I might have passed out from hyperventilation. I giggled as I continued to take in this dream vehicle.

"Hey, Darryl, where are you taking me?"

"Don't worry Jasmine, Marcus has this all planned out and I'm not supposed to tell you a thing."

"Secrets, huh?"

"Yeah, something like that. He made me promise to keep my mouth shut and you know that's my man and I stand on my word."

"Whatever, Darryl, you two are too much."

We both laughed. "We sure are," he said. "Are you ready to go?"

"As ready as I'll ever be."

"OK, we're off then. I'm going to turn on the music for you; oh, and there's a bottle of champagne. Please feel free to help yourself to some."

"If you need anything else just buzz me on the intercom."

"Cool. Right now I'm straight."

But I had gotten nervous again, I didn't know why. I had known Darryl for forever and I knew Marcus was and always would be my life; but every bone and nerve in my body felt like I was on hyper-high alert.

I poured myself a glass of champagne, the bubbles pleasingly tickling my nose. I took a sip, then a swallow, and finally a gulp, emptying the glass. I knew I should slow down, but I poured myself another glass and slammed that one too. Now I was feeling a little more at ease.

I capped the champagne and sat back to enjoy the ride. The alcohol in my blood was whirling around and I started to get warm—which was cool with me, I wanted to be calm and relaxed when I finally met with Marcus so he wouldn't think I was a basket case.

Darryl drove on for about ten minutes and I started to wonder where we were going. I glanced out the window to see if I could see any landmarks but nothing seemed recognizable to me through the tinted windows. This is totally crazy. What is Marcus up to? Whatever, it didn't matter; I was happy—happy to be alive, happy to be here, and happier than I had been in a long time. I knew things could only get better.

Darryl started to slow down. I looked out the window again. The area looked vaguely familiar but I couldn't exactly pinpoint where we were. When we came to a stop and parked, I tried to look out the windows but Darryl had made sure he had parked the limo on the side with the flowers, which pretty much blocked the view.

Darryl came around and opened the door, taking my hand and as helped me out. Then he bent down and kissed both of my hands.

I gave him a big hug. "Thank you, thank you, thank you, I'll never forget this evening."

"You take care, sweetheart. I'll see you later." Then I turned around.

In a far corner of a small, secluded park right along the river was an elegantly set table. The sun was glistening off the platinum place settings, and a gentle breeze ruffled the linen tablecloth. I was mesmerized. In the center, a bouquet blazed with my favorite flowers—orange, violet and magenta, like an African sunset.

Marcus was standing there, next to the table, and I walked toward him like in a dream. His cologne wafted toward me on the soft evening breeze; it almost made me dizzy and I stopped for a moment to catch my breath.

He walked the few steps that lay between us, gently whispering in my ear. "You are so beautiful." I blushed. "You're not so bad yourself," I stammered. He smiled and kissed the palm of my hand.

"Well, Ms. Burrell, you're right on time." Marcus gave Darryl the right-on sign, as if to say, "thanks, my brother, I appreciate you." Darryl slipped back into the car and slowly pulled away from the curb away. I could see his dimples through the window as he drove out of sight. He was smiling and everything in me was smiling too.

Marcus led me to the table, the soft grass yielding under our feet, and helped me into my seat.

"What is all this?" I asked, finally recovering myself enough to ask a question.

"Actually baby, it's nothing—just a token of my love and affection for you. I wanted to show you how the rest of your life with me was going to be."

"Oh, so you think I'm going to spend the rest of my life with you?"

"Yes I do. The ring on your left hand tells me you are."

"Oh yeah—that," I giggled.

"Oh yeah—that." He smiled and gently kissed me full on the lips. I drew his tongue deep into my mouth, something I had been dying to do since I had laid eyes on him this evening, and we kissed as though we had never been apart.

Finally, we drew apart. Then he lifted the cover off of the huge stainless steel platter on a side table to reveal the most magnificent spread of food, which he undoubtedly had cooked himself. There was peppercorn-crusted filet mignon and smoked salmon fillets, along with sweetened baby carrots, cheddar cheese scalloped potatoes, and piping-hot dinner rolls. Next to this huge platter sat strawberry walnut spinach salad and a bottle of Rosemount shiraz.

Replacing the cover to keep everything warm, he served the salad, then poured us both a glass of wine. I was already feeling a little tipsy from the champagne but I couldn't resist the shiraz. I took a deep swallow.

"You must think you're gonna get some tonight."

"No assumptions, sweetheart, I just want to enjoy your company and make you smile."

"But I bet if I do give you some tonight I wouldn't be the only one smiling."

"I'm sure you're right about that."

We laughed and gave each other a high five.

"So let's eat and see where this leads."

I pick up my fork and took a bite of the salad. The delicate flavors blended perfectly. It was delicious, almost as good as his kiss; but I knew better.

I tried to savor my salad as he made up our dinner plates.

"You cooked all this for me?"

"Yes I did. Do you like it?"

"I love it. Where did you learn to cook like this?"

"When I was out in Europe I hired a chef to teach me the art of preparing fine cuisine. I knew you knew a lot about cooking because of all those cookbooks of yours; and don't forget I sat up night after night with you watching those cooking shows. Emeril, Bobby Flay, and that one competition show—what was it called?"

"You mean 'Iron Chef'?"

"Yeah, that's the one. So how could I go away and not come back knowing something about one of your passions?"

Hearing about his experiences overseas was so refreshing. I had grown tired of the lame-ass small talk I was subjected to on the few boring, low-rate dates I had had recently, and was glad to be with someone who stimulated my mind as well as my body.

He was funny and smart and pleasing in every way; and as we sat reacquainting ourselves again the little touches and sexy winks began to make the temperature rise between my thighs. I couldn't believe how we were right back to where we started, as if he had never left. I felt liberated—as if life finally felt like it was really worth living.

We finished dinner as dusk set in. The sun was just dropping behind the downtown skyline and the bright red and orange streaks made the view of the river look as if the water was dancing an Indian rain dance. Marcus took me by the hand and walked me over to the riverbank. We stood there silently, listening to the sounds of our hearts. His eyes shone, and I believe with all my heart it wasn't just the reflection of the setting sun.

Marcus broke the blissful silence.

"Jaz, may I ask you a question?"

"Sure, what is it?"

"Do you believe in soulmates?"

"You know I do, Marcus."

"Do you believe that if two people are meant to be together then they will find their way to each other . . . . eventually?"

"Well, to be honest with you I had a hard time believing that when you left, seeing as though I believed we were the two that were supposed to be together."

"So how do you feel about that now?" Marcus turned to me, his doe eyes looking deep into my soul.

"Baby, right now what I feel is unexplainable. If anyone had told me days before that I would be standing here with you planning our future together I would have laughed in their face and told them to kiss my ass. But after this week I believe anything is possible."

"Anything *is* possible, Jasmine, and I intend to make sure you know that every day of the rest of lives."

He ran his fingers through my hair and gently caressed my face. The look in his eyes was so passionate that a tear trickled down my face, despite my best effort all night to hold back. He wiped it away with the soft pad of his thumb and held my head while he kissed me with mounting urgency. When our lips parted he was crying, too. I brushed away his tears and softly kissed his eyelids.

"Marcus, whatever you want, whatever you need, it's yours. I'm yours."

"That's what I was hoping you would say Jasmine; and I am yours.... forever."

We turned to walk back to the table, and there was Darryl, but this time he was in Marcus' car and had already dropped the keys off at the table. Marcus and I both waved goodbye as Darryl got into his amazing car, which I hadn't even noticed was sitting there. I laughed; "He still has that car?"

"Yes, you know he does, he leaves it stored here because the shipping costs to Thailand are way too expensive. You know he could not live without his sweet baby."

"Wow, it still looks great."

"She sure does."

An eavesdropper might have thought Marcus was commenting on the car. But I knew, as he looked deep into my eyes, he was really talking about me.

We walked slowly walked to his car, arm in arm, reminiscing about old times. He walked over to my side of the car and opened the door for me. I was in heaven. All I wanted to do now was get home and get busy.

The drive home was everything I dreamed. Driving into the sunset with the love of my life, headed for nowhere in particular, but everywhere at once. I was convinced there had to be a God.

# Chapter 33

We arrived at Marcus' penthouse hotel suite and it was all that I had imagined. High ceilings, beige and gold marble columns that rose all the way up to the ceiling, directing your eyes to the skylights strategically placed throughout the room.

The living room had a turn-of-the-century fireplace with a mantel that was covered with magnificent floral arrangements accented with cloth bows that shimmered against the moonlight. Marble figurines flanked the flowers on either end of the mantel, and an original oil painting hung above. The hardwood floors shone as if they had been lacquered that day.

Marcus helped me out of my coat and directed me to the fully stocked bar, telling me to make myself a drink as he went to the bathroom to freshen up. I poured myself a glass of Chardonnay, chilling in a bucket of ice, hoping it would calm my nerves.

I hollered back to the bathroom, "Would you like anything?" He yelled back, "I'll just have a beer, they're in the refrigerator." I opened the small refrigerator tucked below the bar. There was beer and small bottles of wine along with a tray of fresh strawberries. I wondered if those were for me, but decided to wait and see. I opened the beer and placed it on the counter as I waited for him to return.

When he did—oh my God, he looked good enough to eat.

He was wearing a pair of stone-washed baggy Calvin Klein Jeans and the brightest white sleeveless T-shirt I'd ever seen. The muscles in his arms and chest seemed even bigger than I remembered and the beads of water on his skin, left from when he must have rinsed himself off, made me want to run over and bite him. He approached me and asked if I wanted to shower. I was feeling kind of sticky so I agreed. He pointed to the bathroom and said that I could wear one of his shirts.

When I stepped under the stream, I felt warm—not because the water was so hot, but because I was radiating from the inside out. Never had I thought all of this—any of this—possible again. My mind carried me back to the riverbank and how we held hands and talked about the future. I didn't want to cry but my eyes had something different in mind. As I the water ran over me, I cried silently, thanking God for this miracle.

When I was finished I took the towel on the hook in the shower, wrapped it around myself, and slowly opened the shower door. Marcus was standing there, smiling at me, and motioning for me to give him the towel.

"Here, baby, let me dry you off."

I hesitated because I didn't know how I was going to react to him touching me after all this time had passed. But I handed him the towel. He slowly took it from my hands and dropped it to the floor. The look in is eyes told me exactly what he was thinking.

As my mind drifted to a peaceful place, Marcus licked every inch of my body. He started at my forehead and everything was manageable up until the moist softness of his tongue slowly slid circles around my breasts and my nipples. He flicked his tongue over my now rock-hard nipples and I could feel a trickle of cum run down my legs.

I began to cry. He looked up at me and knew why I was crying, but didn't say a word. He picked me up and carried me over to the plush chaise lounge sitting in the bathroom lounge area. He looked at me again, and his eyes told me everything I needed to know.

I couldn't resist any longer. I slid my tongue into his mouth and drew his tongue into mine as we kissed. I could taste the minty mouthwash mixed with beer as our tongues slowly got reacquainted. As they got to know each other better the kissing grew harder and more passionate. Our hands raced over each other's body as I grabbed the back of his T-shirt and ripped it off his body. He grabbed my breast and went to town. Over the years Marcus must have had some practice because what he was doing to me felt like nothing I had every felt in my life.

Hesitantly, I thought about all the women Marcus might have been with while he was away—God knows I'd my share of other men. He was smart, fine, and rich; he probably had women throwing themselves at him. I took his head in my hands, and looked him in the eyes.

"Marcus, why me? I'm sure you've had tons of women in this same position."

He looked up at me. "Yes, I would be lying if I told you I hadn't slept with anyone else since, that I was saving myself for you. Would you have believed me if I told you some bull like that?"

"Hell, no! But Marcus, what makes me so special?"

There was nothing more I wanted *not* to think about was Marcus with other women, because I was finally back in the dream I had longed for the last four years.

"Do you want me to tell you without a shadow of a doubt you're the one?"

"Yes, Marcus, tell me."

Marcus smiled and spread my legs as wide as they would go, propping my left leg up against the bathroom wall. He lowered his head and stuck his tongue all the way into my private place, reaching my g-spot and forcing his tongue in and out, stopping only to flick it fiercely over my clit.

Right at that moment I knew why he was the one for me.

Before he finished I had come four times and could hardly breathe. He asked me to repeat the question, but there was no way I could speak.

He looked at me and asked the question for me: "Why you?

"Baby, you smell and taste like home. No one has ever made me feel the way you do."

He kissed me, and I could taste the clean saltiness of my own cum. I must admit I had never been one to want to taste my own juices before but the nectar coming from his lips tasted as sweet as candy.

The waiting and wanting was over I was there. I had him... and my every waking dream.

We made love for the rest of the evening, exploring anew what we once were and who we were growing to be. All we wanted was to bask in the glory of God's gift of love, forever.

# Chapter 34

THE HOTEL PHONE RANG PRECISELY at six a.m. as we had requested. It shattered the most glorious dream, and I awoke to see Marcus staring at me, smiling.

"Good morning, gorgeous."

"Good morning."

"Did you sleep well?"

"I haven't slept like that in years, if you know what I mean."

"Yeah, sweetheart, I think I do. I haven't had a night like that in a long time either."

"So are you ready for round two?" I asked.

I knew I had to be at work in an hour but I couldn't resist him. I stared directly into his eyes and climbed on top of him. He was already rock hard when I slid myself down on him as deep as he would go.

In a matter of seconds, I could feel myself beginning to climax. Damn, no man had ever filled me up the way he did. I began to ride him like never before. I could see his eyes begin to flutter and roll up in his head; at that moment I decided it was my turn to put in some major work. I wanted him to really feel what he was getting himself into, messing with a notorious Southside Diva.

\* \* \*

When I got to work at seven-thirty, my desk was piled high with files and my e-mail and voicemail were full. Wendy had done the best she could to keep everything organized but in all the commotion, I forgot to sync my calendar and didn't realize there was an important meeting that morning. In the pile of e-mail was a reminder memo from the senior partner about the meeting. I realized I had taken the Benson file home but with the week's events I hadn't had time to work on it.

I called Wendy into my office and asked her if she remembered seeing this e-mail come through her box. She had no recollection of that particular e-mail; I was upset but could not blame any of it on her. I was the one who missed work because of my wild and crazy circumstances.

"Wendy, from now on I need you to help me be more on top of my game. I'm in a whirlwind right now and I'm counting on you to help me get through this," I said.

"Of course, Jasmine. Is there anything I can do to help you finish up the Benson file?"

"There sure is—get me all the initial findings and photocopy five sets, and after that I need you to call Tom and tell him to tell Mr. Hagen that I'll be ready for the meeting at ten-thirty as expected."

I opened my briefcase. It was a good thing I was so anal about how I organized my files because the Benson file was right on top, in alphabetical order. There were only a few things I had left to do so I quickly finished and logged into my voicemail system to go through all my messages, but as I thought about all that had happened, I actually started to feel confident in my decision. Of course, the lovemaking session made it all too easy, but I was finally feeling good about it.

I had to figure out a way to tell my partners, though. I was the tough cookie, their shining star, and I was about to lay some news on them that would definitely cause a ripple in the company. Forget a ripple—I was going to be causing a damn tidal wave. But it had to be done, and sooner rather than later.

# Chapter 35

LEANED BACK IN MY custom leather chair and turned towards the window and stared into space. It was broad daylight, the middle of a sunny afternoon, but all I could see were the moon and the stars. I had just slam-dunked the meeting with the senior partners and was feeling like I had finally reached a new level, one I had been trying to arrive at the last four years of my life. I realized I hadn't spoken with Marcus all day and was yearning to hear his voice.

I picked up the phone and dialed his number. *"The number you are calling is no longer in service."*

The bottom of my stomach dropped to the floor. What the fuck is this? I searched for a reason, thought back. Did I dial the right number? I hung up and dialed again. The chimes rang in again. *"The number you are calling is no longer in service."*

Now I was no longer in shock; I was scared. What was going on? Marcus has had this cell phone number for years. I took a moment to compose myself; there must be a mistake. Even though I didn't believe Marcus would do anything to hurt me, a little voice in the back of my mind reminded me of when Marcus left the last time.

It was our senior year in college and we were driving up to Grand Marais for the weekend, something we tried to do as often as possible. We planned the trip so we could go and be back before fall session started at school.

It was just as the leaves were turning, and the drive up was spectacular, the leaves getting more and more colorful the farther north we headed.

This particular drive seemed different, though, strained somehow. By that time I could tell when something was wrong for Marcus. He usually tried to deny it but his eyes always gave him away.

"What's the matter, baby?" I caressed the back of his head as he looked straight ahead and drove in complete silence. "Is everything OK?" He glanced over at me and smiled.

"Yeah, baby, everything is all right."

I could feel the tension in his neck, but decided to leave well enough alone. He would talk to me when he was ready, I was sure of it. The only thing that kept running through my mind was that maybe he was thinking of proposing. We had had a light conversation about marriage the night before and of course my wheels immediately started turning. I made quick sneak call to Sadie and based on what I told her, she confirmed my suspicions.

When we pulled up to the cabin and started unpacking our bags, the cold air swirled around us like a tiny tornado. It was one of the chilliest days in September but the fresh air was exhilarating. We walked into the cabin. This particular resort was known for their hospitality and service so we weren't surprised to see the fireplace going and a small tray of fruit on the coffee table. We set our bags down and Marcus decided he wanted to take a quick shower.

"Now baby, you know if you get in that shower, I'm coming with you and it won't be a quickie," I told him.

He laughed and put his hands on my waist. He looked me straight in my eyes, then dropped his head, nuzzled underneath my chin, and held me tight—tighter, it seemed, than he had held me in a while.

"You know I love you more than anything in this world," he whispered. But despite the words, there was something in his voice that set off alarm bells.

I held him close.

"I know baby, I know," I told him.

He gently kissed me on the mouth, then pulled away and headed for the shower.

Now I was really scared. I knew he got nervous whenever there was something important he wanted to talk to me about, but this time seemed different. What could be wrong? Wait, don't panic, girl, I told myself. Whatever it is we can handle it, we've always made it through. Together.

I walked slowly towards the bathroom, where I could hear the shower running. I turned the knob, slowly and quietly, and the door opened. I could see Marcus' silhouette through the shower curtain.

He was facing the shower, the water streaming over his head and down his face. I quickly undressed and entered the shower behind him.

"Hey, baby." He slowly turned around and pulled me gently towards his slippery-wet frame. I kissed him. He returned the kiss with a passion I had never felt in him before, so intense it was almost excruciating. I looked into his eyes and knew at that moment everything had gone terribly wrong.

\* \* \*

The buzzer on my intercom startled me and I woke from my trance.

"JASMINE!"

"Yes, Wendy, what can I do for you?"

"Marcus is here to see you."

"Oh, OK. Give me a minute and then send him in." See—calm down, everything is fine. But even though the inner voice was quick to reassure me how great things were, but something in the pit of my stomach was yelling "Run!"

The door opened and all my doubts faded away. There he was, fine as ever. I could not believe how lucky I was; I was marrying the man of my dreams, I was moving overseas and I was finally happy. Life couldn't have been better.

"Hey, baby."

"Hey, Marcus, I was just trying to call you."

"I figured you were, that's why I came up here to tell you I had my cell phone cut off today because I was tired of arguing with the company about my bill."

"Oh, they really must have upset you; you've had that number for years."

"Yeah, I know, I just decided today that I wanted to start anew—a new life, a beautiful new wife. I just want to make sure everything is perfect."

I looked into his eyes; I sensed there was a little more to it than that, but once again decided to leave well enough alone.

"So baby, do you have to work the rest of the day?" He took my chin in his hands and placed a soft kiss on my mouth and a gentle kiss on my forehead.

"Yes, Marcus, I have to work. I've already missed too much work and you see the stack of files on my desk."

"OK, baby. How about we get together tonight?"

"I can't, Marcus. I've been neglecting my girls and I promised them tonight, tomorrow night, and Saturday night. You know before you came back all I had were my girls and I can't let them down."

"You don't have to explain, I understand. Have fun tonight and call me if you get in at a decent hour . . . which I doubt you will." He laughed and hugged me.

"I love you Ms Jasmine Burrell. Correction—*Mrs.* Jasmine Damon. Has a nice ring to it, doesn't it?" he whispered in my ear.

Everything in me wanted to scream but I just kissed him on the cheek and escorted him to the door. "I'll call you later."

"OK, baby, talk to you soon," he said softly.

I closed the door and laughed all the way to my desk.

The day was winding up—five-thirty and getting to be time to leave. I could hear my cell phone buzzing in my purse. Must be Sadie. I picked up the phone and glanced at the caller ID. "Hey, girl, what's up?"

"Nothing. What's up with you?"
"Just finishing these last two files."
"Are you still available for movie night tonight?"
"Yes I am. Whose house is it at tonight?"
"It's at mine."
Whew, I thought; my house was a mess. "All right Sadie, I'll pick up some food and a bottle of wine and be over there by seven. Is that cool?"
"Yeah, girl, that's perfect, see you tonight."
"Bye, Sadie."

I hung up the phone and remembered I hadn't gotten Marcus' new number. But didn't worry because I knew he would call me, sooner rather than later.

## Chapter 36

I got to Sadie's house right before they were about to start the movie. They always joked about how I was *never* late for a court appearance, but always came late to stuff they had planned. It was so bad that I was even late to Carla's wedding. I guess I didn't realize getting married at the courthouse was a very speedy process.

"Hey, ladies."

Hey, Jasmine, yo' ass late again."

"Whatever, Carla shut up, you just mad I was late to that so-called wedding of yours, marrying that African." We all knew the number one rule, and everyone in unison said "*No Africans.*"

African men were off-limits for the Southside Divas. We really didn't know much about them, except for all the rumors we had heard about how they treated women. They beat them, they disrespected them and they used American women to get their green cards. They sweated you the whole night if you gave them a little play and if you gave out your number you would never get rid of them. So that was the creed the Southside Divas lived by and we didn't fuck with it.

But one night when the girls hit the club without me, the enforcer, Carla broke that rule and got involved with one who turned her world upside-down. And if it wasn't for the fact that she was blessed with Brandon, she might have ended up in an insane asylum somewhere.

David was a trip—cool on the outside but has hard as nails if you vexed him. He married Carla and she divorced his ass with such quickness it would have made even Elizabeth Taylor proud. But before he left, he got his green card and went to Africa to bring back his wife and three kids. Now they all live in Eagan happy as can be in their little suburban world. He pays child support for Brandon and sees him occasionally.

Carla took it hard at first, but she's a rider and can't no nigga hold her down. We were all upset about how it went down, but you live and you learn and we had each other.

By way of greeting, I hugged and kissed Carla, then made my rounds. In the back of the room I noticed a face from back in the day. It was Katrina; we had gone to high school together. She was a very quiet spirit but we all knew she had some wild in her somewhere and whenever we were all together we tried to pull it out of her.

I walked over to her and gave her a gentle hug; she was so timid on the outside that her hugs were always very soft. But on the inside Katrina was a fireball who didn't take any shit, even from her boss—she was on the Minnesota staff for one of the state's two senators. In fact, she was his right hand and made sure he had his shit together—at all times.

Katrina had graduated from the University of Minnesota at the top of her class, a political science major. She landed the job with the senator's office after wowing him in the interviewing process, which took over six months. She was competing with some of the Ivy League elites, but she stood her ground and got what she wanted.

Katrina was also one who didn't have a man, and up to just last week, we all wallowed in our self-pity together, trying to keep each other positive.

"Hey, Katrina, how have you been?" She smiled.

"Jasmine, what's up?" Katrina was so meek most of the time; it startled me when she pinched my arm.

"Ah, Katrina what are you talking about?"

"Girl, I heard you were getting married." I glared at my group of divas and gave them the "I'm gonna kill y'all" eye. They smiled and shooed me away.

"Yes, Katrina, I *am* getting married. Marcus proposed to me and we are moving to Europe in the fall."

"Wow, Jasmine that's great. Congratulations—I'm so happy for you." She hugged me again. I could barely feel her, she was such a light hugger. Not like me—I hugged hard.

"Thank you, Katrina. I love him very much and I am finally happy."

"I hear you, girl, life is too short to be bullshittin'." We laughed; I could tell she was sincere. In fact, I felt all my friends had my back. We had been through so much together that it seemed like we were finally growing up.

Then I remembered I hadn't gotten Marcus' new number and the worrier in me began to go to town. I poured myself a glass of wine. The divas always had huge selections of wine because we all liked different kinds. I was a red wine girl—I liked mine dry and spicy, though most of the other girls liked theirs wet and sweet. As freaky as that sounds it was kinda how we were.

As the wine began to warm me, I could feel the muscles in my neck soften and release. I looked around the room at all my friends and they were absolutely beautiful; it was unbelievable that up until now none of us had found true love.

The evening went as it always did. The girls and I laughed and cried all night. After drinking enough bottles of wine, pretty much anything came out. It was always a good cleansing for us; it's probably why we had stayed friends for so long.

As the evening slipped into night, my mind drifted away to my private place, which now included Marcus. I hadn't heard from him and decided I'd just chill, I knew he loved me and would call right on time.

Just as that thought crossed my mind, my cell phone rang. It was a number I didn't recognize.

"Hello, this is Jasmine. Who's calling, please?"

"It's Marcus, baby."

"Oh, hey baby. This must be your new number."

"Yeah, I just decided to change numbers and companies all together."

"You know you could have kept your old number, huh? You've had that other number for forever; now you're gonna have to call all your clients to tell them the new one."

"Yes sweetheart, I knew that, but I wanted to start new. I told you I have a new life, a wonderful new fiancée, and I don't want any ghost from the past calling to infringe on our future in anyway. And besides, I had the new company take my SIMS card out and transfer the numbers that way."

I couldn't argue with him. I also didn't want any of his skeletons popping up on me, seeing as how I always tended to freak out and jump to conclusions.

"So how's the future Mrs. Damon?"

"I'm wonderful, the girls and I have had the best time. They all know I'm moving and they're really supporting me."

"That's good, sweetheart. You do have some really great friends."

I believe the reason everyone was cool with my decision was because deep down the girls really liked Marcus for me. Even though I had ended up a complete mess the last time he left, in retrospect, we all realized he left for the right reasons. Even I had to admit that if he had stayed I probably wouldn't be as successful as I am today. My focus certainly wouldn't have been on law.

"So how late do you intend to stay?"

"Oh, we're not even married yet and we already questioning when I'll be home?" I giggled because I knew Marcus didn't care how long I stayed out.

"Baby, you know I ain't trippin.'"

"I know, Marcus, I just had to get you with that. Well, we're really winding down now, and I'll be free as soon as I help them clean up."

"OK, boo. Why don't you meet me at the hotel when you get done?"

"All right." I looked at my watch. "It's eleven-thirty now. I'll be there in an hour."

"All right, sweetheart, I'll see you in an hour. Love you."

"Love you too."

I hung up the phone and surveyed the scene. Sadie and Carla were still arguing about the butt-whooping she and Angel took in spades at the hands of Sadie and me. They always insist that we cheated, but we never do. Well, most of the time we don't.

Katrina was watching "Girlfriends" while the other girls dozed off into bobblehead mode. Most of the girls had decided earlier to stay the night rather than risk driving drunk. I hadn't had much to drink, which was unusual for me; usually I tried to drink everyone under the table. But tonight something was different; I didn't have the urge. It was like I no longer needed the false sense of security. I didn't feel the sting of loneliness anymore, and for once things were lucid. I could see a clear path to happiness.

"Hey, y'all, I'm gonna go."

"Duty calls, huh?"

"You know it, girl, got to go handle some very important business."

"We know what type of business that is—you ho."

"Don't hate, Carla, we going out tomorrow night and I know you gonna get yours."

"You damn skippy nigga, I always get mine."

"Freak? Freak! Who you calling a freak, Jasmine?"

"You, ol' crazy. Come give me a hug so I can go."

We gathered around in the circle and we all wished peace, blessing, and safety over the whole clique.

Damn, my girls, the Southside Divas. We were more than a clique, we were sisters. We were family.

## Chapter 37

I ARRIVED AT MARCUS' HOTEL room and realized I was winded. Shit, I had been run-walking the entire time since I left the party. I knocked on the door and saw it was ajar. I slowly pushed it open.

The room was beautiful. Candles were glowing in every corner of and petals were strewn across the tables and all over the floor, but the centerpiece was the most incredible—a bearskin rug. He must have had it brought in since I left early that morning.

Now to say a dead animal lying out in the middle of the living room floor was beautiful was an understatement. This rug was amazing. It was pitch black, and as I took of my jacket, knelt down, long black bear hairs tickled my face as I brushed my skin across the silkiest, softest fur I had ever felt.

I rolled over on my back and was startled to see Marcus standing over me, looking at me with pure love in his eyes. He reached for my hand and pulled me up. He held me close, closer than I think I had ever been to someone next to my mother's womb.

He stared at me oddly. I couldn't understand why.

"What? Do I have something on my face?"

"Yes, you do—the most beautiful smile I have ever seen."

Of course now I was smiling even more.

"Marcus, I don't know why all this is happening or care—all I care about is you and being with you and having your children and most of all, loving you."

Marcus embraced me; each time we met, it seemed more passionate than the last. A tear formed in his eye, and as I wiped it away, I placed a kiss on him that would steal the coolest nigga's breath away.

It did. He began to undress me; he started slowly, unbuttoning the first, then the second, then the third button on my shirt.

But I guess he couldn't wait. With one pull, he ripped my blouse open, and I could hear the buttons fall to the floor. He reached behind me and with one swift move unlatched my bra and let it fall to the floor. He held my breasts in his hands and gently caressed them. But as we kissed, his soft touches turned into more of a vigorous massage. It was a bit rough at first, but the intense look in his eyes and the way he kissed me made me concentrate on the enjoyment. "*Marcus!*" I screamed out in ecstasy.

He put his finger across my lips, picked me up, and laid me in the middle of the bearskin rug. He removed his shirt, then untucked the wife-beater shirt he was wearing, but didn't remove it. I could see his perfect muscles rippling underneath and wanted to feel his chiseled biceps wrapped around my body.

"Marcus, *please*; kiss me."

He lay down next to me.

"First, how was your day?" he said.

I was surprised to hear him ask about my day since we were in such a passionate moment, but I welcomed his concern and answered politely.

The day had been a little trying, I said. I explained how I was a little nervous when I couldn't reach him earlier and even had had thoughts of my dreams coming to an end. He winked at me. "How are you feeling now?" he asked me.

"I feel great; this has been the wildest whirlwind week I have ever experienced. But I'm so glad it happened." He touched my face and softly slid his tongue in my mouth. I eagerly returned the favor, softly placing my tongue on his.

We kissed for what seemed like hours. Then he took my hand and escorted me towards the bedroom. I could hear the faint notes of some cool, slow, classic jazz music from the nightstand radio. I got the barest whiff of Egyptian musk incense, just enough to let you know the vibe was right.

## I Surrender All

The bed was covered in rose petals and a tray of different oils, candles, and scented feathers sat under the soft lamp next to the bed.

"All this for me?" I said coyly.

"Girl, please—nothing is too good for my wife-to-be." I giggled and removed my panties.

"Lie on your stomach," he said sweetly.

I turned over on my stomach and rested my head on the pillow, I watched as he poured a considerable amount of oil in his hand. Not knowing really what to expect I closed my eyes and prepared for what was next.

Marcus began giving me a massage. He slowly rubbed the oil into my skin. The warm oil smelled like a mixture of almond oil and lavender. Damn, I was so relaxed; I couldn't believe how good this was feeling. I felt myself getting sleepy and as much as I wanted to stay awake, I couldn't resist.

The next thing I knew, I opened my eyes as Marcus gently brushed my hair from over my eye and kissed me on the forehead.

"What time is it?"

It's about one-thirty, baby."

"I'm so sorry; I didn't mean to fall asleep on you, I must have been more tired than I thought."

"That's all right, I expected you to go to sleep. Now that you're awake though, I have something I'd like to talk to you about."

"OK, I'm up. What's the matter, baby?"

"Oh, nothing is the matter. I just want to tell you how much I love you and everything I'm doing is for us, and our future."

I looked at him with joy and confusion. "I know that. Why are you telling me this? You seem a little stressed."

"I'm not, I just want you to know how I truly feel. I never meant to hurt you before and I would never intentionally hurt you now, or in the future."

"Marcus, I love you and there is nothing you can do to change that."

I began to untie the string on his pajama pants. I gently opened them, then lowered my mouth over his manhood and began to pleasure him, as I had never done before. I had always been good in this department, doing what I had read about and learned from the few pornographic films I had seen. But this time, something in me craved him more than I had ever craved any man, even more than I had craved him in the past. I looked up and saw by his expression that it was a whole new experience for him, too.

I played with my beautiful toy for hours, allowing him to get close to orgasm, then pulling back so that the intensity of his final climb would be unforgettable. When I thought he couldn't take any more I massaged, licked, and stroked him between the testicles and the ass—not close enough to his asshole to make him uncomfortable but low enough for him to really feel me. Not too many women knew about this area, but it's a very arousing area for a man if you know how to do it right.

I slurped and licked all over his shaft, tonguing his testicles as I squeezed them. Then I felt him tense up, and I knew he was going to come; I firmly held his shaft with both hands, squeezing and sucking until a mighty explosion filled my mouth and trickled down my chest. I looked up at him, and we smiled.

I gently continued to lick and suck him until I knew he was completely spent. Men's genitals are extremely sensitive after coming; I had learned to be as delicate as possible after it was all over. Then, when I was sure there was not a drop left, I got up and made my way to the bathroom, where I washed my face and quickly brushed my teeth.

I returned with a warm washcloth and gently washed him off. He pulled me close and kissed me, smiling and laughing at the same time. I think we were both now in heaven.

# Chapter 38

THE NEXT DAY ZOOMED BY. It was hard to leave Marcus's bed, but I knew I had to get to work early because there was so much that I had to get caught up on. I ended up working straight through all my usual breaks and even worked right through lunch. I hadn't even thought of food.

By the end of the day, I had completed every report, every case and all my pre-trial briefs and I was very proud of myself. I couldn't take all the credit though—that massage and sexual healing Marcus gave me the night before truly helped.

I smiled that funny little grin I couldn't control and laughed at myself for being so silly.

Before I had left Marcus that morning, I explained to him the divas' weekly ritual: going out Friday night, shopping all day Saturday, and going out again Saturday night. He was so gracious and understanding; and it was cool anyway, because he had made plans with his boys for the weekend. We decided he would meet up with me later Saturday night at the club.

I was cool with that and I figured the girls wouldn't mind, since Marcus intended to bring a few of his boys through the spot. We divas sometimes dated in the same circles; not necessarily messing around with the same dudes, it was more dating friends or brothers or cousins that ran together.

So the plan was set. Marcus and I had agreed that we would see each other at the club Saturday night, spend the rest of the evening together at my place then go to breakfast Sunday morning, ending the lovely week with me taking Marcus to the airport to board his plane back to home to France.

I rushed home from work and searched through my closet for something to wear. Sadie and Carla had already called me three times and I was still throwing stuff onto the bed to see what looked right. I had a new look I was trying to achieve: An elegant hoochie with a fiancé. I wanted to look stylish, not revealing so much skin it said I was still looking and desperate, but I wanted to reveal a little. I was newly engaged, but I was still a woman.

I decided on a tight-fitting navy short suit. It had a halter-top strap that went around the neck and a short mini jacket with gold and silver rhinestones. I would sport my navy blue leather boots; no one had ever seen boots this color until I found these last year online at Macy's, four-inch heels, tight fitted on the calves all the way to the knee—slammin'.

I showered and changed. I looked in the mirror and I was finally satisfied with the look. I was touching up my makeup just as my doorbell rang.

Damn, Carla's ass was always on time, if not early. She always wanted to get her little drink on at the crib before we got to the club. Just enough of a buzz to get the party started. I ran to the door and flung it open.

"What up, girl?"

"Ain't nothing."

"Dang Jaz, that is a fly-ass outfit."

"You like it? It took me forever to put it together, but I think I got it."

"You sure do, that outfit is what's up."

"You ain't slacking much either, chica, look at all them titties hanging out."

"Yeah, nigga, these bra tops are the bomb. I brought a jacket but don't believe I will need it, if you know what I mean."

"Yeah, I hear you, girl."

"Where's Sadie?"

"She said she, Angel, and Katrina were going to meet us there. They were coming from some happy hour out in Maple Grove and decided to all get dressed at Katrina's house. They're already on the road, so I told them by the time I came by and got you we would probably all arrive at the same time."

"Oh, that's cool. Let me get my purse and my keys."

As Carla and I drove down the busy Minneapolis streets I admired the town I had grown up in and had grown to love. I still hated the winters, but when spring finally sprung and summer rolled in, Minneapolis, Minnesota, was a very beautiful place.

We arrived at the club and gave the valet the keys. I noticed Katrina's car idling at the corner and knew the girls were already in line. It was just starting to form and Carla and I hurried to the front looking for the crew.

Norma Jean's was our favorite club, and sometimes we actually went three times a week. The drink specials were the bomb and we made sure we got there early enough to take full advantage. The club was named after Marilyn Monroe's real name and there was a huge picture of her that graced the front wall of the building. We all loved it and practiced her wind tunnel pose whenever we got the chance.

The bouncer recognized us right away and escorted us to the front of the line. He pointed out Sadie and the girls and we fell in place right behind them.

"What up, niggas?" I snatched Sadie, Angel, and Katrina in a group hug.

"Hey, girl," they said in unison.

"What's going on? Y'all look a little heated."

"We all right, we'll just be better once we hit the bar."

"I know that's right!"

We followed in single file through the door and up to Isaac; he was the one who always carded us. The first time we came, he sweated me about my ID because it said I was a lot older than I looked. And yes, it was a fake; but we had had so much fun and had turned the party out, that the following week it wasn't a problem.

"Hey, Isaac."

"Hey, ladies." Checking our IDs now was just a formality; he knew all of us since we came so often. He just glanced at them now because he had to.

We all paid and got in. Then to the main bar we went.

My guy Sean was working; whenever he saw me he always made it over to our side of the bar.

"What up, Jaz?"

"Hey, Sean, how you doing, baby?" I reached in, grabbed his tie, and pulled him towards me, then kissed him on the cheek.

"There she goes." I could hear Carla in the background, hating, as always.

I was known as the bartender ho. I carefully picked the guy—never a woman—who would be serving us drinks all night and made sure we got several of those drinks for free. With a little extra attention and tips in the beginning, the title of bartender ho was solely mine. I parlayed my charm and sexy looks into drinks for all the divas.

I really liked Sean, though; he was different. He was super-fine and extra-cool for a white boy. We had hung out a few times outside of the club but never really connected. I was just getting over Marcus and my focus was elsewhere.

"Hey, Sean, hook me up with two of those three-for-ones."

Sean started pouring six Long Island teas. I went for my purse to get my money and took my eyes off my drinks for one second. Sadie and Katrina reached for one of my drinks.

"Hold up, niggas, you know how this goes down. These drinks are mine."

I circled my arms around my drinks like a hungry nigga in the jail, checkin' niggas trying to get at his food.

"Move around, ladies, and order your own *shit*."

"Damn, Jaz, your greedy ass."

"Whatever, y'all know what's up. Get yo' own shit."

I paid Sean and gave him a huge tip and a peck on the lips, and carried my drinks to the table. Then I turned, winked, and told him I'd be back. He smiled and nodded.

We all met back the table where we had a prime spot for scoping out the niggas. It was kinda of weird for me; I felt like I was there, but everything around me stood still. All I could think about was Marcus. The little flirting and petting I did with Sean was business—I had to make sure by the end of the night me and all my friends were drunk. So my focus was blurred. But that didn't stop the rest of the diva clan.

The club started to fill up and the girls were itching to dance. We usually waited until the end of the night to dance because we were in no hurry to mess up our hair, nor did we intend to sweat out our designer clothes. But this night was different, there seemed to be an overabundance of fine-ass dudes roaming around. What the fuck was going on?

We were all in our element, niggas everywhere, looking, jockin', walking up to say hello. I almost took the bait, but just as the party was about to heat up, I noticed Marcus coming through the door and he looked more amazing than ever.

I didn't expect to see him tonight, we had planned to meet here Saturday, but this was definitely a pleasant surprise.

Sadie smacked me. "Damn, is that Marcus?"

"Hell, yeah, girl,—my ass is in trouble tonight, and I can't wait."

Marcus saw me right away. He walked straight up to me and kissed me dead in my mouth. I gladly received him, even as I heard the "icks," and "ughs" taking over behind me.

"Damn, nigga, get a room."

"Shut up, Sadie."

"Oh, I'm sorry, ladies, I just hadn't seen her in a while." Marcus flashed his most charming smile at the girls.

"Nigga, we know you was with her last night. Stop lying," Sadie shot back.

The girls all burst into boisterous laughter.

Marcus turned beet-red. "I guess that's my cue." He kissed me on my forehead and politely turned to walk away.

I smiled. "See you later, baby."

"You bet your ass you will."

By one-thirty we were all drunk, tired, and starved. I knew Marcus had already left the club, so I was ready to go as well.

"Y'all ready to go?" I looked around.

"Yeah, let's make it," Sadie chimed in.

Usually the most sober one of the bunch braved the cop-ridden streets to find the closest Burger King or White Castle. But this night we had two cars.

"Are we all going to Burger King?" I asked.

"Hell, yes," said Carla.

"Well, I'm not going to go," Katrina said. She had decided to go home since she had the longest drive, and her ass didn't eat meat.

"Well, Angel and Sadie, y'all just jump in the car with Carla and me."

"Cool."

I drove and we got to the closet Burger King in record time. We pulled up and noticed a couple of brothers chillin' in the parking lot, and the cop car posted up by the bushes. Before I could even get the car all the way in park, Carla's fast ass jumped out and ran over there and started mackin', and the rest of us poured ourselves out of the car and coolly walked up to the door as if we had just come from a church function. Carla caught up to us. "Them niggas was lame," she reported to us.

It was probably your attitude that turned them off, I thought. Carla had a habit of being a bit brusque if things didn't come off like she liked them to.

As we walked by the cop standing in the lobby we put on our best sober face. Cops knew who was too drunk to drive and there was always one or two posted inside or outside the restaurant. Anyone who was too drunk stayed in the car, and we ordered for her.

"Damn, I'm starving."

"I know Jaz, me too, I'm about to get the number two," said Sadie.

"What's the number two, Sadie?"

"Girl, it's the double Whopper with cheese, large fries, and a large Coke."

"Damn, nigga. That's what I want."

"Hell, yeah! Count me in."

Carla tossed me her money and we waited for Angel to order. Angel was taking too long so I ordered everyone's food and paid.

"You gonna have a number two just like the rest of us," I informed her.

"Whatever, girl, you know I don't eat like y'all."

"You are tonight. I'm starving and you slowing up the flow."

The food came and I grabbed the bags and headed for the car. It was still really nice out so we stood outside the car eating and laughing about the night's antics. I thought about calling Marcus, but decided to wait until I got to my house before I used my cell phone. I knew the divas would have something to say, and I didn't want to hear it.

Back in my apartment, I took my clothes off and headed for the bathroom. I sat down on toilet and reached in the shower and started the faucets. I called Marcus.

"Hey, baby."

"Hey, Jaz."

"What's up, boo, are you still coming over tonight?"

"You know I want to, but one of my boys got in some trouble and I have to hang out here for a minute to make sure he's all right."

"Are you OK?"

"Yeah, I'm fine, you know I ain't gonna let nothing happen to me knowing I have you to live for."

"I hear you."

"I'll call you tomorrow; maybe I can have a little bit of your time before you go to the mall with your girls."

"OK, love, I'll wait to hear from you."

I hung up the phone feeling more loved and more comfortable in my own skin than I had felt in a long time.

# Chapter 39

The sound of the phone ringing insistently woke me out a deep sleep; I hazily reached for the receiver, but when I got it to my face and said a sleepy "Hello?" all I heard was the dial tone. Damn, I missed it; fuckin' Long Island teas. I waited for the answering machine light to come on, then dialed the voicemail number.

"Hey, baby, it's me; I guess you're still asleep. I'm going to have to hook up with you later. My boy Rob got into it with his baby's mom last night after coming home so late that she put his ass out. Long story short, he's all torn up and I need to be here for him. I promise I'll see you tonight. I love you."

What a sweetheart. I was a little disappointed I wouldn't see him this morning, but knew what type of friend he was and didn't expect him to be anywhere else when his friends needed him.

I headed for the shower. I had taken one last night before I went to bed, but I could still smell the alcohol and wanted to steam the rest of that scent out of my system.

After showering I decided I'd cook myself some breakfast rather than running out to get something. I hadn't really cooked in my own kitchen for a while and I felt like getting reacquainted. I raided the refrigerator for all the ingredients I could find to make an "everything" omelet and found a box of blueberry muffin mix. I mixed up the batter and popped the muffins into the oven, then I began to chop all the vegetables I could find. This really was going to be an "everything" omelet.

By the time I put the final fold on the omelet, my blueberry muffins were brown; well, light brown . . . well, brown enough.

I didn't eat very much. I was feeling pretty good; I had learned that eating right after drinking helped a whole lot with the next-morning hangover nausea, and the burgers from the night before definitely did the trick. So I just ate a little bit of the omelet and threw the rest away. Eggs were not really what I wanted. I wanted Marcus, badly.

It was eleven-thirty, and the mall was packed. We hated when we had to walk from the far end the parking lot to get to the entrance. Carla, Katrina, and Angel rode together and Sadie and I followed in my car. We were all dressed in our freshest jogging outfits with matching tennis shoes and purses. It seemed sort of juvenile to be dressed that way and looking alike, but who cared; we were the bomb!

We had made it a point to map out a plan for our shopping goals, discussing our outfits for the night; who needed what and what stores we were going to hit up. It was very well thought-out and usually perfectly implemented. It saved us all time and money. We weren't just out spending money for no reason; we all had an agenda and if we stuck to it. It allowed for our wardrobes to be complete, and flawless.

"All right, ladies let's hit it," said Sadie. "We meet up at the food court at one-thirty. Cool?"

"Yes, yes let's get it crackin'," I said. Katrina, Carla and Angel went towards DSW; they all needed shoes. Sadie and I headed for Nordstrom's.

The malls in Minnesota weren't that great. You really had to look hard to find something fly or that didn't have sixteen other exact copies of the same outfit. Even though we all had enough money to buy anything we wanted, we chose to shop smart. Clearance racks had a helluva lot of good deals; I once found a Dolce and Gabbana blouse marked down seventy-five percent.

As I made my customary circles around the racks I noticed someone who looked extremely familiar. He must have been shopping for his girlfriend.

"Sadie, Sadie," I whisper-yelled across the racks so she could hear me but he couldn't.

"What, Jaz?"

"Ain't that Kevin over there?" I asked

"Where?

"Wait, his back is turned to us . . . hold up, wait until he turns around. Is that him?"

"Oh yeah, that's him. Let's go say hello."

"Ah, hell no! That fine-ass motherfucker makes me nervous. He is just too fine."

"What? Jaz, you trippin'. Come on, Southside Diva, he's fine but he ain't as fine as us and don't no nigga make us nervous."

"You right, Doggfather." Sadie was the original Doggfather way before Snoop tried to claim that spot.

I walked up behind him.

"Hello, Kevin," I said.

He turned around and the sunbeam that was shining down on his head was not the same sun that was shining down on us. He obviously brought this great beam of light in with him when he came. Shit, he was actually glowing.

He greeted Sadie first.

"Hey, how you doing?" He wrapped his caramel-covered arms around Sadie and flashed that Kodak smile that he had perfected.

Then he turned to me.

"Hello again, Jasmine." He held out his hand for me to shake. "How are you?"

I hesitantly took his hand, remembering what I felt like the last time he touched me.

"I'm fine Kevin, it's nice to see you again."

"It's really nice to see you too, Jasmine. You look beautiful."

"Thank you, Kevin."

As he let go of my hand his eyes flickered briefly on the engagement ring on my finger. I thought for a moment he was disappointed; but he smiled and said, "Looks like things have changed for the better for you." I hesitated and didn't know why.

I think Kevin was the first man to make me question my decision. I was no longer single. I was no longer on the market, so all the play I was used to getting was going to cease. I knew there were still going to be men who would approach me who didn't care if I was married, but it was going to be considerably fewer, and I wasn't quite sure I was ready for the decrease in attention.

"Oh yeah, I'm engaged. It happened suddenly. I'm very happy."

"Well, Ms. Burrell, congratulations. I'm happy for you."

"Thank you, Kevin."

I realized I was staring at him. Fortunately, he got me off the hook, asking Sadie what we had planned for the day. She told him of our plans and gave him directions to the club we were going to tonight. He seemed interested in meeting up with us later that night.

"OK, Kevin, we'll see you there," Sadie said, and hugged him good-bye. I waited until he had disappeared among the other shoppers.

"Girl, what is wrong with you?" Sadie demanded.

"I don't know, Sadie. Was it that noticeable?"

"Hell yeah, you look like a star-struck teenager."

"Damn, it *was* that bad."

"Uh, yes. Are you all right?"

"Yeah, girl, I'm fine. I guess I'm just trippin' about being engaged and no longer able to do my heavy flirting."

"I don't know, Jaz; he seems to have you all out your body."

"He does and I don't know why. I'm engaged to a beautiful man and I love him dearly."

"I know you do, but it seems to me you got to get the rest of that diva-freak out of you before you walk down that aisle."

"I know. You're gonna help me, right?"

"Hell yeah, girl, I'll help you all right."

"Sadie, you are so crazy, I'm not getting mixed up in any of your shit tonight."

"Naw Jaz, you know I got your back."

"I know; that's what I'm worried about."

We laughed and started looking seriously for the items we came for.

We found what we wanted and checked the time right as we were paying. Perfect timing—it was just about one, so we headed for the food court.

"I bet the other girls are still shopping. You know we always beat them done," Sadie said.

"I know; let's just go to the food court and figure out what we're going to eat."

"Hold up, Jaz, let me move some of these bags around. This shit is kinda heavy."

"See, I told you not to buy all that shit. We were supposed to stick to our list."

"I know, but how could I pass up a full-length Donna Karan leather coat with a mink collar—half off?"

"Whatever. You bought it, so carry it."

"Yeah, yeah, whatever, heifer. You buy things you don't need."

"But I don't complain about carrying it. Let's go."

We found the closest escalator and stood patiently as the moving stairway took us to the food court floor. As I glided upward, I couldn't help but think about how good Kevin was looking and how ridiculous I acted. Was I having second thoughts? Damn. Could I really be faithful until death do us part?

Just as that thought crossed my mind, my phone rang.

It was Marcus. The silly little grin I tried to hide when he called was no longer a grin, but a big-ass cheese.

"Hey, baby."

"Hey, Jaz, what's up? You and the girls having a good time?"

"You know we are; spending money, on ourselves, is our favorite pastime."

"So are you still planning on going out tonight?"

"Yes we are, aren't you coming?"

"Aah well, baby, there's this boxing match on pay-per-view tonight and my boy is ordering it, and it's a really big fight, and I kinda want to see it. Is that cool with you?"

"I really wanted to kick it with you to night. You know, a little bumpin' and grindin' before the real bumpin' and grindin.'"

"Damn, Jaz, I hear you, but I told my man I'd be there; anyway, you got your girls. Y'all better whoop it up all you can cause after we're married you gonna be in the house barefoot and pregnant."

I laughed out loud. "You promise?"

"Hell yeah, baby, I promise."

"I love you, Marcus."

"I love you too. Have a wonderful time tonight and I'll see you later on, be prepared for a long night."

"You're such a freak, Marcus."

"I know, but you like it."

"Yeah, I love it."

"All right sweetheart, I'll call you later tonight."

"OK, Marcus, I'll talk to you later."

I hung up the phone and had forgotten all about Kevin and the moment of insanity I had just experienced. I had and was about to marry the most wonderful man in the world and nothing and no one was going to interfere with that.

# Chapter 40

Norma Jean's, our usual hangout, was always packed with wall-to-wall niggas, wannabe thugs, and a gang of Barbie-doll white, girls. Our favorite club had started out as the white-girl groupie hangout, but we had single-handedly changed the vibe and now we sat back and watched how the niggas began to stroll in, one by one fine as hell. Most of the niggas were cool, but many of them were strictly into white girls, which I didn't mind.

But when they practically broke their necks trying to look at us, it sort of made me mad. "You chose her so stay over there with her." Still, when one of them stared for too long, I'd change my blank stare into a flirty one. I'd smile, wink, and motioning him over like he was standing there by himself. He would try to ignore me but he always flashed me a smile just to let me know he was feeling me. Shit, that was all I wanted. I could care less if he was into white, girls, I didn't want him. He just needed to know black women still had sex appeal and some degree power. The Southside Divas, we had our own show. We rarely got carded, we knew all the bouncers, and I maintained the special relationship with all the bartenders. The DJ shouted us out as soon as we stepped in the door, and all the broke-ass bitches did their usual hater stare. But we didn't give a fuck, we were a class act and them bitches hated us for that. We got much love and we were highly respected—and that's the way we liked it.

But tonight was a different kind of night; we were headed to The Riverview. It was a little nightclub in an industrial area of north Minneapolis, right off the Mississippi River. There were neighborhoods nearby but mostly it was other bars and restaurants. The club had been remodeled to include three bars, a large stage and ceiling-to-floor mirrors, which gave the place a swanky sort of feel.

This club was mostly us black folks, with a few white, girls sprinkled on top for variety. The white, girls that hung out here exclusively dated brothers, and the ones we got a chance to meet were cool. They did their thang and we did ours.

By quarter to twelve, the club was jumpin', the music was on point, and everyone was vibin'—no drama and no bullshit, we had been there for a while so sitting back and watching the place fill up was what we were waiting for. The girls and I made our way to the dance floor and started looking for the lucky man who was going to get to dance with us.

I spotted mine immediately—a tall, built caramel-colored brother with hazel eyes. He had a head of beautiful dreads and he was dressed to a tee; he was wearing a creamy, vanilla-colored button-down shirt and some bomb-ass blue jeans that even I didn't know who the designer was—which was shocking, because I made it a point to know who was making what in the fashion world. His shoes were dark brown Timberlands and his belt had a diamond-encrusted skull and crossbones buckle. A thug swagger, just like I like them. He was bobbing his head to the music when I walked up behind him and stroked the small of his back. He turned around, looked down at me and smiled.

"Hey, sweetie, do you want to dance?" I asked without hesitation.

He set his drink down next to his boy, gently took my hand, and escorted me to the floor. Even though the dance floor was packed, he shielded me; he danced in such a way as to block out everyone who was getting too close to us, and I truly enjoyed that.

His name was Curtis and he was a baseball player, in town checking out the Minnesota Twins. He was in the midst of a transfer from the Chicago Cubs and was delighted that the Twins were interested in him.

He was an amazing gentleman, never fondled me or grabbed my ass, looked me dead in the eyes while we danced and made sure his attention was directed solely at me while we were together. I truly enjoyed his company. We talked about our current situations; he was just getting out of a relationship with a women he had been with for four years, and I told him everything I could about Marcus. He was very understanding and polite; it felt good to talk to someone with some sense.

When the good songs were over, he escorted me around the floor and back to the table where my girls were sitting. He stayed long enough to buy me an apple martini but as soon as it arrived, he got up to leave. I gave him a great big hug and thanked him for the dance and the drink. He kissed me on the forehead and disappeared into the crowd.

"Damn, Jaz, break me off a piece of that," Carla said.

"I know, huh? Girl, he was so bomb, he's a new scout for the Twins and only here for a few days. I told him my situation, and he was really cool, said if anything changed to give him a call."

"Well, since your shit is on lock you can give me the number," Carla said.

"Shit, give us all a copy of his number, best man, or woman wins," Sadie chimed in.

"Y'all some skank-ass hoes go and find your own men, there are plenty to go around."

"Whatever, bitch. Just 'cause you got some dick to go home to, don't be cock-blockin' on us."

"I ain't blocking shit, you hos know the rules. Shit or get off the pot." Everyone laughed and flipped me the finger.

"You niggas are haters." I smiled, raised my drink to my lips, and flaunted my free martini in their faces.

It hadn't really mattered to me that Curtis was so cool; I was just enjoying the moment. I sometimes forgot how to do that, so it felt good just to be there without any preconceived notions, without any anxiety. I was loving being me and I intended to enjoy every moment that life had in store for me—no more crying and feeling sorry for myself. I had come a long way and was ready for the next phase of my life—a husband, a new career, and hopefully a gang of children. It was finally upon me, it was my turn to shine.

I watched as the rest of the girls found men to dance with. They strolled onto the floor laughing and swaying to the music. Damn, I was going to miss them; they were my girls. But I knew even if I lived far away, there was no doubt in my mind that they had my back, and no doubt in theirs that I had them too.

The next couple hours flew by, and before I knew it, it was closing time. Before we left, I decided to call Marcus to see if he still intended to come over, and went into the ladies' room for a little less noise. When his phone went straight to voicemail, I got a little spooked.

Still, I figured, what's voicemail for, so I listened for the beep, then left him a message.

> *"Hey, baby, it's me; I'm on my way home. I have to drop off a couple of the girls but I should be home in a half an hour. Call me if you're still coming over and I'll tell the concierge on duty to let you in."*

I hung up and stood for a minute staring at nothing at all, trying to clear my head and at the same time trying not to panic. Then I got in gear and gave myself the usual pep talk. Don't trip, It's cool he'll be over later.

There, that was it; I picked up my things and went to find the girls. Sadie was going to ride with me; everyone else had found rides, either with the other girls or with the dudes they had met that night. We always had the "call when you get to a safe place" rule and no one ever violated that. We knew how unsafe the street could be so we made it a point to protect ourselves, and each other.

# Chapter 41

There's no way I was going to make myself crazy. I heard the birds singing, and popped up from the couch, where I'd fallen asleep waiting on Marcus to arrive. I looked at the clock; it was five in the morning.

Oh my God, Marcus didn't show up. He must have gotten sidetracked or something really important had to have happened. I got the same jolt I'd had when my call went straight to voicemail, and even a chill, because he always kept his phone on—he had so many business deals going on he never turned it completely off. I reached for my phone and checked for missed calls. I didn't have any.

I dialed Marcus.

"*Please leave your message at the sound of the tone.*"

What the fuck was going on?

I thought about calling one of his homeboys but didn't want to seem like I was checking up on him. I searched through my phonebook for Craig's number and as I was about to dial, the doorbell rang.

Whew, Marcus. I ran to the door and flung it open.

"Hey, baby, I . . ." My face fell, and the look of disappointment written all over my face threw Jonathan for a loop. He wasn't used to seeing me in my frantic paranoid state.

"Oh, Jonathan, hi. I'm sorry, I was expecting someone else."

"I know, Ms. Burrell; a gentleman came by very early this morning and left this note for you."

"OK, Jonathan. Thank you for running it up."

"I figured it was very important, Ms. Burrell, so I thought I'd bring it up right away."

I looked for my purse and handed Jonathan a ten-dollar bill. I closed the door behind him and took the 3x5 card into the kitchen.

*Dear Jaz,*

> *Hey, baby, don't be mad. I know I told you I would be over tonight, but I had some very important business come up that I had to take care of. I turned my phone off because I really needed to concentrate and figure out the solution. I'm sorry I didn't call you but I needed every moment to solve the problem. I came by this morning and dropped off this note because I knew when you awoke you would be either worried or pissed. I need to see you so please be at my hotel room by seven a.m. We need to be at the restaurant by seven-thirty because I'm trying to change my flight to leave out this morning instead of this afternoon. Don't worry, baby, everything is all right. I'll see you soon.*
> *Love always,*
>
> *Marcus*

Everything about this seemed so strange, but I trusted him so I didn't let it get to me. Mistake number one.

I quickly showered and changed into a coral and peach silk sundress—it felt so good against my skin, and I knew that the color flattered me. I took my hair out of the wrap, combed it out, and threw on a tiny bit of makeup. I found my coral sling-back sandals and raced around the house turning off all the lights and double-checking to make sure I didn't leave anything crazy out. I was drunk when I got home, so anything was possible. I picked up my purse and keys and headed for the door.

Just as I reached for the knob, the phone rang. It was so early in the morning I knew it had to be Marcus.

"Good morning, baby."

"Hey, Marcus, is everything all right?" The quiver in my voice had to have been evident, but the relief I felt from hearing his voice quickly calmed that.

"Yeah, baby, of course it is, were you worried?"

"You know me, hell yeah, I'm worried. It's totally unlike you not to keep your word. And lately you've been acting a little distant and it's scaring me. Are you having second thoughts about us?"

"Are you crazy? There's nothing in this world that I would rather do than to marry you and make you my wife. I love you more than I have ever loved anyone, and if you give me the chance, it would be my honor to prove it to you."

"I love you too," I murmured. I felt a little better, but I still was unsettled. "So I was on my way over to your hotel."

"Yes, I know, but plans have changed. I have to leave on an earlier flight than I expected because I have to travel to Rome on business before I go home."

"Well, OK. What is it that you want me to do?"

"Meet me at the French Meadow Bakery Café in fifteen minutes; I have a surprise for you."

"Baby, I thought we were going to the Nicollet Island Inn for their early brunch?"

"I know Jaz, but I have to do a quicker, lighter breakfast if I expect you to get me to the airport on time. You know I want to be close to you and breakfast in a place where they have beds would not be good for us right now. I miss you, your smell, your touch, your body, *your puss . . .*"

"OK, OK, I get the picture," I broke in. If he kept talking that way, who knows where we'd end up, with or without an available bed. "I'll meet you at the French Meadow in fifteen minutes. Marcus, I love you."

"I know. I love you too."

The French Meadow Bakery—its warmth, the delicious aromas—always calmed my spirit. And it was beautiful, decorated with a European vibe and rustic hardwood floors. A huge chalkboard above the counter served as the menu, written every day in a beautiful, decorative style that was like a work of art in itself. The signature bakery item was this huge cinnamon roll covered in a buttery glaze that was to die for.

I walked in looking for Marcus and quickly spotted him in the corner, with his back towards the door. Even from behind I could see he was looking good, as usual. I quietly walked up behind him and covered his eyes with my hands. He let out a small yell, an exclamation of surprise—and somehow I sensed, piercing fear. I jumped a little.

"Hey, hey, Marcus, it's me; are you all right?"

"Oh . . . yeah baby, I'm fine. I've just been so engrossed in this business deal that I had forgotten it would only take you a moment to get here. I actually wasn't expecting you for another couple of minutes and I had a lot of things on my mind."

He stood up and kissed me gently on the lips; but the hug he gave me felt different. His back was rigid, his arms tense; I couldn't help but think—as I had been trying not to since I called him last night—that something was really wrong; something that he didn't intend to tell me about.

Three empty cream containers lay on the napkin in front of his cup, so he must have already been on his third cup of coffee; he only used one cream to every cup of coffee. Not like myself, who had to have at least three, sometimes four creams to every cup.

Something seemed off, and for a minute, I couldn't figure it out. Then I realized what it was. "So Marcus, where are all your bags and the things you're taking home?" I asked him, puzzled.

"Oh, I've already taken them to the airport; I wanted to be able to spend as much time with you as I possibly could before I left. I didn't want to be weighed down and bothered by all them bags."

"I see."

Something still didn't feel right. I prided myself on reading eyes and connecting to people's vibes, and Marcus' were surely out of whack. He was strained but controlled, soft but edgy.

Something was definitely wrong, but I couldn't put my finger on it.

An ugly thought popped into my head: Oh my God, had he cheated on me? He was so good at making me feel comfortable; I always let my guard down when I was with him. Had I let it down too much and let another woman sneak into his bed?

I took a big swig of my coffee and backed my thoughts up. There is no way he had cheated on me, he loved me and he knew I loved him. He would never begin to hurt me in that way; plus his demeanor did not suggest that. It was more of an anxious sort, a kind of nervousness that oozed out of every pore.

"Well, baby, what time *does* your flight leave?" Without looking at me he replied, "At ten-thirty; I found a direct flight on Northwest."

I couldn't take it anymore. I took his chin in my hand and looked directly into his eyes. "Baby, what's going on?"

He looked up from his writing; the peacefulness he usually exuded was nowhere to be found.

I held his hand. "You know you can tell me anything, right?"

"Yes, I know but right now is not the time." His voice was sharp and dry.

"Well, when do you think is a good time?" I said gently, trying not to stir up any conflict, although I was a little perturbed. "I need answers, sweetie; it's killing me to see you like this."

"I know baby, and in due time I'll have them for you. Let's not fight; I have only a few moments to spend with you before I leave and I want this time to be as pleasant as possible." He spoke to me firmly; I'd hear him use that tone long ago, but not since he had been back, so it spun me remembering how short his fuse could be.

"All right, I'm going to let you off the hook this time but just know I intend to be a part of everything you have going on, even if it is painful." I smiled and patted his hand, trying to be as accommodating as possible.

Marcus looked at me; the sweetness and sincerity in his eyes was killing me. He truly loved me and wanted not to hurt me, not even a little bit. He reached forward to kiss me, and with both our eyes closed . . .

*Marcus Damon, would you please stand and put your hands behind your back, you're under arrest.*

## Chapter 42

Shock and fear consumed me. "What do you mean he's under arrest?" I screamed. "I'm an attorney with one of the top law firms in this country and there is no way you are taking him without answering some questions."

"Excuse me, miss, we are going to have to ask you to step back," said one of the policemen.

"But where are you taking him? He's done nothing wrong—tell them, Marcus. Tell them!" I screamed.

The look in his eyes spoke volumes.

"Marcus?"

He was standing there with his head bowed, his chiseled arms pinioned behind his back by handcuffs. He looked up at me with tears in his eyes.

"Baby, I'm sorry, I did this for us. Remember that—I did this for us."

As the plainclothes federal officers walked Marcus out the door, everything in my being exploded. I was left with one question: What did he mean; he did it for us?

The confusion that consumed me was too much to bear; I slowly walked out of the restaurant. Our waitress, hesitant to approach me, touched my arm as I headed out the door.

"Excuse me, miss . . . I'm sorry to bother you, but you haven't paid your bill."

I looked up at her and without a word reached in my purse, found my wallet and pulled out a fifty-dollar bill. "Wait right here, I'll be right back with the change," she said, but as she turned to head for the cash register, I left the restaurant and kept walking.

When I emerged from the fog, I found myself at Lake of the Isles, sitting on a bench, salty tear-stains covering my face. I looked at my watch; I must have been walking for over an hour, and somehow ended up here.

What the hell was going on, what am I going to do? I pulled my makeup compact out of my purse and checked my face. What I was looking for in my face was nowhere to be found; happiness, joy, excitement—everything that had been my life for the last few weeks had crumbled. I was facing a black hole of disappointment, disgust, and fear. I looked deeper into my own eyes in the compact mirror. Pull yourself together, I told myself; there must be some kind of mistake, get your shit together and go find and rescue your man.

I realized I was wasting valuable time. I had to get to the federal courthouse, where they also held prisoners awaiting arraignment. It was Sunday, so I knew they were not going to let me see or even talk to him, but I had to try.

I ran full speed all the way to my car—it was a good mile and a half—and once I got behind the wheel, I practically ran every stoplight on the way downtown.; it was a miracle I didn't get stopped by the police. When I got to the parking ramp I swiped my parking card and proceeded to my assigned spot. I didn't recognize the parking attendant so I didn't try to leave my car right at the door. I ran to the elevator and pressed the button for the processing floor.

As I walked in the processing department I felt a sharp pain in my chest. I had always hated the look and smell of this department. It reminded me of an old rundown country shack, because the employees and the officers were especially rude and the people sitting around waiting seemed to be more depressed than anyone I had ever seen. Even with the place empty I could feel the tension radiating from the lingering aura.

I went straight to the information desk and asked the young lady if any agents had arrived with an African-American man; then, more simple than that, I asked her if she had any information about Marcus Damon. She looked up at me and I could tell she recognized me.

"Hi, Ms. Burrell, how are you today?" she said, smiling

"I'm sorry, sweetheart, do I know you?"

"Well, kind of. I used to live next door to your grandmother; my name is Alicia, Alicia Posten. I guess I was a toddler when you hung out over there."

"Wow, I do remember you, but how in the world do you remember me?"

"I've been following your career every since I was a little girl."

"Wow, thank you so much. Are you planning on being a lawyer some day?"

"I am. I'm in law school right now—and doing very well, I might add," she said, blushing a little but obviously proud.

"Well, good luck to you, although it sounds like you don't need any luck. Just remember, never let the cases totally consume you; they do have a way of changing who you are."

"I won't. You said you were looking for Marcus Damon?" She returned to the subject that had been consuming me, even though I always loved to chat with young, up-and-coming lawyers, especially African-American women.

"Yes. Yes, is there any information on him?" I asked, trying not to show my desperate worry.

"Well, Ms. Burrell—"

"Alicia, you can call me Jasmine."

"All right, Jasmine," she said shyly. She leaned in closer and her bright, perky tone dropped to a low, soft murmur.

"His name is not in the system, but I overheard some federal agents talking about taking him to a private interrogation room for questioning. They were talking about a 'serious offense' and a 'great deal of money'—stuff like that."

Money? "Do you know what room they took him to?"

"No, but I know it's on the thirteenth floor."

The thirteenth floor—that was the floor for major white-collar crimes. *What the hell is going on?* I wondered, for the umpteenth time in the last few hours.

I walked to the interior elevators and pushed the up button. The doors opened immediately; naturally—and thankfully—it was empty. I stepped inside and pressed the thirteenth floor. I felt the elevator rising; as I stood there alone I silently prayed. "God, I'm not going to be able to handle this alone. I really need Your help; and I need it right now!"

The massive doors opened and I stepped out and slowly walked down the hall towards the interrogation rooms. It was a hallway that usually took me a couple of minutes to walk, but today it seemed as if I were walking the last mile to my death.

When I reached the first interrogation room, one of only three on this floor, I saw a familiar face sitting on the bench right outside the room. It was Teri Jorgenson, a well-known prosecuting attorney who had just moved here from California.

"Hey, Teri, how are things?" I said casually.

"Oh, hey Jasmine, things are crazy right now, I just received a case that is a mind-blowing disaster, and on a Sunday at that. I'm really not looking forward to dealing with this on my supposed day off."

"Really? It must be a really important case for them to call you in on your day off."

"Well, I guess someone thinks so."

"Oh really? How bad is it?"

"It's the worst—this young banker has been embezzling money from his company for years and they're just now catching up to him. Looks like he has gotten away with close to a million dollars."

"You're kidding." I couldn't believe she was telling me all of this.

I tried not too sound too interested, but I could feel this newfound information getting the best of me.

"By any chance, Teri, is his name Marcus Damon?"

"Yeah, it is. Do you know him?"

"Uh yeah, we're old acquaintances. I heard about this through the grapevine and wanted to come and check things out."

"Well, he's in there now, waiting to give a statement."

"Do you think I could go in there and talk to him?"

"Uh, I don't know, Jasmine, I don't think that that's a really good idea."

"Please, Teri—he's a good friend of my father's and he might need some advice before he speaks to anyone. I'll owe you big time if you just let me talk to him. Five minutes, *please.*"

"All right, five minutes. Jasmine, you know this is against the rules so if anyone finds out; I wasn't here."

"Yes. Yes I know Teri, thank you. Thank you."

I knocked on the door and slowly opened it; damn, I was terrified.

"Marcus?"

He lifted his head and our eyes met.

He was sitting in the middle of the room behind a small oak desk. The walls were a dingy gray, and the floors were covered in a murky outdoor-type carpet, which was almost worn to the floorboards. The absence of windows made the atmosphere almost unbearable. It stunk—literally.

"Jasmine, why are you here?" was all he said.

"Marcus, where else would I be? Baby, what is going on, they're talking about a felony, embezzlement."

His head dropped to his chest.

"Marcus, Marcus look at me. What have you done?"

"Jasmine, baby, I'm so sorry. It wasn't supposed to be like this."

"What do you mean? Are you saying that you're guilty?" I couldn't believe it. All this time, since the officers took him away, I kept telling myself there had to be some kind of mistake.

"Jasmine, it's very complicated, I can't talk to you about this right now."

I slapped him across the face, and his head snapped to the side with the force of my blow; a look of surprise and even more shame spread across his face.

I looked him dead in his eyes. "You *owe* me! You promised me we were going to be together, and now you don't want to talk? Nigga, don't you know I will kill you?" It all came out in a whisper; I was so angry I could hardly talk. I wanted to reach down his throat and rip his heart out, just like he had done mine.

"Wait, please, baby calm down; I don't want to get you involved." He pleaded with his eyes for me to understand, but I all I saw was a liar, a deceiver . . . a monster.

"Nigga, what, get me involved? How could you do this to me—again?" The tears—tears of anger, tears of complete devastation—that had been brimming now spilled over and streamed down my face.

*"Marcus, what have you done?"*

"Baby, please, just give me some time and everything will work out." He looked up at me with inexpressible sadness and shame in his eyes.

All of a sudden, my anger dissolved; I couldn't bear seeing him locked up. His hands were cuffed behind his back and he had leg chains on his ankles. I sat down next to him and kissed him gently.

"Jasmine, please, I have to work this out on my own and I can't make it through this with you here. I never meant to hurt you and I don't want to hurt you now. So please baby, please leave. I'll call you as soon as they give me my phone call."

"How do you expect me to leave you like this? You are my world."

"Baby, I'll be fine, this will all be over as soon as I can talk to my boss."

"So you *are* innocent, I knew it! I knew this was all a big mistake."

I hugged him around his neck. I kissed him, then got up and ran towards the door. I knew I needed to work quickly to get him out of jail. But when I turned to say good-bye, all of a sudden all my confidence drained away. It was as if this good-bye would be the longest one I had ever known.

I closed the door and thanked Teri, and walked towards the elevators. There's no way I'm going to lose him; if it meant my life, I would find a way to fix this.

*What I didn't know at the time was that you can't fix something that isn't truly broken.*

# Chapter 43

AS A CHILD, WAKING UP in the mornings at Grandma Vera and Grandpa Edmond's was always an especially wonderful occasion. The house was decorated in a "Christian sort of way" with the usual pictures of a white Jesus, Bibles, crosses and Christian sayings displayed in every room.

It was a fairly big house. The main floor had two bedrooms, there was a large bedroom upstairs next to the attic, and the large room in the basement had been converted into a bedroom. My grandparents slept in the front bedroom, and when we stayed over we slept in the back bedroom. I had developed a strange fear of the attic and never went up there, and my uncle Cordell occupied the basement most of the time. So I stayed away from down there also.

My grandma was a great cook so the house always smelled like a country diner, like the kind you could find on the outskirts of any small town. Grandma Vera was an early riser and was always up before anyone else, preparing breakfast for my grandfather and us. She'd make everything from perfectly scrambled eggs, bacon, and salt pork (my grandfather loved salt pork) to the most perfectly round, fluffy pancakes and homemade syrup I had ever tasted. She would make our plates and serve us while we all sat in the dining room quietly waiting, even my grandfather.

It was one of those mornings. I was nestled deep under the covers, with the comfort of knowing it was Saturday and I was free to do whatever I wanted. It was the best feeling—until *"Good morning to you, good morning to you! We're all in our places with bright shining faces, this is the way to start a new day."*

Oh no, please—not that song.

My grandmother entered my room singing. Singing that song bright and early in the morning was her way of letting me know it was time to get up. Dang. I rolled over and looked at the clock—seven-thirty on a Saturday. She has got to be kidding. It was crazy; she woke me up like this every time I stayed for the weekend.

"Jasmine, time to get up," she said cheerfully. In my head I was screaming "Why?? Man, it's Saturday, the only day I get to sleep in. What could I possibly have to get up for?"

As soon as that thought crossed my mind, she said, "Jasmine get up, make that bed and come in the living room. It's time for prayer." Prayer at thirteen years old—what did I need to pray for?

I couldn't believe this; I rolled out of bed and tugged the covers back to the top of the headboard. I found my house shoes and walked lazily to the living room. My grandmother was already on the floor, on her knees with her elbows comfortably resting on the couch seat. She motioned for me to join her; this was going to be an ordeal. I knelt next to her; she paused, looked over at me, and waited for me to bow my head and close my eyes. I did as I was told, as I always did when it came to instructions from her.

With head down and eyes closed, we began to pray—well, she began to pray. "Our Father, who art in heaven . . ." As I joined her in the Lord's Prayer, something I had learned at an early age, for the first time I thought about what this prayer really meant. Most of it I didn't understand, and I was too embarrassed to ask for an explanation. But the part about "lead us not into temptation, but deliver us from evil" was one part that made me shudder.

Were we led into temptation by an outside force? Was I intentionally led to unscrew the light socket covers in the basement and short-circuit the whole house, not knowing that I could have electrocuted myself?

Temptation was definitely everywhere and I was all over it. But that "delivering us from evil," part made me feel a little better—acting up out of spite was easily resolved by asking God to continuously deliver us. Either way, the whole prayer thing was a way for my grandmother to drum into us the importance of living your life for Christ.

Once the Lord's Prayer was finished Grandma broke out in her personal prayer and expected the same of me. Of course I had no clue what to say, but that generally didn't concern my grandmother. She basically forced out of me affirmations and requests that she genuinely believed would take place. While she gave thanks, I knelt there next to her, giving thanks for blessing me with the only thing that came to mind: Healing hands. Grandma had told me since the age of eight I had healing hands; I would lay hands on people who were sick, say a prayer in my head and miraculously they were healed. Over the years, my family believed I could heal people and I began to believe it too. So as I spoke this prayer, my grandmother was right there, egging me on, confirming my gift, praising the Lord. Anything she said or prayed for became law and the entire family and I accepted it—good or bad.

I remembered a time when my uncle Darrin was in a position to play for an up and coming musical genius, Minnesota's own Prince Rogers Nelson's new band. But when Grandma Vera got a hold of the news she prayed against such an atrocity. How dare one of her children join a band that plays secular music when she and his daddy out here trying to save souls? Several days later he broke his arm in a motorbike accident.

There were many prayers like that in our church community so my grandmother was not the only one stealing dreams that didn't fit in the Church of God's way of life. I remembered being in church and a classmate's grandmother also prayed his future away. He was a star basketball player for our high school and slated to enter the NBA after he graduated from college. But those dreams were dashed in a testimony, that time during church service when anyone in the congregation could stand and talk about the glory of God, all that He had done for them. It was an unspoken language that the matriarchs of the Church of God's faith used and used well to discourage, disconnect and completely eliminate anything they felt was not of "God,"—in other words, secular, as they would put it. These prayers were something normal to all of us. We knew they prayed for our safety and for us to be saved, but they also prayed things of the Devil away, things that could draw us into sin.

His grandmother offered up her prayers of closed doors to that NBA path, and of course the classmate didn't end up there. Today he's a preacher.

When things like this happened, it instilled a tremendous fear in all of us; and it sure didn't allow for experimentation in the world. I knew and understood that, but still, most of the time "lead us not into temptation" didn't apply. I wanted to experience life, have some fun, kick my heels up, and I did—but not until I was grown and out of her house.

My childhood was one of naivety, fear and utter obedience. I grew up listening to and pretty much doing whatever I was told. This was fine for me as a child because I was one who craved acceptance and praise. I did whatever it took to make sure everyone was pleased with me, even if that meant doing things I really didn't want to do.

In school I was an A-B student who never got in trouble, and I was teacher's pet in most of my classes. This behavior afforded me the luxury of constant adult reassurance that everything in my life was going to go right. And I was headed straight down Success Road, never looking back—only to lose out when it came to boys.

I shied away from boys for most of my adolescent years. I was afraid of sin, I was afraid of what they expected from me, and I dreaded rejection. I found myself going with boys who were familiar and who really did not pose a threat. I also had a problem with dating my girlfriends' choices. Be it their brothers or their cousins or boys they knew, I was the one who ended up agreeing to be their girlfriend regardless of their looks or my affection for them. I needed my girlfriends' approval and for them to like me, so I did what I could to keep everybody happy.

Over the years, as I grew from a pre-teen and early adolescent into a teenager, things pretty much remained the same. As a high school student I was accepted into a math and science magnet school that pitted me against some of the smartest students in the city. We had to take all advanced placement courses and we had classes with pretty much all the same classmates. Most of us graduated with honors, and practically all of us had way more credits than we needed to graduate.

Our magnet was established for the top in "nerdy" behavior, but my crew and I tried to maintain some semblance of coolness. We all—the nerds, that is—hung together, so amongst ourselves we were what the school was all about. The rest of the school was oblivious to our lives and we lived a separate existence from theirs. We really didn't mind because we felt we were superior to them anyway, and to sit in classes with them was a waste of time.

As a teenager, my acne, my Care Free Curl and my shy, non-combative attitude kept me single. I thought myself an ugly duckling so the guys I liked I usually crushed on from afar. They never knew—in fact no one ever knew except for my notebooks with their names written on them.

The boy in high school I admired from afar was Trevor Carlson. He caught my eye at the summer program we were in right before our first year of high school. When the first days of our freshman year arrived I realized that he was enrolled in the same magnet I was in, and as a bonus we had a lot of the same classes.

I thought Trevor was really cute; light-skinned boys were in at this time, so his smooth, cappuccino-colored skin and his dark curly hair made me weak when he was near. He was already six foot four, even though he was just fourteen, and a bit on the lanky side; he had a huge gap between his two front teeth, which was corrected with braces several years later. His quick wit, charm, and infectious smile made up for any of his physical flaws, but he also had a side to him that was goofy and a little obnoxious, and at times it made it hard to deal with him. I really liked him, though, but fear and stupidity never allowed me to let on.

But by our junior year in high school Trevor and I were really close—as friends, of course. He had developed a liking for DeLana Larkin, my best friend from junior high school. She, I thought, was gorgeous, so I didn't fight him on it. She had long black luxurious hair, flawless caramel-colored skin and an attitude that would kill if you rubbed her the wrong way. She was a spitfire and a hard-nose and I think that's what attracted Trevor. He had even once remarked how he felt she was a challenge and that he was up for the game. Of course, having to listen to him talk about his affection for her really hurt, and on many a night I just listened and then went home and cried myself to sleep.

The whole time he and DeLana dated, Trevor never knew how I felt about him and I had to sit by and watch this couple connect.

During high school my posse included Tabitha, my main road dog. We were so close because we were so smart, and we had almost all our classes together. Then there was Dana, a, girl, who joined the clique because she lived in Tabitha's neighborhood; Arnel, Trevor's homeboy; Trevor; DeLana; and me. We did practically everything together, in and out of school. We studied together, partied together and shared our first experiences with alcohol and weed together. Back in the day, liquor stores didn't sweat much about people buying liquor for minors, and the drunks we gave money to get it didn't mind either, as long as we bought something for them. So drinking became easy. The weed happened after that.

The basement laundry room of Dana's apartment building was where we bonded. With the cement floors and dingy mustard-colored concrete walls, the smell of laundry detergent and dryer sheets made the dank coldness of the basement feel like home. I still enjoy that smell; the secret place where we grew from children to adults has since been demolished, but the memories we had there are as alive as if it were yesterday.

It was a Friday night, and although it was early evening, the sun had set long ago. We gathered at my house and took the bus to Dana's apartment building. DeLana and Trevor had already had someone buy us liquor, so when we exited the bus all we had to do was walk the three long blocks to the apartment building. This night the blocks seemed extremely long to me, maybe because it was so cold outside as we traipsed through the blowing snow and cold until we came to the basement door. Dana entered first, and we waited while she checked to make sure no one was down there. I watched as small funnel clouds of snow swayed against the glittering backdrop. Yes, this night was different.

We had always gone there to drink, but this time we decided to take our experimentation up a notch.

We were chillin', semi-drunk and laughing our asses off about what had happened in school that day. Then someone, I don't remember who, suggested we buy a bag of weed.

The room suddenly was quiet. Were we ready for drugs? All of us in the crew were considered nerds, teenagers who always did what was right. The underage drinking was bad enough; did we dare go further? We looked at each other; then, without any discussion, we sent Tabitha to purchase a dime bag from someone she knew on her block.

Trevor and Arnel went with her while DeLana, Dana, and I stayed in the basement drinking, talking, and laughing. When they returned, we were bug-eyed at how much we could get for just ten dollars.

"Well, let's get crackin'," someone said. The only problem was no one knew how to roll it. We sat around for a while trying to figure out who we could ask to roll it for us and couldn't come up with anything—not one of us could bring it home to our parents, especially me. We knew some kids smoked with their parents, but us, that would never happen. Then Tabitha thought of Charlene, her older sister—she was about five years older and pretty cool. Tabitha assured us she wouldn't snitch, so we all agreed. We followed Tabitha to Charlene's house—it was only a couple of blocks away; Tabitha went inside and we waited by the door, she returned with the whole bag of weed rolled up, about six or seven nice-size joints. We took the bag back to our basement kick-it spot and lit up.

This was my induction into smoking pot, and although we had fun, it was something I didn't really get into until later on in life.

# Chapter 44

We all passed around the joint taking small puffs, coughing and choking, with sips of beer and blackberry brandy in between. I had never taken a puff of anything, not even off cigarettes my uncle Darrin used to have me light for him. So taking puffs of the joint was harsh on my throat at first. I guess I didn't understand what I was really supposed to feel like, but what I felt was definitely nice. I jumped up on the folding table that was attached to one of the dryers, and slouched my back against the wall. I watched as my friends continued to pass the joint and sip the brandy. It was so surreal; everything around me became quiet and still. I could see them laughing and playing, but I couldn't move. My eyes were reduced to small half-moon slits and my limbs had succumbed to the excessive amounts of THC I had inhaled. DeLana came towards me and waved her hand across my face.

"Jasmine, are you all right?"

I looked at her; it took me a minute to focus. But when I did everything about her face was unfamiliar. She looked sort of like a black dwarf. I giggled, and someone in the corner started to giggle. The next thing we knew, our small harmless giggles turned into out-and-out hysterical laughter. All of us laughed, and then the fun began.

For some reason we felt the urge to fight. Play fight, wrestling, attacking each other at will. The girls first attacked the boys, hitting, smacking, and grabbing genitals, laughing, having a ball. But they fought back, jumping on us, grabbing boobs, holding us down as we squealed in sidesplitting laughter. It was the most excitement we had between studying and preparing for college. We had all worked extra hard to keep our grades up and we worked hard on our friendships. We stayed a clique, intertwined and committed to each other our entire high school career.

We were friends, real friends and we loved and genuinely cared about each other—until one of the friends committed the worst betrayal possible.

By the end of our junior year, we had all grown out of the smoking and drinking. Our focus was on college and taking our SAT and ACT tests. I was researching law schools and mentally trying to prepare myself for the perfect future. The last thing I needed was for Trevor—my junior high crush—to move into my neighborhood. We now rode the same bus, stopped at the same corner store before going home, and little by little we starting hanging out more and more—alone, just the two of us. I tried to suppress my happiness so I wouldn't jinx anything, and acted as casually as I could. I got to know him, and he got to know me. My affection grew into love, but I had no clue about how he felt. He was still with DeLana, which was pure torture for me. But we hung tough and that somewhat eased the pain.

Over the year and a half, Trevor and DeLana had become one of the school's signature couples and everyone knew their business. De Lana was hard on Trevor and everyone knew it. She was mean and degraded him, to his face and in front of all of us. And on top of all of that she refused to have sex with him. I never understood why he stayed with her; maybe it wasn't meant for me to understand because I had mixed emotions about it.

The way DeLana was with Trevor was a standing joke throughout the school and I sat by and watched as she hurt him and caused him grief time after time. It was hard, but I said nothing and did even less. All I could do was listen when he needed me to.

Then one night, when Tabitha and Trevor were on one of their many visits to my house, a wrestling match started between Trevor and me. We hadn't wrestled around like that since those days long ago in the basement, but this felt good. Tabitha was up in my room as we play-fought on the stairs. We tugged and pulled at each other, smiling and laughing, trying to catch each other off-guard. He turned me over and pinned me against the stairs.

Our eyes met and the overwhelming sensation that rippled through my body while he held me there was too much to bear. He looked at me and our lips met in the most sensual kiss I had ever experienced. As our shocked eyes consumed each other, we realized what we had just done, cheating on DeLana. We had made a terrible, horrible mistake.

My previous kissing experiences were with two neighborhood boys; both were white. White boys for me were safe; I guess my perception was that they wouldn't threaten or jeopardize my reputation. So as a young teenager they were who I kissed.

But kissing Trevor was new and refreshing; sparks flew, my body tingled in places I didn't realize I had. I felt like love and life were giving me a chance. When we pulled apart, though, the pressure of shame and even disgust descended upon us like a hungry eagle stalking its prey. Our moment of elation vanished as quickly as it had appeared.

That fateful day with Trevor on the stairs of my house slammed my soul into a whirlwind of battling emotions. The selfish, shameful guilt of betraying my best friend, along with the joyous elation of finally kissing Trevor had to be one of the most confusing experiences of my life. How could a simple thing like a kiss send my well-guarded spirit into a tailspin? All my life I had prided myself on being honest and faithful—to friends and to myself; now, in a moment of weakness I had destroyed everything in me that I felt was real.

After seeing Tabitha home Trevor and I walked to his apartment building. We really needed to talk. As we talked, I felt better. We decided that what we had done was totally wrong and that no one should ever know. It would be our little secret and we would go on like nothing happened. That was the plan and we both agreed it was a done deal. I felt like I had dodged a bullet. Even though I was in love with Trevor, I did not want anyone to know of our infidelity—not Dana, not DeLana, and definitely not Tabitha.

Tabitha was the moral majority of the crew; she always had what she thought to be words of wisdom, which made the simplest indiscretions seem like the end of life. She used her superior intellect and maturity to shame and chastise us, and if you couldn't handle the pressure you would cave, kind of like Trevor did. He told Tabitha everything.

When I walked into Trevor's apartment a couple of days after our intimate incident, I could tell immediately that something was wrong. The lights were dimmed and music was playing in the background. I couldn't quite make it out but I knew the vibe that was set was one of serious conversation. Nerves set in immediately.

Tabitha was sitting on the couch and Trevor was nowhere in sight. I smiled and greeted her.

"Hey, girl, what's up? How are you?"

"Hello Jasmine, I'm fine, how are you?" Her cold tone and nonchalant glance should have told me something up.

"Good. What y'all doing, where's Trevor?"

"Oh, he's upstairs; I wanted to talk to you for a moment about something."

At that moment I knew. "You dumb-ass," I thought to myself.

"Yes, Tabitha what's wrong?" I asked as casually as I could; but inside, there was this horrible dread.

"Trevor told me what happened." She crossed her arms, and looked at me with disgust; I stared back in disbelief, I imagined her pulling a scarlet letter out of her bag and pinning it to my chest.

"What did he tell you?"

As I waited for the anvil to drop, I noticed Trevor standing at the top of the stairs looking down into the living room. I glared up at him. Oh my God, you stupid idiot. If only I could scream it at him.

"He told me about the kiss."

"Oh, I see, well it was a huge mistake and we both deeply regret it," I said, the words tumbling out in a rush. "Nothing like that will ever happen again, I'm sure of it. It was a messed-up moment and it happened; now it's over, so there is no need to go any further with this. DeLana doesn't need to know, so let's just keep the peace." I spoke in a firm tone, secretly hoping she was buying it.

"How did it happen, what were you guys doing?"

"We were wrestling around and things got a little too close...." The old Bible phrase "Lead us not into temptation" ran through my mind. "Look," I said, "it really is no big deal, Trevor and I are cool so let's just forget it ever happened."

"Well, I don't think I can do that, but for DeLana's sake I won't say anything."

"Thanks, Tabitha I really appreciate it. I'm truly sorry, it *was* a huge mistake." I felt like I had convinced her to keep this quiet, but wasn't sure if either of them was strong enough to keep their mouths closed.

As I finished my speech, almost tripping over myself to apologize, Trevor slunk down the stairs; you could practically see his tail between his legs. I rolled my eyes at him, then turned and went into the kitchen to get something to drink.

Tabitha must have been cool with my response to him, because she decided that she could leave us alone. She rose and marched toward the door, but before she left, she turned around and gave us both the shame-on-you headshake, then said goodbye and shut the door behind her.

We murmured our goodbyes. His mother wasn't home, so as soon as the door clicked shut behind Tabitha, I laid into him like nobody's business.

"What were you thinking, are you crazy? Out of all the people in this world you tell her, Queen Morals herself?"

"Man, I don't know what got into me, you're right, I never should have said anything. But when I got home I was guilt-trippin' so hard I had to talk to someone."

"Aaah duh, what am I, idiot? If you really didn't want DeLana to know, you sure fucked that up."

"Do you think she's going to tell her?"

"Damn Trevor, I really don't know what to think. It was only a kiss and we talked about it and we squashed it—so I thought."

"I know, Jaz, I messed up. What do we do now?"

"Nothing, Trevor, man; nothing. Just walk me home."

It was a beautiful night, a little breezy but warm. The moon was high in the sky and I could only see a few stars. Trevor had grabbed a light jacket and I had never taken mine off. We walked slowly under the moonlight up the hill towards my house. My mind was in a whirl and I could tell by Trevor's silence that he was thinking hard too. When we reached my house, Trevor asked me if he could come in for a while.

My mother and brother were asleep and my uncle Darrin, who stayed with us occasionally, was out for the night. Trevor and I quietly entered the house and walked slowly to the living room. I flicked on the television but turned the volume down real low. Even though my mother was a light sleeper, I knew she wouldn't care if Trevor were there with me. All my friends loved my mother and she loved all of them. She treated them all like her own children, so hanging out late like this with *him*, but only him, would not have posed a problem.

There was a really weird vibe in the room. The light from the television flickered across the walls and the couch seemed very small. Trevor and I were seated so close to each other that the air around my head seemed thin. Although we were best friends, the real feelings I had for him sometimes surfaced and made me nervous when we were alone. He turned to me and asked, "What now?"

I tried with everything in me to look at him, but the butterflies in my stomach wouldn't let me, so I just looked away—anywhere that wasn't at him. He reached for my face and looked into my eyes.

"Jasmine, what are you thinking?"

"Trevor, I don't know, I'm extremely nervous," I said. Then without any warning our lips met, as though we had been a couple passionately in love with each other for a long, long time. I kissed him as if he were mine and I his; and with the same urgency he kissed me back. I looked deep into his eyes, searching for the answer to the hardest question I had ever asked.

"Do you want to?"

He looked at me and nodded his head.

I excused myself and quietly crept upstairs to my bedroom. There was really no reason for me to have birth control, I wasn't dating anyone and I was still trying to be what the Bible said I should. But with the increase in teen pregnancy and my hormones raging out of control, I begged my mom to take me to the clinic. Of course she scoffed at the idea of her little girl wanting to have sex. But when I explained it was just a precaution, we made the appointment and went together. I never thought about how she might feel, as I looked through my drawer to find the diaphragm case, her only daughter preparing to make one of the biggest decisions of her life. It didn't matter right then anyway, I was going forward regardless.

Wow, this was it—my first time. Could this really be happening? And with Trevor, my best friend; it couldn't be any better than this is what I told myself, as I removed the diaphragm from its case and squeezed the spermicidal gel all over the surface, rubbing it in like the nurse showed me. The thought of DeLana's hurt crossed my mind. How could I do this to her? What kind of friend was I?

But she didn't love him the way I did, she was mean to him and she refused him sexual pleasure. I could be what he needed, and at this moment I was what he wanted. I shut the thought of her out of my mind and inserted the diaphragm, making sure it was in properly. I washed my hands, pulled up my pants, and quickly crept back downstairs, quietly pulling a blanket out of the linen closet; I left the drawer a little bit open so it wouldn't make any noise scraping back in and wake up anyone else.

Trevor was still on the couch. He seemed calm but I knew he was a little nervous; I sure was. I thought it might have been his first time, but the calmness in his smile said otherwise. I ran my hand across his back and felt the tension in his shoulders. I knew doing this at home, with my mother upstairs, was risky, but everything was so right, there was no way we were going to get caught. At least I hoped there was no way. I asked him if his anxiety was because we were in my mother's home or if he wanted to be with DeLana instead of me. He told me he was cool, and I, in return, told him we were protected. I sat next to him. We were ready.

Trevor was a perfect gentleman; he was gentle, patient, and extremely attentive, making sure I was cool. He laid me back against the green velvet sofa and got on top of me. He pulled the large quilted blanket over our bodies. As he tried to enter me, I could feel my body tensing up. I guess he could too. He smiled and ran his fingers through my hair.

"Take a deep breath, Jaz, it's all good." I smiled back, breathed in deeply, and waited for him find me.

As I lay there staring at nothing at all, I could feel the girth of his manhood filling up the inside of my private place, which up until this point had been all mine. I thought, I will never get this moment back. I was giving this man, who was nothing but a fantasy, a myth, something wishes were made on, the most treasured possession I owned. And why? because he showed me a little attention.

Oh my God, he was there, snapping me out of my dream state. The unexpected sensations I felt as he slowly but firmly thrust in and out of me brought me out of regret and into a place of comfort and warmth. I accepted his physical explorations, but emotionally I was a ball of confusion and fear. Was this feeling the natural act of sex or a feeling of love?

This was it; the feeling I had been looking for, it spoke to me, it protected me. And although this feeling was based on deception and lies, I still believed in it. I craved it. And it was a man who had given it to me. It was the first time I had been swallowed up in something that felt bigger than me, and it made me believe in fairytales.

I kissed Trevor on the cheek, silently thanking him for giving me what I needed, and as he raised his hands to caress my face his shallow breaths changed to heavier, deeper ones. I pulled him closer and wrapped my legs around his waist. He arched his back and thrust deeper than I was ready for. My reflex reaction caused him to pause, but the expression on my face told him I was fine. We both breathed heavily, synchronizing our breaths, culminating this special union, and I dared anyone to question our loyalties. We were there together, temporarily in love and temporarily as one.

If he liked it, I loved it. After it was over, we dressed and sat quietly on the couch.

"Jasmine, are you all right?"

"Yes, Trevor, I'm all right. How about you? Are you all right?"

"Yeah, I'm cool. I enjoyed myself, what about you?"

"Well, Trevor, I have never felt like this before and I'm a little confused. We did what we did but you belong to someone else; and now I have to watch you go back to your life while I sit by and wish for what she has. It just doesn't seem fair."

He gently took my hand and walked with me towards the front door.

"Walk with me halfway home, OK?"

"Yeah, I guess." In my heart I so desperately wanted him to stay with me, but knew, with Mama upstairs and his mother probably expecting him to walk in the door any minute, there wouldn't be a chance for that. And on top of all of that the thought of DeLana looking for him made me all the more unsure about my recent decisions.

I opened the front door and we stepped out into the cool night air; we paced ourselves down the front steps and onto the sidewalk. We walked hand-in hand down the sidewalk towards his house. Neither of us said a word.

I believe we were both savoring a moment that would never be again, and I took the silence as a sign of the inner pain we both felt. As we neared the corner he turned to me and said goodbye.

"I'll call you tomorrow, OK?"

"Yeah, OK."

We kissed and I turned to walk away. I could see my house from where we were standing. I just wanted to get far enough away, I didn't know how long I would be able to contain the tears that I could feel surging. I didn't turn around but I knew he was watching, waiting for me to get home.

Back at home, I crawled into bed and lay there for what seemed like hours, reliving the experience over and over again in my head. Having been a virgin I couldn't say if I had had an orgasm or not; I had nothing to compare it to. All I knew was that what had transpired between us was beautiful, fulfilling and as right as any first sexual experience could be. I was in love. With Trevor? I'm not sure, but with love, definitely.

\* \* \*

Trevor and I messed around a few more times in the next month or so; it was easy because we lived so close. But the thought of getting caught and the burden of guilt made the times we got together as a group so frustrating and awkward that those feelings eventually superseded our need for each other. With that I made up in my mind that this was how it had to be, so to keep my sanity while he was with DeLana, I started dating.

My first guy was a football player. He was pretty gross, a not very attractive friend of a friend; I was back to my old ways. But the lesson I learned about having sex with just anyone was that it was way more than I could handle. I realized rather quickly not everyone cared, and for the most part it was all about his pleasure and not mine.

Fast-forward to adulthood; sex and relationships just seemed to get worse.

Damn, that temptation.

# Chapter 45

AFTER I GRADUATED, I THOUGHT a lot about my friendships and the boys I had encountered during high school. Most of what I thought was love was merely a way for me to get the attention I craved. The few boys I dated meant nothing to me except to say I was dating someone. It wasn't until I met Jamil that things in my love life rearranged themselves, though not necessarily for the better.

I first met Jamil my sophomore year in high school when I visited Tony, a boyfriend I'd met through my cousin. Tony was kind of a troubled kid, so he'd been in and out of juvenile detention; he was cool but his problem lifestyle didn't suit me, being that I was Miss Goody Two-Shoes. He kept getting in trouble and when he finally went back to juvenile hall, I wrote him off.

Before that, though, I'd go see him where he stayed in St Paul with his foster parents. The bus ride from North Minneapolis to St. Paul was about an hour and half. I had to ride two buses and walk several blocks to see him; that kind of journey illustrated how desperate my love life was.

That day, when I finally arrived at Tony's house, Jamil was there, standing in the yard with a bunch of other guys. Turned out he was one of Tony's best friends. He was about six foot one, with smooth, cocoa brown skin. I could tell by the shape and definition in his arms and legs that he was a basketball player, my favorite. I spoke to the group of guys standing in the yard and caught Jamil's eye, just like he caught mine. I stared longer than I intended, and when I realized it I excused myself and walked into the house behind Tony. But I daydreamed for a minute. Jamil was so cute; if

Tony weren't here I would try and talk to him. I laughed to myself; who was I fooling? There was no way I was going over to talk to him, especially with all those other boys around. Oh well.

I felt like Jamil was feeling me by the way he stared, but he couldn't approach me because of his boy. I had already decided Tony was on his way out, but I didn't know how I was going to get to Jamil. He became just a dream because I had no way of contacting him; after I broke up with Tony I didn't plan to go back to St. Paul looking for boys—until the winter of our senior year in high school.

That winter, Trevor and I, still friends, heard about a party in St Paul at a club called the Library. It was really cold, bone-chilling cold. I was dressed in a mini skirt and heels, freezing my ass off waiting in line to get inside. Trevor and I waited at least thirty minutes to get in; any longer I for sure would have been frostbitten. We looked at each other and decided to separate just so no one thought we were together on a date. But as the night wore on, we'd meet up every so often to talk and laugh about people. Like the dude and his girl with the matching outfits, and the girl with the jacked-up weave, and the guys who thought they were just too cool. It was all super-funny and we laughed most of the night. As the last few songs played I noticed a familiar face in the crowd. Damn is that . . . nah, can't be. Hell yeah, it is.

It was Jamil, looking as good as ever. He was wearing a khaki-brown long-sleeve button-up with a bomb pair of khaki pants. His tall muscular frame towered over everyone in the club and when he finally looked my way, he smiled, showing that small gap between his teeth that just made me melt. I stopped feeling nervous.

As the party ended and everyone started towards the doors, dreading stepping out into the frozen tundra, Jamil walked over to me and spoke.

"Hello, Jasmine."

"Hey, Jamil, how are you? Long time no see."

"Yeah, I guess so." We both smiled, feeling a little awkward about the moment.

"So you still talk to Tony?"

"No Jamil, Tony and I broke up a long time ago; he was in and out of trouble—too much for me."

"Yeah, I hear you. So who you here with?"

I paused. "Um, I'm here with . . ." and just as I was about to explain Trevor to him, Trevor ran up on me, and wrapped his long, lanky fingers around the back of my neck.

"What up, girl, you ready to go?" I snatched myself away, still smiling at Jamil.

"Oh my bad, I see you're here with someone," Jamil said, taking a step away.

"No, no, Jamil, it's not what you think, Trevor and I are just friends."

Trevor looked at me, then at Jamil, and immediately peeped what was happening. Then, in his goofiest manner ever: "Aw naw, man, I ain't with her," he said. "We just friends, you think I'd like someone like her? Nah man, not me."

I glared at Trevor, turned, and punched him in the chest. "Beat it, fool." Jamil's high-browed look and uneasy smile alluded to the embarrassment on my face. I rolled my eyes.

"I'm sorry he's a nut." I couldn't believe I was still standing there. "Look, Jamil, I gotta go now. You have a nice night," I said, feeling like the whole situation had just crumbled in front of me.

"Hold up, Jasmine—may I call you some time?"

I tried to maintain my composure, but the muscles in my face turned up into the goofiest smile.

"Yeah, sure that would be cool." I furiously dug in my purse for a pen and piece of paper and wrote my name and number on it. "Yeah, call me anytime; even tonight would be OK."

"All right, Jasmine, I might just do that."

As I watched him walk away the warmth I was feeling inside now totally overshadowed the blustery wind that had felt like it sliced through me before. Wearing my usual stupid grin, Trevor and I walked to my car.

# Chapter 46

After that night at the club, Jamil and I had talked several times but it was a few months before we decided to hook up. He was a few months younger than me, but a grade behind me because of when his birthday fell. And in my senior year of high school, I didn't want to get involved with anyone because of all the studying and homework I had to do to prepare for college. When school was almost out we talked more regularly, and as the year ended we set up a date—for the fall, when I'd be in college.

Now that time had arrived. I had finally gotten settled in on campus. It took a while to sink in, what with getting my scholarship straight and moving all my things. But now I was realizing how much living on campus was going to be totally different than living at home. Major freedom.

Jamil and I figured for our first meeting we could go out for dinner. I left my car at home when I was on campus, but rode the bus home to get it when I really needed to go somewhere. The plan was to pick him up from his house in St. Paul—here we go again—and we would find somewhere to eat on that side of town. At least that's what I thought.

It was a beautiful fall day, about sixty-eight degrees and the breezes that floated through my hair were soft and mild. It was shining so brightly I figured even the sun must know I had a date. I felt pretty good about it and got in my car to drive the fifteen minutes to St. Paul.

When I pulled up in front of his house it hit me—if I was going to get to see him on a regular basis, then the traveling was always going to be on me, since he didn't have his driver's license, let alone a car. Damn, was I really this desperate?

He was standing outside; ooh he's so fine; I guess I am.

Jamil was one of six children who lived at home with his mother and his siblings. He was the second-oldest and had assumed the role of caregiver for his family. His older brother was never home; he was a street dancer and lived his life constantly searching for the hottest dance party. Jamil's mother had become addicted to drugs and alcohol, and stayed holed up in her room most of the time. Their father was never around and Jamil didn't talk about him much.

The house was huge—it looked like it was an old duplex turned into a single family home—and it was in terrible shape. The chipped white paint no doubt had lead in it and the windows and doors were in desperate need of repair. The old open front porch was filthy and I could see some of the wood rotting away. The yard had several bare patches where the grass had been worn down; there were bushes that hadn't been trimmed in years, and trees with broken limbs, from children climbing them, I assumed.

I looked through the missing slats on the fence and studied the outfit Jamil was wearing. He was dressed in jeans and a Vikings jersey, which made the unappealing background seem to disappear. He smiled as I pulled up and told me to hold on a minute. I grinned back at him and shut off the car while he said bye to his little brothers.

"Who is she, Jamil?" I could hear his little brothers asking.

"Don't worry about it, go inside I'll be back later." His little brothers laughed and ran up the stairs yelling "Jamil got a girlfriend, Jamil got a girlfriend." As he got in the car I smiled. "Those your little brothers?"

"Yeah. They're some bad-asses."

"Nah they ain't bad, they cute."

"Whatever, girl, you don't know them."

"So you got a girlfriend, huh?"

Jamil smiled and looked me dead in my eyes.

"Yeah, I hope so." He took my hand and squeezed it gently. There was nothing for me to say—the silly grin on my face said it all. He noticed it too, and then I knew I was in trouble.

"So where are we going?" I asked him.

"I don't know, let's just get out of St. Paul."

"Oh, OK. Are you hungry?"

"Yeah, I'm starving. My mother is a mess and there's no food in there, and I don't have any money."

At that moment the pressure in my chest told me to *stop!* and take his ass right back home. But my sympathetic nature wouldn't allow that after his sob story. It was two o'clock on a Saturday afternoon and I drove all the way to Uptown to get him a pizza.

Davanni's had the best deep-dish pizza around and he had no problem polishing off the whole thing. Of course, I had had a couple of pieces, but sitting and watching him finish the rest was nothing short of amazing.

"Are you cool?" I finally asked him, after he had wolfed down the last piece.

"Yes Jasmine I am, thank you so much. I really appreciate it. You just don't know."

"Yeah, I think I do know," I said under my breath. "So what do you want to do now?"

"I want you to meet my homeboys. Let's go kick it with them."

Wow, I thought. That was really cool, he liked me so much I was already going to meet some of his boys.

"OK, where do they live?"

"Not too far from me, in fact right up the street. So back to St. Paul, I guess."

We got in the car and headed back to St. Paul. It was only about twenty minutes but still, back and forth like that was draining my gas tank.

We pulled up in front of one of his boy's house, and from the looks of things, it wasn't much different from Jamil's. I parked on the street and we walked through the six-foot chain-link gate around the back to the side door. The branches and tall grass from the unkempt yard scratched and scraped my skin; the fact that he was not fazed by this miniature jungle made me start to question him and his friends. Was this yard like this all the time? I didn't want to draw attention to myself so when I noticed blood trickling down my arm I quickly wiped it away before it had a chance to settle on my sleeve.

Jamil knocked on the door, then without waiting for anyone to answer, walked inside. I followed close behind and quickly found myself watching my step, being careful not to trip.

The house was dark and full of stuff—lots of stuff. I had been to places where the owners were pack rats but this was ridiculous. We stepped over mounds of clothes and boxes as we headed upstairs towards his boy's bedroom. The sound coming from the bedroom made the blood in my veins pulse; it was hip-hop music and I was kind of feeling it.

The bedroom door was open, and there were two guys sitting low on a mattress on the floor. They were smiling and bopping their heads to the music.

"Hey, what up, Jamil?" said one of them.

"What up y'all, check, this is Jasmine."

"What up Jasmine," the guys said in unison.

"My name is Kyle," said the boy who had spoken first. He put his hand out and I shook it. The other young man gave me the fist; I balled up my fist and tapped him back. His name was Curtis. "Nice to meet y'all," he said. I looked around for somewhere to sit. Jamil, noticing my plight, grabbed a folding chair and handed it to me; he sat on the floor. I moved a few things around on the floor with my feet and opened the chair to sit down. I could see pictures of Kyle and some female taped to the wall so I assumed it was his house. I sat there and looked around and watched the deep engrossment these young dudes had in their music.

I wasn't lame; I had listened to and grown to love hip-hop music but the artists and rappers I was hearing in this house were ones I had never heard before. These rappers were more radical, more progressive—more powerful. Their lyrics were rich with positive messages and the underlying beats and lines were melodic sounds of the motherland.

I was completely mesmerized. I settled back comfortably without saying a word and let the smooth, rhythmic tones soothe my soul. Suddenly, I was in love. I had found something new that caused my heart to stir and my spirit to soar. As I zoned out to the music, I saw Jamil looking at me. I could tell he was deep in thought, but I didn't know if he was thinking about me or if he was, like me, entranced by the beat.

"Who is this?" I asked.

Curtis turned to me and said, "Public Enemy" at the same time Kyle handed me the album cover. I studied the photos. The names were foreign to me; Chuck D, Flava Flav, Professor Griff—but these were beautiful black men who stood strong and tall and represented a new generation of soldiers dying to be heard. I read what I could before Kyle asked for the album jacket back. He replaced the song with something else, and during our silent break Curtis asked me where I was from. I told him I was just across the river in Minneapolis, but now lived on the University of Minnesota campus.

Kyle and Curtis laughed. "Aah Jamil, a college girl, huh?"

"Man, y'all niggas, shut up. She's cool as hell."

I looked at Jamil, a little confused. "Thank you?"

The guys laughed louder. "Aah man, we just giving you a hard time; we can tell she's cool."

"What are you going to play now?" I asked.

"This is X-Clan," said Kyle. "Hell, yeah," Jamil said. "These cats are what's up."

Kyle put the record on the turntable and we all waited quietly for the intro. I motioned for the cover and he handed it to me. This cover was even deeper than the previous one. There were four men dressed in red, black, and green, there were African spears and shields and all kinds of African artifacts. They were wearing "Black by Popular Demand" sweatshirts and red, black, and green medallions of Africa around their necks.

# I Surrender All

I was stunned. Who were these guys and what did they really represent? I put the cover down and focused on the music, joining Kyle, Curtis, and Jamil. Without speaking, we glanced around the room at each other, briefly making eye contact while the soulful beats from our homeland resonated in our ears.

I was done. This is where I wanted to be and I was now looking at Jamil in a whole new way. He was different; he was black. I had lived my entire life in this Caucasian bubble doing good and doing what was right; and finally, finally, someone with the courage of an entire African nation had pierced my psyche and released my inhibitions towards my true identity. I would never be the same again.

\* \* \*

After that night, Jamil and I grew closer and closer. The problems he had at home and my need for some kind of hardcore street adventure threw us together, forced us to rely upon each other. Our need for some semblance of ordinary lifestyles fortified our relationship and we fell in love—or what we knew love to be at the time.

Even though he was still in high school and I was in college, our connection worked out perfectly. My fear of men didn't matter because he was younger and I felt some sense of control. I would pick him and his friends up, take them to eat, take them to his basketball games, and take them shopping. I liked the fact they looked up to me as a woman; I didn't have just one boyfriend, I felt like I had three. Kyle and Curtis loved me and appreciated the way I treated them. The "girls" they were dating did not understand their needs; they continually let me know, and I stepped in right on time to alleviate some of their grief.

At the same time the fellas gave me a sort of peace of mind I had never felt before. I was accepted. I felt needed and that need grew into a sort of codependency. And because of our sheer love and admiration for hardcore hip-hop we became a close-knit family. I was a b-girl and they were my b-boys. What could be better?

## Chapter 47

Jamil was the first man to introduce me to a sort of sexual ambiance. It was amazing how he carefully and meticulously prepared his room for me whenever I came over. Once I entered his home, he would whisk me away to the back of the house where his room was located. I always wondered why he walked me back there so fast, and found out later it was because he didn't want his mother to see me. Not because I couldn't be there, but because when she was drinking she liked to talk and he didn't want to deal with that.

When he opened the door to his room the music, which he always had softly playing was mesmerizing. I asked him once where he had gotten the mix tapes from and he replied that he had made them himself. That seemed so special because the songs he chose were carefully selected and placed in specific order to ensure the right mood, and I felt like they reflected how he felt about me. The scented candles he had lit in every corner flickered nicely against the blue and red colored light bulbs. Sweet-smelling smoke from incense swirled around me, and fresh, clean sheets always awaited our encounter. He was good to me, he respected my family and friends, and he did what he could to please me.

The way he invited me into his space, allowing me to experience his form of sexual foreplay, enticed me into a sexual intimacy with him early in the relationship He was a very passionate lover and I enjoyed being beneath him, on top of him, in front of him. His young, athletic body gave me pleasure and I grasped at it every moment I could. Some of our sexual exploration happened in my dorm room, but most of the time we were secretly making love in his bedroom. That was hard; between his brother and sisters and his very demanding mother, mating time for us at his home was always tricky. We were usually quiet lovers because our lovemaking was sweet and tender. But on occasion, when things got heated, he turned up the music or we covered our mouths with pillows. I knew he always threatened his brothers and sisters before I came, but a lock on the door was necessary to be on the safe side.

I adored his attempts at making me comfortable in a place that was filled with joyless memories. His house was not exactly a place of peace for him, but he did his best when I came around. In retrospect, I think that he appreciated me for allowing him to be somewhere and someone else, at least for the times we shared.

We went out for two months, six months, and eventually we realized we were close to our year anniversary. I had spent most of this time catering to and loving him, and the rest of this time doing homework. I got with the girls on occasion, but mostly I lived my life seeing to Jamil's needs.

On one of our regular meetings, we had spent the entire day together shopping and hanging out. We had bought new clothes, tennis shoes, and cassettes—well, *I* bought him all that stuff—and we hurried up to his room to relax. It was late in the evening and his house was almost empty. All I could hear were the faint sounds of the television in his mother's room. His brothers and sisters must have been out because I didn't hear any of their yelling, and the doors of their bedrooms were wide open, so I knew they weren't in there asleep.

Jamil opened the door to his room for me and I stepped inside. He set down his bags and began his bedroom-conversion ritual. He turned on the colored light bulb and put on some soothing music. He lit a candle, then used it to light the three sticks of incense he had waiting in the stone planter. He looked my way and smiled. "Hey, sweetheart, would you like something to drink?"

"No thank you, Jamil, I'm fine."

He reached for me and gently pulled me down on his bed. I lay back on the mattress, thinking of nothing at all, waiting for him to undress me. I raised my hips to allow him to get my pants and underwear down and waited patiently while he undressed.

His body seemed different this night. He smelled different, as if every emotion that emanated from his pores was different—but I didn't know what. He lowered himself on top of me and I spread my legs.

He entered me with a force that I had not known with him before. I could feel the texture of the ribbed latex condom rubbing up against the delicate walls inside me. The fulfilling sensation wasn't painful, but his strokes were deep and convincing. It was apparent he was leaving his mark on me. I could feel all of him, and I think for the first time he was finally not holding anything back, and I was feeling the same. I thrust my body upwards as he pushed down and deep into me, and we grasped each other in a fit of ecstasy. Then he pulled out of me, lifted me, and walked me to the chair across the room; I slowly bent over it, as I turned to look his way. I stayed focused on his eyes, even though my back was beginning to tense up. He entered me from behind, and when I finally felt his full presence I turned back, closing my eyes as I felt them roll up in my head from sheer pleasure.

As his manhood penetrated into my very soul, images of our ancestral homeland swept through my mind.

There we were, with magnificent trees and wondrous flowers surrounding us. Exotic birds were singing their own special mating call and the beasts of the earth bowed in our presence. I was his African queen and he was my master, my king. It all felt so real, until . . .

"Jasmine, I think the condom broke."

I found out the hard way that it *was* better to give than to receive.

# Chapter 48

Sitting in the abortion clinic with my mother was one of the lowest moments of my life. I had tried all my life to do what was right, to say what was right. And now look at me. I was sitting in a room with other young girls and women, waiting to have the life sucked out of me, literally. I wasn't a bad person, really I wasn't; in fact I felt like I was a really good person. I never tried to hurt anyone, and I always tried to correct my mistakes.

But on this day, I was forced into a decision that would change my life forever, a mistake that I couldn't correct by myself. There was no way I was ready to bring a baby into this world. I was on my way to the top; I was in college now, preparing myself for big things. And a baby would just slow me down. I had no other choice. Right? I had no other choice.

My mother never showed any emotion, good or bad. She asked me what I wanted to do, already knowing my answer. After making the appointment she sat with me and we discussed my decision. My mother always had my back and I was grateful for that, but in retrospect I'm not sure if her continuous acceptance of my negligence was a blessing or a curse. But she was here, sitting with me thumbing through magazines making idle chitchat.

*Jasmine Burrell.* That was my name, I thought; but I couldn't move. *Jasmine Burrell.* The name rang out again; it sounded so familiar but I wasn't sure she was talking about me, until my mother placed her hand on mine and said, "Baby, they're calling your name."

I turned to look at my mother; she was so beautiful and so strong. How was she able to sit here with me and not be angry? "Go ahead baby, it's gonna be all right. I'll be out here waiting when you get done. I'll be right here."

I stood up and slowly walked towards the blond lady in blue. Her gentle touch on my shoulder sent chills screaming through my body, but her calm voice made it at least *seem* as though everything was going to be all right.

I followed her into a pristine white medical room. The narrow examining table seemed to beckon; I tried to retreat but my feet wouldn't let me. You can do this; you have to do this. Everything was swirling furiously, and I began to feel light-headed. I inhaled deeply, gasping for air, just a little bit of air; when I found it, I grabbed hold and tried desperately to disappear within the oxygen molecules floating by. Then, in utter failure, I exhaled and began searching for a familiar place, a place I knew no one could hurt me, a place where I was free and all things around me were sacred; once again I had failed. I stood in a daze, helpless.

"Please undress from the waist down and the doctor will be in, in a moment." I gazed at her as she left the room and proceeded to take off my clothes, then scooted up on the bed. I placed my feet in the uncomfortably wide stirrups and covered my lap with the sheet. I lay back and stared up at the ceiling. As if I searched the ceiling, like I might find a trap door up there that I could escape through, a nice looking white man walked in. He was tall with dark hair and peaceful ocean-blue eyes. He was wearing a long white doctor's coat and had his face covered with a surgical mask. The nurse who had been with me before followed behind and quietly shut the door.

"Good morning, Miss Burrell, how are you?" the doctor greeted me.

"I'm fine, I guess; a little scared."

"I know, Miss Burrell, but in a moment everything will be all right."

Why did everyone keep saying that? How did they know? Was there some magical potion that they were going to give me to make me forget about all of this or were they just trying to pacify me to keep me sane? Lying back, expecting the worst, I realized that the people in this room were on my side. It had been many years since the Roe vs. Wade decision legalizing abortion was handed down. And the two medical professionals who were here with me had chosen to assist in a procedure that, while unfortunate, was considered a life-saving commitment, a choice they made, I assumed, after long agonizing days of weighing their options. A choice they made to help me.

"OK, Miss Burrell, I'm going to explain everything as I go." I glanced over, as he removed the piercingly white sheet off the metal table. I guess in my dazed state I didn't even notice it. There were several strangely shaped instruments lying on the metal plate, and a plastic container nearby. The doctor began picking up metal rods, which increased in size as he proceeded down the row.

"These are dilation rods," he explained. "I must dilate your cervix to a size large enough to allow me to insert this vacuum." He lifted up and showed me a plastic tube about ten centimeters around. It was about the size of those extra large Pixie Stix, the ones you had to cut open with a scissors like we used to eat as kids in front of my grandmother's house. My mind floated back to my grandmother's house.

"Darnell, Darnell, come here; look what I got."

"What?" Darnell ran to the front door.

"Look. Me and Christine just came back from the corner store."

"Where did *you* get money?"

"I *found* some change on Grandpa Edmond's desk."

"Ooooh, I'm telling."

"Look," I said and lifted up the long narrow straws right into his line of view. I had bought two of those huge super-long Pixie Stix, one cherry, and one grape.

"Here, Darnell, you want one?"

"Yeah, Jaz, give me one."

"I'll give you one if you go in the house and find the scissors, and if you don't tell."

Darnell ran like a champion into the house looking for the scissors. I heard him bumping around the house, then finally asking Grandma Vera where they were.

"Boy, what do you need scissors for?"

"Jasmine has candy and we need them to open it."

"When did she get candy?"

"She went to the store and brought me one."

Grandma Vera reached in the junk drawer and pulled out the sharp metal scissors and walked Darnell back to the front of the house.

"Jasmine."

"Yes ma'am?"

"I don't recall saying you could leave this yard and go to the store." I looked at Darnell and gave him a scowl.

"I know, Grandma, but me and my friends went right there and came right back."

"Yeah, well, from now on you make sure you let me know when you plan to leave this yard, OK?"

"Yes ma'am, OK."

She motioned for me to come to the top of the porch stairs. She took the large pair of scissors and cut the tops of the Pixie Stix; she handed one to me and one to Darnell. Without a word she turned and walked back to the kitchen.

"Dang, Darnell, why you tell I went to the store?"

"I'm sorry, Jaz, I didn't know."

"I should take that candy from you; getting me in trouble."

"I said I was sorry."

"Whatever. I'm leaving."

"Can I come with you?"

"No. You can't come, you're too young."

I was always so mean to Darnell; all he wanted to do was hang with me. I suddenly became aware of where I really was. Damn, this was one time I wished my baby brother were here.

"OK, Miss Burrell, the dilation process will go really fast and then I'll insert the vacuum and after a few minutes you will be all

## I Surrender All

done," the doctor said. "All right now, scoot all the way down to the edge of the bed; are you ready?"

"Yes," I said, my voice quivering. The nurse sat there with me, her chair right next to my head. She opened her hand and I placed mine in hers. "Here we go, sweetie, take some deep breaths," she said.

I looked up at the ceiling and began to breathe. I started to close my eyes in fear, but the nurse said, "Jasmine, open your eyes; keep your eyes open and breathe." As my eyes fluttered open, I felt it.

Oh God, the pain. This pain was like nothing I had every felt before. I could feel the tears welling up as this strange man inserted then removed seven or eight metal poles into my vagina, dilating my now heartbroken womb. And then . . . swoosh. The sound of the vacuum turning on stunned me, and every fiber of my being was flooded with remorse.

"Ms. Burrell, I'm now inserting the vacuum." I must have nodded yes, because there was no way in hell I wanted him to put anything else in me.

And with no more notice, he inserted this life-sucking tool, intended to give me my life back; but what I felt was my life being taking from me, even though I had given him permission to do so. The strong pull against my abdomen sent me into a silent shock and I could hear the remains of my unborn child being sucked from its biological safe haven into its new foreign home.

"*Five, four, three, two, one.* We're finished. It's all over."

But was it truly over? He walked out of the room carrying my little he or she to a place I'd never know.

My eyes filled with tears. I looked over at the nurse while she helped me up from the bed. The intense cramping kept reminding me of what had just happened. The nurse handed me an extra large sanitary napkin, which I placed sticky-side down into my underwear, and then she escorted to a recovery room.

After the procedure patients had to remain at the clinic for a minimum of twenty minutes, longer if you had come by yourself. Another nurse gave me two extra-strength Advil, a small glass of water, and slice of toast, and led me to a nice comfortable lounge chair. The other ladies in the room were motionless. Some seemed at peace with their decision while others were wretched with anguish. Either way my experience was over. I was relieved that I had decided to secure my future, but I agonized over the way I had to do it.

As I lay waiting for my twenty minutes to be up, I realized my entire world would different now, and I tried with all the courage in me to salvage the little bit of dignity I had buried in the bottom of my soul. I had just committed what seemed to be an unforgivable sin, taking the life of my unborn child, and with that what I felt to be a permanent separation from God. But God was a forgiving God, wasn't He? At least that is what I was taught. So why were pro-lifers so ready to condemn anyone who even thought about abortion? Well, my sin had been committed, I could only hope for the best.

I took some deep breaths and thought about my future. There was no way for me to make amends to the tiny little spirit I had given to God way before its time. But I had to find a way. I lay my head against the recliner chair and closed my eyes; tears formed as I prayed.

"God, please forgive me. I'm truly sorry for what I've done." I waited for a response, but there was nothing.

The nurse came and told me I could leave if I was feeling up to it. I told her I was, but knew I was nowhere near ready for what I was about to face. I walked slowly towards the heavy wooden door, pushed it open and followed the lobby signs through the whitewashed hallways, back to where I started. I searched the room for my mother, and she was right where I had left her. She approached me cautiously, hoping not to trigger any leftover remorse, took my hand and led me out the door. I wrapped my arm around her waist and lay my head on her shoulder. She said, "Baby, everything is gonna be alright—alright?" I nodded yes, but knew deep down in my heart, "everything being alright" was not going to be as easy as everyone said.

## Chapter 49

It was six, and I had awakened without the alarm clock; the night was consumed with tossing and turning, nightmares, tears and tequila. Damn, it seemed as if I had dreamt about every wrong move in my past that had to do with a man, and why I couldn't get it right.

How could this be happening? I kept wanting to reach over and call Marcus so I could hear him say yesterday's events hadn't happened.

But I couldn't; yesterday *had* happened and once again I was alone. I couldn't figure out what I had done to deserve this. There had to be a good explanation why God was punishing me once again. Was fornicating so bad that I had to lose everything all over again? That was the only sin I knew I was out of control with.

"OK, God," I screamed. "I'll repent, if You give me Marcus back. I won't have sex again until I am married; and this time I truly mean it."

This wasn't like all the other times, when I had said it right after some way-wrong drunken one-night stand. Was He listening to me? He had to be listening; He had to save me from this nightmare. "God, are you there? God, please...."

Just at that moment I felt it, and it wasn't God. Fluid rose in my throat, and I ran to the bathroom, releasing all the disappointment that was welling up inside of me. There was no way for me to rebound from this. I walked back to the bed to lie down and dreamt about all that I thought was to be.

The day was sunny and warm, lightly teased by a cool autumn breeze. The birds were singing and the flowers that surrounded the beach club were in full bloom, and I could smell their sweet fragrance.

Preparation had gone perfectly, from picking out the bridesmaid dresses and tuxedos to the florist, the menu, and the music.

My bridesmaids were all present, as were the groomsmen, and everything and everybody was beautiful. I hadn't seen Marcus; he didn't want to see me before the wedding so I stayed in the dressing room and primped and smiled and nursed the butterflies in my stomach with warm tea.

I heard the music, the music is playing; it must be time. I slowly got up from the chair and took my place in line behind my bridesmaid, I was ready; this was it. All I wanted to do was see his face, to touch his face. He was there, right there, so close; I knew he was waiting for me.

Standing tall at the end of the aisle, I appeared and walked casually toward my dream. He was wearing a crisp black tuxedo and was smiling at me with tears in his eyes. There was no need to rush; this was forever. *Brrriiing... bring;* who the hell forgot to turn off their cell phone? I was furious. Please. Stop. The ringing.

I woke up angry, realizing it was my phone. "Oh my God, it could be Marcus." I jumped to my feet and ran to the phone. "Hello? Hello?"

"Hey, Jasmine, it's your mother."

"Oh, hey, Mom." I was extremely disappointed that the phone call wasn't Marcus, but I was glad to hear my mother's voice.

"Hey, Mom? A little more enthusiasm would be nice you, know."

"Oh I'm sorry, Mom, I'm just a little bit under the weather. What's up?"

"Nothing, baby, I hadn't heard from you in a while; just checking in. You feeling sick?"

"No, just tired. I have a big day ahead of me and I didn't get much sleep last night."

"Jasmine—what is going on, baby? I know that voice; something is going on."

"Mom, I really don't want to talk about it right now."

"Well, you've been playing me to the left a lot lately; it must be this new boyfriend you got. Got your nose wide open."

"No, Mother, it's not that." Sometimes I changed and called her "Mother" in order to drive home a message. To confirm to her that whatever it was she was thinking was way off.

"Then what is it, Jasmine? Don't make me come over there."

"No, I promise I'm all right. I'll call you later, OK?"

"All right, Jasmine. But if I don't get a call from you today, I'll be on my way over there or to your job if I have to. Try me."

"I know, I'll call you later today and fill you in on everything. Is that cool?"

The phone beeped, and there was a strange click.

"Yeah, Jasm . . . ."

"Mom, I got to go, someone is on my other line. I'm waiting on a call about a very important case. I promise I'll call you back."

I clicked over before she could say goodbye. Boy, was she going to kill me.

*You have a collect call from an inmate in the Hennepin County correctional facility. Press one if you accept the charges.*

I quickly pressed one and waited. A series of clicks rang loudly in my ears and . . . "Hello, Jasmine?"

"Marcus!"

# Chapter 50

THERE WAS NO EMOTION IN his voice. Our entire conversation was me asking questions and him replying with one-word answers. He couldn't give me anything. After a week of giving me everything, I was forced into accepting nothing. This was more than unbelievable.

But when his time was up and the phone ended our conversation, I had no more information than I started with. I had to take matters into my own hands. I was going to get to the bottom of this and I had all the education and accomplishments to prove I could do it. I had expected to hear from one of the girls, but they never called, so I didn't call them. I needed to do this by myself.

I had never gotten dressed so fast before; my entire existence was running on autopilot. I really don't remember much of anything until I pushed the button for the elevator at the courthouse. Shit—I completely missed the elevator ride at home, the front desk, the drive; it was a sheer blessing that I didn't have an accident because I don't recall stopping for any lights or signs.

I ran to my office and shut the door. It was seven-thirty and Wendy was already there making coffee. She didn't hear me come in so I didn't speak. I turned on my computer and waited for the black screen and flashing lights to give me what I needed: Teri's number. I had to find Teri to find out what the charges were and if they were going to release him on bond.

Scrolling through my contacts page I found a number I thought might be hers. A lot of the numbers had changed because of a big move the district attorney's office had just completed. I dialed and waited.

"District attorney's office, how may I direct your call?" Came a soothing voice on the other end. Thank God, I was so nervous that any other response probably would have sent me into a serious breakdown.

"May I please have Teri Jorgensen's office?"

"One moment please while I connect you." I waited on hold, listening to some classical piece of music playing.

*"You have reached Teri Jorgensen with the district attorney's office. I am not available at this time to take your call; however, I'll be in the office today so please leave a detailed message and I'll get back to when I return"*

Shit! "Teri, this is Jasmine Burrell, I really need to speak to you about a case you are working on. The name is Marcus Damon; I don't have a case number or anything, all of this just happened. Please contact me as soon as you get this message, it is of dire importance that I speak with you. I can be reached at"—then I gave her practically every number I ever had, including my home and the front desk of my apartment. I guess after the fact it seemed like overkill, but I couldn't risk her not contacting me. I figured if I left all those numbers, she would see how important this was.

I sat back in my chair and glanced over at the flowers. What the hell was going on? This has got to be a dream, or a big fucking nightmare. I closed my eyes and thought about Marcus. He has to have a good explanation for this, there is no way he is guilty of embezzlement and fraud.

The knock at my door startled me; I had forgotten Wendy was in the office.

"Yes, come in."

"Jasmine?" Wendy appeared at the door with a big cup of coffee in her hand and a peculiar look in her eyes.

"Hello, Wendy; girl, I'm sorry I didn't speak to you when I came in, you know me and my mad rush all the time. How are you?"

"I'm fine."

I looked back at her. "Well, good. That's good."

"The question is, how are you?" Wendy looked at me as if I had a big-ass zit on my forehead.

"I'm fine, why? You're looking at me like I just escaped from a mental hospital."

"Well, I'm not sure if this is some sort of new fashion statement for you or if you had a long night last night but . . ."

"What? What's wrong?" She looked at me and motioned to my shirt. I looked down and screamed. "Oh my God." I was still wearing my blue and pink terrycloth nightshirt. I had put on an entire suit but had forgotten to change my shirt. Wendy laughed.

"Wendy, please do not laugh at me; this is way far from funny."

"No, I'm sorry, Jasmine, this is funny as hell."

I looked at myself in the mirror and had to agree. This was funny and I couldn't help but laugh, almost in spite of myself; I was glad, because it really calmed me down. In fact it, allowed me to refocus, take a breath and collect my thoughts.

Wendy set down the cup of coffee and headed for the door. Before she could leave I spoke.

"Wendy?"

"Yes."

"Thank you."

She smiled at me, not really knowing what she had just done, but knowing she had helped, and nodded. "You're welcome, Jasmine, anytime.

There was no way I was going to have time to go all the way home to change, so I decided to call Sadie to see if she could bring me one of her shirts. I also needed her ear. I finally felt it was time to tell her, but I was going to tell only her. The other girls would have to find out later. The less badgering and "I told you so's" I got from them the better.

I was just about to dial her number when Wendy buzzed in and said I had a call from Teri. "Oh great, Wendy, thank you; put her right through."

I picked up the phone. "This is Jasmine," I said, hoping I didn't sound too anxious.

"Hey, Jasmine, this is Teri. I got your message."

"Yes, I was hoping I could talk to you about Marcus Damon."

"Uh, yeah, Jasmine about that—you see I'm not at liberty to talk to you about this case."

"What do you mean, Teri? I'm just trying to get a little information so that I can help with his legal defense. In fact, I'm trying to see if there is even enough evidence for a pre-trial hearing."

"Well, Jasmine, I hate to be the bearer of bad news, but this case is more than what you have been told. In fact, this man is looking at spending most of the rest of his life behind bars. This is a very serious federal case and I don't see him wiggling free under any circumstances."

"Come on, Teri, you know the system—innocent until proven guilty, right?"

"Yeah, Jasmine, I know, but the evidence they have against him is more than enough to convict him ten times over."

"Are you kidding me? What do you mean?"

"Look, Jasmine, I've probably already said too much; in fact you might need to get yourself a lawyer, too."

"WHAT?"

"Yes, I got an e-mail asking me questions about you, and your involvement with Mr. Damon. The feds have been watching him, and they know that you've been together; they have pictures, phone records, everything. They're trying to figure out how to approach you as we speak; but you haven't heard it from me, all right?"

Everything around me disappeared. I believe I hung up the phone before I replied, said goodbye or anything. Talk to me? What would they possibly need to talk to me for?

## Chapter 51

Sadie actually called me before I could call her. She wanted to know what the finale of Marcus' stay was like and if he made it to the airport OK. I couldn't believe she was asking me these questions just as I was about to call her, but I knew how our Capricorn third eye worked. She asked just enough in the right tone to let me know she knew something was wrong, and she was just waiting on me to 'fess up and give her the details.

"Sadie, I have a big problem."

"What's the matter, Jaz?"

"It's Marcus."

"I knew it, what did he do to you?"

"Well, Sadie, what he did, he did to himself, but now that we are engaged it has spilled over to me."

"Jaz, you are really scaring me. What the hell happened?"

I gave Sadie the quick and dirty version of my Romeo and Juliet tragedy and begged her not to tell the other girls until I had more answers. I explained to her that the FBI now wanted to speak to me, and that they had been watching us the entire week. She was floored. All she could say was "Oh my God."

"Sadie, what am I going to do?"

"Jasmine, stay calm. You are the bomb attorney and if anyone can get him out of this mess it's you."

"I know, Sadie, I thought of that, but the way the prosecutor is talking and the way Marcus has reacted to this whole thing, it really is not looking good."

"OK, baby, don't panic. I'll meet you at your house tonight so we can strategize."

"All right, Sadie; thank you, girl, I really appreciate it. I don't know what I would do without you."

"Girl, I got you, don't worry."

"I love you, Sadie."

"Love you too. I'll see you tonight." I sat back in my chair trying to think about my next move when Wendy's buzz on the intercom startled me.

"Hey, Jasmine, you have a call on line one; they say it's from the Federal Bureau of Investigation."

"Oh shit!"

There was no way I was prepared for this, but I had no choice.

"OK, Wendy, I got it."

I paused for a moment. Then, knowing I couldn't put this off, I picked up the phone.

"Hello, this is Jasmine Burrell."

"Hello, Ms. Burrell, this is Agent Tom Boskel with the FBI, how are you today?"

"Well, you're calling me, so I think I have been better." He chuckled, and got right down to business.

"The reason for my call, Ms. Burrell, is it seems you are acquainted with a Mr. Marcus Damon. Is that correct?"

"Yes, he is my fiancé."

"I see. Well, Mr. Damon has found himself into a lot of trouble and we are now holding him for questioning. Because of your acquaintance and the last week of our surveillance, it has become necessary for our agents to speak with you."

"Why me? I don't know anything about what is going on. I hadn't seen Marcus in years, he showed up at my home and . . ."

"Yes, I know, but we believe the time you spent with him might shed some light to the dealings he has had with another man affiliated in this case."

"I promise you, I know nothing about it. He never said or mentioned anything to me about his whereabouts, or his business. The only thing I know is that we were to be married."

"All right, Ms. Burrell, that's fine. But we're still going to need to talk to you. Can you be at our office in Bloomington tomorrow morning at seven-thirty?"

"Umm . . . do I have a choice?"

"Actually, you don't; if you don't show up tomorrow morning then we will come looking for you. Have a nice day, Ms. Burrell."

The sound of the dial tone blaring in my ear informed me our conversation was over.

The next few hours were filled with frantic phone calls to everyone I knew who had had any experience with the FBI. I first called a colleague, John, to see if he could help me with Marcus' defense. I knew he was going to want to know the details, but unfortunately I had nothing to give him.

We made arrangements to meet for coffee after I met with the FBI agent; I figured maybe after talking with them I would have some more information for him. I also made a call to the courthouse to see if Marcus was going to have a bail hearing. The clerk said it was set for Wednesday morning at eight. I was little upset about why it would take so long for his bail hearing, but knew how the system could be at times—slow as hell. But even more, I wondered why there were no plans to extradite him back to Europe. I had had so little experience with federal cases other than drug-related crimes, that a lot of what was going on with Marcus was new to me.

Then it hit me. I'll call Tonya—she was once an agent for the FBI and she could help me sort through some of this and maybe, help me with my questioning tomorrow.

Her voicemail picked up, so I left her a very detailed message begging her to call me as soon as humanly possible.

The last call I needed to make was going to be the hardest. Calling my mother and explaining to her how I went from being a successful single lawyer to getting engaged to moving out of the country to finding out my husband-to-be is apparently a criminal—and to top it off, possibly going to jail myself; without ever even mentioning any of this earlier on.

I knew my mother was going to hand it to me, so I decided to invite her to lunch. It was ten forty-five and if I took her to her favorite spot to eat, then maybe I could get everything out before she killed me. I picked up the phone, dialed, and waited for her to answer.

"Hello."

"Hey, Ma, it's me. What you doing?"

"Oh, hey, Jasmine, I was just going over some of these files. I have a couple of closings this month so I wanted to make sure everything was in order. How are you? You sounded so disconnected the last time I spoke to you."

"Yeah, Mom, I know a lot has been going on and I haven't had a moment to breathe."

"Well, Is everything all right, baby?"

"Well, . . . yes and no. Mom, can you meet me at Little Tijuana in an hour?"

"Sure, sweetheart, I just have a couple of phone calls to make."

"I have a few, too. So let's meet there and I'll fill you in on everything that has happened."

"Everything that's happened? Are you in some kind of trouble?"

"No, Mom, no it's nothing like that," I lied. "No, I'm fine. I just need to get some things off my chest and I need you to help me."

"OK, baby, I'll meet you there in an hour."

"I love you, Mom."

"I love you too, baby."

I hung up the phone-feeling semi relieved. I knew if I could get my mother to understand what I was doing then things would somehow work out.

When I pulled up at the storefront Mexican restaurant I saw her mint-green Jaguar already out front. Dang, I forgot how clean that car was.

I entered the restaurant and saw my mother sitting at the table drinking pink lemonade. She was always so poised, dressing like a movie star everywhere she went, even to the grocery store.

Like the rest of us, my mom, growing up under Grandma Vera's rule and being the oldest child, got the worst of Grandma's Christian love. My mom was still a work in progress, even as a business owner. She had grown up so smothered and sheltered by that strict Christian rule that most of her teenage and early adult years were spent trying to placate the very people who had imprisoned her true self. Her identity, usually almost completely masked, would spill out every so often, but for the most part she stayed caged in a sort of cocoon-like shell.

As a child I watched her give and give until there was nothing left. Everyone in the family and all her friends—even her acquaintances—knew what they could get from her, which was practically everything, and most of them had no problem taking advantage of her unbridled generosity. But my mom was a force that a lot of people didn't understand; her sweet, loving outer shell, encasing a sassy, independent core, over time became worn down by years and years of self-neglect. My mother had given away so much that as I got older, I found her trying to take on the problems of someone else's world, even when she didn't have to. At times I had to point out that those were not her problems to deal with and that the person involved had made their own bed and they should have to figure out how to sleep in it.

Generally, my barrage of objections fell on deaf ears and she usually did what she could to help; more times than not those she helped usually let her down. She just let it go, which never made any sense to me. But that was her way—who was I to try and change things? And she never held any animosity or anger towards them.

Myself included. My mom had bailed my brother and me out of a ton of unnecessary situations and never once stopped loving or giving. That was why I loved her so much and knew that if I couldn't trust anyone else in this world I could trust her. It was killing me not to have talked to her about Marcus and all that had happened over the week, she was truly not going to understand why I had kept all of this from her, but I was determined to put such a positive spin on this nightmare as humanly possible with my well-thought-out presentation.

When I got to the table I smiled and hugged the top of her head, kissing her gently on the forehead. "Hey, Mom."

"Hey, sweetheart, how are you?"

"I'm fine, how are you?"

"I'm good, baby."

"You look cute, Mom."

"Oh thank you, baby, just something I threw together." I laughed, trying to postpone the inevitable a bit longer.

"So, what's up, Jaz? You've been extremely weird lately," Mama said, cutting to the chase.

"Uh yeah, Mom, I know." My strained smile told my mom more than I had ever intended to, but now that I had her full attention my mission was to tell her everything and hope for the best.

Before I could speak, Mom noticed the ring. I had forgotten to take it off before I stepped in the restaurant.

"Jasmine, what is that on your finger?"

I looked down at the ring; I had a hard time looking up and facing my mother.

"Jasmine?"

"Yes, ma'am?"

"What is that?"

"Mom, it's an engagement ring."

"A *what*? What? Who? Where did you get an engagement ring and why don't I know anything about it?"

The shrillness in my mother's tone sent my hopeful scenario into a 180-turn, straight towards disaster.

"Mama, wait—calm down, let me explain."

"Yes, I'm waiting, girl." She put her cup down and looked directly at me, as if she had never met me before; this couldn't be her daughter speaking.

"How do I say this? Mom, I'm getting married."

She looked at me with disbelief, like I had not been the firstborn of her womb.

"Getting married? Getting married? To whom, may I ask?" Her tone was frigid—icy even.

"Marcus, Mama; Marcus has been here all week and he asked me to marry him."

She said nothing, just dropped her head—looking for the right words, I guess. Finally, she looked up.

"Baby, I'm not sure how to react to this. You know how I feel about him."

"Yes, I know."

"He really hurt you the last time he was here, and I don't know if I can forgive him for that."

"I know, Mama. Look, we talked and he explained to me his reasoning for leaving so abruptly and why it had to be; and I totally understood. Mama, you know how hung up on Marcus I was—and you were too, don't forget."

"Girl, this ain't about me."

"I hear you, but if Marcus had stayed I probably would not be as far in my career as I'm. My focus would have been all out of whack and who knows what else. Marcus leaving was for a good reason, even though I did not agree with at the time. Now that he is back, he and I were able to hash out the negative feelings, getting to the bottom of how we truly feel about each other and what we found is that we are still very much in love with each other."

"Jasmine, are you crazy? You don't decide to marry someone in a week, I don't care how much you think you love somebody. Don't get me wrong, I love Marcus too, he was a wonderful man and at one point I did think he would do right by you, but baby, you need time to sort things out; to really sit down and get to know him again. He's been gone a long time and people change."

Deep down I knew she was right; especially after all his recent lies and deceit. I was hard-pressed to disagree with her.

"So where is he, baby?"

"Well, there's more."

"There's more? More than you making a life-altering decision without my input?"

"Yeah, Mama, there is more. I'm leaving and moving to Europe with him."

"You're moving to where? Europe? Where in Europe?"

"France, Mama, he already prepared a place for me."

"I don't believe this—you're going to pack your things, leave your family, your friends, and the firm after only a week of thought?"

I looked deep into her eyes, which were filled with tears. "Mama, I have to do this, I love him and he loves me. If I don't do this now I'll never know what we could have had."

"Jasmine, this is way too much," Mama said.

The waitress appeared to take our orders. This break in our dramatic confrontation was definitely needed; I still had to figure out how to come at her with the embezzlement part of the saga.

I was so anxious I felt like it was eating me alive; I knew my mom felt the same. I hated to drop all of this on her. She was strong, but I was a big part of her strength. She had spent all of her life on my brother and me and a good portion of it was her living through us. I knew it was torture for her to hear me speak of leaving.

"I don't know, Jasmine—Europe is a long ways away; how am I supposed to get along without you?"

"Mom, I wouldn't be leaving right away and you know we are more than capable of flying you out anytime you want to come and visit."

"Yes, I guess." She paused, then said slowly, "It seems like you have your mind made up and you really do seem like a different person, happy . . . finally."

"I'm happy, Mommy, and you'll see it will all work out."

"But . . ." This was going to be the hardest part.

"But what, Jaz?"

I squeezed her hand gently. "Mom, Marcus is in jail right now."

"What? In jail? Why is he in jail?" The anger she was feeling showed all over face.

"I'm not really sure what's going on yet, but I'm going to get to the bottom of the situation, and I assure you, everything is going to be all right."

She snatched her hand away and started spewing a strange kind of venom all over me; it kind of felt as if Grandma Vera had showed up to take her place.

"How can you assure me of anything? You have no clue as to what's going on yourself! Girl, you have lost your mind. You must be crazy if you think I'm going to let you leave with someone who has obviously been lying to you. If you don't know what's going on, Ms. 'Top Lawyer,' then he has not changed; he is selfish, deceitful, and thinking of only himself. He has only been here a week, and once again has managed to turn *your* life upside down. Shit, you might be in trouble for just being around him."

I winced. Oh my God, is she psychic?

"Baby, this time I won't stand for it; I'm not going to let him do this to you again."

"Mom, please, I'm sure it is a huge mistake. I spoke with him for a moment and he said something about speaking with his boss to straighten everything out. As soon as I leave here I'm going down to the courthouse to get him released and to get the charges dropped. In fact an agent from the FBI wants to speak to me tomorrow morning and I'm sure it is to confirm his alibi. So relax, Ms. 'Top Lawyer' has this thing under control."

She was just about to launch her rebuttal when the waitress arrived with our food. Mama gave me a look I hadn't seen in years, a look that reminded me that she wasn't playing with me and whatever it was that I was doing I had better stop it right now.

She had no clue; she would never understand the love Marcus and I have for each other. She had always had a hard time with men because of her overly giving nature and at times it seemed as if the guys she was dating were just using her. As an adolescent I never knew what she knew about men or about dating. Since her and my father's divorce I only remember a few guys that hung around consistently. Maybe she was keeping them from us, not trying to involve them in our lives too much, or maybe she just hadn't found the right one. Either way I don't believe my mom ever felt the type of love I felt for Marcus. He was everything to me and regardless of what she said, I intended to stand by my man.

We spent the rest of our lunch eating in near-silence, occasionally playing a strange charade where we just talked about current events and family gossip, as if nothing was wrong. I knew Mama was confused and frustrated and I knew that she was plotting one more showdown with me before this was going to be considered a done deal. She usually had a pretty strong argument when it came to things that could possibly harm my brother or me, and in a normal situation I probably would have folded. But when it came to Marcus we both knew things were different. She had intentionally raised a very independent-minded child—she wanted to be sure I could and would stand up for myself if I needed to—but that, coupled with the fact that I was a notoriously stubborn Capricorn goat, meant that the fight she had ahead of her was not going to be easily won.

After we had finished, I went to the cashier to pay, while Mama gathered her things and headed for the door. She looked back at me and waited until I had caught up with her before walking out.

She turned and gently placed her hand on my shoulder. "Jasmine, listen—I know you think Marcus is it, and that's fine; but you have to be smart about this. Take your time, baby, there is no rush; you have plenty of time to plan your life, you are still young and if Marcus loves you the way he says he does, then he will wait until the time is right.

"Oh, and by the way, I am going with you tomorrow to meet with those FBI agents—just so you know."

I just shook my head and gave her a hug.

"All right, Mama, all right, Mama." I didn't want to upset her any more than I had.

"The meeting is scheduled for seven-thirty a.m. in Bloomington; I'll pick you up at seven so we can be sure to be on time."

"OK, Ms. Jasmine. You think about what I said and I'll see you in the morning, if I don't talk to you before then."

"All right, I'll see you."

# Chapter 52

I helped her into her car and closed her door, and as she waited for the oncoming traffic to pass so she could pull out into traffic, I thought about all the things she had said.

From a rational standpoint, she was right. What was really going on? Why was Marcus in jail and what else had he lied about?

A sick feeling in my stomach began to make its way up into my chest. Did I need to vomit? I ran back into the restaurant, almost knocking over the waitress, praying no one was in the bathroom. I opened the door to the first stall, and everything I had just consumed—not just the food, but Mama's tirade, the week's events, the jail, the FBI agents, everything—all came spewing out, landing me, and my sanity, in a sea of regret, unbelief, and chicken fajita salad.

Damn, this shit really got me twisted; I couldn't seem to keep anything down. I rinsed my mouth and stared at my watery eyes in the blurry restaurant mirror.

There had to be an explanation why I couldn't get this love thing right. I had seen it done before, so I knew it had to be possible. Why did there always seem to be a dark cloud hovering over my head whenever a man was concerned? Was I too needy, too quick to encase my view of love into a beautifully packaged fantasy? Maybe I just was not meant for love; maybe love and I were two different entities, never meant to meet.

All I had been through in what I considered love seemed to replay itself right before my eyes. My fictitious notion of love seemed to completely dissipate; I was falling fast, swallowed up by a belief that was now nonexistent. There was no chance of this working even if Marcus was innocent—who was I fooling? I had once again set myself up for failure, and everyone who truly loved me knew it too, and had tried to warn me. It was crazy; my insatiable need to be loved by some random man always took precedence over my true self; always blinded me with this perfect portrait of my life as I thought it should be. But unlucky me, here I'm again—all alone.

The reflection in the mirror changed; damn, here she is again. The woman in the mirror was no longer an image of me. Everything about her was different—her hair, her eyes; she purposely projected a sort of presence that consumed the entirety of space. She was larger than life, beaming confidence and grace, strength and fortitude. Everything about her represented something that was not like me. Nothing about her looked or felt familiar so when she appeared before I usually ignored her, except for the time she asked me about my love for Marcus. It seemed as if I only related to her when I wanted her to approve something I wanted to do, and I ignored her when it came to actually getting or doing something just or right. I looked at her closely, more closely than I had ever looked before, and this time something in me longed for her. I had always feared giving in to her, so my ego kept me from truly connecting. But now my ego had diminished, and I realized how much I needed her. How much my heart needed her. The tears once again resurfaced. She is so angry with me; I spoke to her this time.

"What am I supposed to do? I can't seem to make you happy." She looked back at me with unforgiving eyes,

"I messed up; I'm sorry—please forgive me." But when she looked at me I knew she was never going to forgive me this time.

I closed my eyes. One day she will be proud of me, and I won't have to look away when she beckons for my presence. One day she won't have to look at me with such disgust and contempt; one day she will love me, one day we will be one.

# Chapter 53

I DECIDED NOT TO GO back to the office and I even neglected to check on Marcus. I had to have some serious "me time," and one of the ways I got that was by going shopping. I never understood why shopping always made me feel better when I was feeling sorry for myself; I guess it must be the shopping endorphins, and finding the cutest Gucci handbag with matching sunglasses. I had heard that compulsive shopping was an addiction but at the point where the sales clerk was ringing up my bag it really didn't matter.

I walked into my apartment carrying so many bags that I almost didn't notice an envelope with my name on it. Someone must have slid it beneath doorsill. I set down my bags and flipped it over to see who it was from; nothing. I tore open the envelope, wondering who it could be from.

> *Ms. Burrell, you don't know me, but I know you. There are a few things you need to know before you meet with the FBI agents tomorrow. Let's just make this easy—you don't know anything. That's it; stick with that and everything will come out all right for you.*
>
> *Signed,*
> *A very close and personal friend of Marcus*

"What the hell?" I immediately went to the phone and dialed the front desk. I pay way too much money for this kind of shit to happen.

"Hello, this is Jasmine Burrell, may I please speak to Jonathan?"

"Hold, please."

"This is Jonathan. May I help you?"

"Jonathan, this is Jasmine. I found a note slipped underneath my door. Do you know anything about it?"

"Well Ms. Burrell, a gentleman came in today and asked if I would give the note to you. I figured you wouldn't be in until after my shift so I slid it under your door. Is there a problem?"

"Umm, no Jonathan, thank you. I thought maybe someone had got past security that was not supposed to be roaming around up here. There was no name on the note so I got suspicious. Could you describe him to me?"

"Well he was Caucasian, tall and thin, with short blond hair."

"Short like how? Crew-cut short?"

"Well, close to that Ms. Burrell. The sides were very short but there was a little more on the top."

"Was there anything else that stood out?"

"Well, yes, Ms. Burrell, he had the bluest eyes I have ever seen."

"OK, Jonathan. Thanks again. I appreciate your help."

"You're welcome."

I hung up the phone and studied the letter; there was nothing about it that helped me in any way. Someone was warning me not to get too involved, so maybe their intentions were good, but the fact that they seemed to know a lot about me made me nervous.

I called Tonya again to see what she knew.

I dialed her number and waited, praying silently that she'd answer.

"Hello, this Tonya."

"Hey Tonya, it's Jasmine."

"Hey Jasmine, how are you? I got your message. What's up, girl you sound pretty stressed out?"

"Tonya, girl, I really need your help. An FBI agent is questioning me tomorrow and I'm scared to death, I don't know what to do or what to say."

"Jasmine, calm down. Tell me what happened; did you do something?"

"No, I don't think so . . . well, let me tell you quickly what happened." I hesitated. "A friend of mine resurfaced this past week and as it turns out he has some pretty serious baggage he brought along with him. Tonya, he's in jail for some type of fraud and embezzlement scheme."

"So, if he's just a friend why has it been brought to you?"

"Well, he's more than a friend. He's my fiancé; while he was here he proposed to me and I agreed to marry him before all of this happened."

"Damn girl, what did he do to get a yes out of you? I know how you are about men so this brother must be the bomb."

"Tonya, honey, its Marcus."

"Oh my God. No, not my baby brother!"

You see, Tonya not only had FBI connections; she had Marcus connections. I just couldn't have left the message about Marcus on her voicemail; that would have been too cold. But it still felt terrible to have to be the one to break the news to her.

It was even harder, because Tonya and Marcus were very close in age, so close emotionally; and out of all of his sisters, Tonya was the nicest. She loved her brother almost to a fault and liked me a lot too. She had always said that we should have gotten married and was very upset with Marcus when he left, not just because he was leaving her and the family, but also because of the way he had done me.

"Jasmine, tell me all you know."

It was apparent that Marcus had not contacted any of his sisters or his parents while he was here and her fear and concern for her brother were mixed with anger and disappointment.

"Tonya, all I know is what I've told you, and now the FBI wants to speak with me and I don't have a clue what to do. They have him locked up at the courthouse with a hearing scheduled for Wednesday. He called me once but didn't say much, and then this evening I got home and there was a note under my door telling me I'm being watched and not to say anything about what Marcus and I did over the week. It was signed by someone claiming to be a friend of Marcus.

"Tonya, I really need your help, but I need your confidence in this. Please don't tell your family until I can get some more information on what's going on. I don't want to worry your parents unnecessarily."

"Neither do I, Jasmine; let me make some phone calls down to the bureau to see if I can find something out. I'll get back to as soon as I know something. Don't worry, Jasmine, I'm sure this is all a big mistake; Marcus is way too smart for this type of mess. Call you back in a few, OK?"

"OK Tonya, but please hurry. I'm going crazy over here."

"I know, sweetheart. I'm still in shock, but try not to worry. Everything is going to work out, I promise."

I hung up, trying to hang on to some shred of composure; there was no way I was going to make it through the night without having some sort of help. I looked towards the kitchen and realized my help was patiently waiting for me to call on them.

My kitchen stayed stocked with all types of liquor, from wine to the best of the hard stuff like Grey Goose and Tanqueray. I also kept a few bottles of flavored rum around, just in case someone wanted a girly daiquiri. Myself, I'd stopped drinking the frozen fruity stuff after trying my first martini. Now I made sure I had every liquor and mix necessary to make all different kinds I liked.

Tonight felt like a tequila night but I had already drunk the entire bottle of Patron the night before, so vodka martinis it was. I mixed a large shaker of vodka with a little fresh squeezed lemon juice, sugar and ice. I gave it a good shake and poured my first of many martinis I intended to have that night. There was no reason for me to sip, so I threw the first one back, eagerly awaiting the jolt to my system that would eventually blur all those sharp edges. I picked up the glass and shaker and headed to living room balcony. It was a beautiful evening; maybe a little air would help to clear my thoughts.

The second martini went down a little easier than the first, so I poured the third; just pouring it, I felt even better. There was enough liquor in my system that things seemed less scary; there was no doubt in my mind that once I had a chance to talk to Tonya again that my meeting with the FBI, Marcus' incarceration, my life—everything would be just fine. I sat in my favorite chair on the balcony staring at the sky, thinking about Marcus and our wedding day, which surely would happen once this terrible mistake got all straightened out. I slammed the third drink and floated to the kitchen to make another round.

As I poured once again, I heard a knock on the door; it must be Sadie. I slouched to the door and opened it.

"Hey girl," I smiled, glass in hand, speech slurred, eyes at half mast.

"Hey baby girl, how you doing?"

"I'm fine baby, just sitting here getting my drink on."

She followed me into the kitchen. I leaned back against the countertop, not realizing it was several inches further back than I expected. Sadie saw what was happening and grabbed the glass out of my hand as I slammed backwards into the edge of the granite countertop.

"Jasmine, are you all right? Girl, how much have you had to drink?"

"I'm fine, I just lost my balance. Give me back my drink."

"I don't know, girl, you seem a little over the top."

"Look, sweetheart, I'm cool. I just need something to calm me down. Do you want me to make you a martini?"

"No, I'll just have a glass of wine, and I know where it is; you have a seat."

I reached for the barstool and sat down. A sharp pain in my back was an unwanted reminder of how out control I was, but right then I didn't care. The vodka was my fiancé now and I wanted him. I sat back and sipped on my drink, waiting for Sadie to get herself a glass of wine. Then I remembered I had Apple Pucker in the cabinet so I figured time for a change, time for apple martinis now.

Sadie watched warily as I filled the shaker with more vodka, the green stuff this time, and a few ice cubes. As I shook the drink she looked at me cross-eyed.

"Is there a problem?" I asked her, feeling a little defensive.

"I don't know, is there?" she said, the question hanging in the air like a dare.

"Well, you looking at me funny so I thought you might have something on your mind."

"The only thing on my mind, Jaz, is the glass in your hand and the way you're handling this situation. I thought we were going to work through this together—but with you sitting up here drunk, how do you expect me to help you?"

"Look Sadie, I'm not drunk, I'm just feeling good. We can talk about anything, in fact this way you'll get all the dirt you need so you can run and tell the girls what's really going on. Like I know you're itching to do."

I jumped down from the stool and stumbled toward the living room. Sadie grabbed me and looked at me with disgust.

"Look, bitch—and I mean this in the most sincere way possible—I'm not your enemy. I did nothing to you, so you can miss me with all this animosity bullshit. Marcus is the one who did this to you, neither the girls nor I had anything to do with your pain, so you are not going to take this shit out on us."

I looked at her, her eyes flashing, standing firm; the tears were streaming down my face now. I dissolved.

"Sadie, I'm sorry, I don't mean to take this out on you. You're my best friend in the world and I didn't mean to hurt you. I'm so confused, what am I going to do? I love him!"

"I know, baby and I'm going to do everything in my power to help you through this, no matter what the outcome." Her grip on my arm loosened and she enfolded me in her arms. I started crying even harder.

"Sadie I don't think I can live without him, if he goes to jail...."

"Don't say that, sweetie, we're going to get him out of there and everything is going to be fine."

"Sadie I don't know about that, I got this note today. Here, read it."

I fished it out of my pocket, gave Sadie the note and waited for her response. "Jasmine, where did this come from?"

"It was underneath my door when I got home."

"Jasmine, this is very strange and kind of scary."

"I know, Sadie, that's why I'm tripping; I called Marcus' sister Tonya and she's going to call the bureau to see if she can find out what's up. The note is creepy as hell, I don't know if I should report it or what."

"Well, Jaz, let's just wait to see what Tonya says; she's got to have some information for you."

"I sure hope so, Sadie. This is really getting out of hand."

I walked to the living room and sat down on the sofa, Sadie settling next to me. The phone rang and I jumped.

"Hello?"

"Jaz? This is Tonya."

"Hey, Tonya, what did you find out?"

"Jasmine, it doesn't look good. They've had wiretaps and computer infiltration on him for some time now. It seems as if Marcus was funneling money from several clients into separate offshore accounts. The company numbers were so large, I guess he assumed no one would miss the little bit he was taking. But the company had set up dummy corporations as a catch and Marcus for whatever reason got caught."

I couldn't say anything. I just sat there, dreading what she might say next.

"Baby, I don't know what to say about his mess, but you just need to tell the truth. They don't know a lot about you as far as this case goes, I think they're just grasping at straws where you're concerned, so be careful and don't give them anything extra. You know how to do it, counselor."

"Yes I do, Tonya, and thank you so much. I will do my best."

I couldn't believe I could even formulate words, much less seem so calm; it was as if someone had taken over for me so I could function, while inside I was still stunned.

"As far as Marcus is concerned, will he be getting out on Wednesday?" I asked her.

"Well, they're setting his bail at five hundred thousand dollars, and the only way I see getting him out on that is if I tell Mom and Dad. They're going to have to post bail for him to get out. I don't have that kind of money."

"Tonya, I do. Don't tell your mom and dad yet until I've talked to him and have worked out his defense."

"Are you sure you want to do this, Jasmine?" Tonya asked me. Her voice was as somber as I'd ever heard her.

"Yes Tonya, he's my fiancé and yes, I love him very much. I would do anything to save him."

"OK, Jaz. Don't do anything yet—remember, you're not to know this information."

"I know, Tonya; I'll play it cool until Wednesday's court date. As for tomorrow, Tonya, all I can say is what I know, which is not very much."

"All right, I'm going to leave it in your hands for now. Take your time, they'll try to trip you up every chance they get, so just listen to the questions and give as little information as possible."

"OK, I got it. I'll call you as soon as I'm done."

"Good luck. Oh, and make sure you pray before you go in to speak."

"Girl, I know that's right. Prayer—never leave home without it."

Even though I hadn't been to church in forever, I still really believed in prayer. Besides, in this situation, I knew prayer and God were my only hope.

## Chapter 54

I filled Sadie in on what Tonya and I discussed, and we used the rest of the night to strategize. We decided I would play the sweet, innocent role, leaving nothing to chance. I figured I would maintain as much of the truth as possible—that was the best way not to get caught in lie. And besides, I really hadn't had anything to do with him for the past four years, except for this past week. Anyway, I would answer only when asked, they would have to take only, and exactly, what I gave them. Being an attorney would really pay off, which I knew they would probably try to use against me; that's why matching wits with them would be so important—got to get to them before they get me.

The plan was set. I had to do my best to get Marcus out, and I intended to do what it took.

Sadie agreed, and decided she could go home. I walked her to the door and kissed her good-bye. I told her that Mom was going with me so it wasn't necessary for her to come. I would be all right, I reassured her, and said I would call her as soon as I was finished.

By this time the liquor was finally wearing off and I felt like I could finally sleep. I felt better having a plan, but I was a little anxious about seeing Marcus. I knew if I spoke to the agents they would understand it was all a huge mistake, and this whole thing would be all over, they would free him and we would continue with our life together, just like we planned it.

I set the alarm for five-thirty because I wanted a little more time to pray and meditate on God. I just felt like He was going to work it out. I hummed a few bars of one of the hymns

I remembered from church, and headed to the bathroom for a quick shower before bed.

And before I drifted off to sleep that night, I said a few words, beginning with "Our Father who art in heaven, hallowed be thy name..."

My phone rang two minutes before the alarm was scheduled to go off. I knew it must be Mama so I jumped up and answered it without looking at the caller ID.

"Hey, Mama," I said sleepily.

"Is this Jasmine Burrell?" I didn't recognize the voice.

"Who's calling?"

"Is this Jasmine Burrell?

"Yes this is, who's calling?" I said again, more sharply.

"I have a message for you from a Marcus Damon."

My heart stopped. "Yes, yes what is the message?"

"I was told to tell you not to worry and to just tell the truth to the FBI agents. He also said to tell you he loves you and he is sorry."

"He's sorry? What do you mean he's sorry?"

"That's all, miss."

"Wait, wait, could you tell him I love"—but the caller hung up before I could finish.

I was feeling like a character in a creepy movie; how does he know I have to speak to an FBI agent? There is some really strange shit going on and I had to get to the bottom of it.

The alarm was now blaring, the sound mixing with the confusion swirling in my head, an especially bad combination especially after all of those martinis. I shut off the alarm and called Mama.

She picked up after two rings.

"Hey Mama, I was just calling to make sure you're up."

"Yes baby, you know I'm up, been up since four-thirty."

"You're still waking up early like that?"

"Yeah, baby, I don't know what it is, I just can't sleep some nights."

"Well, what do you think about getting breakfast before we go?"
"That's fine, what time should I be ready?"
"Can you be ready by six-fifteen?"
"Yes, I'll be waiting."
"OK, I'll call you when I'm out front."
"All right, Jaz. See you in a little bit."

Just like that, we discussed it as if we were talking about getting together for lunch, or for a little shopping outing. I hung up the phone and headed for the shower; I was already semi-hung-over, and the weird phone call, along with what I knew was coming in the next couple of hours had me on edge. Everything I learned in college and beyond about stress control just wasn't working.

I suddenly realized, as I was walking toward the shower, that I really had no choice; I had to call upon the only one who could really help me.

As I took off my pjs and got into the shower, I prayed silently, searching for the right questions to ask God and listening hard for the answers. As I got out of the shower, I felt like the prayer had refreshed my soul just as the warm water streaming down had cleansed my body, and I felt like the thoughts ricocheting in my brain seemed to slow down, maybe even organize themselves; I began to feel like there was the possibility of some semblance of control.

He was with me and I could feel Him, His presence took over, leading me on a journey that challenged everything in me I felt was strong. I wept and knew all things would work in God's favor. I knew God loved me, even if I just couldn't understand why. I had never really completely submitted to God before, I was always half in and half out and finally coming to grips with this realization left me naked, and I cringed, finally seeing myself as I truly was. Clothed and hiding—there was no way I was coming out of this without it being God's will.

Finally, there were no more tears left to cry. I dressed and headed to get Mama. I felt confident for the first time since this whole ordeal began, because this time I really prayed and I knew God was not going to let me down.

I was so calm that when Mama got in the car she wondered what was wrong with me. I explained to her: I had prayed and God had told me everything was going to be all right, so not to worry.

She nodded but said nothing. I could tell by her silence she was scared and trying to keep it from me. We drove most of the way without talking.

The restaurant was relatively empty; Mama and I sat in a corner booth and talked about the case and my planned responses. We figured they would try anything to get to me, so she was going to stay with me to keep me cool. They'd have no chance if Mama stayed with me, she was my rock and I knew if anyone had my back she did, no matter what.

We ate a quick breakfast and as we headed for the car. Mama looked at me. I knew exactly what she was thinking. I nodded and she smiled.

"It's going to be all right, baby," Mama said. "It's going to be all right." And this time for some reason I totally believed it.

When we arrived at the FBI building, I parked in the two-hour visitor parking space, figuring there was no way I was going to be there longer than that. I had no information to give them, and on top of that I wasn't going to volunteer anything at all, so presumably it would be a short interview. Mama and I approached the front desk and asked for Tom Boskel. The blond receptionist asked us to take a seat in the lobby, assuring us "Mr. Boskel will be with you soon." I could hear her whispering into the telephone as she alerted Mr. Boskel that I was here. I sat down and picked up an old Time magazine and flipped through the pages. When I looked up, I saw a familiar face approaching.

Oh my God. It was the Ice Cube lookalike who had arrested Marcus.

As the agent came closer, I could feel the presence of the Lord slipping away; please don't leave me, I begged Him. Then, as the agent introduced himself, fear took over.

"Hello, Ms. Burrell, my name is Tom Boskel. I'm with the FBI."

I nodded and shook his hand. "And you are?" He turned towards my mother.

"This is my mother, Bernadette Burrell," I said. Mama turned towards him and firmly shook his hand. I had seen that look in her eye before; it was the look she had when she nearly beat down the chaplain at my brother's elementary school for God knows what reason.

"Hello," she replied, never taking her eyes off of him.

"Nice to meet you both. Ms. Burrell, will you follow me to the back room?"

I informed him that my mother was coming with me. He stopped, turned, and looked at the both of us. "Oh, she is?"

"Yes, she is," I said firmly.

"Well, I thought there might be some things you might not want to talk about in front of your mother."

"No, I tell my mother everything, she knows everything about me."

"Are you sure?"

"Yes I'm sure."

"Look, Mr. Boskel," my mother broke in. "I'm not leaving. I'm going right into that room with my daughter."

He stared at her suspiciously; then, with a smug, "it don't matter she's guilty anyway" shrug, he turned again and continued down the hall. "All right, suit yourselves."

He walked us to a room with three chairs and a big wooden table.

The room was a bit chilly—because of the air conditioner, but also the frost coming off of Mr. Boskel. He was a cold piece and I could see in his eyes he wasn't going to cut me any slack.

The questioning began. Surprisingly, I had most of the answers. Well, not surprisingly, when I thought about it—I felt like God had given me the words to say. Then Mr. Boskel asked me again if I wanted to speak to him without my mother present. I told him she was staying.

He continued his questioning. If I didn't know the answers I told him straight. At one point, he went as far as to ask me where

Marcus was keeping the bulk of the money he took. He hinted that they could cut me in on some of the money, a couple of hundred thousand if I could tell him where it money was.

I had to laugh. "No, Mr. Boskel, I don't know where his money is."

He seemed to accept my answer at face value, as he had done throughout the entire session. Finally, after what seemed like ages, he stood up.

"Well, Ms. Burrell we're done here. Thank you for your time and I will keep in touch. Here is my card if you think of any other information you would like to give me."

"OK, thank you. It was nice meeting you," I said, even though it really hadn't been nice at all. But at least it wasn't as horrible as I imagined it could be.

He shook my hand, then my mother's, and directed us to the lobby.

We walked out of the building as fast as we could; when we got to the car we both thanked God.

When I got to the car, the first person I called was Tonya. She seemed relieved that my interview seemed to have gone well, but she was still worried. She told me she had decided she had to tell her mom and dad because she was risking getting herself into some serious trouble with them if they somehow found out from someone else. I agreed, but reminded her that I was going to be working the case with some of the best lawyers in town and that I had already planned to secure his bail. She thanked me and once again reassured me that everything was going to be OK.

God had come through for me, I could feel it. Marcus was going to be out on bail and he would be able to tell me what really happened and we would put all of this behind us and move towards our future. For the first time in what seemed like forever, I smiled, feeling now that maybe everything was going to be all right.

I dropped Mama off after I called Tonya. On the way back, I decided to stop off at my favorite coffee shop. I didn't mention it to Mom because she would have wanted to come, but I needed the time to deprogram and strategize. The SunnysideUp Café was just the right place for it. It was quiet and discreet and I could get a lot of thinking done. I had major work ahead of me and I had to be sure I was on top of my game. God had given me a reprieve and I was going to be prepared for whatever came my way.

I took the newspaper I had just purchased, my journaling notebook, and my favorite pen and sat down at a table toward the back. The waitress came and I ordered a cup of coffee with extra cream and sugar. I paged through the paper looking for the feature and entertainment section; I hadn't looked at the crossword puzzle in over a week now, and I was starved for the peace and relaxation that the puzzles gave me. It was Tuesday, so the puzzle was going to be relatively easy.

But I couldn't concentrate on the puzzle. I set it aside, and turned my attention to what I had to do: Marcus and his case. I took out my notepad and wrote down everything I knew that had happened in chronological order. The day the pendant arrived, when I received the first phone call, down to the day they handcuffed Marcus and took him away from me.

Nothing that I saw on paper made sense: Why would he deliberately come to Minnesota to woo me, knowing full well he was involved in this serious criminal activity? I sat there in a daze for a while, then I picked up my coffee. It was cold now, but I didn't care; I drained it in one gulp. Then I got up, and left the money on the table, grabbed all my things and headed for the courthouse. I was going to speak to Marcus, and this time he was going to answer.

# Chapter 55

THE COURTHOUSE WAS FULL OF people, all kinds; black, white, Latino, most of whom I'm sure dreaded being there. It wasn't surprising that the ratio of minorities to whites was always the same—way more minorities than whites. It seemed as if the powers that be had a certain quota to meet, and the people of color were always there to fill it. It was sad how listless everyone seemed—it almost made me lose hope for my own goals. I had forgotten how depressing the intake floor could be, watching all those people waiting to learn their inevitable fate. I always assumed if you were in that room then you had some issues to be resolved, and no matter what you did, you always felt guilty until proven innocent.

I shuffled my way through the waiting crowd, trying not to draw attention to myself; I knew some of them knew who I was, but I didn't have time, let alone the energy, to answer any question about anyone's case. I reached Harold, one of the courthouse guards I knew, and asked him if he could bring Marcus to one of the holding rooms; he nodded, and motioned for me to go through the door and wait there.

Sitting in the holding room, sweat poured down my spine. I had no idea what this meeting would bring but I needed to have it. I needed to see him, look into his eyes, and feel his presence—to know he was innocent.

The door opened, and Harold stood there—without Marcus. I jumped to my feet. "Where is he?" I screamed.

"I'm sorry Ms. Burrell, Mr. Damon was transferred this morning."

"Transferred to *where*?"

"He was transferred to a federal prison in South Dakota."

"What? What are you talking about?"

"Look, Ms. Burrell, that's all I know. You need to speak to someone else about all of this."

Harold closed the door; the emptiness in the room couldn't come close to matching the emptiness in my chest. A caustic chill slowly and meticulously wrapped itself around my throat, squeezing tighter and tighter. I began to cry.

\* \* \*

Instead of trying to find Marcus I drove home. My head hurt, my stomach was queasy and my heart was broken. Why was God punishing me like this? I didn't understand. Once again, God had betrayed me; he had set me up and let me fall.

When I arrived home, I went straight to the bathroom, passing the Footsteps poem hanging in the hallway. The poem was a conversation between God and a man who has come to see him. God revealed to the man the vision of them walking together, with two sets of footprints. But when the hardest times in the man's life appeared, there was only one set. When the man asked why God had left him during the most difficult times in his life, God told him, "My son, I did not leave you. It was at those times I carried you."

It always resonated, instantly calming me; but this time as I stopped to read the words, I didn't feel the same.

"This is bullshit!" I screamed, snatching the painting and throwing it to the floor. I heard it crash as shards of glass flew about my feet, and the corner of the heavy metal frame gouged a divot out of my hardwood floor. I smirked; I didn't care. From now on I'm doing me, whatever *I* wanted.

I poured myself a glass of vodka, added a little orange juice, and downed it in one long, deep swallow.

# Chapter 56

I AWOKE TO THE PHONE ringing; I hadn't planned on going to work, but I had forgotten to call Wendy to let her know. I was in such a state of shock that my family, my friends, and especially my job no longer made sense. If I couldn't be happy in love, then what else was there? The soothing feeling of vodka flowing through my veins had dissipated overnight, and I let the voicemail pick up the call, as I hustled to the kitchen to find my salvation. I opened the freezer door and retrieved the bottle of Grey Goose; surprisingly, there was still a good third of a bottle left.

A glass seemed like it would take too much time, so I tilted my head back and let the icy liquid trickle down my throat, instantly soothed. All of a sudden, things seemed clear again: Yes, I was in love—but with a man, no way. It was the vodka that had me sprung now and nothing or no one was going to change that.

I glanced at the caller ID on my kitchen phone and saw that it was a call from the district attorney's office. I snatched up the receiver and frantically punched in the number.

"Teri Jorgenson's office."

"Hello, this is Jasmine Burrell, may I please speak to Teri Jorgenson?"

"Hold one moment, please."

I listened to the annoying elevator music coming through the phone while I tipped the bottle almost vertically, draining what was left. In mid-swallow, I heard someone answer again.

"Hello, this is Teri."

I gulped down the last few drops, and tried to catch my breath. "Hello? Um, hey Teri, this is Jasmine Burrell. I just got a call from your office and assumed it was you."

"Yes, Jasmine—I wasn't sure if you were aware of what was going on with Marcus Damon's case?"

"Well, no, Teri, I don't know what's going on. I heard something about him being transferred to South Dakota. What happened?"

"After we spoke with Mr. Damon and explained the evidence we had against him, he decided to plead guilty to a lesser charge, and he also gave us information on how he was able to embezzle the money and where the accounts were located. He requested to be sent straight to the federal prison as soon as possible, waiving any rights. We were able to get him out on the first flight to the South Dakota federal correctional facility. He didn't ask to speak to an attorney or want to have an attorney present. We presented him with that option but as I said, he waived everything."

"I don't understand, how long is he supposed to be *there*?"

"That's all I have; you may want to speak with his family or his co-workers, they might have more information for you."

"OK, thank you, Teri. I'll check on things from this end. I really appreciate the information."

"You're welcome, Jasmine. I know that he was a good friend of yours and I just wanted to make sure you knew what was going on. You have a nice day."

"I'll try. Thanks again."

I hung up. He pleaded guilty; why would he do that? Was he actually guilty?

There was no turning back now. I had already drained the bottle of Grey Goose; I headed towards the kitchen for a bottle of wine. It didn't matter that it was nine-thirty in the morning. It mattered even less that I was mixing vodka and wine; and the fact that I hadn't eaten anything made it even sweeter. The quicker I could get my high on, the better.

I found the corkscrew in the utility drawer and began twisting out the cork. The smell of the Black Opal shiraz was a welcoming and familiar scent. I really loved wine and intended to enjoy this bottle as if were my last. I took the bottle and stretched out on the couch. I flicked on the flat-screen and began to channel-check. At the rate I was going, I was going to be good and drunk by noon, which was all right with me. I decided to turn off all my phones and spend sometime with myself.

I figured out long ago when I was drinking red wine that if I gulped deeply, I could literally feel the warmth of the wine coursing through my body and numbing my senses—which is what I wanted, to be totally and completely numb. I smiled in spite of myself.

Then it hit me. "Damn, I know what I really need; I need a joint."

I hadn't smoked weed in a long time—I couldn't even remember the last time—but now I was craving its potent calming effect. I picked up my phone and called my boy Drake.

Drake was a cool-ass brother I had met at the car wash about a year and a half ago. I was vacuuming my Benz while he was washing a classic peanut-butter-colored Chevy Caprice Classic; it was so clean I had to ask him where he got it. His laid-back aura intrigued me right away. He was a roughneck for sure—and he was fine as hell: a beautiful brother, with a well-sculpted nicely shaped beard and gorgeous eyes. His chocolate skin made his eyes sparkle and the gleam in his smile radiated for miles. Over the next year we developed a real friendship. He was smart and very articulate. He had worked in the mortgage business for a while, but was hit hard when the real estate industry collapsed. He sold weed on the side to make ends meet, but was really trying to start his own company. The fact that he sold weed didn't bother me, he was discreet, and always professional even if it was an illegal substance he was selling.

He picked up after a couple of rings.

"What up, Ma?" "Ma" was an endearing new word that men had picked up from the East Coast and started using. I guess it was short for "Mammi."

"Hey, Drake, what you up to?"
"Nothing, girl. How have you been?"
"Man, Drake, I've been better."
"So what can I do for you, Ma?"
"I need you stop by—can you come right now?"
"Uh yeah—well, in about an hour."
"Come on, Drake, you know your hours be more like two days."
"Ha ha, you're funny, girl. What you need?"
"Not a whole lot, something small."
"All right, Ma, I'll be there in a little while."
"Drake?"
"Yes, Ma?"
"Drake? Don't take all day; I ain't gonna be waiting on you."
"I know Jaz, I'll be there."

I really liked Drake, but we were just friends. I had never thought about sex with him, even though I knew for a fact he had a nice-size package—I could tell by the way he walked and stood, the brother was packin'.

I hung up the phone and continued sipping my wine. I was feeling really saucy and better than I had felt for a long time. It was time for me to get off my ass and do some new shit. The tired-ass church-girl act was already old again and I wanted some excitement—shit, I *needed* some excitement. I knew just what I was about to do. I bathed, brushed my teeth and began searching.

When I heard the knock my nerves suddenly went haywire. I ran to the mirror and looked deep, searching for the woman who always showed up when I was about to do something crazy. I didn't see her. After all I'd been through in the last few weeks, I knew she didn't really and truly have my back either—so now what?

It's on and poppin'. I calmed myself and made myself slowly walk to the door.

"Hey, Drake."

He stopped for a minute, taking in my midnight-blue negligee and the four-inch pumps I was wearing. From his half-cocked smile and expression on his face I knew he was shook—and that my outfit was having the desired effect.

"What's up, Jaz?" He tried to sound casual.

"Nothing. Come on in."

I smiled. "You like what you see?"

"Hell yeah—but what are you doing?"

"Something I probably should have done long time ago."

"And what's that?" he asked—I couldn't tell if he was trying to be coy, or trying to avoid the obvious.

"You know what that is, boy, don't play stupid with me. You got my weed?"

"Of course I do. You want to smoke some now? I got a blunt already rolled."

"Hell yeah, boo, fire that shit up."

I walked Drake to the living room and as he settled onto the couch, I lit a candle and long stick of Egyptian musk incense. I made sure he got a nice view of my ass as I bent over to pull out an ashtray. I sat down next to him as close as I could get without sitting directly on his lap, then I took his lighter from his hand and lit the chronic-filled blunt he held between his soft, full lips. I used the evil eye as he inhaled my insatiable long-lost friend, but it seemed like my look wasn't doing its job, because he stared back at me with a seductive look all his own. I held his gaze as I took the blunt from his hand, then saw his eyes flicker over at the half-empty wine bottle.

"Jaz, have you been drinking already this morning?"

"Why, yes I have. And?"

Drake was not much of a drinker; every now and again he would indulge in a little Hennessey but overall liquor was not his thing; weed was.

"I don't know, Jaz, this seems to be a little much. Are you sure you know what you are doing?"

"Of course I do, Drake, I wouldn't have called you to come over if I didn't know what I was doing."

"Hey, Ma, you know what, baby? I think I'm going to leave. I see you had a little bit too much to drink and after you smoke this weed I know what's up, and I value our friendship way too much to take advantage of you in any way. But, check, don't get me wrong, on another day when you're not drunk and I'm not super-high I would love to oblige you—in fact, it would be my pleasure to pleasure you. OK, Ma?"

I looked into his eyes, and then I dropped my gaze. I knew he was right, and I was feeling a little embarrassed about the way I was acting.

"Drake, I'm sorry I don't know what has gotten into me. Thank you."

"It's all good; I like you—I like you a lot, and I don't want to jeopardize our relationship."

"Hold on, Drake, I'm a run put something on."

"Oh hold on, Jaz—you don't have to do that, do you?" He smiled; I smiled harder.

"I'll be right back, sweetheart."

As I ran to the bedroom to throw on some jeans and a T-shirt, I noticed I was still wearing my engagement ring. I took it off and placed it in my jewelry chest; I wasn't sure if he noticed it, but if he did he didn't say anything. I figured he probably knew I was having man troubles, and because he was such a thoughtful person he just left it alone.

I went back to Drake and we smoked weed, laughed, and talked for the rest of the morning and well into the afternoon; his cell phone was ringing, but he didn't answer it.

I was glad to have him there with me. The conversation and just his voice was so soothing that I felt good—so good that I felt myself nodding. We lay back against the sofa and I nuzzled his chest and he held me as I drifted off to sleep.

When I awoke, Drake was gone and I was snuggled up under the throw blanket I kept on my bed; against all the odds, it had turned out to be a really nice day. Still high and a little groggy, I thought about Drake and his gentleness in my time of need. I hadn't told him about Marcus, but it seemed as if he already knew. What was even odder was that out of all the people I could have called, Drake was someone who, although he did his dirt on the side, was a very strong believer. His true heart and spirit lived there and our unwavering belief had always created a bond between us.

Damn. Had God set me up?

As I stood there, surveying the room and into the hallway, I realized the floor was clean. I walked over to where the painting had been—the glass was all gone, and the painting was lying face-up on the hallway credenza. I read the poem again, and for the first time, it seemed, I really understood it meant. God had not left me—in fact, He had sent Drake to carry me. I slid to the floor, sobbing.

## Chapter 57

"Kevin," I shook him, "Kevin, shut off the alarm."
Kevin Owens was so fine, when I looked at him, lying there naked, totally quiet and at peace, I knew I had happened into a wondrous dream.

"Good morning, baby." I kissed him gently on the lips and ran my fingers through the softness of his black curly hair. *Damn, he looked so good."*

I had to be at work by but I couldn't resist him. I pulled the bed covers off him and climbed on top of him, softly stroking, licking, and touching the warmth of his caramel body. I loved the way he looked. I lowered myself on top of him and slowly moved towards the foot of the bed to position myself over is manhood, which was now beautifully firm. I kissed him there and placed him in my mouth, using my tongue and jaw muscles to gently but firmly massage him to excitement. I could tell by his soft moans that he was enjoying me as much as I was enjoying him.

For some reason I enjoyed giving him head. Maybe it was the satisfaction I got from being with such a fine specimen or maybe I was just horny; either way, Kevin was it. He pulled me up to face him and kissed me, guiding his eight inches, into the folds of my throbbing wetness. I loved when he made love to me—his beauty matched with his sensual nature made sex amazing. He had ignited in me a new flame, one that I finally accepted.

After losing Marcus, the incredible yearning for love in my life became irresistible. I had spent the first two years of Marcus' incarceration trying to convince myself that I was waiting for him. But after he pleaded guilty to a lesser crime, and still received more than eight years, my faith in God and my faith in the system had been challenged. There was no way a first-time offender with a mere traffic ticket on his record should receive that sort of time—and there was no way God would take him from me . . . again.

But He had. Everything that I had always lived and believed was shattered. I covered it all up with a martini and smile.

Marcus and I kept in contact through sporadic phone calls, letters, and cards at holidays. But as time passed the infrequency of our contact hardened my heart as well as my commitment. I had met a few men who I had tried to get next to, but it always failed miserably.

So when Kevin re-entered my life after our meeting long ago through Sadie, I thought, this is absolutely my last try. Kevin was fine—how could anyone that fine hurt me? He was successful, and so suave that I just knew he would be drama-free. And because he was a close friend of Sadie, I believed he would genuinely care about me.

Running into Kevin at a private party for one of Sadie's clients was inevitable; she had been trying to get me together with him for the longest time, and finally she had done it.

When I walked into the ballroom at the Hilton, I knew I was in trouble. Kevin was standing directly in my line of view and he noticed me as soon as I had noticed him. He was wearing a black-on-black Armani suit with a crisp white shirt that fit him perfectly; he looked as if he had just walked off the cover of "GQ."

I was instantly nervous. I looked at myself in the ballroom mirrors; I had worn my cream-colored Dolce and Gabbana halter dress, sequined, and matching pearl-lined sling backs. I was happy to see that I was looking pretty damn, good. I straightened up and tried to build up my nerve.

He glided towards me as if he was floating on air, and every shred of courage I had just drummed up flew out of my body, dissipating into thin air. I tried to smile but it felt like my entire body had gone into an involuntary state of rigor mortis. I wanted to run, but couldn't move. I took a deep breath and waited for him to approach.

"Hello, Ms. Burrell, how are you tonight?"

"Oh, hey Kevin, I'm fine. How are you?"

"I can see that you're fine; I asked how you were doing."

My flushed expression gave him the answer. But he just smiled, letting me know he was truly feeling me. He took my hand. "Would you like a drink?"

His touch was so soft, and coupled with the look in his eyes, it made even the simplest questions complicated.

I swallowed hard. "Yes, that would be nice."

"What can I get for you?"

"I'll have an apple martini, please."

"I'll be right back—don't disappear."

I giggled like a giddy schoolgirl. "I won't; I'll be right here."

He kissed my hand and headed for the bar.

I thought I would just crumple into a heap right there, my physical reaction was so overwhelming. OK, girl, keep your cool; he is just a man, nothing special. But as I watched him walk away the soft wetness between my legs was whispering something else. It had been a long time since I had been with a man, and my body was betraying me, as usual.

As I waited for Kevin to return, I spotted Sadie—and she spotted me. She grinned slyly as Kevin handed me the drink. She sauntered up to us, patting Kevin on the back. Then she welcomed me with a big hug, whispering in my ear, "Get him, girl."

I shook my head and motioned for her to get the hell away from me. She turned away laughing. I turned my face away from Kevin so he couldn't see. I silently mouthed the words "I'm going to kill you" as she trotted away. Then I turned to thank Kevin for the drink.

He nodded, then asked if I wanted to sit down. He gestured for me to lead, and as I walked ahead him he placed his hand on the small of my back. I hoped he hadn't felt me shudder, but I knew he could feel me shivering. We sat at one of the small tables in the back and that's where my new fairytale began.

## Chapter 58

WE LAUGHED AND TALKED FOR most of the night. He was such a gentleman, smooth, suave and very seductive. At one point, he motioned to the dance floor and I happily agreed. The DJ had been playing old-school music all night and when I heard Luther Vandross' "If Only for One Night" start up—one of my favorite songs—I thought the night couldn't get any better. He led me to the dance floor, wrapped his arms around my waist as I placed my hands around his neck, and he pulled me close. Suddenly, a feeling—wonderful yet frightening—enveloped me, and took me to a place I hadn't been in a long time. He was so fine and he smelled even better. I relaxed and laid my head in the crease in his neck, but inside I felt like screaming. All the emotions and the several martinis I had caught up to me. I was finally feeling uninhibited and free.

"So, Kevin what are your plans for this evening?"

He pulled back and looked me in the eyes, "Well, Jasmine, I was hoping my plans this evening included spending more time with you."

That stupid grin I always tried to hide had a mind of its own, and despite all my efforts, I could feel it spreading across my face. "We could leave here and go back to my place."

Had I said that out loud? Oh my God, what are you doing?

He moved his hand from my waist and caressed the back of my neck and asked where I had parked my car. I told him I had left it with the valet. He asked for the ticket and told me to go tell Sadie we were leaving. I immediately agreed, as if I had no mind of my own. I found Sadie, who was posted up with this fine-ass dark-skinned brother and excused her from her company.

"What up, chick?"

"Um, Kevin and I are leaving."

"Oh, you are? She grinned so hard she reminded me of the Cheshire cat from "Alice in Wonderland.""

"Bitch, shut up, I know you set me up."

"Jaz, what are you talking about? I had nothing to do with this."

"Whatever, heifer, I'm'a get you back."

"You ain't gonna get me back, he getting ready to get yo back." She laughed, louder than I could stand.

"Shut up, ho, best believe I'm gonna kick your ass later."

"I know, nigga, just go, and get some for me."

I gave her the evil eye and a smile. As I walked away I could hear her hootin' and hollerin', and in spite of myself, I couldn't help but laugh.

When I got outside, both my car and Kevin's car were waiting. He was driving a brand-new black Ford Probe GT Coupe with beautifully chromed twenty-two-inch rims. I could hear the Notorious BIG bumping from his back seat and realized we had the same taste in music. He had already paid and tipped the valet for both our cars and proceeded to open the door for me. I thanked him and got in.

"Just follow me," I said.

He smiled. "I'll follow you anywhere."

I drove through the streets of Minneapolis over-thinking, analyzing, and plotting the night ahead. I had made up in my mind that I wasn't going to sleep with Kevin, but hadn't figured out yet how I intended to accomplish this feat. With sex appeal oozing from every pore in his body, and my own magnified level of my horniness, I knew that it was going to be damn, hard to keep my composure. Then it hit me—I'll put in a movie or something. That could give me time to get my own hormones in check; maybe then I could resist any of his advances, obvious or otherwise.

I drove on, completely confident in my decision. This is gonna be cool; I can handle this, I thought.

We parked in the underground garage of my apartment, and I got out to wait for him so we could take the elevator up. But the way he walked towards me turned me on so much I had to make myself think about something else, like quantum physics.

He opened the door that led to the lobby and I slowly walked through, eyeing him warily and grinning slightly, hoping I wouldn't give my nervousness away. He followed me to the elevators and I pressed the up button. I could see out of the corner of my eye the woman working at the concierge desk and the older lady she was talking to, looking him up and down. I smiled, thinking, Yeah, bitches; he's with me.

We silently entered the elevator, both looking directly in front of us, neither saying nor doing anything. We rode the elevator in silence. I was trying to gauge his demeanor, but through his calmness, I was at a loss. So, feeling like I had to break the awkward silence, I asked him if he was having a good evening. He smiled and his pearly whites damn, near blinded me.

"Yes, I'm having a wonderful evening. And you?"

"Actually, this is one of the best nights I've had in a long time."

"Good."

He took my hand as the doors were opening and we walked hand-in-hand to my apartment.

As he walked in, he glanced around and nodded his head in approval.

"What do you think?"

"Very nice, you really have great taste."

"Thank you, I try." There was another awkward silence, then: "Would you like a drink?" I asked him.

"Yeah, sure. What do you have?"

"I have beer, wine, vodka, and a bunch of other stuff."

"I'll just have a beer."

He followed me into the kitchen; I handed him a beer from the refrigerator, then I poured myself a glass of wine. As I walked to the living room he trailed behind; I could tell by the way my ass heated up that he was watching me. I invited him to sit down while I lit incense and turned on the radio. KMOJ was doing its late-night "Midnight Love" radio show, and the view from my balcony window was breathtaking.

We sat and got to know each other.

He was so gentle—respectful, kind, and extremely laid-back. We chilled and talked about his upbringing, his mom being from the Virgin Islands and his dad growing up in New York. Damn, that's why he looked like a fine-ass Puerto Rican. He told stories of his teenage escapades in England while visiting his aunt over the summer, and his visits to the islands—places I had never been, mostly because I was always too busy. I had always dreamt of traveling but could never find the time to get started.

"Kevin, as fine as you are, how come you don't have a girlfriend?" I don't know what made me ask him that bold-faced, but somehow it had just come out of my mouth.

"Well, I'm very busy and having a girlfriend doesn't fit into my schedule right now."

"Then why are you here with me?"

"I have to be honest with you; I've had a thing for you since the first day I met you at the Asian restaurant with Sadie."

Wow you had a thing for me, I thought. I smiled inside.

"I was kinda waiting to see if you were going to come around. But after seeing you at the mall that day and realizing you were about to get married, something in me faded. I started focusing more on my work, and dating and other women got put on the back burner."

"So I should be flattered, right?"

"No, no you don't have to be flattered—shit, I'm the one that's flattered, just to be sitting here talking with you now has been more than I could ever dream of."

"Wow, mm, thank you," I said. I could feel my body heating up even more, evident by the beads of sweat that formed in the small of my back.

"I was sure you had women knocking down your door to get with you."

"To be totally honest, there are a few that are quite persistent, but they have nothing on you. When Sadie told me you were no longer getting married I was going to try with everything I had to get next to you."

"Kevin, I know Sadie set me up."

"Yeah," he smiled, "we were kind of working on this together, but believe me I forced her hand."

"Yeah, right, I know that heifer and I'm sure she was on board full-throttle." We laughed.

"Yeah, you're right." He looked at me so earnestly. I could feel the tension in my neck and back release. It felt good—really good.

"Would you like another beer?"

"Sure, but let me get it. Would you like another glass of wine?"

"Yes please."

He stood up and walked coolly towards the kitchen, and I decided it was a good time for me to excuse myself to go and change—something form-fitting but not too suggestive. I walked to my bedroom smiling inside. OK, Jasmine stay cool, everything is going fine, don't get crazy.

I looked through my closet. What could I wear that would still make me sexy and appealing, but not lead him on? I sifted through the hangers and found my favorite Juicy Couture jogging suit; the soft velour material and the way that it hugged my curves would let him see what I was working with, but wouldn't give him the wrong idea about the evening. I changed into a thick pair of slipper socks and grabbed a comforter off the bed. Even though it was a nice evening, I wanted to open the window to let in some fresh air, and most nights, living up so high, the breeze that cascaded in could be downright chilly.

When I returned to the living room, everything had changed. All the lights were out and there seem to be more incense burning, as well as candles lit. The music had changed, too. He had figured out how to turn on the CD changer, which I had filled with Jill Scott, India.Irie, Dwele, and some CDs I had burned myself.

I walked towards him, not sure what to expect. Kevin handed me my glass and escorted me to the couch. But instead of us both settling on it, he took the blanket from me, laid it across the back of a chair, then pulled me close and swayed softly against my body.

"Would you like to dance?"

"Yes," I whispered, mesmerized.

We danced, and I could feel my body awakening to the possibilities; maybe there was a chance for me after all. Holding him tightly, not wanting to let go, not wanting this evening to end, I began to cry.

"What's wrong?" He asked softly.

"Nothing. If you didn't already know, I'm a big baby and what I'm feeling here with you feels so good that I don't want it to end."

"It doesn't have to end. We can go like this forever if you want."

I lay my head on his chest. "I hope so," I mumbled.

With every song change, the evening slipped away. Finally, we sat down to exchange numbers and information.

"I know you must go, so I won't keep you," I said.

"And out of respect for you, Ms. Burrell, I'm going to go. Because if I stay any longer, who knows what would happen?" We both laughed.

"All right, Mr. Owens. I'll walk you to the elevator."

We walked to the elevator in silence, but something in me screamed: You deserve to be happy, as happy as anyone else. I pushed the down button and took Kevin's hand. "I had a wonderful evening. Thank you."

"It was my pleasure; I hope this is not the last of our evenings together?"

"I would love to see you again."

"All right, how about I give you a call later this week and see where you're at? I have this special place I would like to take you."

"Oh, OK. Just let me know, and I'm there."

He smiled and looked deeply into my eyes so deep it felt like he could see right through me. "May I kiss you?"

"Yes, please do."

The softness of his lips and the sheer intimacy of his kiss were enough for me; he was the one.

Just at that moment Marcus' face flashed in my mind. Oh my God, Marcus, I'm sorry but I have to move on, please forgive me.

I return Kevin's kiss; he shifted his weight and held me closer than I thought I could be to someone. We stood there kissing and smiling and kissing again. This was the first time I was glad the elevator took so long. When the doors opened I hesitated. "Wait . . ."

No, Jasmine. Let him go. And I listened to the voice; you're right, whoever you are.

"Call me when you've made it home, OK?"

"I will."

He kissed my hand and as the elevator doors closed in front of him, I stood silent and motionless, thinking, this could finally be my chance.

# Chapter 59

WHEN KEVIN GOT OUT OF the shower, the water glistening off his caramel-covered body was amazing. Damn! I stood there in awe, thanking God; He was everything I knew to be righteous and I loved him.

I walked over to Kevin and kissed him. "I know you will be gone by the time I get out of the shower so I'll see you when you get home."

"OK, baby. If I get a chance I'll call you to see if you can do lunch."

"All right, sweetheart, I love you. Have a good day."

"You too, baby."

As I watched Kevin get dressed, I thought, Oh the beautiful babies we were going to have.

It had been three years now that Kevin and I had been together. I did everything in my power to keep him satisfied and happy. I was really doing well at the law firm and I had started getting used to having a live-in boyfriend.

Kevin had moved in with me six months after we met. He had practically moved in after the party, spending every night with me. Early one morning, I suggested he stay and we could save money, as well as be together. He agreed, moved his things and our life as a couple began. We established a stable relationship and grew more in love as time went by. I finally felt comfortable in my skin, enough to let my guard down to trust again. Kevin had a calming nature and his effect on me spoke volumes. Our connection seemed to lead us right down the path towards marriage.

I really wanted the perfect family. Like every little girl, envisions, I wanted the house, the picket fence, the two-point-five children, the dog, and the *fine-ass husband*. I had been given another chance at love, and I wasn't going to let anything take it away.

I looked at the clock. Shit—I was going to be late. I jumped in the shower for a quickie, touching all the major points and making sure to rinse off thoroughly. I pulled out the first suit I saw and quickly got dressed, unwrapped my hair and threw on just a little make-up; I was done in fifteen minutes flat. I grabbed my cell phone and briefcase, hoping everything I needed was in it, and proceeded to the elevator doors.

Getting to work this week was tough because of the construction re-routing. I had mapped out a route that would get me there in seven minutes and used it when I was really running late, which now had turned into most of the time. I had fallen off a bit on getting to work and business meetings in a timely matter since I had been with Kevin. It was always some extra kissing or another round of sex that threw my time off. But taking easier cases and changing my schedule to start later and work later gave me a little more playing room. There were a least three of four days out of the week that I had to use my quick route—or my "quickie route," as I called it.

I arrived at work at six fifty-eight, but by the time I got to the elevator and to my desk I'd be considered late. My partners in the law firm didn't care much, but I hated setting a bad example for the associates. I needed them to understand what being on time really meant, and how does it look for the person in charge of their team to always be late? But even though I did my best, Kevin had put a "thang" on me and I was enjoying every minute of it.

When I finally reached my office Wendy was on me with several messages, two of them urgent.

One of the urgent ones was from Kevin and the other one was from Mrs. Damon—Marcus' mother. What could she want? Had something happened to Marcus?

I thought for a minute. Do I call Ms. Damon first? No, girl, call your man first.

I ran to my desk and called Kevin's cell phone. While the phone was ringing I looked at the last message and realized it was a call from my girlfriend Paige. I wondered what was up with her; I hadn't talked to her in ages.

When Kevin answered the phone, I could tell from his voice that something was wrong.

"What's the matter, baby?"

"These motherfuckers are tripping."

"What Kevin, who?"

"These motherfuckers here, at this job are tripping."

"Baby, what happened?"

"They let me go today."

"What?"

"Man, they fired me; well, they asked me to resign."

"Why?"

"Remember the day I was running late for that very important meeting, and I told you about the parking pass I took out of that dude's car?"

"Yeah, I remember."

"Well, I lied to them when they asked me a week ago—I told them that I had found it."

"Yeah, and?"

"Well, they're saying since I didn't turn it in to the parking desk and I started using it without proper authorization, it's considered theft."

"But you told them you found it, right?"

"Hell yeah, that's what I told them, but they talked to the dude whose pass it was and he said he had left his car window open the day it came up missing. And by him reporting it right away they knew exactly what day and time it got lost, or taken."

"Ah baby, I'm sorry. Don't worry, have you talked to your boss?"

"Yes, I spoke with him today."

"How come it took a whole week for them to say something?"

"They were waiting to interview the owner and to look at the tapes."

"Tapes?"

"Yeah, there's a camera in the parking lot and they say they have me on camera taking it."

"Wow, do you need me to come down there?"

"Nah, baby, to hell with these people. I was done working here anyway."

"Have you talked to Sadie?"

"Yeah, I saw her earlier."

"What did she say?"

"What could she say, she ain't my boss."

"I know that, Kevin, but she could vouch for you."

"Yeah, she could but fuck it, I'm cool, I'm'a' just chill for a little while, take a break from this nine-to-five-grind shit."

"Are you sure?"

"Yeah, baby, I'm sure. I'm getting my shit packed right now and I'm going home."

"OK, baby, just take it easy, everything will be all right. I'll try to come home early."

"Cool, baby. I'll see you when you get home."

"OK. I love you."

"I love you too, Jasmine."

I hung up the phone. Damn, this is fucked up. It wasn't that we needed Kevin's income to help us survive; it was more of a convenience. We'd been able to do whatever we wanted—shopping, traveling, buying things for fun. It was like we were teenagers who had hit the lottery. Practically everything we did had a high price tag. So when he came home last year and installed a brand-new projection-screen television along with the new Playstation III that had just come out, I only shrugged. Even though he had spent most of the evening playing video games, his days were spent working hard and bringing in a paycheck.

I didn't mind him playing while we were home together; in fact I enjoyed watching him play, I even played from time to time. But now things would be different. He had made up in his mind to kick back for a while and not work, and something under my skin began to crawl.

Why does he get to stay home and hang out, while I continue to work?

Then, thinking about the man that I had and the way he made me feel, I drew in my rebellion and checked myself. He won't be out of work for long, he'll get bored and get back into the grind soon enough. I was going be the supportive girlfriend, not the nagger I heard men talk so badly of. I loved Kevin and wanted him around so I didn't want to stir up conflict in the peaceful home we had created.

All those feelings safely stuffed away, I sat back down at my desk and confronted another puzzle as I held the message from Mrs. Damon in my hands. I knew it must be important because she hardly ever called me anymore. She had been so disappointed and embarrassed by what Marcus had done it was like she and Mr. Damon had disappeared.

I picked up the phone and dialed her number. While I waited for her to answer I poured myself a glass of water to help calm my nerves.

"Hello?"

"Hello, Mrs. Damon, this is Jasmine."

"Hey, Jasmine, how are you, sweetheart?"

"I'm fine, Mrs. Damon, how are you?"

"Jasmine, baby, I'm doing OK. Not feeling the best today, though. I got a call from Marcus and he wanted me to call you and tell you a few things."

"Oh? What did he say?" I sat back in my chair trying to remain calm, but something in me was stirring.

"First, he wanted to apologize again for what he's done to you, he's really sorry, baby. He got into the money scheme without knowing what was really going on, a mistake on his part. The other men who were involved were the ones really making the money. Marcus was more or less their courier; his position with the company allowed him easier access to the accounts. He did make a few cents but overall a lot of the money that was made was transferred to off shore accounts for his co-defendants. The kingpins of the organized ring are still on the loose."

I wonder if one of them left me that note, I thought, as I heard her say that.

"Oh, and Jasmine, there is another thing."

"Mrs. Damon, what else could there be?"

"Marcus did not have the courage to tell you but I think you need to know. I know you have moved on with your life, and I also know you still have strong feelings for Marcus. Those kinds of feelings just don't go away. You are a beautiful, girl, and I only wish the best for you, but you have to understand that my son was very much in love with you. He would do anything for you to be happy."

"I know, Mrs. Damon; I loved your son very much as well. What else is there?"

"He called to tell me they're going to be transferring him to a minimum-security facility up in Waseca, so that means he will only be a few short hours away. He didn't want you to know because he says he doesn't want you to see him locked up like that. But as his mother, I know he's dying to see you. I don't know if you have it in you, Jasmine, but I think it would be really good for you if you go up there and see him."

"Mrs. Damon, I'm in a relationship and I don't think Kevin would like that at all."

"I know, baby, but Marcus is dying, I mean his spirit is dying. When I spoke to him he was really beating himself up about what he had done to you—that hurt him more than anything. He said he can handle jail, jail is a cakewalk compared to how he feels about hurting you. Jasmine, please just think about it; I don't want to pressure you, but I do want you to know what's going on. Maybe if you go, you can once and for all settle this thing between you two."

"I hear you, Mrs. Damon, but I don't think I can do it. I'm so busy and seeing him would only infuriate me."

"I understand, Jasmine; I just ask that you think about it. OK?"

"OK, Mrs. Damon, I'll think about it, but I can't make you any promises."

"No, no, baby, that's all I ask, that you just think about it."

I hung up the without saying good-bye.

Damn you, Marcus.

# Chapter 60

It was Monday, six in the morning.

"Sweetheart, will shut off the alarm?" I asked Kevin.

He did, but my tone this morning was different, more than any of the other mornings I had told him to shut off the alarm. It had been six months since Kevin got fired, and he still had made only minimal attempts to find a job. An Internet search here, a phone call or two there—nothing seemed to pan out.

"Baby, are you going to look for a job today?" I asked him, now feeling like the hundredth time I'd asked in the past two weeks. He rolled over, his back to me; I guess that was my answer, my cue to leave him alone, which I did most of the time.

I was still stuck on being the perfect mate, not wanting to anger him or ruffle his feathers. But so much time had passed and things around the apartment were getting tight. I was still making enough money to support us, but with all-new fancy things and the trips charged on credit cards and his—not to mention my—need to shop, everything we had saved was quickly depleted. I did have a 401(k) but I had promised myself I wouldn't touch it. He had cashed out his 401(k) and used it to put a down payment on a motorcycle, which I now had the privilege of making payments for.

"Fine, Kevin, whatever; I'm going to work."

I left the situation there in bed with him and headed for the shower. It was getting harder and harder to cope. I was finding myself, more days than not, moping and feeling like shit. I didn't have an illness a doctor could diagnose, but I felt more tired than I had ever been, my head seemed to pound constantly and all the muscles in my body ached, particularly along my back and shoulders.

It was crazy, I was the one constantly worrying about him and what he needed, while he kicked back and chilled. He wasn't letting the situation bother him to the point of sickness, so maybe I should just let it go.

The shower was beginning to steam up the air around me; I could feel the tension in my spine start to release. I slowly walked over towards the shower and moved the curtain back, as a white billowy thickness of the steam engulfed me. Lord, please help me, I whispered—and in that instant, I felt a sense of peace wash over me. "Everything is going to be all right," I quietly prayed for Kevin. Lord, give him the strength and wisdom he needs to do the right thing. Please help us to get through whatever this is. I really do want this to work. Amen.

Now if only I could get him to believe in what I just prayed.

Kevin was raised Muslim, so his beliefs in how God worked, faith, tithing and all the things I was raised to believe were a challenge for him. He didn't understand a lot of the Christian doctrine, and quite frankly didn't care to learn. I tried several times to explain the concept of paying tithes, giving back for blessings already received. But when the discussions got heated he always remarked that God wants us to be stable first before we give our money to Him. He would say God would understand if we use our money to pay bills first, then with what is left over we give to Him. He couldn't come to grips with the notion that you paid God his ten percent *first* and then you had faith that God would take care of all the rest of your needs.

That was my mantra. I grew up on that, in fact, I had memorized my grandfather's favorite scripture on tithing: Malachi 3:6, "Should a man rob God?" My grandfather preached that sermon every first Sunday for sure. And I believed him. It wasn't until now that I had strayed from tithing; even during my wild college years, I tried really hard to get my tithes to church. Sometimes they made it, and sometimes they didn't. But I gave myself an A for effort. Kevin and I were paying my bills first, hoping this would somehow get us out of the hole. It wasn't working, but I couldn't get Kevin to understand. I really hadn't thought about our religious beliefs before we started dating, so finding out firsthand how being unevenly yoked could cause so many problems was a serious blow.

On my drive to work, I sat thinking about the relationship—good thing I knew the route so well, because my driving was completely on automatic pilot. It was like I needed to play the whole relationship over again, remembering in the beginning being truly happy with Kevin. And now everything and everyone began to change, including me.

In the very beginning, my friends were so glad to see me happy too, and they were happy it looked like I had finally found a good man in Kevin. But their feedback had begun to change even before this mess, as my friends and family started to question his work ethic and his input into our future. Now, thinking about what they had said, I had to wonder if he really was serious about us and where we had talked about going. As far as I could tell, he had pretty much checked out of the financial and supportive side of our relationship in the last six moths—which included his support of how our home was kept and how much he invested in seeing to my comfort, seeing as that I was still working a full day and came home to cook and clean. He even got irritated if I got home late, because that meant his dinner would be late, too. He never said anything outright, but I could tell it was there.

Kevin got used to me cooking for him. I was the consummate housewife—I cooked, made his plate, and even brought it to him while he sat and watched TV. The scenario really didn't bother me because it was what I saw, how I was raised. I watched my grandmother do it for years and learned it was customary to bring your husband his plate. The difference may have been that my grandfather worked three jobs, and Kevin was not yet my husband—but who's looking at that? Kevin was my man and I wanted to keep him happy.

The thing that made this hard was his attitude when I wasn't there to do it. On days when I came home late or when I just didn't feel like cooking Kevin would get mopey. Not a loud, yelling anger, but a quiet, solemn mood; it would have been better if he just got mad and screamed at me. Instead, he would withdraw into this shell and refuse to speak; in fact, he would refuse to do anything. I would question him on how he could be upset with me, seeing as how I just walked in the door. He'd say he wasn't upset and that there was nothing wrong. But having lived with him for over four years now, I knew something was wrong.

It was only after I kept badgering him about his mood that he would say something about not eating all day. "You haven't eaten all day?" I would ask. "How is that my problem?" Then the argument would begin.

I had gotten so tired of arguing about the same issues over and over that I'd just come home later and later. Shit, he was a grown-ass man and should have been able to feed himself. And even better than that, why couldn't he have dinner waiting for me? I was the one working while he sat at home. I don't think it even occurred to him to prepare a meal for me—or us for that matter.

OK, so maybe things weren't as wonderful as they used to be between us anymore. But the fighter in me wanted to fight for this relationship; I refused to be a failure again. I decided at that moment I would do everything in my power to comfort and support Kevin through this obviously difficult time. Maybe he was depressed, and anyway, nagging was not going to change things. When I got to work, I started making some phone calls. I know plenty of people who could help him find a job.

I called my mother first; she picked up on the first ring.

"Girl, I was just getting ready to call you," she said.

I laughed. We had this crazy thing about calling each other at the same time. We already spoke three or four times a day but when the phone calls started to overlap we knew we had issues.

"Hey, Ma, how are you?"

"I'm fine, baby. How are you?"

"Not so good. Mama, Kevin needs to find a job."

"Yeah, I know he's been out of work for too long. What is he doing to find one?"

"Not a whole lot, Ma. I think he might be a little down. All he does all day is smoke and play video games."

"Well, he needs to get off his ass and get to lookin.'"

"Yeah, Mama, I know. Do you know of anyone hiring?"

"As a matter of fact, I just got an e-mail from a friend of mine at American Express, and they have some openings in their customer service department. Do you think that he could do that sort of work?"

"I'm sure he can, all he has to do is go over there and apply. Mom, will you call and tell him? I don't want it to seem as if it was my idea."

"Yes, Jaz, I'll call him."

"Thanks, Ma, I'll talk to you later."

"All right, baby, I'll let you know how it goes."

"OK, bye—love you."

"Love you too, baby."

My mother loved Kevin; her only beef was with his lack of get-up and go when it came to finding and keeping a job. She hated to see me working so hard at the firm as well as working so hard at home. She just wanted him to do his share, and so did I.

As I settled in, I saw the beeping red light on my phone; I had been so focused on calling my mom that I hadn't even checked when I got in. I pressed the message button and waited. One message was from Mr. Johnson, the father of the twins who had pleaded guilty—before I could intervene—a few years ago: "Ms. Burrell, could you please call me as soon as you get this message? We have a serious problem and we need your help."

He sounded really distraught. I hadn't heard from Mr. Johnson since his two boys were incarcerated. I wondered what had happened. I made a note to call him as soon as I was through checking my other messages.

The next message was from one of my partners; he wanted to meet with me this afternoon to discuss a big case he was working on. I believed he needed my help but didn't know how to ask without sounding helpless. He had been dropping hints for some time now and maybe it had gotten so bad that he was ready to break down and actually ask. I marked the time on my calendar and waited to hear the next message.

As I listened to it, everything in me stopped.

"Hey, Jasmine, it's Tonya, Marcus' sister. Sorry to bother you with this, but Marcus called me from jail and asked me to call you on a three-way. I refused at first but he begged me, and you know I can't resist him. Marcus, are you there?"

"Yes, I'm here."

The sound of Marcus' voice coming through the phone smacked the life out of me. His voice sounded exactly like the day we met.

"Jasmine, baby I miss you. I know you probably don't want to hear this but I had to call. You stopped writing and I can't seem to get through on your cell phone. This was my only option. I know you're in a relationship now and I hope that you're happy. I just want you to know how sorry I am for hurting you and that I still love you, very much. I gotta go, but I hope someday you can find it in your heart to forgive me. I love you.

"Thanks, Tonya, I'll talk to you later," he said to his sister, and hung up.

"Jasmine, it's Tonya. Girl, I'm sorry, I hope I didn't ruin your day. I'll talk to you later." The she hung up too.

Dazed and confused, it took me a minute to hang up the phone. I was so stunned I didn't even know what I was feeling. It had been over four years since I had heard from or talked to Marcus. Why now?

I tried to compose myself; I poured myself a glass of water and gulped it down, nearly choking on it. The loneliness and neglect I had been feeling lately, coupled with Kevin's apparent lack of concern for my feelings, had stirred up my old feelings for Marcus. I wanted to see him again.

The itch had actually started after hearing from his mother that he had been transferred to a minimum-security prison in northern Minnesota, but I was so caught up in Kevin I had no intention of visiting there. Kevin had fulfilled my needs up until recently and I was trying to be the honest and faithful girlfriend. But this was Marcus—the love of my life, the man I had intended to marry. What would it hurt to pay him a visit? I sat staring at the picture of Kevin and me on my desk.

I'm gonna go see him, tell him I'm in love with Kevin and close this chapter in my life for good; my brain had kicked into gear trying to override what my heart was feeling. I knew I was in love with Kevin, but a big part of me needed to see Marcus—one last time.

# Chapter 61

Satisfied with my decision, I picked up the phone and scrolled through my Rolodex to find Mr. Johnson's number. I dialed, wondering what could have happened.

When Mr. Johnson answered the phone I knew right away something was wrong.

"Mr. Johnson, this is Jasmine. You called?"

"Yes Jasmine, I have some devastating news. My son . . ." he stopped and took a deep breath. "My son died."

"What? Who? Which one?"

"Timothy. Timothy had asthma; he died from acute suffocation from an asthma attack."

"No, Mr. Johnson. Did they know he had asthma?"

"Yes, they knew, and up until he was sent to prison he had very good control over it."

"Tell me, Mr. Johnson what happened?" I was overcome with sadness—and outrage.

"I don't really know a whole lot because they're trying to keep it quiet, but I did speak to Thomas and he told me his version of the story.

"I guess there was an altercation up at the prison and the guards had to use pepper spray inside the building. And Timothy was caught in the mist. Thomas was right there, with him but in the fracas no one but Thomas noticed that my son couldn't breathe. He tried to get the guards to help him but everyone was in such an uproar that no one came. Thomas watched his brother suffer, then lose consciousness. He was right there screaming for help and they wouldn't come. By the time someone got to him he was dead. My baby was dead."

"Oh my God, I'm so sorry Mr. Johnson. What can I do to help?"

"Jasmine, I need two things."

"Anything, Mr. Johnson, anything. I'll do anything you ask."

"First, I need you to get my son Thomas transferred out of that prison, preferably somewhere close to home, but we have to get him out of there. He is not doing so well, he will either kill somebody or harm himself, and I can't let that happen."

"I understand, sir."

"Next, I need to see if we have any legal rights against the prison. Those men killed my son and I want someone to pay for it."

"I understand, Mr. Johnson; first I'll work on getting Thomas transferred. He certainly does not need to be there. I'll start looking for a facility closer to home, maybe a camp or something. He has done quite a bit of his time so moving him shouldn't be a problem considering the extenuating circumstances.

"The second part is going to be a little harder," I continued, "and is going take a little more time. I'll have to make a lot of phone calls in order to get to the bottom of this. Please understand, Mr. Johnson—you've already said they're trying to keep things quiet so I may have a difficult time getting any information, but I'll certainly do my best."

"I know, you have always done your best for us. So whatever you come up with we will appreciate."

"OK, Mr. Johnson, I'll get right on this; please, please take care of yourself and trust I'll do my best. How is your wife?"

"Not so good; she hasn't left her room for a week, and I don't know what I'm going to do."

"Well, tell her I'm working on this and we'll get to the bottom of this, whatever it takes. I promise."

"Thanks, I know you won't let us down. Have a good day."

"I will, and you too, Mr. Johnson. I'll be in contact."

I didn't realize I was crying until I hung up the phone. Timothy's death along with the call from Marcus was way too much to handle.

I had to leave, but where would I go? I didn't want to go home and look at Kevin's ass lounging on the couch—*my* couch. I grabbed my purse and told Wendy to clear my schedule for the day.

Everything was in disarray; I needed a drink. It was just about eleven, time for my favorite Chinese restaurant to open; I'd go down there and chill for a little while.

The Red Dragon was like the "Cheers" bar to me. I went at least three times a week, sometimes more, so everybody really did know my name. When I walked in the regulars were sitting at the bar, having their usual cocktails—Frank, Sandra, and a couple of other people I recognized but didn't know personally.

"Hey, Sandy." I greeted one of my favorite Red Dragon bartenders.

"Hey, Jasmine, how are you today?"

"I'm fine, I guess."

"You want a punch?"

"Yes, ma'am!"

"You're here kinda of early today. I wasn't expecting to see you until tonight."

"Yeah, I know, got a few things on my mind. I needed to come down and sort them out."

"Do you need a menu?"

"Yeah, give me one—not that I don't already know everything on it."

"Yeah, I know." We laughed.

"Here you go, and here's your drink."

It was the infamous "Wondrous Punch," my new drink of choice—Bacardi light and dark, 151, Meyer's Rum, a little bit of mixed juice and a splash of grenadine. There was no reason at all to drink these unless you wanted to get totally messed up—and I dare anyone to have two. Everyone who came to the Dragon came for the punch and by the end of the night you knew why.

The Red Dragon was one of the last bars that still free-poured their drinks by hand. All the other bars had started using some measuring contraption that stopped the pour right at an ounce;

go figure. The Dragon was the spot—the drinks were strong, the food was delicious, and the crowd was cool.

I sat down in a booth and slowly sipped my drink. As the cool, intoxicating liquid trickled down my throat I began to feel better. Just a few more sips and all the stress would be gone.

As I sat there contemplating all that had just happened, my mind floated to Marcus' voice. There was something about it that took me to another place, to a whole new existence. Damn. I truly missed him and I needed to see him, sooner rather than later. I reconfirmed my resolve to go visit. It would be easy for me to go as a lawyer rather than trying to get placed on his visitors list. I could skip all of the background-check hoops and maybe even get a private visit.

That was it; I would go to see him on Sunday. It made the most sense to go on a Sunday, because it would take a good four or five hours all told—enough time to drive up to the facility, visit for an hour or so and drive back. The drive alone was going to be about an hour and a half, so leaving early was my main focus.

I would get up earlier enough to shower, dress and have something to eat, which I never did on Sunday. My church-going had gotten so sparse that I usually got up right before it was time to be there, and even then if I didn't get moving right away, I'd end up missing it.

Kevin never wanted to go to church, so getting I'd be able to get out of the house easily. I could use church as an excuse to get away for a while; he might wonder why I was leaving so early, but other than that he wouldn't care. It would give him the time he wanted to watch whatever game would be on. It was late fall, so football would be on all day. The only thing I would have to worry about would be getting back to feed him.

I sat at the Red Dragon, now on my second drink, reminiscing about Marcus and how things were. It didn't matter to me that he had committed the ultimate betrayal—or at least didn't matter enough to keep me from seeing him; a part of me still was in love with him and needed to be with him.

When Maggie came in for her shift she was surprised to see me already sitting there, half-drunk in the middle of the day. Maggie was my usual waitress; she was an athletically built white girl in her mid-forties with blond curly hair, cute as a button, and very cool. She was definitely one of the reasons I frequented the Red Dragon.

"Hey, Magnolia," I said, calling her by the nickname I gave her.

"Getting started early, Jasmine?" she asked with a hint of concern in her voice.

"Yes ma'am. Why not?"

"I hear you—is everything all right?"

"Yeah, I guess, Maggie; it's been one of those days."

"I see you have a menu—are you hungry, do you know what you want?"

"Yes, just give me the usual."

"OK, Jasmine, coming right up."

She took my menu and headed toward the kitchen. I got up too, heading toward the jukebox. I decided I would play something to change my mood, and who else to do that than Bob Marley? I had loved Bob Marley since my uncle Felix hipped me Marley's "Legend" CD, back when I was in high school and I had been hooked ever since. As "No Woman No Cry" poured out of the speakers, I began to sway to the mesmerizing beat. The rhythm of Marley's voice put me in a kind of a trance; now, thoroughly drunk and feeling good, my body relaxed. All I needed now was a joint and my food.

When I headed back to my booth, I saw my old friend Paige walk in the door. It was funny; we were also close, but while she still lived in the Cities, we had often gone months without seeking each other, even talking to each other. But whenever we got together, we always picked up like we'd just seen each other last week. I'd run into her cousin Mario from time to time, too, and he kept me up on her news.

I was surprised to see her now, because last I'd heard, she'd moved to Mississippi. She had divorced Shane and was doing the damn, thing in the Dirty South. From what I had heard, the separation from Shane was too much for her to handle. So she went to Mississippi to stay with family for a few weeks, and a few weeks turned into months, then years. It seemed like a lot of big changes all at once for her; but I hadn't worried about her. She was one person who consistently took care of business—her business, that is. I had worried a little bit when I heard she'd run into some rough situations down there, though. Anyway, I guess I'd be finding out exactly what was going on.

"Paige—hey, girl!" She looked as beautiful as ever.

"Hey, Jaz." She grabbed and hugged me so tight I almost lost my drink.

"What's up, my nigga?" I asked her. We slapped five and I invited her to join me.

"Girl, ain't shit up. Just doing me, you know how I get down."

"Yes I do!"

"I called yo' ass when I got in town but you never called me back."

"I know, dog, had some major shit going on at the time and I seriously forgot."

"It's cool."

"So what up, girl, where yo' husband at?"

"Nigga, please. I divorced him a long-ass time ago."

"What happened?"

"You know me; we were both trying to run the shit, and both of us being Leos, you know that shit didn't work."

"I hear you. So what's been up, I hear you been kicking it in the Dirty South."

"Nigga, hell yeah, Mississippi is the bomb; niggas galore, money everywhere, and on top of all that, I ain't got to worry about this cold-ass Minnesota weather."

"Hell yeah, I hear that. You know your cousin has been telling me all the dirt."

"I know, that nigga probably done told you everything huh?"

"Well, some of the shit he said had me scared. I hear you were down there getting shot and shit?"

"Them some hatin'-ass hos, you know a nigga like me went down there and the bitches couldn't stand my independent

Northern ass. I had all they niggas running in behind me. The brothas were shook on my game. They didn't understand how I could be so cool one minute and so cold-blooded the next. Shit, I had to show them how we Northerners get down."

I had always envied Paige that. She was a real dime—beautiful, strong, smart, and didn't give a fuck. It was all about her. We had grown up together but we were so different. My slow, sheltered existence, compared to her fast-paced, non-conforming individuality allowed for us to become two separate but very equal entities. I gave her what she needed from me, and she forced on me what I needed from her. Completely accepting with no prejudice, resentment, jealousy, or fear.

Our lives had gone different ways once we grew up, too. Me with my successful career and nice apartment, but she hadn't been so lucky. But we never changed when it came to each other. No matter how far away she was, there was no forsaking our friendship or our bond.

"What you drinking, Paige?"

"I'm going to have a frozen, margarita."

"A frozen margarita, kinda frilly huh? Why you drinking that light-ass shit?"

"Girl, the last time I was here and had one of them damn, punches, my ass thought I was going to die the next day. My heart was fluttering around and my chest felt like it was going to explode. I ain't fucked with them since."

I laughed. "I hear you."

"So Jaz, what up with you?"

"Girl, my shit is all stressed out. Kevin's ass still ain't working and the shit is starting to get tight."

"Damn, Jaz, you still working, cooking, and cleaning for that nigga?"

"Yes, you know it."

"Girl, you crazy as hell, I wouldn't be doing shit for him. He can't at least have the house clean and dinner made for you, he home all day."

"Yeah, yeah I know; I feel like I'm stuck."

"You better get unstuck and kick that nigga to the curb. There are way too many men out here who would love to take care of a woman like you."

"I know, Paige, but I love him and I want this to work."

"Whatever, girl." She waved me off and started sipping on the drink Maggie had placed in front of her.

The red and gold paisley wallpaper and the Oriental lanterns strategically placed throughout the Dragon were beginning to blend into one blurry backdrop. The air was beginning to thin, and the room was swirling lightly. I took one last sip of my drink; number two, history.

"Paige, I was thinking about going up to the prison in Waseca to visit Marcus on Sunday."

There was no telling which way she would respond when I dropped bombs on her. Sometimes she was like a ticking time bomb herself. I sat back and braced myself for her response. When she looked up from her drink, I could see that the tequila was starting to take effect, so I didn't know if the look in her eye was confusion or disgust. She took another deep sip of her margarita and smiled.

"Marcus? Marcus?"

"Yeah, heifer, what other Marcus do you know in jail?"

"Girl, you are really trying to get yourself in some trouble aren't you?"

"No, Paige, it's not like that; I'm just going up there to see how he is doing, just going to check on him."

"Yeah, right, nigga. I have known you all my life, ain't no way you going all the way up there, three hours away just to see if Marcus is all right; you going for a conjugal visit."

Her laughter ripped through my chest like a jagged knife.

"Paige, what are you talking about? You know damn, well I can't go up there to fuck him."

"Whatever, nigga—you got mad pull and if you wanted a private meeting with him I'm sure you of all people could pull it off."

I sat there for a minute contemplating her response and had to laugh to myself. Shit, she's right—if I wanted to I could probably go up there and get really broke off.

"Naw, Paige I ain't on that, for real. I just want to see how he is doing."

"OK, then, Miss Prim and Proper, are you going to tell Kevin?"

My glare should have given her the answer, but yelling "Hell, no!" felt a whole lot better. She burst into laughter and raised her hand in the air to get five.

"That's my nigga, I knew I trained you right."

"Girl, you're crazy."

"I know, but I ain't the one going up to the jailhouse to see my ex-fiancé while my current nigga is at home thinking I'm at church. You a dirty dog, Jaz, do that shit."

# Chapter 62

Sunday couldn't come soon enough. I spent most of the rest of the week preparing for my trip up to Waseca. Going to get my hair and nails done, shopping for the shortest skirt and the tightest top. I was in a perpetual cyclone, my thoughts were spinning in my head a mile a minute and I couldn't keep still. It was lucky for me that Kevin had been in his own little world that entire week, or else he'd have been asking me a lot of questions I wouldn't have had answers for. And since I had gotten up so early and his night had been long, up late watching television, I figured I could slip out before he even realized I was gone.

It was now quarter to eight, and I knew I needed to get on the road in order to get back at a decent hour; I grabbed my purse and Bible and headed for the door.

"Jasmine."

I stopped dead.

"Where you going?"

"I'm going to church."

"Why are you leaving so early?"

"I was going to try and make it for Sunday school—why, do you want to go? I'll wait for you."

"Nah, I'm cool, I'm just gonna lay here and watch the game."

I knew that if I asked him to come he'd back off. "Oh, OK. I'll be back around three or so."

"All right baby, have a good time."

"I will."

"Hey, can I have a kiss?"

I hesitated, realizing what a big mistake I was about to make. I loved Kevin and wanted to be with him, in spite of the last six months. But something in me needed to see Marcus one last time, so instead of going with what I knew to be right, I went with what was seriously wrong—just one more time I let me get in the way.

I walked over and kissed Kevin passionately, eagerly searching his eyes for one glance, for one thing to stand out and beg me to stay. It wasn't there. I whispered "Bye" under my breath as I headed for God knows where.

I spent the drive to Waseca listening to old love songs, mostly the ones Marcus and I used to listen to. I was truly doing a number on myself—torturing myself with the fantasy and memories of my days and nights with Marcus.

Seeing the exit sign to the city of Waseca startled me because I hadn't realized I had gotten there so fast. Damn, what was I doing? Of all the crazy things I'd done, this was by far the craziest—the lies, the deception. This was not who I was. Or was it?

I pulled into the parking lot of the prison and sat for a moment trying to compose myself, trying not to cry, trying not to scream and most of all, trying not to turn around and drive away.

I reached for the rearview mirror to check my makeup if need be—and of course, there she was, that reflection of me/not me.

What, what do you want? I demanded of her; then she faded away.

I closed my eyes. You have to do this. Just go, get it over with and be done with this for good. And that was exactly what I intended to do—checking in, going through the security pat-down, waiting in the bare room with just a table and two plastic chairs. Until they brought Marcus in.

Damn!

# Chapter 63

MARCUS WAS ALWAYS A STAR, he could shine brighter and represent harder than any man, regardless of his situation. Seeing him standing there, only five feet away from me, proved it once again.

From his beautiful dark-chocolate skin, from the top of his smooth head to the gleam in his smile to his perfectly creased prison clothes, and brand-new Nike tennis shoes, Marcus looked good. Shit, he looked *damn*, good—except for the prison clothes, he looked liked he had never left. I was smitten all over again; in my heart we were meeting for the first time.

He walked up to me, and as clean as he looked, he smelled even better. He got as close as he could get to me and smiled.

"Hello, Jasmine."

"Hey, Marcus."

We hugged—just a short friendly embrace because the guards were watching, but it was enough to send every sexual atom in my body stirring into its own separate orbit.

"How are you?"

"I'm fine, Marcus. I should be asking you."

"I'm cool, Jasmine, just doing what I have to do."

"Yeah, I guess."

"So I see you got my message. Don't be mad at Tonya, I made her do it."

"I'm not mad at all, in fact I wanted to see you one last time just to tie up all those loose ends floating around."

His face fell; he looked so disappointed I knew what his true intentions were. But he spoke with confidence. "Yes, I heard you were pretty serious about Kevin; you two are living together now?"

"Yes, we are, and we're very happy."

"I'm glad to hear that, Jasmine, you deserve the best. I'm just sorry I wasn't able to be the one to give it to you."

"Well, as a matter of fact, Marcus, you were able to give it to me but you fucked that up!"

Damn, where did that come from? I had to check myself; I wasn't there to bash him, he was already in a bad place and there was no reason for me to get ugly. "I'm sorry, Marcus, I didn't mean that," I said quickly.

"Don't worry about it, Jaz. I deserved that."

"No, you didn't, I didn't come all the way up here to fight with you; I just wanted to see how you were doing."

"I know, sweetheart; I'm fine."

In the back of my mind I thought, You sure are.

The next hour and a half went by so fast. It was like old times, we touched and held hands, we laughed and joked, and talked about everything we could think of. Smiled and several times caught each other gazing, first him looking away, then me. What was I feeling?

"Marcus Damon," the sound of the guard's voice pierced our little bubble; and at that moment I knew we were over.

Marcus took my hand and looked me in the eyes. "Jasmine, I know what I did was wrong and I cannot change the past. All I can do is do what's right and that begins with finishing out my time. I have only two years left and I don't intend to ever come back here. But I want you to know: Someday I'll make this all up to you, if you let me."

"Marcus . . ."

"Look, Jaz, don't say anything right now; I just want you to know how I feel."

I closed my eyes to keep back the tears and when I felt his lips touch mine, everything around me disappeared; there were no guards, no metal detectors, no people, no nothing, just Marcus and I kissing like we were one again.

When we parted, the tears that had made their way down my cheeks caressed my chin. As I felt them drip onto my chest, they felt somehow felt happy, exuberant. And so did I.

"Marcus, I love you."

His eyes fluttered open and he smiled. "I love you too, Jasmine."

The astonishment I felt as he floated away hit me like a brick. Oh my God, what had I said? Before I could recant, he was gone, head high, walking through the cream-colored door marked "holding cell."

# Chapter 64

THE DRIVE BACK TO THE city was the worst. I felt like I was being torn up inside—love, betrayal, guilt, pleasure, and a whole slew of other feelings I couldn't even begin to describe. Was I crazy? I must have been; what was I thinking? I fumbled around for my cell phone and called Paige. I was so relieved when she answered.

"Hello?"

"Hey, girl, what you doing?" I said, trying to sound casual.

"Nothing, just getting off work."

"Could you please meet me at the Dragon? I just left Marcus and I need to talk to you."

"Oh shit, Jaz, I'm on my way."

"No, wait I'm still driving back from Waseca so give me about forty-five minutes, cool?"

"OK. Cool, I can go home and change."

"All right, Paige, I'll meet you there."

It was quarter after one, and church would be close to letting out. I'd told Kevin I wouldn't be back until three, but I figured I'd call him and let him know I was going to run down to the Red Dragon to get something for us to eat. He would be cool with that.

I dialed the house phone and got no answer. Damn, I wonder if he's still sleeping. I tried his cell.

"Hello?"

"Hey, baby, what are you doing?"

"Hey, what's up baby, I just left the house to go get my car washed. How was church?"

"Oh, church was good; I was just about to go down to the Dragon to bring something home to eat."

"Oh that's cool, how about I meet you down there?"

SHIT! I was still a ways away from the city, so here I go trying this lying thing.

"Well, I won't be there for a while, I have to stop by Paige's house for a little while. Do you just want me to bring you something home?"

"No, since I'm already out and about, I'd rather meet you there. How long do you think you're going to take?"

"Oh, about forty-five minutes or so."

"All right, baby, I'll meet you there in an hour, cool?"

"Um, yeah, that's cool."

"I love you, Jaz."

"I love you too.

By the time I got to the restaurant I had sweated out my hair and I looked like I had been on a damn, safari. My stomach was tied up with cramps and my head hurt from all the stories I was making up in my head. Kevin didn't deserve this, but what he needed and what was good for him didn't matter at the time—I wanted what I wanted, which always got me into trouble.

And even though seeing Marcus had unleashed a flood of feelings like fear and confusion, being near him had re-ignited in me a fire that was slowly consuming my entire being—starting from in between my thighs.

It was like I was a virgin all over again. I wanted more; I needed more. I thought about Marcus for the rest of the drive, as I parked my car and even as I walked into the Dragon. Before I even saw Kevin sitting in the booth by the bar, I had made up my mind that I had to see Marcus again.

Kevin was looking so good; he must have gotten a haircut after he got his car washed. He was wearing a nice pair of sharply creased Polo slacks and a navy blue Polo shirt. He smiled with the excitement of a newborn baby.

"Hey, Kevin." I was just trying to keep cool.

"Hey, baby." I walked over to kiss him, hoping he wouldn't smell the scent of another man all over me. "You look nice, you get a haircut or something?"

"Thank you, baby. Nah, I just went and had Jimmy line me up, he was at the barbershop cleaning up. How was church, did you have a good time?"

"Yes I did. Um, could you please order me a punch? I have to use the bathroom." I said the words all in a rush; I just wasn't good at pretending like nothing was different.

"Baby, it's Sunday and you just left church. You sure you want a Wondrous Punch?"

"Yes I do! You know what? Never mind; I'll get it myself," I snapped. I turned away from him and toward the bartender. "Pat, can I get a punch?"

Kevin looked at me as if I had two heads.

Damn, I'm tripping; the tension was too much to bear. I practically ran to bathroom and flung open the door, startling the girl who was primping in the mirror.

"Oh, sorry," I mumbled.

"It's cool. Are you OK?"

"Yes, I'm fine, thank you; just need a punch."

She laughed. "I hear that."

"You too."

I entered the stall and squatted over the toilet seat trying to figure out a way to calm down. Just a sip or two of that punch and I'll be fine. Just let me get to that punch. I thought about Paige—damn, I needed to call her. I don't want her walking into this mess. I fished in my purse for my cell phone, then dialed her number.

"Hey, girl, where you at?"

"Oh hey, Jaz, I'm just leaving the house. Are you there?"

"Girl, yes, but I got a slight problem."

"What's up?"

"Kevin is here."

"What??"

"Yeah, girl, I called him to see if he wanted me to bring him something home to eat and he was already out, so he decided to meet me here."

"What do you want me to do?"

"I think I need you in here, but I don't want to put you through any more of my mess, in case this things get ugly. Because if he goes to asking me a bunch of questions you know I ain't good at lying."

"Yes, I know that, all them times you got us in trouble as kids going back and telling my mom the truth after we had got the lie all straight." She laughed.

"I know, my bad."

"Well, I'll come in for a minute, then give some excuse to leave. I need a drink anyway."

"OK, but first I told him I had to stop by your house before I got here because I was still on the road trying to get back. So you know what to do."

"Yeah, I know. I got you!"

When I got back to the table, my drink was there and Kevin had ordered himself a beer; he was looking at the menu and chatting to somebody on the phone. I sat down quietly and sipped my punch; the tension between my shoulder blades seemed to dissolve into a light mist and floated off my back into the restaurant. I looked at the menu, already knowing what I intended to order.

"Kevin, do you know what you want?"

He looked over at me, and still talking on the phone, pointed at the pepper steak.

I ordered yushan with chicken and told the waitress what he wanted. I was beginning to get irritated with Kevin because he was so into this phone call, but I didn't say anything, considering where I had just been. When he finally hung up I didn't even bother to ask him who he was talking to, and he didn't volunteer the information either. I felt the jealousy bug biting me in the ass and realized I had already started to implicate him based on my guilty conscience.

Man, I need another punch. I called the waitress over and ordered another one, even though I had just barely finished with the first. Kevin looked at me with concern.

"Baby, are you all right?"

I glared up from my drink. "Yeah, I'm fine. Why?"

"No reason, you just look a little stressed. Is there anything I can do?"

"No, Kevin, no there is nothing you can do, I'm cool. By the way, Paige is meeting us down here."

"She is? Didn't you just leave her house?"

"Yes, I did. Dang, you sure have a lot of questions today."

"Damn, Jaz, why you snapping at me, did I do something?"

Just at that moment I realized my mistake. I was taking all my frustrations about Marcus out on Kevin.

"Baby, look I'm sorry; I'm just a little out of sorts. I think I'm about to start my cycle."

That was my out. I always used my female issues to get me out of tight situations and usually it worked. As I sat there thinking about my selfish emotional infidelity and waiting for Paige to show up to save me, our food arrived, along with my second punch. I took a deep swallow and let the freedom that the liquor brought quench my thirst for salvation—something I should have gotten from church but missed because of a need to quench something else.

We sat and ate, not saying much. It was apparent that Kevin didn't have a whole lot to say to me; he focused on the flat-screen television situated above my head. I didn't have a lot to say, either, but the alcohol buzz snuck up on me and forced me into a chatter I found hard to control.

"So who was that on the phone?"

He glanced up from his plate. "It was my boy Tony."

"Oh, what's up with him?"

"Nothing much, just doing the family thing, his, girlfriend is going to have another baby."

"Wow, that's cool. So how's your pepper steak?"

"It's good. How's your food?"

"I love it; it tastes really good. So what are going to do when you leave here?"

"I'm going to the crib to finish watching the game. You coming home?"

"Yes, I'm so tired."

"You do seem sort of drained. Church had you going like that?"

"Yeah, it was really good."

"What did the pastor preach about?"

Uh oh. "He preached about faith and tithing," I lied.

"That whole thing."

"What do you mean by that?" I said sharply.

"Nothing, Jaz, I'm not trying to get into a serious discussion right now."

"Whatever, Kevin."

I finished my second drink and decided I had had enough. I asked the waitress to box our food and called Paige to tell her never mind showing up; we were leaving. She didn't answer, so I left her a message and sat staring at Kevin trying to figure out why I even bothered. I didn't know why all of a sudden I was feeling like this; something wasn't right.

When the waitress brought the bill I waited a moment to see if Kevin was going to pick it up. It took longer than I liked, but he took it and started fishing around in his wallet for some change.

"You got it?"

"Yeah, I got it, you just get the tip."

I smirked and thought, You got it.

I rummaged through my purse for a few dollars to pay the tip and realized my phone was flashing; I had missed a call. How could I miss a call when I was just on the phone? I didn't recognize the number so I called to listen to the voicemail.

"Hey, Jaz, this is Marcus."

Oh my God. I felt the bottom of my stomach drop out.

"I'm sorry to be calling you, but I just wanted to let you know how much seeing you meant to me. You are the best thing that ever happened to me. I love you. Hope to talk to you soon. Bye, baby."

I could only imagine the look on my face; I hoped Kevin wouldn't say anything, because there was no way I would be able to explain it to Kevin. But I wasn't so lucky.

"Who was that?" he asked.

"Nobody—someone from the office trying to get in touch with me about a case."

"Trying to get in touch with you on a Sunday?"

"I guess; you know how my business is."

"I guess. So, you ready to go?"

"Yes. Let me say bye to my people and I'll meet you at home."

Inside, I heaved a huge sigh of relief that he had let it go at that.

"OK, Jaz. I'll see you at home."

# Chapter 65

WHEN I ENTERED MY APARTMENT building I realized how tired I was. I had been driving for hours and had eaten and drunk way too much. I shuffled past the concierge and pushed the elevator button. While I waited for the doors to open, my cell phone rang and Kevin's number was on the caller ID.

"Hey, baby, what's up?"

"Hey, Jaz, are you at home yet?"

"Yes, I'm at the elevator right now."

"OK, good. Listen, I'm going to stop by my boy's house for a minute, is that cool?"

A part of me wanted to snap, but the other, more exhausted part of me replied, "Yeah, whatever, Kevin, do your thing."

"Baby, are you all right?"

"Yes, I'm fine."

"OK, baby, I'll see you later on tonight."

I guess my tone of voice prompted him to ask, but his desire to kick it with his boys superseded any desire to come home to check on me.

"All right, Kevin. Bye."

I hung up, realizing I had heard Kevin say, "I love you" while the phone was closing. Oh well.

But when I got home and walked into the kitchen, it was so nasty, it just made me feel even more exhausted. Fuck it! I went to the liquor cabinet, found a half-full bottle of red wine and started drinking straight out of the bottle. I can't believe this shit. I took a deep swig and headed towards the bedroom.

Damn, what a mess! Staring at all the clothes and shit thrown around, it took everything in me to keep from screaming. I drank deeply, kicked some things around and jumped in the bed. I ain't doing shit, I decided.

I called Paige to see if she had gotten my message and to see what she had decided to do. She had just missed me down there so she stayed and had a couple, then went to find some trouble. Just like old times. I told her the entire Marcus and Kevin story and she couldn't believe the mess I was getting myself into—that was usually her MO. She laughed at me: Better you than me.

"Fuck you," I snarled, "you better help me out of this shit."

"Ah hell nah, chica, you on your own."

"What kind of friend are you?"

"The best kind, nigga. Handle yo' shit and get at me later with the details."

"Thanks a lot, Paige," I said sarcastically.

"You're welcome, babe. I'll holla."

I hung up the phone. She always made me laugh, but there really wasn't anything funny; I was in a dilemma that I had created all by myself and there was no easy way to get out.

When Kevin came home later that evening, I didn't even bother to look at the clock to see what time he strolled in. I was so upset with the way the apartment looked that if I had said something we would have ended up in a huge fight. I lay in the bed drunk, pretending to be asleep.

But when he got in the bed naked I knew what was up. I was in no mood to sleep with him, but something in me felt like it was my obligation. Most of the sex we were having recently was based on his needs, and my need to please him—my duty, so I thought.

He scooted close to me and started massaging my breast. I gave him the "Go away, not tonight" moan, but that didn't stop him. He rolled me over and began to take off my panties. I really didn't feel like anything, but I didn't fight him; I figured he'd get on top, do his thing and be done and go to sleep.

I lay there while he entered me and stroked back and forth. My body, my physical being, still enjoyed it, but inside I was torn. How could I be in love with two men? It's been said that it is impossible to truly love two people, but lying there, thinking about being with Marcus while Kevin came inside of me, seemed to prove the naysayers wrong.

Then he finished, rolled off of me and lay facing the other direction. He had never done that before, so I was worried that he may have been feeling something in my energy. I turned away and prayed. Lord, please get me out of this mess.

# Chapter 66

By Monday morning, everything I knew to be normal and right had spiraled into a black hole of disillusionment. My entire life was turned upside-down by the selfish choices I made. I had always told Kevin I would never cheat on him, but I found myself fantasizing more and more about Marcus, even though I hadn't physically cheated. It was still only a kiss, but it was a more-than-friendly kiss, and the thoughts of making love to Marcus while lying underneath Kevin felt like betrayal. The Bible does say something about thinking about a sin is the same as if you committed it.

It all felt wrong, but I couldn't help myself. Marcus was like a drug; I had to have him. And there was no way Kevin could find out about my desires, because Marcus was the only man Kevin was intimidated by. He knew how much I had loved Marcus, and kept asking me before we got serious if I was over him. I told him yes—but I didn't believe it, so why would he? If he knew or even suspected anything going on between Marcus and me, conversation or otherwise, there would be hell to pay on my part. I had to keep everything—that I'd talked to Marcus' mom, much less that I'd gone to visit him—under wraps.

As I was leaving for work, I noticed Kevin's cell phone sitting on the dining room table. It wasn't like me to pry, but all my guilt streaming through my veins seemed to make me suspect him, like I was suspicious of everyone. I scrolled through his call log while he was sleeping, and wrote down some of the numbers, especially the calls that seemed to have been made a little too late for my comfort level. Who the hell would be calling at two a.m.? I took the slip of paper and carefully put his phone back where I had found it. Then I scooped up my keys, my purse, and my briefcase and headed for the door. I didn't bother waking Kevin up since he had had such a fulfilling evening. I left the apartment without a word and shot to the elevator before Kevin would know I was gone.

When I pulled into the parking ramp at work, I recognized Kurt, a guy I had met at the club quite a few years back. He was dressed very casually, which was unlike him, so I figured he wasn't there for a court appearance.

He was the first man I was into after Marcus left. He was a highly educated brother, tall, thin with beautiful cappuccino-colored skin. He wore the coolest wire-rimmed glasses and dressed like a college professor. I really dug him, but what you saw on the outside was a far cry from what this brother was really about on the inside.

When we met, the attraction was instant and evident. He was smart, intellectual, and very well-spoken, which intrigued me the most. I was a sucker for a good conversation and he and I would talk for hours about everything under the sun. He was a teacher and a poet and had traveled all over the world doing and seeing things most of us only dream about. He had me hooked right away, but he played this game of cat-and-mouse that I hated but had to learn to accept.

On any given day we would have a wonderful time, talking, getting together, going to bars with poetry expos or live bands, art exhibits and jazz venues. H/he was all that, and I fell for him hook, line, and sinker. The only thing that confused me was his constant disappearing act; and I mean he would disappear for months at a time. He would stop calling and answering his phone, never returned voicemail messages and became a complete ghost—until he needed me again. It was crazy, but at that point in my life I was searching for the perfect dude, and for me he fit the bill. So even though I knew better, whenever he called, I answered.

He was so different, and underneath the hard exterior he had spent years building around him, I could see a man who truly desired an authentic love. And of course I thought I was the one who could give it to him.

One night we ended up at the Underground Bar on campus. When the bartender came, I ordered us a round of beer.

Kurt was a beer drinker and a real slick cat, but he never hid that; early on he made it clear he didn't have any money—being a starving artist and all that—and that I was going to have to "carry him." When he said that, a little red flag went up, but strangely, I think it was this confident up-in-your-face attitude that had amped me about him the most. And I had money, so I just ignored those little alarm bells going off in my head. Besides, I had finally found a man who aroused my intellect as well as everything else, and on top of all that I really enjoyed his company—loud, out-of-pocket antics and all. Shit, what's a couple of dollars?

So that night when I looked around and saw beer was only two dollars a bottle, I thought once again, it's cool—it's literally a couple of dollars. I could buy quite a few and not feel like I was being played.

When our drinks arrived, I gave the bartender a twenty for the two I bought. She returned my change and I tipped her a dollar, leaving me with two tens and a five, all the cash I had on me that night. I put the money in my pocket and turned to watch the show.

The soft touch of his hand to the back of my neck helped to erase any suspicions about him. He was the real deal, the type of guy I could really get into. I liked his vibe, his style and the fact that he carried himself like a man. Strong, daunting, and totally in charge, he know how to give me exactly what I was looking for.

I paid for another round, but before we could finish them he was ready to go. He was weird like that—everything at a whim. It didn't bother me, though; I was leaving with him and that was all that mattered.

When we got to my car, I asked, "Where to?"

"Your place. I got some things I want to show you."

"OK, fine." I started the car and headed for home. At that point, spending the night at my house was usually a no-no for guys I had randomly met. But I'd spent hours on the phone with Kurt just talking, and he had taken me to so many cool places something in me trusted him.

The cool midnight air sailed in and out of the windows as we headed toward my place. He pulled a CD out of his backpack and stuck it in the player; damn, Miles Davis never sounded so good. He softly caressed my neck while I drove, quietly listening carefully to every note coming from Miles' horn.

When we got to my house, I turned off the car, I removed the CD, returning it to the case and handing it to Kurt.

"No, you keep it. Just make sure I get it back," he said.

I smiled. "I will."

Kurt was gracious like that. Even though I paid for everything when we went out, still, he was always giving me something—music, incense, DVDs to watch, magazines, books to read; things I think he intended for me to learn from, things that were supposed to help me elevate myself. I think he liked that I listened, without judgment or prejudice.

When I opened the door to my apartment I could tell he was impressed. He walked around carefully studying every artifact, painting, and sculpture I had carefully arranged.

"Do you like the artwork?" I asked him, impressed that he seemed to be interested.

"Yes. It's really nice."

"I get them from the hair salon I go to. The owner is from Mozambique and travels there quite frequently. I've tried my best not to buy up the entire store."

"Would you like a drink?"

He asked for vodka and orange juice, so I poured two heavy shots, topping them with a splash of OJ. If this didn't get the party started, nothing would. I brought them into the living room, bending down seductively to give Kurt his glass from his perch on the couch, then I thumbed through my CDs looking for something I knew he would enjoy. John Coltrane—perfect.

As the smooth, mystic sounds of Coltrane floated through the air, Kurt took a huge sip, then set the glass down on the coffee table.

"Would you like to dance?"

I hadn't felt like this since Marcus, so the feeling of Kurt's body so close to mine lifted me—lifted me in such a way that once again I believed all things were possible for me. I finally felt like I could give in, freeing my heart and removing the hurt from my soul.

We swayed dreamily to the music for I don't know how long—an hour maybe? Then he slowly and gently walked me towards the bedroom. He lowered me to the bed and began to slowly undress me, as I started to tremble. I smiled and lifted my behind enough for him to remove my pants. When he undressed, I was pleasantly surprised; he was slender but not narrow, and the sight of his naked body seemed to unlock a sea of sexual desire.

I studied him slowly. There was no room for error; I wanted him, forever, and tonight was the night I was going to make it official. I didn't care that he was aloof; my intentions were to love him so good in one night that he would never leave.

I reached to tease the soft hair that covered the center of his chest, and placed small, delicate kisses there. I moved slowly to each nipple, kissing and sucking, taking my time to please as much of him as I could. He moaned, as did I, and before I could speak, he brought me up face to face, kissing me like we were meant to be.

We spent the evening exploring each other's bodies, tasting and teasing, touching and pleasing, until we were both entirely spent.

Maybe love was meant for me after all, I thought. Kurt was more to me than just a quick passing of time, and he had given me something I had never had, not even with Marcus.

Kurt had given me vision, a glimpse of myself. His uncompromising attitude made me sit up and take notice to all the things I truly desired to do—writing, freedom of expression, saying and doing exactly what you wanted. Those were the things that were missing from my life and Kurt was there to give it to me, and then some. I appreciated him for that; he showed me something deeper than love could ever show: He showed me who

I was, or was meant to be. We lay intertwined, sleeping peacefully, a serene silence surrounding us.

But the next morning was havoc. Kurt had to be home to get his daughter; the baby's mother was dropping her off at six o'clock, before she had to go to work, and the clock was showing five-thirty, so we rushed to get dressed and practically ran to the car. We made it to the freeway in record time. When we got to his house, before he got out we kissed and sealed our fate.

"Goodbye, baby."

"Goodbye, Kurt. I hope you have a beautiful day," I said, still half-asleep and dreamy from the beautiful night we had spent together.

"I'll call you when I get off work, OK?"

"OK." I watched as he sauntered to his one-room in a rooming house. I smiled, and like I always did when this happened, thanked God for something I had been praying for, for a long time.

As I drove home, I felt like I was seeing things I had never seen before. I was ready for anything, taking charge and finally doing what I wanted. This was a new beginning and I welcomed the challenge.

In my apartment I readied my mind for church. I had missed the last two Sundays and knew the pastor would be looking for me if I didn't show up today. It was still very early so I decided to wash a load of clothes.

I separated the laundry into light and colored clothes; I'd wash the colored clothes first. The jeans I was wearing needed to be washed, so I reached into the pockets to get the money out that I had left in them from the night before.

I fished around, but my pocket was empty. That was odd, I was sure I had put the bills in there last night before I went out. I had two tens left and knew they were supposed to be in my pocket. I pulled the pocket inside out—nothing. I checked the other pocket; empty too.

Maybe I put it in my purse. I ran to the kitchen to find my purse, unzipped it, dumped everything out on the kitchen counter. I rummaged around in the pile, but nothing. Then I ran back to my bedroom and checked the bed, the floor, underneath the bed, my pockets again. Nothing.

"I know that nigga did not take my money," I thought, as the first little sprouts of doubt started to creep into my mind. Then I looked through everything—the things on my dresser, the bathroom; I even ran down to the garage to check the car.

My money was not there, and anyway I know where I put it. It was gone.

Shit! That motherfucker took my money!

Everything in me seized. I was stunned, angry, hurt, ashamed, and most of all confused. How could I let this happen to me? Tears mixed with last night's mascara welled up, stinging my eyes.

I punched in his number. He was going to get a tongue-lashing he wouldn't soon forget.

But it all dissipated when I heard his voice on his voicemail message.

"Kurt, this is Jasmine," I said into my phone. "I'm missing twenty dollars, I know I had it and I know where it was. It is not here," I said in a strangled-sounding voice, trying with all my might to hold back the tears.

"OK, you win, I get it. The lesson I just learned is so way more important than any relationship we developed. You really know how to make a point. I hope that you use that money for something you actually need, because you didn't have to take it. If you had asked I would have happily given it to you. I guess that is what you don't understand about me, and where we differ as people. You just don't know how much stronger you have made me; or maybe you do. Good-bye Kurt . . . ." I trailed off. Fearing that I would start sobbing into the phone, I quickly hung up.

Then the floodgates opened. I sprawled out on the living room floor, bawling and asking God why? There was no way I was going to make it to church now; Pastor is going to kill me. I better call them and let them know I won't be in service again. I scrolled through my phone numbers to my pastor's home number; I knew they would already be at church so I could leave the message and avoid talking to them. I knew it would take a couple of days before they could get to me, and hopefully by then I would be somewhat straight.

The answering machine came on and I left tear-filled message, telling them I was in a bad place and that I would contact them when I had gotten my stuff together. I knew they wouldn't buy that excuse for long, but it would buy me some time.

I spent the rest of the day crying and kicking myself for being such a fool. The bottle of vodka kept me from completely losing it, but the aftermath of the hangover caused me to miss a couple of days of work.

There was no turning back now. God had forsaken me for the last time.

## Chapter 67

"Jasmine, what's up, girl? Long time no see."
I walked over to where Kurt was standing by the elevator entrance in the parking lot. I had forgotten how tall he was, and his "basketball player" body—my favorite.

"Soooo, Jasmine, what have you been up to. You still got that boyfriend?"

"How do you know I have a boyfriend?"

"Girl, you know I get around, word on the street is that you and that dude are pretty tight. Aaah, you fell into that monogamous trap, huh?"

"Well, Kurt, just because you have a fear of commitment doesn't mean every man does. And if you must know, we are doing it big."

"How come he gets to be so lucky?"

"Kurt, don't start. You know how come, you had your chance, you know why he is in my bed and you ain't."

"Damn, girl, are we having another domestic? How come every time we see each other we get into an argument?"

"Don't ask me, you're the one that be trippin.'"

"You still upset with me about the twenty dollars?"

"Hell nah, Negro, yo' ass obviously needed it. I hope you took care of yo' business."

"Why you acting like this, Jasmine? Here, you want your money back?" He started fishing in his back pocket for his wallet and pulled out a stack of twenties.

"Kurt, get away from me, you're crazy."

"Nah here, take it."

"You know what, sweetheart, I'm not going to argue with you; I'm late for work. You take care of yourself, OK?"

I walked towards the elevators, but I found myself turning to teasingly wave bye. It was strange—something in me really liked him, really liked him, but re-handing him control over my psyche I couldn't do.

When I finally got to my desk I sat there for a minute trying to figure out what type of karma I had attracted. Seeing Kurt was not what I needed; I was already feeling a little vulnerable—mostly because of my emotional infidelity, but seeing those late phone calls to Kevin had me on edge as well. I took the slip of paper out of my purse and stared at the phone numbers to see if I recognized any of them. The only number that really concerned me was the one that came in at late-night hours.

I decided I would do a reverse search on the phone number. The phone was registered to a C. Larson—damn, that could be anybody. I sat there staring at the number, contemplating the drama if I called it. Don't be stupid; this could be anything or anybody, I told myself. You'll only make an ass out of yourself if you dial that number.

I decided to just hold on to the number and see if it came up any more. I could check the phone bill records to see how often the number was being called; then I could confront him.

I had somehow completely turned my guilt trip into a quest to catch Kevin cheating. I had no reason to suspect it—I had just convinced myself that if I was feeling this way, he had to be feeling the same. I was tired and fed up with the complacency of our relationship.

I didn't have any pressing cases, so I decided I would turn around and go home and talk to him; something had to change. I buzzed Wendy and told her I was going to leave and that I wouldn't be coming back.

As I drove home, I went through the conversation I would have with him. Trying to come up with all the most important points I wanted to make, I was basically preparing myself for trial, with him as the defendant and me as the victim, but I had to be

## I Surrender All

careful not to implicate myself or my whole interrogation could go terribly wrong.

I opened up the front door, expecting to see Kevin in front of the big screen playing video games like always, but he wasn't there. I walked into the bedroom and looked around; the bathroom door was closed and I could hear the shower running. I walked over and opened the door.

"Kevin?" He didn't answer.

"Kevin, we need to talk." I could see him moving behind the frosted class of the shower door, but he still didn't say anything. I reached out and opened the shower door.

"Kevin. I really need to talk to you." He looked at me at with disdain, then suddenly he grabbed my hand and pulled me inside, fully dressed, shoes and all.

"Kevin," I screamed, "what are you doing?"

"Ah, stop tripping," he said as he ripped off my shirt and began tugging at my skirt. "Take that shit off, I've got something I want to show you."

"Kevin, stop! I'm getting all wet!"

"I know, that's why you're in here, so I can get you wet."

"But my hair, my clothes."

"Baby, don't worry about all of that, just let me take you away for a minute. Is that OK? Can your man take you for a little ride?" He smiled.

All of my suspicion, all of my anger seemed to be washing down the drain as I felt him pressing up against me. Ooh, he is so fine; I took the rest of my wet clothes off and threw them onto the bathroom floor; those urges were getting the best of me again.

But still, it wasn't our ordinary routine sex. "Kevin, why are you doing this?"

"Look, Jasmine, you've been kind of distant lately, and I don't know why. I just want to please you, is that all right? Damn, can I please my woman?"

I looked in his eyes and wholeheartedly said, "Yes, yes you can."

The reconnecting we did in the shower made me forget all about the phone numbers. It felt like he touched me in ways he had never touched me before, or at least not for a long, long time. He took me for a ride just like he said he would, and all my negative feelings about the relationship suddenly seemed so distant. He was all that I had asked him to be.

We left the shower and lay down in the bed, exploring each other as we once did. We spent the rest of the day and evening in bed, like we used to do back when we first started dating, and the next morning, it seemed like we had left all our animosity and anger behind, in some other past. I was up early changing the sheets, cooking breakfast and preparing myself for a wonderful day ahead. Kevin was even up, and cleaning too. It was like we had started all over again—and all thoughts of Marcus seemed to have disappeared.

Maybe I had been wrong about Kevin; maybe it was *me* who hadn't given the relationship a chance. I was always looking for something better, something more intense. Kevin was feeding off my negativity and regurgitating it back on me. I had given him the ammunition to fight against me. He had never really done anything wrong from where I was standing. The fact that he hadn't worked in a while was because of a semi-depressive state that I must have put him in. It was my fault that he couldn't be all that he could be. I had to make it up to him somehow.

I decided that I needed to let him know how much I truly loved him, right then. I walked into the study, where—I couldn't believe it—he was on the computer looking for a job. I thought at first I wouldn't disturb him but I needed to let him know what I was feeling.

"Kevin, baby, can I talk to for a minute?"

"Yeah, sure, what's up?"

"Baby, I would like to apologize for the way I've been acting lately. I guess I felt like *you* were being distant so I separated myself from you even more. I know you're having a hard time right now, but I have faith in you, you'll find something soon."

"Yes, baby, I know—as a matter of fact, I have an interview scheduled for tomorrow morning." Wow. I guess he hadn't been such a freeloader after all; I should have given him more credit.

"Wow, that's great, who is it with?"
"Oh, it's with a graphics arts company in Edina."
"Oh, that sounds cool. I hope you get it."
"Yeah, I do too. Sitting around this house was getting depressing."
"Yeah, I know baby," I said sympathetically. "I don't have to tell you good luck; I know you'll charm them to death."
"Yeah, Jaz, I hope so." He paused. "By the way, what made you come home so early yesterday?"
"Oh nothing, I just wanted to see how you were doing; we haven't spent much quality time together lately and I really didn't have a whole lot of work to do," I lied.
"Anyway, I'm going to do some work here at home, then make you lunch. Is that cool?"
"Yeah, baby, that's fine with me."
I walked away feeling really good. Now that he was up and actually trying, I could focus more on him and us, rather than Marcus and me. Kevin seemed different since last night, and since he must have been already looking for a job without me knowing it, maybe his complacency had passed and he was ready to move on to bigger and better things—our relationship, our future, our life, together. I could forget about Marcus and move on with Kevin. He had proved to me that he would be there for me no matter what, and I welcomed our newfound commitment. Now, no one or nothing could separate us.

Except for a positive pregnancy test.

# Chapter 68

When I had missed my period two months ago, I didn't think much of it—I was never one of those women who had periods you could practically set your watch by, like some of my girlfriends. But when I missed it the next month, I got an uncomfortable little twinge; it wasn't like me to miss two in a row like that. I had been taking my pills, but lately, I'd been forgetting a day, then trying to catch up; I'd been on the pill long enough that I figured there must be enough of those hormones in my system that it wouldn't really make a difference, so I put off thinking about it for about a week. But then I thought, OK, I'll just do the test and it'll be negative, and then I won't have to think about it anymore.

I looked over towards Kevin as he lay in bed staring at the ceiling, covers pulled up to his neck. He was silent. I believe he knew I hadn't had a period in a while, but he never said anything or asked any questions. I opened the pregnancy test packaging and left the room.

When I walked out of the bathroom with the urine-covered stick and both windows showing dark blue lines, I paused to figure out a way to break this to Kevin. We had been going strong for the past two months; he had gotten that job in Edina, and it was going well. I was working hard and bringing in new clients. My workload had skyrocketed, and so did my income. We were comfortable. I hadn't tried to contact Marcus since that one time; he had called me for a while, but when I never answered, he must have finally gotten the message, because he had stopped. I guess he figured I had moved on.

The bedroom seemed much colder when I walked back into it. Kevin was sitting on the edge of the bed. He seemed mesmerized, almost, and he was staring at me—but the look in his eyes was not one of anticipation or joy; it was closer to disgust and disappointment.

"I'm pregnant."

He looked up from his trance. "Are you sure?"

I handed him the stick in silence, and then walked to the kitchen to get a drink. Wait—I can't drink; I'm pregnant.

I could see Kevin on the phone. I took a bottle of water from the fridge. I don't think the concept of being a mother had sunk in yet; I was way too calm. I opened the bottle and swallowed deeply as I tried to put everything in perspective. I'm in my early thirties; I have a stable home, a great career, and a man who loves me. I could pull this off; *we* could pull this off. I drained the bottle and went back to the bedroom to talk to Kevin.

But as soon as I looked at his face, it was clear he didn't feel the same.

"What's wrong, baby?"

"Nothing, Jasmine."

"Baby, I can see that something is wrong, talk to me."

"We can't keep this baby."

I stared.

"What do you mean, we can't keep this baby? What else would we do? I'm not giving it up for adoption, and an abortion is out of the question."

"Why?"

"Why what, Kevin?"

"Why can't you get an abortion? Jasmine, I'm not ready for a baby."

As confident as I had been feeling minutes before, now I had never felt so alone. "You know why, Kevin," I said, and stormed out of the room. I grabbed my keys and jetted to the elevator. I was half-hoping Kevin would try to stop me, but he didn't.

I should have realized how he felt about children when he had told me he had had a child when he was still in high school. They had been together for a while but after he found out she was pregnant, he and his parents made some arrangements that kept him from really taking responsibility for the situation. That should have been my first clue.

The fact the baby's mother never came sniffing around our way when we got together was even better. In retrospect, I realize my own selfishness kept me from delving into that situation. I wanted Kevin all to myself and I was not about to share him with a baby's mother—or a baby, either. Because his daughter was not a part of his life—by his choice—I didn't ask any questions and he didn't offer any answers.

But now that I was pregnant with his baby, the anguish of the mother of his first child seemed to radiate through my womb, and I struggled to find the perfect apology to the sweet little girl who never knew, or had a connection to the man that helped to conceive her.

I was really in no condition to drive, so I decided to go for a walk. I pressed the up button on the elevator and rode to the top floor, thinking about the new life growing inside of me.

Light rain was falling, so the walking path was empty; raindrops had coated the leaves, the flowers, and the grass. I looked at them, in awe of their resilience. The smell of the wet grass reminded me of the days when I would help Mama mow the lawn.

I couldn't understand what was happening to me. Shit, thinking back, the baby was probably conceived the day I left work early to chastise Kevin on that phone number shit. Go figure.

Maybe God was speaking to me, trying to get me to truly understand His power and love for me. But why use a baby to do that? And why now, when everything with Kevin was beginning to work itself out?

I decided I needed to get away for a while. Kevin needed some space and time to think and so did I. My girlfriend Tiffany in Louisiana had been begging me to come visit her but I couldn't, or wouldn't, make the time. Now, it suddenly seemed like the right time. I could relax, get some sun, and figure all this out.

Kevin could do whatever he wanted to for the few days I would be gone. Maybe this baby had just stirred up old feelings about his first child; once he realized this was a different situation, he'd see everything differently. Now all I had to do was to call Tiffany to make sure it was a good time for me to come down.

I had met Tiffany during the summer of my senior year in college. We were among twenty students from around the country to do a six-week legal study on the airline industry, when we toured major hubs throughout the country.

We hit it off immediately and we did everything together. Since the first few weeks of the program were in Minnesota, I got the opportunity to show Tiffany around the Twin Cities. We hit up the malls and the clubs, the clubs getting all they could stand from us. We partied, drank, kicked it, and we had stayed friends ever since, despite the distance between us.

I was drenched by now, but walking around the rooftop path, thinking about old times felt good. Something in me was happy; maybe that something inside me was my new life, my new destiny.

# Chapter 69

My bags were all packed and I had asked my brother to take me to the airport. Kevin was still on probation at work, so I didn't want to be the one to make him late. When I called my brother, he immediately said yes, even though the flight was at the crack of dawn, because he knew I was going down to Louisiana to see Tiffany, whom he thought was hella fine. I teased him that she was happily married, but he didn't care; he still wanted me to hook him up.

After I had hung up I sat there a minute smiling, thinking about my brother and how he would feel to be an uncle. I guess I must have been really cheesin' because the automatic "what you smiling at" that came from Kevin's lips snapped me out of my daydream.

"Oh, nothing. I was just thinking about something my brother said. He's going to take me to the airport in the morning. OK?"

"Yeah, that's cool, that way I can sleep in a little longer."

I stared him down even though he was not looking my way. "Kevin, don't be late for work tomorrow trying to sleep in."

"Nah, I won't, I'm'a make it on time."

He sounded agitated, so I just left it alone. "I'm going to take a shower; do you want to join me?"

"No, I'm cool, I'm just going to get something to drink and watch TV for a little while. I'll be in there later."

"Oh, OK. I'll be in the bed then."

I walked to the bathroom and tried to reassure myself that everything was going to be fine. Kevin and I had been together for a while now. He'll come around, I was sure of it, and when he came to bed tonight I'd help it along by giving him exactly what he liked most—me.

In my dream, I was falling from a place I had never been before. The visions I experienced as I spiraled towards the ground weren't frightening but were revealing; the astonishment of hitting the ground woke me up.

Damn! If you hit the ground it means you're going to die; I remember hearing that somewhere. I reached over to hug Kevin, praying for comfort, it seemed so real.

The bed was empty. I sat straight up and looked at the clock. It was four-thirty; he must have fallen asleep on the couch. I put on my robe and walked into the living room. The television was on but the volume was turned down to just a murmur.

"Kevin?" No answer.

I looked around, poked my head in the other rooms. He wasn't here.

What the hell? I walked over to the phone and dialed his number.

"Hello?"

I was silent, shocked at the fact that he answered his phone, out God knows where.

"Hello, Jaz?"

"Kevin! Where are you?"

"I'm out at my homeboy's house."

"At four-thirty in the morning? You expect me to believe that?"

"Yeah, because that is where I am."

"You mean to tell me that you left out of this house and didn't have the decency or respect to tell me you were leaving? What if something were to happen to you? You know what, never mind!"

I hung up the phone, fuming. This motherfucker thinks I'm stupid. I stormed back into my room, thinking of all the things I was going to say to him when he finally got home. There was no way I was going to be able to go back to sleep so I just lay there staring up at the ceiling, trying to figure out which bitch he was just fucking with.

I heard the key in the apartment door lock, and then the door opened and I heard him softly call my name. I pretended to be asleep as walked into the bedroom and quietly took off his coat and shoes, trying not to wake me.

"Kevin, where were you?" I couldn't stop myself from speaking up.

"Damn, I just went to my boy's house for a minute."

"Oh, for real, and you couldn't wake me to tell me that?"

"I could have but I didn't want to. You were asleep."

"Kevin, do you realize how disrespectful and insensitive that is?"

"What are you talking about?"

"Kevin, if something was to happen to you I wouldn't know shit. What you were wearing, where you had gone. Don't you think that that would be pertinent information for me to have? You just get up and leave in the middle of the night, what kind of shit is that? What if I were to do something like that?"

It was obvious he had been drinking; I could smell the liquor on him as soon as he got in the bed. He didn't say anything.

"Kevin, are you just going to ignore me?"

"Look, Jasmine, I told you where I was; I'm through with it."

He rolled over to his usual spot in the bed and went to sleep. I lay there fighting back tears, rubbing my stomach and praying for the sun to slip through the small opening in my curtains.

# Chapter 70

WHEN I FINALLY BOARDED THE plane I could feel the tension in my shoulders begin to release. I really wanted the waitress to bring me a glass of wine, but the little person growing inside me didn't care for wine.

The airplane was already pretty full when I got on and searched for my seat among the other coach travelers. I had intended to ride first class but no seats were available by the time I booked my ticket at the last minute.

My seat was located mid-plane at the window next to a thin, balding white man. His lightly frosted blond hair and his very obvious comb-over reminded me of a young Donald Trump. He looked studiously out of the window as I approached his row; he might as well have been wearing a sign that said, "Don't even try to talk to me." It didn't matter because I had no intentions of talking to anyone; my main focus was to get to New Orleans and just chill. So I was surprised when he struck up a conversation. His opening line was so formal I almost had to smile.

"Hello, miss, how are you today?"

"I'm fine, sir. And you?"

"I'm all right, just ready to get this trip started. I'm in need of a serious vacation."

"I hear that, you and me both."

"So is New Orleans your final destination?"

"Yes it is, I have a girlfriend down there I'm going to see."

"Have you ever been to New Orleans before?"

"No, this would be my first time."

"Well, you are definitely in for a treat; New Orleans is the place for anything under the sun. Whatever it is that you're interested in, New Orleans has it."

"I'm really not into a lot of partying right now. I just found out I'm going to have a baby, just going down here to relax with my friend and her family."

"Wow, congratulations! Is this your first?"

"Yes, it is."

"Your husband couldn't come with you?"

"Oh, I'm not married, but my fiancé couldn't get off work." That wasn't the reason he wasn't with me, but it wasn't a lie, I figured.

"Wow, what a lucky man. A child is such a blessing."

"Thank you, sir. I really needed that."

"Call me Paul."

"OK. My name is Jasmine."

It was so nice to have someone finally on my side. I hadn't talked to anyone about the baby except Kevin and it felt good to have someone tell me not to worry, everything was going to work itself out.

As we got off the plane Paul took my carry-on bag and walked with me to the top of the ramp and all the way to baggage claim. Tiffany was waiting; she must have seen me first, because when I spotted her, she was smiling and waving. I turned to Paul to thank him and give him a huge hug. I wanted to let him know how much I appreciated his kind words, and to ask for his e-mail. He was such a kind, generous person, and I wanted to keep in touch. But when I turned back toward him to take my bag from him, it was sitting at my feet and he was nowhere to be found. I scoured the area, looking at faces and clothing trying to figure out where he had gone so fast.

I turned to Tiffany. "Tif, did you see the man that was with me?"

"What man, girl?"

"The white man who was helping me, carry my bag."

"No Jaz, I didn't see anyone, what are you talking about?"

"There was a gentleman who sat with me on the plane and I just wanted to thank him."

"Jasmine, baby, I didn't see anyone. Are you ready to go, love?" I looked around the airport one last time, hoping to catch a glimpse of him, but he was gone.

I didn't completely understand the meaning of our chance encounter, but knew that whoever he was, he was a wonderful man, and a true blessing. He had put my spirit at peace in a way I hadn't felt for a while, and I thanked God for the tiny miracle he had just provided.

Walking into Tiffany's house, I knew I had made the right decision to come down here. Her presence and the warmth of her home was just what I needed. She showed me my room and asked if I wanted to freshen up. I thanked her, set all my things in the small guest room and hurried to the bathroom to change and do something with my hair. She had already mentioned on the drive in that she had major plans for us, and I just wanted to be ready for anything she was willing to throw at me.

I walked out of the bathroom feeling refreshed.

"Tiffany, where's Malik and your sweet little girl?"

"Oh, girl, Malik is at work and Destiny is at school. They'll be home later on tonight. You'll get to see them soon enough. Right now, though, we can have some private time together."

I laughed. "All right, sweetie, whatever you say. So what do you have planned for us today?"

"Well, first let's go have breakfast. We got this place here that servers a crazy breakfast, any kind of seafood you want with grits and gravy and shoot, girl, whatever you can think of they'll make it."

"All right, sounds good to me."

As she drove, I looked out at New Orleans. All that I saw amazed me; it was so different from home. There was an elegant richness about this place, even the poor ghetto streets we passed through on our way. There just seemed to be a warmth and depth about the people, and with the flowers, the warm sun, and soft breeze and I felt like I had been set free. I leaned back, thinking about my life and the new life growing inside of me. Now felt like the perfect time to tell Tiffany. I turned to her and smiled.

"Tiffany, guess what?" There must have been something in my voice, because she looked at me, a little confused.

"What, sweetie?"

I smiled even harder. "Guess."

"What, girl, you sure got a goofy grin on your face. What's going on, Jaz?"

"Tiffany, I'm pregnant."

"What?" She screamed. "When, how, what? Oh my God, congratulations! Why did you wait so long to tell me, when did all this happen, how far along are you, what did Kevin say?"

"Dang Tif, hold up a minute, one question at a time. I found out right before I came here, you know how it happened, and Kevin, well Kevin is trippin'. He wants me to get an abortion."

"What? Why?" Her excitement turned to concern.

"I don't know, girl, he thinks that we aren't ready, I guess."

"Well, what do you want to do?"

"I want to keep it, Tiffany; I have already had more than my share of abortions."

"What do you mean, baby?" The frown in her forehead grew even deeper.

The sun streaming through the car window suddenly felt too hot, scrambling my brain and the tears began to flow.

I had never told anyone about the abortions except for Mama and Kevin, and even Mama didn't know about the second one. After Marcus went to jail, the missed birth control pills and the positive pregnancy test took me right back to the same clinic I had been to before as a teenager. Now a woman, I sat in the lobby all alone, waiting all over again to be stripped of the baby I had conceived with my now jailbird ex-fiancé. As I told Tiffany, the pain I felt reliving the two worst mistakes in my life seemed almost worse than what I had gone through at the time.

With tears in her eyes, Tiffany pulled up to the restaurant and parked the car. She looked over at me and hugged me.

"Tiffany I cannot abort this baby, I can't. God is not going to give me another chance at this. I know that."

Tiffany squeezed my hand. "Don't worry about it baby, Kevin will come around. He ain't crazy. You are a beautiful woman and you are carrying his child. He *will* come around, just give him some time."

I looked at her as she wiped the tears from my face with her hand.

"I hope you're right, Tif. If I have to get rid of this baby I don't know what I'll do."

"Don't worry, Jaz. If you need me to talk to Kevin I will, and I'll explain to him what a blessing a child brings to your life. Destiny is exactly that, my destiny, and I couldn't imagine life without her. And if he don't get right, then you move down here with me and I'll help you raise that baby."

I hugged her as hard as I could. I knew she was dead serious and a part of me seriously thought about doing it. "Thank you, Tiffany. I love you."

"I love you too, sweetheart. Now let's go get something to eat, I know you and li'l mama are hungry."

"What, do you think it will be a girl?"

"Yes. Jasmine, actually I do; the way you are glowing right now, I can see her smile shining right through you."

Looking down, I caressed my tummy and said hello to my little miracle, my little girl.

The restaurant was decorated in an old Creole style with a Latin feel, and the food smelled delicious. Even better was the tall handsome man who approached us, smiling from ear to ear. As we followed him to the only available booth in the back of the restaurant, I looked him over.

"Damn, do all the men look like that down here?" I whispered to Tiffany.

"Hell yeah, girl, we got a lot of together brothers down here just waiting for the right woman to come along."

"Well, damn, he is so off the chain, can he make me forget all about, um, what's his name?"

We giggled as we stared at the chiseled arms and chest of the Nubian prince gracing our presence.

"Will this be OK, ladies?"

"Yes," I was quick to answer.

"All right, you ladies relax; I'll be right back with water and a couple of menus."

Everyone seemed so happy; at least it's what I saw. The servers were smiling, the guests were smiling, and all seemed right with the world. When the waiter returned, he quietly set the glasses of water on the table and gently handed the menus to us. It was odd, but it felt like he was staring at me.

"You ladies take your time and I'll be back in a little while to take your orders."

Our eyes met and a smile I didn't intend squeezed its way through my lips and onto my face. Without hesitation he smiled back and innocently winked at me, giving the go-ahead to proceed with the flirting. Then he walked away to wait on another table.

"Tiffany, did you see him flirting with me?" I said

"No, I saw you flirting with him."

"I was not!"

"Yeah, right, girl, it's OK. You're thousands of miles away from home, ain't nothing wrong with a little bit of flirting; in fact it's good for you, keeps the juices flowing."

"Girl, please—I'm the last person to need any more juices flowing. I've got enough flowing right now; for me, you, and the two tables behind us."

"You are so crazy. What do you want to eat?"

I laughed, finally feeling relaxed and ready to enjoy myself.

When the waiter returned to take our orders I realized I was so hungry I could have ordered everything on the menu. In the last couple of days I felt like was eating everything in sight. It couldn't have been because of the baby, I was only a few weeks pregnant, so I chalked it up to a psychological thing. Restraining myself, I asked for the honey-wheat pancakes, grits, and the beer battered shrimp with crawfish gravy. I also ordered some of their Southern sweet tea, which Tiffany said the restaurant was known for. Tiffany ordered a seafood omelet and the hash browns with everything, and they weren't joking about the "everything." I had never seen anything like it.

"Is that really good?"

"Girl, just wait, I'm'a let you taste it. OK?"

"All right, if you say so." I gave her the high eyebrow look, and she gave me an "All right, doubt me if you dare" smirk.

The place was filling up fast and there was a steady stream of people coming and going.

"This must be the spot."

"It is, they've been down here doing this for over twenty-five years and it's never empty."

"Damn, so it's a family-owned business."

"Yep totally, run by an elderly man and his three sons."

"Wow, it's just like the barbecue restaurant I used to work at when I was in college."

Why at that moment did a picture of Marcus pop into my head? I decided I'd better not think about him anymore, so I told Tiffany I had to go outside to call my mom and Kevin and let them know I made it here safely.

I walked outside and found a wrought iron bench surrounded by a rectangle of light green grass, obviously newly planted. I could feel the heat radiating from the bench even before I sat down, but it didn't bother me; I was trying to soak up all the warmth it offered. It would be no time before I was back home, where it was winter half the year.

It was close to noon and I knew Mama would be waiting on my call, so I called her first.

"Hey, Mom."

"Aah, it's about time, what took you so long to call?"

"Oh, nothing in particular, Mom, just getting settled down here. Tiffany and I are at this restaurant right now, getting ready to get our grub on."

"How was your flight?"

"It was good, the flight itself was really smooth, went by really quickly."

"Is everything all right, baby?"

"Yeah, I'm cool. It's really hot down here though—shoot, about 85 degrees today."

"Wow send some of that this way, we only pushing high sixties."

"I know, it's really nice down here. Tiffany is taking real good care of me."

"Good, baby. Well, I won't keep you—you have fun, OK?"

"OK, Mom, I will. I'll talk to later on tonight."

"All right baby. Tell Tiffany I said hello."

"I will, love you."

"Love you too."

I knew my mother could tell something was wrong with me, she always knew by the way I spoke and would mention it if I didn't sound right. I guess the explanation of the heat satisfied her enough to leave it alone, for now. I hung up the phone feeling pretty positive. My mom didn't know about the baby yet, but I knew she would be cool. I was older now, way more stable than I had been, and I had a boyfriend who loved me. This whole mess between Kevin and me was all a misunderstanding. He would come around; he had to. We had been together for a while now and everything we had been through was leading to marriage, so why not have this baby?

Calling Kevin now was going to be a lot easier; I had psyched myself up and was feeling more confident. Kevin really and truly loved me, so this wouldn't be as serious a problem as he was making it out to be. I scrolled back through my cell phone for the last time I had called him and hit the send button. Happy and excited to hear his voice, I patiently waited as the phone rang.

But it just kept ringing. After the seventh ring, I started feeling nervous. I better have my argument ready just in case he was still tripping. Hopefully he had had enough time alone to realize how much he missed me and how much a baby would change our lives for the better.

After the tenth ring, his voicemail came on.

"Hey, Kevin, its Jaz," I said into the phone. "I made it to New Orleans. Tiffany and I are having lunch, call me as soon as you get this message. I love you."

He'll call. I'm sure he's at work and can't get to the phone.

When I returned to the table my food was waiting for me and Tiffany was already eating.

"Dang, girl, is it that good?" I said, laughing.

"Hell yeah, thought you knew—you outside playing while I'm in here getting my grub on." We laughed.

"OK, let me see what's poppin.'"

Everything looked amazing, and smelled even better. I had never imagined eating seafood and grits, but this simple combination blew my mind.

But the best thing at the table was the homemade sweet tea. I had never tasted anything so good. I prided myself on being able to recognize the ingredients in what I was eating or drinking, but couldn't for the life of me tell what they had mixed together to make this exquisite concoction. It was like every sip tasted better than the last.

"Damn, Tiffany, what are they putting in this drink?"

"Girl, I know, right, they will not give the secret away to save a life. Everyone down here has been trying to get them to tell or better yet, trying to figure it out. No one has even come close."

"Well, they need to stop playing and market it."

"I know but they won't do it because it would mean they would have to put the ingredients on the label."

"Wow, that's crazy!"

"Look, Jaz, you gotta understand, we are down here with a bunch of old-time folks who have these crazy beliefs, beliefs that have been passed down from generation to generation. Girl, I'm sure some slave from way back came up with this drink and somebody from the family learned how to make and it has just been going on and on, like normal."

"I hear you, girl. Well, before I leave to go home I want to come back by here to get some to take to Kevin. I know he would love it."

"Oh by the way, speaking of Kevin, did you talk to him?"

"Uh no, he didn't answer his phone. He must be at work. I'll just call him later."

We left the restaurant feeling happy and satisfied. I was thoroughly full and Tiffany, who was generally full of energy, was walking a little sluggish herself.

"What do you want to do now?" she asked me as we walked back to the car.

"Truthfully, I would like to go to the house and take a nap, but my time is short here and I don't want to miss a thing. Let's go down to Bourbon Street. I hear that's where everything is jumping."

She laughed. "Sweetie, this whole town is jumping. Let's go have some fun."

"It's one-thirty now. What time do you have to pick up Destiny?"

"I called Malik and he said that he would get her today. He told us to have fun and take our time and that he was going to barbecue for us tonight."

"Wow, that's cool. I can't wait."

"OK, let's get going. How about we go downtown first and then double back and hit Bourbon Street and the riverboat casino?"

"All right, love, I'm with you whatever you want to do.

"And Tiffany?"

"Yes?"

"Thanks again."

"Ah, Jaz, you know the deal. I love you."

"I love you too. Tif."

She smiled and held my hand as we walked to the car.

I drank in the air that seemed to be filled with a special kind of freedom, filling my lungs with gratitude for the gifts God had given me.

# Chapter 71

WHEN WE GOT DOWNTOWN, I couldn't believe it—it looked just like it did on TV. It was a wonderful place, with an extraordinary atmosphere and tantalizing aromas everywhere. The Old World architecture was gorgeous, and there seemed to be flowers and growing things everywhere. There was serenity in the people; they went about their business doing whatever it was they were there to do. I stood quietly taking it in. One day I too would be in a place of serenity, a place where I could just *be*.

All the stores we ventured into had tons of black people shopping in them. It wasn't at all like Minnesota, where we only had a couple of malls that black people frequented and it was rare to see black people in the city shopping. Minneapolis, seeking to bring baby boomers back into the city, had spent a lot of money to rejuvenate downtown. It worked for a while until a white man was killed during a robbery.

We strolled amongst the New Orleanians, window-shopping and talking about just about everything. I jumped when I heard my phone ring; my next thought was it might be Kevin. But when I looked at the caller ID, I didn't recognize the number.

"Hello, this is Jasmine." I answered with my "business voice."

"Hey, baby." I was surprised to hear Kevin, since I didn't know the number he was calling from.

"Hey, Kevin, what's up?"

"Nothing much, just took a quick break and saw that you called. So you made it, huh?"

"Yeah, I made it."

"How is it down there in the Dirty South?"

"It's great; I love it. It's about eighty-five degrees, the sun is shining and there ain't nothing but beautiful black people walking around. I'm really enjoying myself."

"That's good. How are Tiffany and her family?"

"They're doing fine, really great. They have a beautiful house and doing it big down here. So what time do you think you'll be getting off work? I have something really important to talk to you about."

"Is it about you being pregnant?"

"Of course it is. We really need to discuss this."

"Look, I told you how I felt; I don't think we are ready for a baby."

"Let's just talk about it tonight—I'll call you later on this evening, OK?"

"OK, fine. I really don't know how much good it's going to do, but I'll holler at you later."

"Bye, baby," I said.

He hung up without saying good-bye. I pressed "end" on my phone and stared at it for a moment. I was still feeling semi-sure of myself—I know he loves me and if he just gives me the chance to explain, I know he will see things my way. He just has to.

Tiffany looked at me. I could tell she wanted to know what we had said, but "Hey, Jaz, let's go in here" was all she said.

I turned around and looked at the window. It was a baby-clothing store.

I hadn't even started showing and I was already geeked about having this baby and doing all the shopping I could, especially if it was a girl. I picked up the cutest little pink and white dress and almost started crying. I stood there holding the dress up to my stomach and asking my little girl if she liked it. A little feeling came over me; it was her, telling me she loved it, and I started laughing. I'm having this baby no matter what. She needs me—almost as much as I need her.

I placed the dress back on the rack and motioned to Tiffany that I was ready to go. "You've had enough, sweetie?"

"Yeah, I'm tired. I guess I can catch Bourbon Street and the casino another day."

As we drove back to Tiffany's house, I felt even more sure that I was doing the right thing. Yes, there was Kevin, but I knew how to work him. All I had to do was to get emotional on him and I could get him to fold. There was a soft spot in all men for tears and if I had to, I was going to pull out all the stops. He needed to know how important this baby was to me and that there was no way I was going to give her up. I was ready to talk to him that evening.

When I hung up the phone that evening, Tiffany gently touched my shoulder.

"What did he say, sweetie?"

With tears streaming down my face I explained to her how adamant he was—just dead-set against having the baby. The timing wasn't right, he insisted.

"Damn, it, Tiffany, he knows about my situation, my abortions. I told him I felt like this was my only chance to have a baby; God is not going to keep letting me steal the life away from my unborn children. This is my last chance."

Then I just lost it and started sobbing.

Tiffany put her arms around me as I sobbed. Was I fooling myself to think that Kevin would change his mind about this baby? Would I be making a mistake by trying to raise a baby on my own? Did it matter to him that this was my body and I should make the decisions about it?

All my life I had allowed my body to be used for the pleasure of others. Allowing men to take what they wanted. And each time a different man came into the picture I relinquished my power, giving them my soul as well as my body. My innate need to be desired was a curse but with every new encounter, the promise of something bigger and better always rekindled the hope of true love. Their words were always exactly what I wanted to hear, and time and time again I gave in to their desires, suppressing my own just to keep them near. I was a slave to men and I couldn't for the life of me break free.

Kevin was no different. All that I had to give I gave to him, leaving me with nothing for myself. And I could never blame him for seeing what it was he wanted and taking it, because it was so freely given. I had never understood what it meant to demand to be loved and respected. I never wanted to rock the boat.

But this was different. There was a life involved that I felt a connection to right away. My other children didn't have a chance because I was nowhere near strong enough to protect them. But the one I carried now was way stronger than me and demanded that her presence not be ignored. I could feel her spirit and I knew she would be the one to change my life. In fact, I needed her to be the one to change my life. She was going to be the redeemer of my soul.

# Chapter 72

After that first day of highs and lows, the rest of my visit was definitely on the low end. I was starting to feel some of the discomfort of pregnancy, coupled with the heat. And Kevin's response to "my" situation left me drained. I decided to leave a day early because I knew I wasn't making life any better for Tiffany or her family.

Tiffany and I were silent as we drove to the airport, but as I stood in line to go through security, she made one last effort.

"You don't have to leave, Jasmine."

"I know, baby, but I'm not good company right now. Plus, I need to go home and face Kevin on this and make him understand my feelings."

"OK, Jasmine, I understand. But I loved having you here—and remember what I told you. I'll help you raise that baby, so if he gets to trippin' call me and it ain't nothing for me to come up there to make sure you're straight."

I hugged Tiffany, not wanting to let her go; my tears were tears of admiration and gratitude. I don't think she truly knew how much she meant to me, and there were no gifts or words to explain. All I could do was hug her.

"Jasmine, I know, baby, I love you too," she said gently.

We parted and the look in her eyes said it all. I handed my ticket and ID to the security officer, then turned to wave goodbye. She smiled that perfect smile of hers and somehow I felt in my spirit all would be fine.

Even before the plane landed I had been bracing myself for a long drawn-out fight with Kevin; when I told him I would be home early his response was vague and unsympathetic. But I didn't care. I had a newfound strength and nothing he could say or do was going to move me. If he wanted to leave, then so be it. I had family that loved me, and friends that had my back no matter what. I left the plane feeling confident and strong.

I had called Kevin from the plane and knew he was running late, so I took my time and strolled through the airport looking at the people with children as I walked by. Some of the children were asleep in their parents' arms. Others were running rampant from gate to gate yelling, screaming and playing tag.

Damn, was I ready for that? As I looked around and saw all the different shapes and sizes, kids from tiny babies to teenagers, I smiled. I believe I am; besides, my child ain't going to be running wild like that anyways. She is going to be perfect. Just perfect.

I walked down to the baggage claim area and waited outside for Kevin to pull up in the passenger pick-up lane. He had called to say he was a couple minutes away so I found a bench and sat down, thinking about the words I would use to make all this right.

I often had whole conversations in my head—I never knew why but it made things easier for me when I was trying to convince someone of something, which worked really well in my profession. Every word in my head I used would be countered by a reply from the other party; I always swung the reply biased my way, so it wasn't exactly the best way to prepare for a confrontation but it helped. It was a way for me to feel confident about my conversation. On a good day in the courtroom or if I was the center of attention or there were lots of people around, I could dominate the conversation.

But in private conversations, I had a hard time saying what I really felt. Over the years, I had watched how my brother and Paige and my other friends who had the gift of gab practically forced people into giving them their due; and though at times I knew what to do, there was always something . . . something that held me back. I let fear and not wanting to hurt someone's feelings keep me from getting what I wanted.

I closed my eyes. Lord, please help me to change his mind, just a few words from you and a little bit of understanding from him. I promise I'll be the best mommy in the world.

As I opened my eyes I saw Kevin pull up and pop the trunk.

"Hey, baby."

He walked over, lightly kissed me, grabbed my bags and put them in the trunk.

"You ready to go?"

I opened the car door as he raced to the driver's side. He seemed to be in a hurry.

"What's going on, Kevin, why the rush?"

"Oh. that patrol officer back there was trippin' as I was slowing down to look for you. I just want to keep moving so I don't have to cuss his ass out."

Great—he was in a bad mood, so now was not the time to bring up the baby.

"So how was your trip?"

"It was fine, I really had a nice time, and Louisiana is a beautiful place. We should go together sometime; I know you'd love it."

"How are you feeling?"

"I'm feeling fine, I guess, just a little tired. I think I have serious jet lag; I just want to go home and sleep."

"Yeah, I hear you, I'm kind of tired myself. Work was tough today, seemed like everybody was trying to stress me out."

"Are you all right?"

"Yeah, I'm fine, just got a lot on my mind."

"Yeah, I know. Me too."

The drive home was quiet; I stared out the windows looking at nothing, hoping for something. We pulled into the garage and I let out a deep breath, thanking God my baby and I made it home safely. I reached for my carry-on bag while Kevin took the suitcase and we walked silently to the elevator. I looked towards him, hoping to catch a glimpse of some softness in his eyes. But he didn't return the look, so I figured he was still in a bad mood, and we rode up in more silence.

When I walked in, to my surprise the house was clean. The floors were swept and the garbage was taken out.

"Wow, the place looks nice," I said.

"I know; I spent all day yesterday cleaning it."

"Well, thank you, love, I really appreciate it."

"Ah, it's all good. Do you want me to take your bags to the bedroom?"

I followed him to the bedroom and set down my purse and bag, then went into the bathroom. I looked at my face in the mirror, noticing bags under my eyes. I unbuttoned my pants and pulled everything down.

"Oh my God no, please God no!"

The bright red bloodstain in my underwear was a cruel reminder of my past mistakes. Had God not heard my prayers, my apology?

"Kevin," I practically screamed, "I need to go to the clinic, I'm bleeding."

Kevin ran into the room. He stared at the red stain.

"Baby, what's wrong?"

"I don't know. There's blood in my underwear. I need to go to the hospital," I said, an awful fear in the pit of my stomach.

"OK, baby, calm down. Get some of your things and let's go." The softness and concern in his voice touched me. Maybe he really did care.

He kept his arm around me from the moment we closed the apartment doors until he opened the car door for me and helped me in.

Dear Lord, please don't let me lose this baby. I'm so sorry for what I have done with my children in the past. Please God, give me another chance.

There were only a few people in the waiting room when we got to the clinic—a little Asian girl and her mother, an older white man in the wheelchair, and an Indian family with three kids.

Dang, I hope all them aren't sick, I thought—I don't want to be getting any infections that might hurt the baby...

Kevin and I chose a corner in the back of the waiting area and waited for my name to be called, as I tried to keep my fear from taking over.

"Are you OK?" Kevin asked.

"Yes, I'm fine, just a little scared."

"Don't worry, baby, everything will be fine."

He caressed the back of my neck so tenderly I almost started to cry. I scooted down in my chair and lay my head on his shoulder.

I picked up a month-old women's magazine that was in the waiting room to distract myself until they called my name, but my eyes kept straying up to the "If you have been sitting for more than twenty minutes or more" sign. Finally I looked at the clock; it had been twenty minutes, so I decided to get up to ask how long it would be before I would be seen. Then the nurse called my name. I turned to look at Kevin with tears in my eyes. He stood up, took my hand and we followed the nurse to the examination room.

The nurse was an older lady, maybe early fifties, her strawberry-blond hair cut short.

We stopped in the hall outside a row of examination rooms.

"Hello, Jasmine, I'm Kathy, your nurse. Can you please step on the scale?" I slipped my shoes off and stood very still while she recorded my weight. Damn, 165 pounds; way more than I expected. I followed her to the small white room and sat in the first chair while Kevin took the one next to me.

She took my temperature, then checked my blood pressure, then took my pulse.

"OK, Jasmine, I'm finished; tell me why you are here today."

"I'm pregnant and there was blood in my panties this morning."

"OK. Were you cramping at all?"

"No. There were no cramps."

"I'm going to need you to undress from the waist down and sit up on the table; the doctor will be here in a moment." I nodded my head without saying a word.

She left the room.

"Jasmine, look, I know we have our differences about this baby," Kevin said, "but I don't want my feelings about this situation to get in the way of how I feel about you. I love you and I don't want you to forget that."

"I know you do; I love you too. So why can't we have this baby? We're in a healthy, stable relationship, aren't we? You just got a good job and I'm doing great at the firm. I don't understand why this is so hard for you."

"Baby, I don't want to talk about it right now, you just relax and we'll deal with all of this later."

"What do you mean later? We don't have time for later."

Then he clammed up and took a magazine from the shelf and started leafing through it like there nothing wrong. I sat there on the cold table, frustrated, scared, and naked from the waist down.

There was a knock at the door, then "Hello, Jasmine, my name is Dr. Kamsheeh."

The stocky balding Indian man surprised me in more ways than one. He was way older than I anticipated, he was Indian—India Indian, not Native American—and he was a male. I had never had a male doctor before, so this was a little hard, but I trusted he knew what he was doing.

"So Jasmine, I hear you're pregnant and you're having some problems with vaginal bleeding."

"Yes sir, I noticed a significant amount of blood in my underwear this morning and I got scared."

"I understand your concern. I'm going to do a couple of things, OK? First I'm going to do a pelvic examination, and then I'll use the sonogram to listen for the baby's heartbeat and to see if we can see a picture of the baby. Is that all right?"

"Yes, that's fine."

"OK. Lie back and put your feet in the stirrups, please."

Then he pulled the curtain around the examination table, and I lay there, my feet in the stirrups, trying not to think about anything at all, trying not to burst into tears. It felt so similar to the abortion clinic I thought at any moment I would lose my mind. If there was anything wrong with this baby I would never be able to forgive myself.

"Now, I need you to scoot all the way down to the end of the table, let your knees relax to the side and take a deep breath. I'm going to touch you so that I can insert the speculum."

I took a deep breath and waited for the cold steel of the speculum to penetrate me. It was always an odd feeling; they tell you to relax, but how can you? As I lay there, I heard the words, faraway at first but clearer as the speculum was removed. I raised my head to listen.

"Everything down here looks fine. The cervix is fully closed and I see no signs of dilation. Let's check for the baby's heartbeat."

I lay back again and silently prayed. There was no noise or movement coming from Kevin. I was hoping he was still in the room so he could hear his baby's heartbeat. Maybe realizing this baby was real would change his mind about having it.

Doctor Kamsheeh squeezed the gel onto my stomach. He removed the sonogram wand from its holder and placed it on top of the gel, moving it around in a circular manner.

"Quiet; listen." I lay very still, concentrating on the sounds coming from the ultrasound machine. "Do you hear it?"

The beat . . . . beat . . . beat sounded more like a swish . . . swish . . . swishing sound, but I could hear it. Steady, constant, alive.

Dr. Kamsheeh smiled. "That's the sound of your baby's heartbeat."

"Oh my God, thank you!"

The beating of my baby's heart was more than I could handle. I clapped my hand over my mouth to keep myself from screaming and shut my eyes tight to keep from crying, listening so I could synchronize my heart to hers.

"Wow, this baby has a strong heartbeat. Let's check the sonogram picture to make sure this baby is in the right spot," said Dr. Kamsheeh. He turned on the TV screen and moved the wand to the right then to the left again. "Oh, OK—there it is."

I rolled to my right to see the picture on the monitor. There she was, no bigger than my index finger, lying comfortably in my womb. Not moving, not even questioning why she was here, just knowing that she was to be.

Kevin looked too, and as he did, something in his eyes changed. He smiled, not thinking I seen it. This was it. I'm having a baby—I mean, *we're* having a baby.

# Chapter 73

"**K**EVIN, WAKE UP. I THINK my water broke."
It felt like a bubble popping in between my legs; the warm fluid that oozed onto the bed sheets forced me out of my dream state and into a state of panic. I slid out of the bed and rushed to the bathroom. I sat down on the toilet, wiping at the fluid that was dribbling down my legs and onto the floor. Was this the moment I had been waiting for all this time? After crying through lower back pain and excruciating heartburn, waking up out of a deep sleep to nightly leg cramps and weeks of false labor pains, the time was finally here. Damn, am I ready for this?

I was certainly ready to get the pregnancy part over with, but I was a little scared about being someone's mother. I had always heard that once a baby came into the world the mother was magically infused with a wise patience and maturity; but would that mean I would know what to do with a new life, a baby that would be mine? Out of my daydream I could hear Kevin moving around, getting my bags with all my things (including my boombox and music tapes—I wanted her to come into the world hearing something special). Then he started making phone calls.

I screamed from the bathroom, "Kevin, I feel serious tightening and cramping in my abdomen—we should go right now. You can call whoever you're calling when we get to the hospital."

He didn't say a word, just put down the phone and we left the house. It was bitterly cold and unusually dark that morning, even for the middle of winter. Sometimes Minnesota winters had a funny way of making one feel totally helpless. When those nights hit that were twenty and twenty-five below, with forty and forty-five below wind chills, everyone and everything in sight stood still. It was so cold that the simplest movement was a problem. But even though this night was a cold one, I didn't notice the least chill. All I could feel, all I wanted to feel was the sensations of labor; the uninterrupted vibration of life forcing its way into the world. We were on our way.

We got into the car and Kevin drove to the hospital as fast as he could—fast enough to get me there in record time, but no so fast as to scare me to death. I could tell he was nervous but the cool in him wouldn't let it show. We arrived at the emergency entrance and he let me out; I waited while he parked the car at a nearby meter, specially labeled for situations of our sort.

We entered the hospital together; we rode the elevator to the maternity floor together and at four forty-five p.m., with Bob Marley playing in the background, my mother, my aunt Denise, my girlfriend Paige, and my brother's girlfriend Sadiq helped Kevin and me welcome Sasha Demi Owens into the world, all of us together.

# Chapter 74

Physically exhausted but emotionally soaring, I felt the nurse place Sasha's warm, naked body on my chest, introducing me to her as if I had never met her before. But she was wrong; I had met her, in fact—I knew her. When I looked in her eyes, every story we told together, and every joke we laughed at filled my soul, reminding me of what life was like way back then. Way back when we actually first laid eyes on each other. She was definitely a spirit that had been here before.

The nurse took her away while Kevin and I watched them thoroughly check her out. They wrapped her in a blanket and returned her to my arms. I held her close, realizing she was everything I was searching for, everything I desired, and all that I had longed for; she, only taking one breath, had fulfilled and made relevant my entire existence, my entire being, my reason for living. She was the epitome of what was to be, my future, my heart, my love.

And once again I thanked God for one more chance.

# Chapter 75

※❦※

SASHA WAS GROWING AND THRIVING—EIGHTEEN months old, and bringing us joy with every new thing she learned. Our lives seemed to be at a place of balance—but the apartment didn't fit our lifestyle anymore.

"Kevin, I think we need to move. Do you think we can buy a house?"

"A house, Jasmine? Why? Don't you like the apartment anymore?"

"Well, baby, I was thinking a house would be better to raise Sasha in. She could have her own room and a yard and a whole bunch of room to run around. We've lived in this apartment for a long time now and I just think a house would be a better place to raise a child. Don't you?"

"I guess, Jasmine. You know buying the type of house you're going to want is going to be expensive."

"I do have some money saved that we can use for a down payment. I figure all we have to do is get Mom to help us look for one and then we move. It will be easy."

"I hear you, but . . ."

"But what?"

"Whatever, Jasmine, do what you want."

Kevin and I were getting along—we both loved Sasha more than anything in the world—but a part of me could tell he was distant. Whenever I asked him to do something that might create change, he would rebel and retreat into his shell. My suggestion we buy a house was just cause for him to regress.

To me, a house meant a lot of things, all positive—a nice place to raise Sasha, a place we could own and call home, somewhere we could grow and live for as long as we wanted. To him it meant more money, more work and more headaches. He seemed to always be years behind what I wanted to do whenever I looked at our future beyond the next six months. To top it all off, he was adamant about leaving Minnesota. I could understand why—the winters were harsh, the people were harsher. But I wasn't leaving my home base for some place we had no connection to, at least not on a whim.

Every time he mentioned leaving I listened, but wasn't budging. I explained to him it didn't make sense to pack and move somewhere with no jobs and no support. We always got into an argument about it. If Kevin had found the city he wanted to live in, moved there without us, found a job and had a place for us to come to already laid out, then no problem—as his girlfriend and the mother of his child I'd feel I'd have no choice but to move. But it never went like that; it was always "I don't want to buy a house because I don't plan on staying here," but he never had a plan to leave, so we never left.

The very next day I called my mother and told her I wanted to start looking for a house. It didn't matter to me that Kevin was not feeling buying a house, I wanted one and I was going to get one.

My mother had been in real estate for over twenty-five years and had held on to her license for situation such as this. We discussed the possible neighborhoods I'd be interested in, and began to search the Multiple Listing Service website. It didn't take long for me to find what I wanted; in fact, it was perfect.

It was a three-bedroom split-level in the up-and-coming suburb of Brooklyn Park, about fifteen minutes from the city and both our jobs. The house was beautiful; it sat in a cul-de-sac with about four other beautiful homes, and the tree-lined street and yards were meticulously maintained with professional landscaping.

It was a for-sale-by-owner property, so when my mother, Sasha and I went to look at it the owners were home. The couple, the Hendersons, greeted us warmly at the door, told us to call them Cindy and Frank, and took us through the house, showing us every little detail and all the things they enjoyed while they were there. It was apparent they really loved this house.

"Cindy, this is a great house, why are you moving?" I asked the wife.

"We're relocating; my husband's company is transferring us to Colorado so we really have no choice."

"Oh I see. Is that why it is priced so fairly?"

"Yes, we have to sell it as soon as possible so we decided to price way below market value in order to get it sold."

I looked at my mother and could see her mouthing "This is it." I nodded back, "I know."

"Is there a back yard?"

"Yes, there is; in fact, we were saving the best for last."

I walked up to my mother and nudged her as we followed the Hendersons up the lower-level stairs and through the kitchen towards the patio doors, whose vertical blinds hid the back yard from view. When the doors opened, my heart stood still. I wanted this house.

We stepped onto a bi-level deck, surrounded by tiki torches, with a patio table and chairs shaded by a large, moss-green umbrella. A privacy fence enclosed a garden of red, pink and yellow rosebushes, a functioning fountain moving crystal-clear water along a three-foot span of aqua-colored concrete. In one corner stood a play set including a swing, a slide and climbing bars.

"Oh my God, Cindy, this is it. Let me call my fiancé."

I set Sasha down so she could go play on the swing; my mother followed her. I excused myself and called Kevin. I referred to Kevin as my fiancé so that it would sound like I was in a stable relationship headed towards marriage, even though when I thought about it there were serious fractures in our relationship, despite our shared adoration for Sasha.

"Hello, it's me."

"Yeah, what's up?"

"I think I found our house," and before he could retort I dove in headfirst, explaining how wonderful the house was, how reasonable the price was, what a great area it was in, leaving no detail out except for how much our payment would increase from what we were paying at the condo.

"I want you to see it."

"Slow down. Where is the house?"

"It's in Brooklyn Park and it is the bomb, you have to see it."

He hesitated—not a good sign.

"Is that all right, do you want to see it?" I pressed him.

"Yeah, I guess, how much did you say they wanted?"

"They're asking $249,900, which if you see this house is a steal. I think we should jump on it before someone else gets it."

"Wow, that's a lot," he said slowly. "What are the payments on that?" I would have pretended that I hadn't figured that out yet, but he knew I had because Mom was with me and that was what she did.

"It's about seventeen hundred a month."

"Seventeen hundred? What makes you think we can afford that?"

"We're both working and it's not like this isn't an investment," I said hurriedly. "Either way it goes we win, because when we sell it, I'm sure we can make a large profit."

"I don't know Jasmine . . . we just had a baby and I . . ."

"Just come and see the house," I broke in. "I guarantee you'll love it."

The silence on the other end told me he was thinking about it, but was not going to make up his mind on the spot.

"All right, tell them I'll come and see it this weekend."

"Oh no, we can't wait until this weekend," I jumped in again. "It will definitely be gone by then; you need to see it tonight."

"OK, baby," he sighed. "I'll come out."

When Kevin showed up, his slow methodic saunter was a dead give-away he was none too pleased. I didn't care; I was so excited about the house, I ran down the sidewalk to greet him.

"You made it! You have to see this house, you're going to love it."

I grabbed his hand and practically dragged him up the concrete sidewalk. "Look, baby, isn't it beautiful?"

Kevin looked around slowly, taking it all in; he was in no rush and he showed no expression. I took him on the grand tour as the owners smiled and made small talk with my mother and Sasha.

"So, do you have any questions?" I asked him breathlessly.

Kevin smiled slightly, but it was really more of a grimace than a grin. He wasn't thinking about buying this house, he was thinking about how to pay for this house. I pulled him aside and asked him what he thought.

"I don't know. The house is nice, but how much will our payments be?" he asked *again*.

I called Mom over and had her explain the formula to calculate the payment and why in the long run everything would work out for the better, but he was not impressed. He liked the house, no doubt, but the payment had him shook. I walked him to the back yard again, hoping that he would see how wonderful it would for raising Sasha; and whenever we decided to sell it, we'd make a pot of money on it. We could really start our future out on a good note.

Kevin shrugged. "Whatever, Jaz—go ahead and get it."

I smiled and kissed him on the cheek. "Thanks baby," I said, overjoyed at the thought of our wonderful new house and new life we'd have. I was so wrapped up in what I wanted, I couldn't see the disappointment on Kevin's face; all I heard was his affirmation, and that was all I needed.

I ran to my mother and told her we were going to get it. She was pleased, not only because it was a great house for me and Kevin and her grandbaby, but she would also get the couple thousand dollars commission tied to the contract.

Cindy and my mother started going over the contract at the kitchen table, and I walked around the house, soaking up all its wonderful details again. Then my mother called me over for one big part of the contract that I had forgotten about—earnest money.

"Jasmine, you're going to need an earnest money check tonight in order to have them take the house off the market."

I looked at Kevin and he looked at me with question marks in his eyes.

"OK, Mom, how much do I need?"

"Between five hundred to a thousand dollars is sufficient. The more you give the more serious the owners will take you."

"All right, how about a thousand dollars?"

I reached in my purse for my checkbook as Kevin looked on, baffled at how I could write a thousand-dollar check just like that.

But to me it was a no-brainer. I wrote the check out to Frank and Cindy Henderson and signed my name. Cindy smiled and took the check but said she wanted to have her lawyer look over the documents before they signed anything. That seemed reasonable.

"OK, Cindy, Frank, thank you so much. We look forward to hearing from you when you're ready to proceed." I smiled and shook hands, as did Kevin (though less enthusiastically) and we left.

As we left, I fantasized about the move we were going to make, how it would solidify our relationship and provide a stable home for Sasha and the babies to come. I had no idea Kevin was thinking something totally different—or maybe I did and I just didn't care.

# Chapter 76

When my phone rang at work, the call from the Hendersons the next day was like music to my ears; their lawyer had reviewed our offer and they had accepted it with only one condition: that if we were not able to secure a mortgage for the home, we would have to forfeit the thousand-dollar earnest money check. I agreed to those terms, but I was a little worried about losing my earnest money, so after I hung up I called my mother to make sure that was something that was normal or just to see if that was all right to do.

She was a little concerned too, but reassured me we would get approved for the mortgage, so it was fine just to go with it and not to worry. The earnest money would be taken off the bottom-line cost of the house anyway, once we closed. I knew my mother knew what she was talking about so I trusted her and went with it. Then I called Kevin and told him the good news.

When he finally answered the phone, I heard the same sigh in his voice I'd heard yesterday.

"Hey, Kevin, it's me. What's wrong?"

"Ah nothing, just another day in paradise."

I knew when he said that that he was not having a good day. Something at the job was bothering him.

"Are you OK?"

"Yeah, I'll be all right eventually, what's up?"

"I just got the call from the Hendersons. They agreed to our offer."

"That's good."

"Damn, you don't sound excited."

"Well, to be honest, I'm sitting here thinking about how we're going to be able to afford such a jump in our payment."

"I think that we can do it, this is an investment and I believe we should go for it. You know God will make a way, if we have faith and believe."

"Yeah, I hear you, but . . ."

"But what, Kevin?"

"I just don't know; I'm already stressed out as it is."

"I know, baby, just go with me on this—it will all work out."

"Whatever, Jaz, whatever you want."

"I'm going to call the mortgage lender and get him started on our file," I said, ignoring the resignation in his voice.

"Cool, I'll call you later. Better yet, I'll see you at home—what's for dinner tonight?"

"I don't know yet, I took out some ground beef, so maybe I'll make meatloaf or something."

"That's cool, I'll see you at home."

"I love you."

"I love you too, Jaz."

I hung up the phone feeling only semi-content; why couldn't he share my excitement just a little? Well, whatever; I wanted this house and I was going to get it. I called our mortgage broker and told him to move forward with the paperwork.

I was feeling good; I decided to finish early, go get Sasha from my daycare and go home to start dinner so it would be ready when Kevin got home.

When Kevin walked in the door the meatloaf was on the table and his plate was all set; all he had to do was sit and eat.

"Hey, baby, what's up?" I said, smiling. "How was the rest of your day?"

"It is what it is." Wow, another one of his flat "I'm in a bad mood" responses.

"Are you hungry, do you want to eat?"

"Yeah, let me go wash my hands."

"OK, Sasha and I'll be at the table."

I walked Sasha over to the table and put her in her high chair and brought all the plates and drinks to the table. Kevin walked over, kissed Sasha on the forehead and sat down to eat. I sat down next to him, hoping to gauge his attitude about the house.

"So what's going on? You seem kind of upset."

"Ah it's nothing; that job is getting to me, though—everyone got shit for me to do. It's always something."

"Well, don't worry; it'll get better," I said encouragingly. He smirked but didn't reply.

"So have you heard anything from the mortgage guy?" he asked. I was surprised he was even bringing up the house, but I took it as a good sign.

"No, not yet. He said he'd call tomorrow. Oh, and by the way, I had to give notice on the apartment so that we don't get stuck on our deposit."

"Are sure that was a good idea? What if we don't get the house?"

"I really had no choice; we set the closing date sixty days out and I had to let the property manager know. She says there is a waiting list for this unit, so we better get this house."

"Whatever. I just hope you know what you're doing."

"What do you mean by that?" I snapped.

"Nothing—forget it."

We finished the rest of the meal in silence. When he was done, Kevin got up and planted himself in his usual place in front of the television. I finished feeding Sasha and cleared the table and cleaned the kitchen, then I took Sasha in to give her a bath and I put her down to sleep. I lay down next to her, feeling dejected and defeated. I breathed in her innocent toddler breath, hoping she could breathe new life into me, praying she could keep me from suffocating. I kissed her and fell asleep snuggled up to her, almost like she was holding me, not the other way around.

# Chapter 77

THE NEXT MORNING, HENRY FROM the finance company called. I couldn't wait to pick up the phone when Wendy put the call through, but my excitement was dashed when I heard the news: He was having a hard time getting me approved. I had defaulted on a car loan in my early twenties, but since it had happened so long ago, he said if I wrote a letter explaining what happened, that would clear it up.

But that wasn't what was really bothering him. It turned out that the several credit cards I had now were all more than fifty percent over the limit, and that posed a significant problem. The bank didn't like the fact that the cards were all nearly maxed out. I knew my balances were high, but they were all being paid on time, so I hadn't thought about the maxed-out limits at all. But he told me my credit score dictated that I needed to put three percent down.

That was nearly eight thousand dollars.

I was flabbergasted. "Henry, what do you suggest?"

"There are a couple things you can do. Do you have the three percent down?"

"To be honest with you, I was hoping to get a zero down program, but if I have to I can work on that. But it will be tough."

"Can you pay off any of your credit cards, or at least try to get them down below the halfway mark?"

Damn, I had five cards and the halfway mark on all of those cards would mean coming up with close to five thousand dollars.

"I don't know if I can do that, I don't have that kind of cash on hand."

"The other option is taking the money out of your 401(k) or borrowing the money from a family member and we call it a gift. You can send a gift letter in with the application to underwriting and they will accept that. And if that doesn't work, then I'll have to try and shop you around to some BC lenders."

"What are BC lenders?"

"BC lenders are lenders who underwrite loans, but give them to you at a higher interest rate, which unfortunately will cause your payment to be higher and you might have to do an adjustable rate mortgage or an eighty/twenty, with one payment at one rate and another payment at an even higher rate."

"Damn. Oh, excuse me, Henry."

"It's quite all right, I understand."

"Which option do you think is better?"

"It would be best to get you in a regular FHA or government-backed loan, but if you can't come up with the down payment, then we need to look into the other options."

"Please do what you can do on your end, and I'll do what I can on mine. I need to make some phone calls and I'll get back to you later on today."

"All right. I'll look forward to hearing from you later on this afternoon."

I had no one to call but my mother. I couldn't call Kevin and listen to his "I told you so" bullshit.

When she answered the phone, the excitement in her voice was quickly deflated by the disappointment in my voice.

"What he say, baby?"

"Mama, he said a bunch of stuff—first off the car loan thing, but he said we can get around that."

"What else?"

"My credit cards, they're all maxed or close to being maxed out; and on top of all that I might need three percent down."

"Damn—that's what he came up with?"

"Yep, so far. I told him I had to make some phone calls and I would get back to him."

"And you know those figures don't include the closing cost monies you need either," Mama said with trepidation in her voice.

"Damn, I need more than what he already said?"

"Yep. I told you, you were going to possibly need down payment money plus money to close. I was just hoping you could get a no-money-down program, then you would only have to pay the closing costs."

"Oh, I see."

"Did you call Kevin yet?"

"Hell no, I'm not trying to hear his mouth until I have something figured out."

She laughed. "I hear that." Then, getting serious again: "OK, let me think. What kind of money do you have saved?"

"I have my 401(k), which is about ten thousand dollars and I have no idea what Kevin has saved. I believe he spent his 401(k) when he left his last job, so what he has built up with this new company may not be that much. The mortgage broker also said I could get a gift, but I know none of y'all got that kind of money."

"You right about that. All right—I'm going to come over tonight and we're going to work these numbers and come up with a plan. Call Kevin and see what kind of money he has saved and we'll go from there."

"Cool, but what about Henry? I told him I'd call him back later on this afternoon."

"Henry will be fine, we'll call him first thing in the morning when we have it all figured out."

"OK, thanks. See you tonight."

I hung up the phone. Then, screwing up my courage, I called Kevin; thankfully, his office voicemail picked up, so I left a simple "see you at home" message just to keep things light. Then I sat back in my chair and prayed. Lord, I really want this house, please work this out.

And that was that. The boost of confidence I got when I finished telling God about it made me feel better. I was getting this house some kind of way; this was my house, I just knew it.

When I got home Kevin was already there, fixing himself something to eat. It was his day to pick up Sasha, and she was happily playing with her toys in the living room. I scooped her up, gave her a kiss, and took her into the bedroom to change her diaper. All fresh and clean, I brought her back out to sit in her walker.

"Hey, Kevin, how are you, baby?" I greeted him.

"Hey, baby, ain't nothing—just trying to put something in my stomach, I ain't ate all day."

"So I talked to the mortgage lender today," I began cautiously, "and we need to do a few things before he can get us approved." It was a like curtains closing on his face; he was shutting down. "What did he say?" was all he asked me.

"Well, because of some past credit issues I had and the fact that our credit cards are close to maxed out, we need to have three percent down and/or we need to pay down the cards. I have about ten thousand saved in my 401(k) that we can use, but that won't cover everything, the down payment plus the closing costs would be around fifteen thousand. How much do you think is in your 401(k)?"

"Look, Jaz, I don't know. I have them taking a minimal amount out of my check, and they don't do matching, so it's not going to be that much."

"Could you find out? Mama is coming by tonight to so we can work out some of the numbers to see what we can come up with."

He walked towards the living room without responding.

"Kevin, did you hear me?"

"Yeah, I heard you, I just don't think this is a good time to try and move. That payment is really going to put a strain on me and I'm stressed out as it is."

"Look, I know the payment is quite a bit more than we expected, but I think that we can do it. If we rearrange some of our finances and cut back on a few luxuries I know we can make it work.

"And why are you acting like this, anyway?" I asked him, my temper starting to fray. "You act like you don't want to progress, like you want to stay stuck in this same place doing the same thing."

"I told you I don't like Minnesota, never have and I don't plan on staying here, so buying this house seems ridiculous to me."

"Ridiculous?"

The doorbell rang, which was fortunate, because I was just about to get on his ass. I turned to go to the door and he plopped down on the sofa to eat.

"Hey, Mom, how are you?" I greeted her as I opened the door, and kissed her on the cheek.

"Hey, baby, how are you?" She paused and looked me up and down, and then walked over to Sasha and gave her a big kiss on the forehead. "What's wrong? You look a little upset." She turned back to me.

"Ah nothing, Mom, Kevin is tripping about the house. I whispered to her: "Would you go and talk to him?" My mother was always calmer with him than me.

She looked over at him and smiled. "Yes, I'll go talk to my son-in-law." I winced, because we weren't married now, and the way things were going, that wasn't going to happen.

I went into the kitchen to give them some space, but listened from the other room. I didn't know how my mother was going to get him to change his mind, but I was hoping she could. I sat on the barstool pretending to read a file while they laughed and joked and played with Sasha. What could possibly be so funny? I thought. They were having too much fun, and it was beginning to get under my skin, so I interrupted them.

"So what did y'all come up with?"

"What we need to do is get those credit cards paid and maybe over a month or so your credit score will go up and then you can get the no-money-down program."

"Why will it take so long for the score to come up? And if it doesn't come up enough, then we will have spent most of the money to pay them off and be short the down payment if it's needed," I objected.

"I know, but that's the chance you have to take. You need to start calling the credit card companies and letting them know what you're trying to do so that they get your payments processed as soon as possible," my mom said.

"Damn, that sounds like a lot of work," I remarked.

Kevin smirked. I glared at him, trying not to lash out.

Sasha started to fuss, so I picked her up and left the room. I could hear Mom tell Kevin she was leaving and that she would call us later. "Give my grandbaby a kiss for me," she yelled from the other room.

I started Sasha's bath and was getting her ready for the tub when Kevin walked in.

"Are you all right?" he asked.

"I'm fine," I said shortly, then snapped, "You know what? This is way too much—just forget it." Then I turned back to Sasha, who was splashing happily, ignoring his questioning stare that I could just feel boring into my back. He stood there for a minute, then turned and left. I heard him getting ready for bed.

When Sasha was finished with her bath, I dried her off and put her in her pajamas. She was sleepy and ready for bed, so I took her to the bedroom and laid her in the bed in between Kevin and me. Holding her close, I cried myself to sleep.

Kevin was silent. He knew if he had opened his mouth to say one word to me I might have snatched his tongue out.

## Chapter 78

When the call from Henry came through the next morning, I struggled to figure out what I was going to say. I didn't want to tell him I didn't have what I needed to get the house—shit, I didn't want to tell myself that. I needed more time to figure things out, but I didn't want Henry spending a whole lot of time on a deal that wasn't going to fly. And on top of all of that, there went my thousand dollars.

"Hey, Henry, how are you?"

"I'm fine. And yourself?"

"I'm not so good. I spoke with my mother and my boyfriend last night about the house and what we needed to make it happen, and it looks like there is too much stuff floating around out there. Coming up with all that money in such a short time is just not possible for us right now. So I think I'm going to let it go and try later when I got my stuff together."

"Are you sure? I've been looking at your file and there are several other avenues we can take to get this done. I'm sure I can find something for you to make this work."

"I'm sure you can, and I appreciate your efforts, but I'm tired. Kevin is really not feeling it and I just don't want to fight anymore. I really appreciate your help; thank you so much for all your hard work. I'm really sorry."

I hung up the phone, feeling completely defeated. That was *my* house, and I had been sure God would answer my prayers.

Then I called my mother to tell her I had decided to let the house go. She was more upset than me about losing the earnest money, but I just didn't care anymore. I asked her to call the

Hendersons and tell them what happened; there was no way I was going to be able to face them. She agreed, and said she would call me later. "I love you, baby," she said as she hung up.

"I love you too, Mom."

So that was it. I was done.

I felt terribly alone. I decided I would run down to the Red Dragon for lunch where I could get a drink—a good one. I hadn't had a hard drink in a long time because of breastfeeding Sasha; but that was over now. There was nothing to stop me, and shit, I was thirsty.

Right at noon I shut down my computer and told Wendy to cancel the rest of my day.

"Are you all right?"

"No, not really. I didn't get the house and I'm so upset with Kevin I could spit, so I'm going down to the Red Dragon to have me a couple. I would ask you to join me but I need you here to cover the phones.

"You know what? Fuck that, would you like to come have lunch with me? Let's just take the rest of the day off and go have some fun—matter of fact, let's go shopping, I haven't bought myself anything in a long time. Why don't you just put the phones on sleep and let the answering service get it?"

Wendy looked at me in shock, but by no means was she going to turn me down.

"OK, give me a minute and I'll be right down."

I smiled. "I'm going to get the car, and I'll wait out front for you. If you see anyone or if anyone asks you any questions, tell them we have an out-of-office meeting that I need you to take notes at."

"OK, no problem—and thanks."

"It's cool, you've been a godsend for more years than you know. You deserve some time away from here, and so do I. You do drink, right?"

"Yes, a little bit."

I laughed. "Well, that's nice. Me, on the other hand, I *drink*."

"Yes—I've heard about you and the divas."

We laughed and I headed for the garage.

At the Dragon, we decided we would order a whole table of food and two drinks apiece—might as well get this party started off right. I looked around the restaurant for Maggie and spied her behind the bar, totaling up an order. I waited for her to come over to my table. When she looked up, she spotted me and smiled, then made her way over.

"Hey, Jasmine, long time no see."

"I know, sweetie. I've been trying to do the family thing. You know my little girl is eighteen months now."

"Oh my God, has it been that long?"

"Yeah. Here, let me show you a picture." I clicked through a few photos on my phone.

"Oh, she is so beautiful!" Maggie gushed.

"Thank you, Maggie. She's my girl."

"Oh, and this is my office assistant Wendy. We decided to blow off the rest of the day, have some food and drink, then go shopping."

"Well, ladies, sounds like you got the day all worked out."

Then she took our drinks order, and was back in a few minutes. She set down the glasses and told us to let her know when we were ready for the second.

"Oh, we will," I said definitively.

I took a deep sip of my drink and sat back as the liquor hit my bloodstream. If felt good—damn, good.

For the next two hours, Wendy and I sat and ate and drank and laughed and cried, but through it all I felt renewed. I had already decided to ask Kevin if he could pick up Sasha so that I could spend more time treating myself and not have to worry about getting her while I was intoxicated.

I dialed his number and waited for him to answer, shushing Wendy so he wouldn't know where I was.

"Hey, Kevin, what's up?" I said when he picked up.

"Nothing, just sitting here in the office tying up some loose ends. What's going on?"

"I have a few things I need to do tonight so I need you to pick up Sasha from daycare. Is that cool?"

"Yeah, that's cool. Hey, did you talk to the mortgage guy?"

"Yeah, I talked to him and told him we decided to wait."

"You did?" He was trying to stay cool, keep any hope out of his voice, but I knew he was happy to hear this.

"Yeah, I did."

Then he thought of something. "What about the thousand dollars?"

"I guess I just lost that, whatever." I brushed it off, and quickly rushed through a quick goodbye before he could say anything else. "All right, so I'll be home later, just make sure you pick up Sasha up by five-thirty."

"Yeah, right, but . . ."

I cut him off. "Thanks, baby. Talk to you later."

I hung up, and slammed the rest of my second drink. *Now* I was feeling just like right.

We left after the second round, and spent three hours of intensive shopping therapy. Three hours later, when I got home from the mall, Kevin was feeding Sasha. I found a McDonald's bag on the kitchen counter with a few chicken nuggets left so I ate one, then walked straight to the bathroom to urinate and brush my teeth; I really didn't need Kevin to know I had been drinking, so I brushed, flossed and used the last bit of mouthwash to disguise the scent. I just hoped it worked.

"So how are my two most favorite people in the world?" I said brightly. The liquor and the shopping had taken my mind off of losing the house and the thousand dollars, at least for a while. I had left all my shopping bags in the car so Kevin wouldn't know how outrageous I had just been.

"We're fine, Mommy," said Kevin as he lifted Sasha out of her high chair and handed her to me.

"Hey, little girl, Mommy missed you."

Sasha smiled at me, then reached up to hug me with the strength of ten thousand men, and right at that moment all was right with the world.

"So what have y'all been doing?" I said, trying to be casual.

"We actually haven't been home that long. I ran by my mom and dad's house so they could see Sasha, then we came straight home."

"McDonald's, Kevin?" I laughed. "Don't be feeding my baby that garbage." "Yeah, I know, it was getting late and she wouldn't eat what my mom cooked, so I stopped at Mickey D's. I knew she would eat that."

Carrying Sasha, I walked to the stack of mail and thumbed through it, passing over the bills and junk mail. Then I stopped cold on the letter from the Waseca correctional facility. Had Kevin seen it?

I stuffed the letter in my pocket and took Sasha to the bedroom to get some of her toys. Damn, Marcus, what could he want? I wanted to rip open that letter right then and there, but knew I had to wait until I was alone or Kevin was asleep.

The rest of the evening was kind of a slow agony of waiting. Kevin watched some TV, and I played with Sasha, gave her a bath, put her to bed. Then I even tried to coax him into the bedroom with sex—that always made him sleepy afterward. But nothing worked. He was so into his online video game that he stayed up well past his usual eleven o'clock bedtime and was still up by midnight.

My patience was wearing thin; I wanted to see what was in that letter. I contemplated locking myself in the bathroom and quietly reading it there, but it would be just my luck that Kevin would need to use it or something. Shit—it looked like I was just going to have to wait until tomorrow morning, after I had dropped Sasha off at my mother's before I went to get my hair and nails done.

"Kevin, I'm going to bed, are you coming?"

"Nah, I'm going to play for a little while longer; I'll be in there in a minute."

I checked on Sasha and got into bed, thinking about Marcus and the mysterious letter.

The next morning I woke up earlier than usual and got myself and Sasha dressed. I whispered in Kevin's ear that I was going to drop off Sasha and then go to get my hair and nails done. He muttered something and rolled over. Great, I thought. He's good and asleep, he won't even miss me.

I packed Sasha's bag—bottles, cereal, diapers, her favorite blanket, and her favorite toy, Tickle Me Elmo. I actually loved it too; I thought it was adorable how it laughed and Sasha laughed right along with it. I grabbed my purse and the letter I had slipped in my dresser drawer and headed for the elevator without making a sound. Kevin didn't move.

When the elevator doors opened I thought about trying to read the letter then, but with Sasha and all the stuff I was carrying, I decided it would be better if I just waited a little longer, until I was alone. I needed to be somewhere with no interruptions.

My mom was in the kitchen cooking when we arrived. She immediately dropped everything and snatched up Sasha as if she hadn't seen her in years.

"Hey, how's Grandma's baby?" she said. Sasha laughed and hugged my mother tight around the neck. Sasha loved her grandma.

"Hey, Ma."

"Hey, baby, what y'all doing here so early?"

"Oh no reason, needed to get up and moving, my hair appointment is at nine."

"Jasmine, it's seven-thirty—what's going on? Is everything all right at home? Is Kevin OK?"

I laughed. "Yes, Mother, everything at home is fine. I just wanted to get up and out. Is that all right with you?"

"Yeah, it's fine, but you know I know you better than that." She looked hard at me.

I could never keep secrets from her. I took a deep breath.

"Mom, I got a letter from Marcus."

She looked at me as if I had two heads. "And?"

"I didn't want to read it at home."

"So you brought it over here, all excited and stuff," she said.

"Yes! What should I do?"

"Open it, silly—you know you can't wait. But be careful, girl,—you playing with fire."

"Ah, Mama, it ain't nothing, probably just writing to say hello."

"Whatever," she said skeptically. "But you remember what I said."

I scowled at her back as she took Sasha to the other room to play. I quickly removed the letter from my purse and studied everything about it, his handwriting, the stamp, and the type of envelope. I slowly broke the seal, thinking about his tongue sliding across the gummed edge.

What was I doing fantasizing about a man I had long ago given up? I shook my head to clear it, then pulled the letter out, unfolded it and began to read.

*Dear Jasmine,*

*I have been thinking about you and about writing this letter to you for some time. I know that this may be bad timing but I had to write. There is no way for me to put into words how sorry I am for hurting you. I never meant for what I was doing to go that far. I just got caught up in the moment and the excitement of it all. You meant the world to me and still do and I'm now paying the ultimate price for messing things up with you. I'll never forgive myself for ruining your life, our life. What we had was so special and I regret every day the choices I made, which have now got me in the predicament I'm in. I want you to know that I, in all of these years spent behind these bars, have still been able to hear your voice, feel your lips against mine, imagine your embrace, make love to you in my mind. I miss you and I needed you to know that. I know you have moved on, and I hope that you are happy. I spoke with my sister Tonya and she told me you had a baby. Congratulations. I'm sure she is as beautiful as you are. I just hope that Kevin is treating you the way you deserve to be treated. If at all possible, I would like to call you sometime. I have your mother's number if that makes it easier. I don't want to disrupt your life at home. In fact, I have a time slot this Saturday, and if it is OK, I am going to call your mom and maybe we can do a three-way call or something. I know you may not want this but I have to try. I just need to hear your voice. Take care, love and hope to talk to you soon.*

*Sincerely yours,*
*Marcus*

Nothing could have prepared me for this. Tears were streaming down my face, and I felt like I had a jungle full of butterflies in my stomach—proof enough that I still had unfinished business. In fact, it was enough business to make me question the pertinence of my current life. I started to question everything—feeling like I had always known deep down I hadn't gotten over Marcus but I had forced myself into a new life, being in a committed relationship with the father of my child, planning big things and moving on.

Of course Kevin and I had some issues but we were a family and we were going to make it work. There was no reason to question my choice. I was happy—wasn't I?

I sat there, reading the letter over and over again, trying to convince myself I was living the life I wanted, the one that included Kevin.

The phone rang.

When my mother appeared from out of the other room holding the phone in one hand with her other hand over the mouthpiece, I knew I was in trouble.

"It's Marcus," she mouthed.

Why was he calling so early, how did he know I was here?

# Chapter 79

How did I get here again, driving back up to Waseca? Lying about church again, getting dressed, and dressing Sasha. I had to bring Sasha with me this time—not because she couldn't stay home with her father, but because I wanted Marcus to meet her. It was funny, after talking to Marcus the day before I realized there was so much I wanted to say to him, so many things I wanted to do with him but had been robbed of the opportunity.

Now was my chance to tell him everything I was feeling, all that I had been going through since he had been gone, mostly about how it felt to be a new mother and how the life of a pretend wife had changed me. How I was committed to the relationship I was in and how I wanted Kevin and Sasha and I to be a family, without any interference from him. It was going to be hard, but I would explain it as straightforwardly and as clearly as I could, so there wouldn't be any misunderstanding on either of our parts. I purposely decided not to tell Marcus I was coming, so that his reaction would be honest.

My plan was set, all I had to do was tell him and all he could do was listen. Everything in my mind was in order; I waited in line with Sasha by my side, poised and ready to speak.

Until I caught a glimpse of the little girl he was holding and the young lady who was with her and my carefully thought-out plan was obliterated.

They were leaving right as we entered, after we had been frisked and checked. We passed the little girl and who I assumed to be her mother in slow motion, each of us eyeing the other uneasily. I didn't understand why I was feeling this way; it was an energy I couldn't explain. Wow, the, girl, really looked like Marcus. But I must be crazy; there was no way. I turned and approached him, only half-smiling now, but smiling nevertheless.

"Hey, Marcus—surprise."

Marcus looked stunned, but his natural graciousness and warmth kicked in like a reflex.

"Hello, Jasmine," he said, and he hugged me. He held on a little longer than I expected, but it felt good.

"Whoa, who is this beautiful little lady?" He smiled that perfect smile and introduced himself to Sasha. Sasha looked him over and gave him a half-cocked smile.

"Jaz, she is beautiful—she looks just like you."

"Thank you. So how have you been? I know you weren't expecting to see me so soon but I thought why not, we were in the neighborhood and thought that we would drop by." I smiled.

He laughed. "The neighborhood—right." Then, gathering his wits, he continued.

"I've been fine, just trying to make the best out of a messed-up situation."

"Yeah, I know; it's pretty tough, huh?"

"Well, you know me, I do what I have to do."

"Yes, I do know you. So Marcus," I stopped for a minute, but I couldn't wait any longer. "Who was that who was just leaving, one of your nieces?"

"Um, yeah that's my oldest sister's daughter and her little girl. They came to visit with me right before you got here."

He halted a little as he spoke the words—not exactly what I wanted to hear, but his explanation sounded plausible. I hadn't met his oldest sister; she had moved away from Minnesota long before we met. It was highly likely that that was his niece and great-niece, but his eyes and body language spoke of something else, I just didn't know what. I didn't want to get into it while I was there with Sasha so I just let it go, with a final "She sure looked a lot like you."

His eyes bucked and he began to sweat.

"Marcus, what's wrong?"

"I have to go."

He stood up and motioned to the security officer to open the door to the visiting room.

"Marcus?"

"Jasmine, please, I have to go, I'll call you later on tonight, I'm sorry."

He walked towards the heavy metal doors.

Stunned and confused, I picked Sasha up and headed for the checkout point. I had driven all the way up here . . . for what? I turned, hoping to catch a glimpse of his eyes—they never lied—but all I saw was the back of his shining, smooth head as he went through the doors.

The drive home was strange; Sasha was unusually talkative. I really expected her to be tired from all the driving, but she was wide awake, trying to talk to me in her toddler gibberish. But with all the confusing thoughts running through my head I found it hard to concentrate on what she was saying.

When we finally got home Sasha had fallen asleep. I took her to her room and laid her down. I spent the rest of the day thinking about Marcus and the child he had held, wondering what really was going on. I avoided Kevin at all costs, by pretending to be working, because I had no explanation for my distant behavior. I furiously wrote to Marcus, sending him four letters, hoping his response would ease all the tension I was feeling about the little girl.

And respond he did. Over the next couple of months, the friendly cards and the casual letters started coming more frequently, so it was always a mad dash to the mailbox to keep Kevin from seeing all the correspondence. But Marcus never mentioned the girl and neither did I. I just wanted to keep everything nice and light, and it was.

# Chapter 80

TWO MONTHS AFTER LOSING THE house, we decided we'd still move. Several couples had come by to see our condo and finally we had buyers. We closed on the property and received a check we put towards moving costs and storage. We ended up moving in with his parents and his younger brother in a townhouse on the border of downtown Minneapolis. His parents were planning a move to the Virgin Islands and Kevin thought it would be good for us to take over their townhouse. It was cheaper, way cheaper, and we'd be helping his parents out.

Waking up on a Sunday morning now had a totally different feel. The shabby dust-covered ceiling fan and the shoddy metal window blinds were a far cry from the exclusive apartment we had just left. I had put most of the furniture from our apartment into storage, even though his parents' furniture was a little outdated. They prided themselves on being frugal shoppers, buying higher-quality items and keeping them longer. But when we found out we would have a room to ourselves, we brought our bedroom set and a lot of our dishes and knick-knacks because Donya was taking all her small art items.

I tried to make their home feel more like ours, but it was difficult, since we more or less lived in one room.

After about a month of all six of living under one roof, Donya and Hassan left for the islands. She had been ready to go, but she needed to make sure the property she owned and rented out when she wasn't there was vacant. It was starting to get cold again and she hated the cold.

Kevin's father, on the other hand, had to stay and wait to hear about his transfer. He had been a manager for the postal service for over twenty years and was ready to leave the cold too, but his transfer was taking a little longer than he, or we, expected.

Because I felt like we were in his space, and not really in a place of our own, I tried my best to stay under the radar. I kept Sasha from fiddling with things that weren't ours, and I spent most of my time with her, in our room. Sasha was a good girl, so it was easy keeping her out of stuff, but cutting our living space in half was hard on all of us, including Kevin's father.

# Chapter 81

MY DAYS WERE WAY DIFFERENT now that we had moved, the small luxuries I had known—the sensational views, the concierge service, and other amenities—were gone. And simple things like stopping at the corner store in the building to pick up something for dinner turned into major chores, driving all the way to the grocery store several miles away.

Because of our move, I wanted to find a new daycare for Sasha, one nearby—somewhere clean, not too expensive, and a place where my daughter would learn something and not just be sitting around playing. I looked at several places before finding New Dimensions, a daycare/preschool, just blocks away.

The first thing I noticed was how immaculate it was, and Sasha, who had come with me, immediately liked the bright colors it was painted. I asked the receptionist for the director in order to see if there was space, before we even took a tour; I knew this might be the place. When the director appeared, I knew this was the place.

A tall, well-dressed white woman with shoulder-length blond hair walked out from a back office. Her well-maintained nails and her high-priced wire-rimmed glasses added to her aura of competence and professionalism.

"Hello and welcome to New Dimensions. My name is Annie Leimann—how can I help you?"

"Hello Annie, my name is Jasmine Burrell and this is my daughter Sasha. We are looking for a new school for her."

After politely shaking my hand, she reached down and shook Sasha's. "What a beautiful little girl. How old is she?"

I looked at Sasha. "Baby, tell Ms. Annie how old you are." Sasha looked up and held out two fingers. I smiled. "She's *almost* two."

"She's very smart."

"I know, that's why we need to have her in a preschool setting verses just a regular daycare."

"You came to the right place. Let me show you around."

We walked through all the classrooms and spent a few moments talking while we watched Sasha play in the cozy, fenced-in yard with wonderful equipment. It was definitely a perfect fit and as luck would have it, she had one spot open.

Ms. Leimann took us to another room to fill out the paperwork and even offered to have Sasha stay for the day, but I decided to it would be better to prep her for the idea of a new school; but I was thrilled we could start tomorrow. Annie smiled and said she was excited to have Sasha join the preschool. I was just as happy; I knew this place would be great for us.

I hadn't expected to find a place for Sasha so soon, so I didn't need to visit all the other daycares on my list. I had taken off the whole day to do it, but it was still early so I called my Grandma Vera to see if she could watch Sasha for a few hours while I went to work, which I had been neglecting with all the stress and chores of the move. I dropped Sasha off and drove straight to work, trying to make sure I hadn't forgotten anything important at work that I would have to answer for when I walked in the door.

When I got to the office the atmosphere was sullen and heavy. Damn, had someone died? I walked through the outer reception area, taking in everyone's expression. No one would look at me and no one spoke.

I got to my office where Wendy was sitting behind her desk, talking on the phone. As soon as she saw me, she hung up and motioned me to the back room, where we kept the supplies.

"Girl, what is going on?" I asked her.

"Jasmine, I have been trying to call you all morning, but you weren't answering your phone." I reached in my purse for my phone; I had put it on silent while I was at the daycare.

"What?"

"The partners called an emergency meeting this morning; our company is being bought out."

"What? What do you mean?"

"Some company out of Europe offered each partner enough money so they could retire comfortably, and they took it."

"Wendy, wait—I need to sit down." I sat heavily on waiting room sofa.

"So what's going to happen to us?"

"We don't know yet—some of us may keep our jobs, some of us may not. They haven't said anything; Marco down in the mailroom had the information first and slipped it to Francine, and the rest is history."

"Oh my God. I can't believe they're doing this without telling me. I'm going in to speak with Tom. I'll be right back."

"Wait—I don't think that is a good idea; they're still meeting."

"I don't care what they're doing, this is my livelihood and I'm going to find out what is going on."

Wendy grabbed my arm. "Wait, Jasmine!"

I broke away from her and stormed down the hall towards the main conference room and swung open the doors. Everything stopped, and all eyes were on me.

I turned slowly, studying all the faces. I knew all but two of them, and those two seemed the toughest and stared the hardest at me.

As Tom, my senior partner approached me, something in the back of my mind sprang forward. The man in the far left seat, with short-cropped blond hair and his expensive tailored suit seemed familiar—not like I had seen him before, but something about him was familiar.

"Hello, Jasmine, we were just talking about you," said Tom smoothly. "For our guests, this is Jasmine Burrell, one of our most promising attorneys. She is definitely next in line for a partnership." I smiled—not for real but I did the best I could.

Tom quickly went around the room, naming the investors; my attention was focused on the man on the left, looking at me intently.

"And last but not least, Jasmine, I would like to introduce you to the men who will be taking this company towards the future. Jasmine, this is François Chadwick."

I reached over to shake his hand; when he stood, a chill ran down my spine that made my knees weak. I stumbled, and grabbed the table. He reached out and held my arm tightly.

"Are you all right, Ms. Burrell?" he asked. I looked in his eyes and thought, I know you.

His deep blues eyes seemed to pierce me, and I felt my eyelids fluttering against my will. He stood me up, shook my hand, and returned to his seat. I watched him fold his tall, thin frame into his chair, grinning bizarrely. As I studied him, he winked at me.

That was all I needed to know. He was the "friend of Marcus" who had dropped off the note at my apartment.

Tom nudged me; I must have been staring at Mr. Chadwick. I turned and nodded. "I'm fine," I said. "Must have been a little too much coffee this morning."

The other gentleman approached, but instead of shaking my hand, he greeted me in an Old World fashion, kissing both of my cheeks.

"Jasmine, this is Mikhail Schuyler."

"Hello, Mr. Schuyler, it is a pleasure to meet you."

"You too, Jasmine. My partner and I have heard a lot about you and we are looking forward to working very closely with you."

"Um, that sounds great," I stammered. "I'm excited as well."

The meeting had been about to break up when I entered, so after a few pleasantries, everyone rose from their seat. I eyeballed Tom to follow me as I said my goodbyes and excused myself from the meeting. He followed me, smiling. He was obviously excited about the sudden turn of events.

"Tom, what's going on?" I asked him, bewildered.

"Jasmine, these gentlemen are offering us triple what the firm is worth, and Steve and I have decided to take them up on their offer. We will have a considerable say in the day-to-day operations of the company, up until we fully get them integrated into the company process, but Mr. Schuyler and Mr. Chadwick will be responsible for the entire operation, taking us to the next level. Jasmine, they're talking about taking us global—do you know what that means?"

"Yes, Tom I think I do, and I'm not sure I want it to go that far." Something about these men had me nervous. I didn't want to go anywhere with them.

I turned to walk away.

"Jasmine, you'll see, everything is going to be fine," Tom said, unfazed by my lack of enthusiasm. "Just wait—we'll be the top law firm in the country, and you'll be the new face leading us into the future."

I kept walking.

Something was wrong. I knew the letter I received about Marcus had to come from the blond guy—blond hair, piercing blue eyes; I remembered what Jonathan had said when I called him about the note. And now he was buying out the partners in my company. Something was up and I had to find out what.

# Chapter 82

In my current state of mind there was no way I was going to get any work done. I went back to Wendy and told her I wouldn't be back until I didn't know when. I had to think.

I grabbed all my stuff and a couple of the files I had been working on and headed to the elevator. The doors opened and I stepped inside; but right before the doors could close all the way a hand slipped in and forced the doors open again. Mr. Chadwick stood there, smiling at me.

"May I join you?"

I grimaced and whispered under my breath, Do I have a choice? "Yeah, sure, of course." I half-smiled.

"So Ms. Burrell, what do you think about my partner and me coming over here to work with you?"

"Um Mr. Chadwick, if you don't mind me saying, I don't know what to think. It's all so sudden, wouldn't you say?"

"Yes, Ms. Burrell, you're right. But I think that given the opportunity, we can make this company more successful than it already is—and we need your help to accomplish this."

"I hear what you're saying, Mr. Chadwick, and I'm flattered. It's just going to take some time for me to get used to the idea of new management."

"That's understandable; just know my partner and I are willing to give you all the time you need to adjust. Just think of us as your new best friends."

Before I could reply, the doors opened at the lobby level. "Good day, Ms. Burrell," he said, and stepped out of the elevator.

I watched him walk away. Then the doors closed and I fell back against the elevator wall, trying to figure out what the hell was going on.

The bottle of vodka was waiting for me when I got home; I had picked Sasha up from my grandmother and put her down for a nap. Kevin was still at work, so I had plenty of time to be by myself and to think about all that had transpired today. All right, Jasmine, think: What's the connection? I figured the two men who had bought out our company were connected to Marcus in some kind of way—but why weren't they in jail and why were they buying out my company now? It didn't make sense. What could they want with me?

Maybe Marcus could shed some light on this bullshit. I had to talk to him, which meant another trip up to the prison.

I could go tomorrow. It would be easy—Kevin would be at work and Sasha would be at her new daycare. I could leave first thing in the morning and get back in time to pick up Sasha and get home without anyone knowing what was up. The plan was set; I would interrogate Marcus and find out who they guys were and they wanted. He would have to tell me now—they were moving in on my territory and I was not about to have that.

I went to check on Sasha; she was sleeping soundly. I walked back to the kitchen, picked up the bottle and took a deep swig, finally able to relax. The next two swigs cleared my mind and there I was once again, floating to my favorite place, my private place, a place meant just for me. Yes, gotta love that vodka.

# Chapter 83

The next morning I got up early and got Sasha ready in record time. I sat her at the table and let her eat her cereal and fruit while I had a cup of coffee and toast.

Kevin's father had to be at work by five a.m., so he was already gone, and Kevin was sound asleep; the alarm wouldn't go off for another forty-five minutes or so. I packed all of Sasha's things, grabbed my purse and briefcase, situated her on my hip, and headed out the door. I put Sasha in her car seat and sped to the daycare, getting her there right when the doors opened at seven. The receptionist and her new teacher were at the door waiting for her, as they did every morning to greet the kids as they came through the door. I loved it.

"OK, Sasha, Mommy has to go to work. I'll be back to get you later."

She smiled and walked off happily with the teacher, studying her new surroundings and waving as she headed for her classroom.

I took the nearest freeway entrance and for the next few hours, plotted how I would find the answers I needed to solve this mystery.

The visitor parking lot at the prison was nearly empty. I walked directly to the gate and had my bags and my body checked for weapons and contraband. The prison guard cleared me and I proceeded to the visiting area.

Marcus walked over towards me, a puzzled look on his face. All he knew was that the guard had informed him he had a visitor, which turned out to be me. He was obviously confused, but he would know why I was there soon enough.

"Hey, Marcus," I said.

He bent over and kissed me on the forehead, then sat down in one of the hard chairs. He was looking as good as ever and I had to compose myself because I was there on business, not pleasure.

"Hey, Jaz, I wasn't expecting you, is everything all right?"

"No, Marcus everything is not all right," I said, getting straight to the point. "What can you tell me about François Chadwick and Mikhail Schuyler?"

He stiffened.

"What the hell? How do you know them?"

"The better question is how do *you* know them?" I snapped.

"Jasmine, stop this interrogation bullshit and tell me what the hell is going on."

I briefed Marcus on the previous day's events and also told him of the letter I had received years ago when the FBI questioned me. He rose to his feet and began pacing.

"Marcus, what is wrong? Who are these guys and what do they want? I'm not stupid—they obviously have an interest in me and I need to know how to defend against them."

Marcus sat down again, and took my hand.

"Look, baby, you don't want to mess with these guys. They're very rich and highly connected. I suggest you do whatever they say or you will end up like me."

"Are you serious? Do whatever they say? When have you ever known me to be intimidated when it came to my work?"

"Baby, I'm not talking about your work and what you're capable of. I'm talking about your life. These guys play rough; and when they play, they play for keeps. I don't want anything to happen to you or your family."

"My family? Are you saying they will threaten my family?" This was getting weirder by the minute.

"Yes, that is what I'm saying. Look, Jasmine, the reason I'm in here is because I refused to do what they asked. I started out making deposits and doing little odd jobs for them, simple stuff. But as the deposits got bigger and the errands got more complex, I started to question them about what was going on. They didn't like that. So when they refused to tell me what they were doing I decided I wouldn't do it anymore, and I told them to find someone else.

"That was a big mistake. The last job I did for them was the job that put me in here. They had set me up, making sure I would take the fall for everything. Made sure they didn't do anything to implicate themselves—they came out of all that junk squeaky-clean.

"Four of us ended up going to jail, one of the guys ended up dead in a freak boating accident, and the other guy involved disappeared before they could find him.

"I'm telling you, Jasmine—don't try to be Superwoman, just for this one time. Just do as they say or quit your job."

"Quit my job? Are you crazy? I'm up for a partnership in the next two years, there is no way I'm quitting my job." I couldn't believe what I was hearing—it just sounded so bizarre, like out of a movie or something. These things didn't really happen to real people—did they?

"Listen, I know this shit sounds crazy, but you cannot win this one. You have to believe me." He was almost pleading with me.

I was just about to let him have it, explain to him how don't no one scare me into doing nothing I don't want to do; then the little girl, from the last visit ran up to him, jumped into his arms, and yelled "Daddy, I'm here!"

Daddy? I looked at Marcus as he held the little girl, smiling at her while looking across at me, trying to explain to me with his eyes how this little girl was his daughter.

The young lady from last time appeared, following the little girl. She stood looking at me as if I had two heads. And at that moment I felt like I did.

"You have a daughter?" I asked, ignoring the little girl, ignoring the young lady standing right next to us,

"Yes, Jasmine, I do," Marcus said, a mixture of pride and guilt in his voice. "Jasmine, this is Astyn, my little girl."

Astyn turned to me and smiled.

"Hi."

"Hello, pretty girl, how are you?" I said, smiling at her.

"I'm fine. How are you?"

"I'm fine, sweetheart; you sure are a sweetie pie."

"Thank you—what's your name?"

"My name is Jasmine."

"Mommy, this is Jasmine," Astyn said, innocently introducing me to the woman standing next to her, who had stood silently since she arrived. I looked over at her. She eyed me suspiciously. I stood up. "Marcus, I think I better go. Thanks for your help—I will take care of this situation on my own. You have a nice life."

I turned and without looking back, I left the visitor's room as fast as I could without actually breaking into a run. I got in the car and sat there for a moment.

Shit, that little girl had to be about six or seven years old, meaning she was conceived around the time Marcus and I were together. What the fuck, I can't believe this shit; that motherfucker.

I started the car and began driving home. My body felt like it was filled with feelings so harsh and so brutal that I finally had to pull over to compose myself before getting back on the road.

There was no way possible Marcus had a child that age. That bitch must be lying, trying to pin her baby on him. But damn, Astyn sure did look like him. But how? We were together then. Had he cheated on me?

Everything was crazy now; there was no turning back. I had opened up a door that I couldn't close, and it was all my fault. If I had just left him and his drama alone I wouldn't be in this predicament. Work issues, baby mama issues, infidelity issues—they were all swirling around in my head like one messed-up tornado. My own man and my own baby and my own life—I was jeopardizing it all to run behind a nigga in jail who obviously never really cared about me.

The visual of that little girl jumping into Marcus' arms replayed over and over in my head as I drove back to the city, a cruel reminder of my complete inability to cope with men, and with reality. Once again I had let my needs smother the needs of my family and what was right. I had had no right to blame Marcus; I was no different. Here I was pining for a man who had turned my entire life upside down and all I could think about was how could he do this to me again. We weren't a couple any longer; we hadn't been a couple in years. I had a life, a good one, with a baby and a man I loved, even if he wasn't perfect. How dare I risk all of that for a man imprisoned for being a high-class crook?

This was it: I was going to give everything I had to my family from now on, and no one was going to ruin it—not even me. Marcus was history, a thief who had stolen my heart for the last time.

# Chapter 84

Over the next year, I submerged myself into my family and my career. Kevin and I had been doing well, no major drama, and I had given up on Marcus and begun to pursue the dream of wedlock I had wished for as a child. No one ever explains to you, as a young, girl growing up, that marriage and having a man doesn't define you as a self-sufficient individual capable of all things possible. So like most women, even though I had a beautiful child and a successful career, the fact that I had had a long-term relationship that hadn't yet led to marriage, was like a fracture running through to my still fragile womanhood.

All my life I had dreamed of getting married, having the perfect wedding, having the perfect life. I had spent the majority of my adult life chasing the ultimate feeling of love. The elusiveness of that emotion forced me into situations I'd rather not have had to experience but as time passed, I used those experiences as stepping-stones to a more concrete and stable place. Kevin didn't understand this, but even if he had, he had no intentions of marrying me based on my feelings about this. He had his own views about marriage, convincing himself of the man's perspective—which for my part, I couldn't care less about. He felt like he had to have a financially stable household, that he needed to have "made it" as prominent member of society, with money saved and security beyond all means before he would even consider marriage. Everything had to be perfectly aligned, which in turn would keep him sane. It was like a funhouse mirror, because the one thing I felt would preserve my sanity was to get married, become legit. I had given Sasha his last name, so that left me feeling like an outsider, just another woman birthing his child, not really a part of his family.

"Kevin, we need to talk," I said one Sunday morning, as he and I and Sasha snuggled in bed. I knew this was the totally wrong approach, the words that made men run screaming from the room—or worse, just shut down entirely. I didn't care; I rearranged myself so he could see my face and moved Sasha to the other side of the bed. He casually sat up, looking at me with "here we go again" eyes.

"What's up?" he said, sighing.

"Don't you think we need to get married? We've been together for over five years and now that we got Sasha, I think it's time we become a real family."

"You don't think we are a real family?"

"No I don't, it don't feel that way to me."

"Damn, Jaz, why are you trippin?" He was losing his composure fast.

"My life and my security, you call that me trippin?" I wasn't hanging on to mine very well either.

"I don't know. I'm not really ready to get married, we ain't stable, we living here with my father and I was hoping to have some money saved before we did that."

"What do you think is going to change in next few years?" I demanded. "The money we making now ain't gonna get too much better unless I make partner, and they tripping down at my job, some new European company has bought us out so I don't know where I'm'a go from here. I think we need to just do it and get it over with."

"Man, I don't know; I'm really not ready for marriage."

"Look, you need to pick a date. I'm tired of doing this as single individuals. I'm doing everything a wife would do and then some; don't you think I deserve to be called your wife?"

"Now you know, it ain't like that. I just think we . . ."

I wasn't having it anymore. "You need to pick a date, and I wasn't playing."

Kevin looked at me and knew something in me was different.

"What about December of next year?"

I couldn't believe he had changed his mind so quickly after all these years, but I wasn't going to question him if he'd gotten this far.

"December of next year, that won't work. You need to pick something sooner, I'm not waiting that long. Look, it's July now, Sasha is will be two in February, how about we plan something in late August or September next year?"

His silence was his answer, so I decided for him.

"OK, what about September twenty-eighth? That's more than a year away. It should give you enough time to get whatever it is you need to get done, done."

His mouth was set in the stubborn way I knew. I knew he didn't want this—but I did, and I was going to get my way on this, as I had on everything else.

In my own little world I was king, and I didn't care one way or the other, how anyone else felt about what it was I wanted. I was trapped in two worlds; trying to exert some sort of control over my life, while at the same time giving all I had to please others. It was crazy how these two impulses were just two sides of the same coin. I rarely gave into this kind of unrestrained desire, but when I did, that was it—I couldn't control it, nor would I if I could have. It was the only time outside of my work when I felt like I was strong, and it didn't matter if the things I wanted weren't good for the other people involved.

# Chapter 85

That same day, I called up my mother and told her we were going to get married. She was happy—she knew that was what I wanted—but she also knew we were embarking on a costly event that she and my dad—who had always been a part of my life, even though they divorced—were more than likely going to have to pay for. When I told her, she said we better start looking for a place to hold it as soon as possible. There were three things I knew I wanted: I wanted the wedding and the reception to be in the same place so moving around would be easy; I wanted my grandfather to perform the ceremony; and I wanted the wedding to start on time. Three simple things; everything else was negotiable.

Then I started contacting everyone I wanted to have a significant role; I called Paige first to let her know I wanted her to be my maid of honor. I followed with calls to the divas, letting them know what I needed them to do, and then to anyone else I could think of at the moment that I wanted to have a spot. Everyone was excited about his or her responsibilities and the ball started rolling way before I had a ring or a real engagement. But this was how I liked to roll, it didn't matter that I hadn't had a formal proposal or that I didn't have a ring. I was finally getting married and no old-school tradition was going to keep me from doing it, and doing it well.

That evening, after Kevin got home from work, I started telling him about all my ideas—how many groomsmen he was going to need and where we were thinking about having it. He just listened to all I had to say, nodded his compliance and walked away.

"Kevin?" I called after him.
"Yeah?"
"What's wrong?"
"Nothing."
"Kevin, I know when something is wrong with you, are you all right with this?" I asked him—not that it mattered.
"Yeah, I'm cool."
"Well, do you want to help with anything, like music or food or colors?"
"Nah, you go ahead. You do what you want, and I'll just show up."

Great, I thought. I'll make all the decisions, and this wedding will be exactly what I want it to be.

Of course, it was reckless for me to think that I could get away with planning an entire wedding without any input from the groom, but Kevin was on board, and that's all I wanted—no drama or no stress. Shit, I'm the bride, so this is *my* day anyway, so I'm going to have it just like Burger King, my way.

Ignoring Kevin's silence, I smiled and walked away thinking about the dresses, the flowers, the food, my bachelorette party; everything was going to be the bomb, and I was going to make sure of that. But as I walked towards the kitchen to start dinner a picture of Marcus flashed across my mind, and my heart stopped.

Come on now, Jaz, don't start this shit, Marcus is history, and you know that. You're marrying Kevin; this is want you want. My mind was working overtime, trying to convince me I was making the right decision—but my heart was stirring up something else; something I didn't need or want.

Or did I?

# Chapter 86

With the wedding planning and all the errands and coordination that went with it, the next few months seemed to fly by. I hadn't realized we were eight months out until I looked at the calendar and my birthday was coming around again. Sasha was about to turn two and winter had set in on us so harshly that a lot of my pre-wedding activities were slowed or completely brought to a halt. I continued to make phone calls, setting up appointments and making arrangements as I could. The only things I needed to check out personally were the photographer, the place where we were going to have the wedding, and the company I had selected to do the cake tasting. I wanted to give the girls ample time to try on dresses, lose weight and pay for everything, so Mom and I decided we would check out bridal shops over the weekend instead of putting off until later. In spite of the slowdown, everything seemed to be running smoothly and all plans were falling into place.

Work was another story. I had been going to work every day as usual but with the new management everything was different. I rarely saw Tom anymore; he and Steve and the other partners were always out of the office, traveling or playing golf. Their careers had turned into vacations while I was stuck with a lot more of the case files, and the two European con men.

The new owners were not very friendly. They wanted things their way or no way and I started to see what Marcus was talking about when he said not to mess with them. They were hard-nosed dudes with a touch of the sadist, and they were misogynistic on top of that. I had thought about quitting, but with the wedding coming up and Kevin on edge, there was no way. Most days I avoided them as best I could, coming in early and staying late. I kept my door closed and asked Wendy not to interrupt me unless it was a dire emergency. Most of the time that worked, but sometimes I had to sit and listen to their foreign accents tell me how to do my job. I never said much and they never got too out of hand, but I knew I wasn't going to be able to take them much longer.

This morning seemed even worse—no sun, just gray, dreary clouds and bone-chilling cold. It was so depressing; I really wanted to stay in bed, but knew there was too much work to do at the office.

Luckily, it hadn't snowed in while, so the streets were clear and my drive to work was relatively swift. As I walked into the lobby, I looked toward the door to greet the doorman, but he was not at his post. That was unusual, I thought; maybe he went to get another cup of coffee or to the bathroom or something.

It took me no time to get to my floor, since no one stopped to get on in between the lobby and my floor. In fact, when I thought about it, the entire building seemed strangely empty. When I got off on my floor, I was unnerved to see the lights in my office. Had I left them on overnight? I didn't think I had, but knew the answer as soon as I opened the door. There, sitting at my desk drinking coffee and thumbing through my files was François. He was dressed to the nines, as usual, wearing a dark blue pin-striped suit with a powder blue dress shirt, a clearly expensive silk tie of many different blues and gold, and I got a good look at his midnight black Cole Haan shoes because his legs were crossed and resting *very* comfortably on my desk. Although I didn't care very much for the man, his taste and style in clothing was off the chain.

"Mr. Chadwick, is there a problem?"

He looked up from the file he was reading and smiled.

"Good morning, Jasmine. How are you?"

"I'm fine, Mr. Chadwick. Is there something wrong? Why are you in my office?"

"Well, I have been studying you and your work for some time now, and I think it's time we had a talk. I have a proposal for you."

# I Surrender All

I stood there, remembering what Marcus told me, thinking about the letter that was slipped under my door, wondering what in the hell kind of proposal he could possibly want to make.

"What does this have to do with, Mr. Chadwick?"

"Have a seat."

He motioned to the chair sitting across from my desk, the one I usually asked people to sit in.

"Jasmine, I've been thinking about how I could be of more assistance to you. How I could more effectively use your talent."

I didn't reply.

"I have a new client for you. He's an international banker and a very close personal friend. He got himself into a little bit of trouble and the European government is trying to extradite him back there to face charges of embezzlement, and I want you to handle his case. He will be flying in from New York tomorrow, and I want you to drop everything you're doing and put all your energy into making sure there is no conviction."

"Um, Mr. Chadwick, I'm really not comfortable deserting my clients to work on something I know nothing about. Don't you think you can find someone else? I have a lot of work to do as it is, and adding another case to my workload is really going to put me behind."

He got up and walked around the desk towards me, narrowing his eyes. Coming around behind me, he placed his hand on my shoulder. "Ms. Burrell, I don't think you understand. This is a very important client and I need you to take this case."

"I'm sorry, Mr. Chadwick, but I'm not going to be able to do this for you. I have way too much on my plate. Maybe Tom or Steve can help you out."

I slid out from under his grip, got up out of my chair, and walked to my desk to survey the scene. I rearranged a few things and noticed out of the corner of my eye Mr. Chadwick closing my office door. Then he walked back towards me and leaned in close—so close I could smell the hazelnut coffee on his breath.

"Ms. Burrell, it seems we have a misunderstanding. I'm not asking you to take this case, I'm telling you, and if you have a problem with that, then *we* have a serious problem."

"Mr. Chadwick," I stood firm, "you will not intimidate me, and I will not do anything that it is immoral, unethical or that will cause problems for my family and me."

"Ah yes, your family. You mean your fiancé Kevin Owens. You two are getting married this fall, right? And what about that precious little girl of yours—what's her name again, Sasha?"

I cringed at the thought he knew so much about my family. "Mr. Chadwick, if you're implying you will cause harm to my fiancé or my child, you better think again. I'm no punk and if you come near my family, I will kill you."

He laughed loudly. "Yes, yes . . . that's what I'm talking about. You have that killer instinct I need to get this job done. I'll bring you his file tomorrow morning; I'm out of the office for the rest of the day. Have a pleasant day, Ms. Burrell."

He walked out of my office, laughing to himself as he dialed someone on his cell phone. I could hear him as he walked around the corner, confirming with the other party my enthusiastic response to his request.

He must be crazy if he thinks I'm going to drop what I'm doing to take this case. Who does he think he is?

# Chapter 87

THE NEXT MORNING, MR. CHADWICK knocked on my office door and motioned for the tall African-American gentleman standing behind him to enter first, and I knew my day was going to be shit. Chadwick's companion entered smiling broadly, and reached for my hand to greet me. I stood there motionless, in awe of his unbelievably attractive presence. I had a hard time looking at him without letting my face show what my mind (and body) was thinking.

When I shook his hand, his skin was so soft it almost set me to shivering. His skin was the color of milk chocolate, smooth . . . nice. He was clean-shaven and impeccably dressed in a Versace suit, but the corporate impression was turned upside-down by his gorgeous dreadlocks that he wore pulled together tightly in a ponytail. They hung down neatly, ending in between his wide muscular shoulder blades.

He was beautiful, and once again my body began to betray me. Damn, I smiled on the inside; I must truly have a problem.

"Hello, Ms. Burrell, I've heard a lot about you. How are you today?"

"Um hello, Mr. . . ."

"Oh, I'm sorry—Galileo; my name is Galileo Prince."

"Galileo," I laughed. "Come on—your name is actually Galileo Prince?"

He stared, obviously not amused. "Yes, that is my name; my mother had this strange fascination with science and astronomy before I was born, so here I am."

"All right, if you say so." I smiled, trying not to stare too hard at him.

"Jasmine, this is the client I was telling you about," said Mr. Chadwick. "I'm going to give you his file and I want you to give him your full attention. I have transferred all your other files throughout the office so there will be no need for you to worry about them. I need you to give Mr. Prince premier service and if you have any problems with anyone in the office, you come and find me right away. I have given instructions for you not to be bothered until this case is finished. Do you have any questions?"

I looked over at Mr. Chadwick, then back to Galileo.

"No . . . no, Mr. Chadwick, I don't have any questions. I will do my best to make sure I give Mr. Prince everything he needs."

Shit, that didn't come out right.

Mr. Chadwick grinned slyly and left my office, closing the door behind him.

I hesitantly glanced sideways at Mr. Prince to see if he had noticed anything. I turned beet-red when I saw him obviously pretending to thumb through the Essence magazine had he picked up from the coffee table, trying to suppress a smile.

As I tried to compose myself I noticed Wendy settling in at her desk.

"Excuse me, Mr. Prince," I said, getting ready to go out and talk to Wendy. But before I could leave he said, "Jasmine—is it OK, for me to call you Jasmine?"

"Yes, Mr. Prince, that's fine."

"Jasmine, I need you to do me a favor."

"Yes?"

"If I'm going to call you Jasmine, I need you to call me Galileo—is that cool?"

"Yes Mr. . . . I mean, Galileo, that's cool."

I walked out of the office feeling a little queasy; this was not going to be easy.

All right, Jasmine, keep it together. This is business, strictly business.

Wendy was standing there with a cup of coffee in her hand. I pulled her to the side.

"Wendy, girl, I'm going to need your help. Do you see that man standing in my office?"

"Yeah, I do. Who is that?"

"He's the new client Mr. Chadwick had for me."

"Damn, Jasmine. Excuse my French; he's fine."

"Wendy, I know, that's why I need your help. Man, this dude is killing me and we haven't even begun to work yet. Married... what the hell am I thinking about?" I raised my hand to slap five with Wendy.

"I hear you, Jasmine. I'll do what I can, but I surely don't envy you; well, maybe I do."

We laughed, trying not to let Mr. Prince hear us, but I knew he was listening. He had to be listening.

I reentered the office with two cups of coffee; I handed him a cup, and proceeded to prepare my coffee as I liked it. Galileo stared at me as if I had three eyes.

"Is there a problem? Is your coffee hot enough?" I said.

"My coffee is fine. I'm worried about yours."

"What do you mean?"

"I've never seen anyone put that much sugar and that much cream into a cup of coffee—you might as well have had the cream with a dash of coffee in it," he said, smiling.

I smiled, too, and blushed, looking down at my cup of coffee that looked like lightly tinted milk.

"Yeah, I know Galileo. My ex-boyfriend used to reprimand me about the way I drank my coffee, too."

"Ex-boyfriend?"

"Yeah, my ex-boyfriend didn't like me messing up coffee either. He's in jail now, for embezzlement." Shit, what was I thinking? I don't know this man and I'm telling him all my business like he was my new best friend.

"I'm sorry Galileo," I said hastily. "I don't know what made me say all that, something in me is feeling really comfortable around you, I guess." There, I was doing it again. He smiled, but he had a strange look on his face.

"Are you talking about Marcus Damon?" he asked.

My eyes widened as I realized that Galileo probably knew Marcus, seeing as though they both had dealings with Mr. Chadwick.

He walked over towards me, reached for the cup in my hand and set it down on the desk. He gently lifted my chin with one finger until our eyes met.

"Jasmine, I knew Marcus well. He is a good man. We worked together on a few projects and I found him to be an honest and upstanding gentleman."

I looked at him, confused. "What are you talking about? If he was such a good upstanding man, why the hell is he in jail?"

"Look, Jasmine, what happened to Marcus was a big mistake. He's not supposed to be in jail. He was supposed to go to trial and everything would have been fine. They needed him, so they didn't want him to go to jail."

"What do you mean? Were you involved in all of this mess, are your case and his case related?"

He dropped his head and turned away from me. I grabbed his arm and swung him back around as hard as I could.

"Galileo, talk to me. Tell me what's going on."

He took my hand and led me to the leather sofa in the corner of my office and returned to pick up our cups of coffee, which, I was sure, were cold by now.

"I can't say much but I can tell you that Marcus really didn't know what he was getting himself into. He was just doing his job and unfortunately became a casualty of war.

"Mr. Chadwick and Mr. Schuyler are very powerful men with ties to the Italian mob and business stakes that go all the way up through European government. But as quiet as it is kept, they're also deeply involved in some undercover business involving the United States government. Marcus' citizenship here was the key."

My entire body was shaking now, rattling the lukewarm cup of coffee I was holding. I tried to take a sip, but I was shaking too hard to be sure I could get it to my mouth without spilling. The chill running down my spine had left me as ice-cold as the coffee. I set the cup down and looked at Galileo.

I couldn't believe what I was hearing. Who was this man, and how did he know so much? I struggled with what he was saying; he sounded like he knew what he was talking about, but I really didn't know if he could be trusted. He didn't know me, and the fact that he was spilling his guts the way he was made me nervous.

"Listen to me." His spirit was so calm, and for a moment I forgot all my fears and lost myself in his beautiful almond eyes.

"Jasmine, I know how to take them down, but I need your help. If you don't already know, the charges I'm facing aren't real. They paid the district attorney and a few judges to trump them up to make it look like I was the ringleader of all the money laundering and embezzling. There's going to be a trial and I'm going to be found guilty, but before they sentence me some new evidence is supposed to surface that will get me off. They just need the time to create it. So all I'm supposed to do is sit back and wait for all of this to blow over. This way it will look like I was the criminal who got off on a technicality. They'll be out of the spotlight, as always, and business will go on as usual."

"So what the hell do they need me for?"

"When we were all in Europe, all Marcus did was talk about you. How wonderful, and beautiful, and what a talented lawyer you were. He had promised himself that whatever the situation, he was coming back here to make you his wife.

"Well, we all listened very closely, especially Mr. Chadwick. He had developed a strange fixation on you and decided he wanted to get to know you for himself. He knew his whole operation was close to being exposed, so he recruited Marcus into the group in order to have a reason to get to you, so that if anything went down he could use you to represent him. He figured a prominent

African-American woman representing him would give him extra leeway, make him look like he was accessible."

"But when Marcus found out what was really going on and refused to do any more deals, threatening to turn Mr. Chadwick in, they fixed it so that the last deal Marcus had done would put him under. They had initially set it up so Marcus could walk away from all of this, but his stubbornness and, I guess, his conscience made him plead guilty."

"You see, if his case had gone to trial, Mr. Chadwick knew Marcus would try to get you to represent him, which would have given him the opportunity to meet you, pretending to be Marcus' friend, someone truly concerned with Marcus' well-being. At the same time he could use you as leverage against Marcus, in case Marcus tried to implicate him. Marcus pleaded guilty to keep Mr. Chadwick away from you. He figured if he was in jail Mr. Chadwick would have no reason to pursue you. He would take the blame for the crimes and the European government would hopefully end their search for Mr. Chadwick.

"But that didn't work; they intensified their search and started uncovering information that threatened Chadwick and Schuyler and their whole criminal enterprise. And that's where I come in. I had been involved from the very beginning and felt very loyal to Mr. Chadwick, because of what he had done for me."

"And what was that?" I asked; I could barely get the words out, the story was so amazing.

"Don't ask; that's another story for another time.

"You need to know, Marcus left without saying a word. He was in Hawaii for a while and then ended up here with you. But Mr. Chadwick had him followed and knew every move Marcus was making. He anonymously sent the evidence against Marcus to his shady lawyers and Marcus ended up in jail."

I stood up and walked towards the window; so many different thoughts were swirling around in my head. I shut my eyes. How could this happen, the love of my life stolen from me because of someone else's bullshit? Marcus wasn't guilty; he was a victim. Oh my God.

"Jasmine, we have to play this very carefully," Galileo continued. "Mr. Chadwick will stop at nothing to get what he wants. You see, it only took Chadwick a few years to set up the deal to buy your law firm, and now he is right where he wants to be—next to you."

My eyes fluttered open—snapped, really, and I forgot all about Mr. Chadwick, Galileo, Kevin, Marcus' infidelity, his lies and deceit. I just had to see him. *It wasn't his fault.*

I smiled and returned to Galileo. "OK. What do we do?"

"Meet tonight and every night from here on out to get this straight. But remember, no one—I mean no one—can know anything about what we are doing. Mr. Chadwick has spies everywhere. You would not believe who he has on his payroll. Agreed?"

"Yes Galileo, agreed. But I can't meet every night, I have a family and that won't work."

"OK. That's cool, you tell me when and where, and I'll be there."

He gave me his business card and told me to call him later on in the evening. I agreed.

As he stepped away to make a phone call, I figured we'd have to spend a majority of our time in the office, with several sporadic meetings elsewhere. If Mr. Chadwick knew we were meeting outside the office, I'm sure he'd get suspicious. I began jotting down all the places I could think of that were inconspicuous, where we could meet to begin putting together a case to take down the European connection, our new name for the two men who had ruined so many people's lives, including mine.

When he finished his phone call, I handed him the list of possible meeting spots and told him I would contact him with a date and directions when I figured out a time. He nodded, and we shook hands. I watched as he walked through my office door and out into the hallway.

What was I getting myself into now? I cringed at the thought.

# Chapter 88

I WAS MEETING GALILEO AT the Palomino Restaurant in downtown Minneapolis, upstairs from the in-house Rock Bottom Brewery. Both the Palomino and Rock Bottom were very popular nightspots downtown, but I chose Palomino for its more secluded setting.

I approached the hostess and informed her I would be meeting a gentlemen for dinner and could she please direct him to the bar area where I would be seated. She smiled and escorted me towards the circular bar stocked to the ceiling with every kind of liquor and spirit imaginable. I was in heaven.

I sat down at the bar, ordered a lavender martini, waited as a really cute bartender poured the crisp cocktail into a tall, thin-stemmed, sugar-rimmed martini glass. I thanked him and took a slow, deliberate sip. As the cool liquor slid effortlessly down my throat I noticed Galileo scopin' out the bar area, apparently studying faces and memorizing his surroundings. When he recognized me, his smile illuminated the dimly lit room—even the other diners noticed it, giving them a taste of what I had been dealing with all day. He was different, special, and because I was soon to be married, I couldn't believe I was feeling what I was feeling.

He was dressed a lot more casually than the last time I'd seen him—not that it was any less impressive, it was just a side of him that I hadn't seen. A heavy dark-brown leather jacket—clearly a designer item—was draped over his arm and his tailored cotton shirt hung just snugly enough around his shoulders for me to see the definition in his back. His shoes were some sort of leather loafers that looked like they were handmade, maybe in Italy. I couldn't take my eyes off of him. I took one more deep swallow of my drink before he got too close, and prayed for some kind of relief. But as he reached down to give me a light hug, his dreadlocks, no longer pulled back, wrapped around my face and neck; the scent that lingered sent me heading towards a place I'd hadn't been in a while.

God, I thought, if You're playing a joke on me, it is no way funny. Damn, if I could just see what was underneath all that soft-ass material he was wearing. I laughed to myself, a little tipsy from the martini that was now circulating through my bloodstream.

"Hello, Jasmine," he said. His smile was so intoxicating that for a moment I almost forgot to respond.

"Hey, Galileo, how are you?" He took my hand.

"I'm fine, and yourself?"

I took another sip. "I'm great, just sitting here having a drink and thinking about some wedding arrangements I have yet to make." Shit, why did I say that?

From the look on his face, he wanted to know the answer to the same question.

"Oh, so you're getting married soon, huh?"

"Yes, in September." I tried to keep the disappointment from showing, but my voice was so flat, it was evident I wasn't excited about it.

"Congratulations—I'm sure you will be a beautiful bride. Where's your ring?"

I looked down at my hand, which he was still holding in his.

"We haven't had a chance to go and pick out rings yet. Just been so busy with work and our daughter and stuff like that—you know how it is."

"Actually Jasmine, I don't. If and when I propose to my wife, whoever that will be, I will be sure I have a ring for her."

"I hear you," I said, "but Kevin and I have been together for so long it's like we're already married; we're just going through the motions to get the paper."

"Oh, his name is Kevin; I was going to ask if you were seeing anyone, seeing as Marcus is tied up right now," he said. "Well, he must truly be a saint to capture a beautiful woman like you." I blushed.

"What does he do?" Galileo asked. I couldn't tell if he was just being polite, or if he had some other reason.

"He's a graphic designer for a major ad agency here in the city. He's a great guy and we've been making these plans for a few months now."

"Wow, that's great. Let me get a drink so that we can toast to your big day."

I really didn't want to toast. It wasn't that I had had second thoughts about Kevin; it was just that Galileo was so bomb. I kept thinking bout his dreadlocks wrapping around me, protecting me like a cocoon protects a butterfly.

I finished my first drink and ordered another while Galileo started on his Miller Genuine Draft. He asked the bartender for the tab and paid it without blinking. I was thoroughly impressed by now and knew it wouldn't take much more for me to be all outside of my body, trippin' and thinking dirty. I looked in the mirror behind the bartender and promised myself as I took a swig from my drink that I would behave, but the direct path the liquor took towards my private parts was telling me something different.

All right, girls, calm down, this meeting is strictly business, you got it? Strictly business. I spoke to my nipples as if they were human; they would appear out of nowhere, whenever they felt like it, refusing to listen to reason, just standing at attention whenever a man that aroused me was in the vicinity. I reached for the jacket I was wearing and pulled it close to hide my girls.

"Are you ready to find a table?"

"Yeah, I'm ready.

He reached to the side of me to pull back the barstool and help me out of my chair. I clutched my glass and stepped down to the floor,

We were face to face, and looked up into his eyes. We held each other's gaze for way too long; then he smiled, caressed my cheek and stepped aside, allowing me to lead the way towards the hostess' station. I could feel my entire body warming up; I knew he was staring at my backside. He casually placed his hand comfortably on the small of my back and all that was holy about me evaporated into thin air, a cruel reminder of my weakness for men.

I wonder what's going through his mind right now? If it was anything like what I was thinking, we were going to be in for a long night.

Our table was in a far corner, so walking through the restaurant was like a scene from a movie. The magnificent high ceilings and carefully laid tables with their crisp white tablecloths and glowing glasses captivated me. The room was filled with flowers. Even Galileo was impressed as he walked through the room, checking out every detail. We sat down, eyeing each other uncomfortably. I tore my eyes away from his, recognizing a scent that was very special to me. I inhaled deeply as the aroma of fresh roses from the vase on the table made me feel higher than I already was.

"I love the smell of roses," I said, exhaling dreamily.

"Oh you do, huh?"

He picked up one of the roses and gently ran it across my nose and chin, watching my reaction carefully.

"Galileo, you're teasing me. The smell of roses is one of my favorite scents."

"I hear you. I feel the same way. The natural beauty and smell of a rose, there's nothing like it. Well, almost nothing." He looked at me meaningfully.

I returned his gaze, and the reckless intent of seduction became almost overwhelming. I could see it, smell it, taste it—and it was working.

I needed to change the subject.

"Aren't all the tables beautiful? It's almost like being on an island, don't you think?"

"Yeah, I do. I would love to be on an island with you, Jasmine."

I smiled; well, I tried to smile. My skin felt like it was smoldering—deliciously—so I took a gulp of my drink. Now my throat was burning because I had swallowed it so fast.

I reached for my menu, even though I always ordered the same thing. Galileo opened his menu, reading out loud.

As I sat waiting for Galileo to decide, I listened to the jazz playing softly in the background. It was hypnotizing both of us—we both started swaying our heads first to the music, then, it seemed to the rhythm of each other. Fortunately, our waiter arrived to take our order, breaking our trance. I ordered my usual seafood ravioli and another martini, and after a few questions, Galileo ordered their signature paella and another beer. I smiled.

"Hmm, good choice, Galileo," I said. He looked at me intensely. I feverishly looked away, finished up my second martini and took a couple sips of water, trying to cool the air, which seemed to be soft and sultry. This was definitely going to be a long night.

As we waited for our dinner, we talked about our life experiences and things that we had in common. He was into writing poetry and loved music. He explained that he had been a rapper in his former life and had released a few underground tracks that he collaborated on with a couple of his partners. I laughed and explained my love for rap music when I was younger and begged him to burn me a copy of his music. Surprised, he hesitantly agreed and said I'd have it by tomorrow.

The waiter returned with our meals; I took a forkfull of my ravioli and watched as Galileo took a bite.

"How do you like it?"

"Actually, Jasmine, it is rather good, but I make it better."

He winked at me, and I almost choked on a piece of lobster. I reached for my glass of water.

"Oh, so you can make it better than that? Let me try it."

I went to reach for my spoon to get a taste of his meal, but before I could, Galileo had scooped up some of the paella onto his spoon and brought it to my mouth. Hesitantly, I allowed him to place the spoon in my mouth while I slowly removed the contents with my tongue and teeth.

"Hmm, that *is* good; I doubt you can make paella better than that."

He laughed. "Oh, is that a challenge? How about I make some for you sometime? I will be here in Minnesota for a while, while we work on this case, so I will have plenty of time to prove you wrong."

"Umm, I don't think so, Galileo," I said, reasserting myself. "We're strictly business, no meals cooking and all of that, I can barely control myself with you in this public place; so just keep your seductive methods away from me—I'm cool!" The liquor in my system was talking now.

He burst into a belly laugh and nodded. "I hear that Jasmine, I hear that."

Smiling nervously, I took a swallow of my martini, hoping he couldn't recognize how rattled I was. Sipping on my third martini, the evening seemed a little calmer. Galileo and I sat and talked about everything under the sun. After finishing my third drink, I had decided against another even though my body was craving it; the conversation had turned to Mr. Chadwick and Mr. Schuyler, so I figured I better sober up some in order to mentally prepare for what was about to happen.

For the rest of the night, Galileo filled me in on all the details of their elaborate embezzlement and money-laundering scheme, exactly how Marcus was involved, and how much money he supposedly moved around; how Mr. Chadwick had convinced Galileo to take the fall, promising to get him off, and how I was the key to all of the pieces falling together in place.

I sat in astonishment listening to all the horrible things Mr. Chadwick and Mr. Schuyler had done—the lying, the cheating, the stealing, and worst of all, the mysterious deaths of two co-workers.

"Galileo, you never mentioned anyone dying!"

"Yes, I know Jasmine. I didn't want to scare you; but after talking with you I figured you of all people could handle it."

Someone has got to stop them, I thought—and at that moment, I decided it would be me. These men had ruined my life, starting with my relationship with Marcus; then to show up at my house, and then to threaten my family. Something sparked in me; I could feel my blood begin to boil. Yes. I was going to take these men down, and with the inside information Galileo had given me, it would only be a matter of time.

I looked at my watch; it was close to ten, and I knew Kevin would have had enough of being home alone with Sasha. I wasn't worried about how he would feel about me being out so late because I had phoned him a couple of times throughout the evening explaining the case to him, and he seemed OK. But once I got home, I knew things might be different. I knew I had to leave, but we stayed for another fifteen minutes, just to make sure I was cool to drive.

We decided to meet at the office at around nine to keep working on the case—our secret case. We knew it would be important for Mr. Chadwick to see us together so he would think we were working on Galileo's case—when in fact we were working on him.

I thanked Galileo for a wonderful evening and told him I looked forward to working closely with him. He smiled and kissed me on the forehead, telling me how much he had enjoyed himself. I looked up and when our eyes met I knew, he knew I had enjoyed myself as well. He walked me to my car, making sure I was in safely, and before I could get my seatbelt on good he had slipped away like a gentle breeze into the cool night air.

# Chapter 89

THE NEXT COUPLE OF MONTHS seemed to vanish into thin air. The wedding was right around the corner; the florist was in place, the cake was ordered, my brother had contacted the DJ and the bridal party had ordered and been fitted for the tuxedos and dresses. Everything was running like a well-oiled machine and I was proud of all that I had accomplished.

I was working really hard on the Prince/Chadwick case, sorting through all the evidence and hidden memos and messages that Galileo and I had steadily uncovered, while hoping and praying Mr. Chadwick wouldn't catch on to what we were doing. He was in and out of town so much I figured he'd be too busy to notice our little investigation. But I was still extremely nervous. He would pop in on me from time to time, checking on my progress with Galileo's case, and I'd smile and give him the standard "It's going well, Mr. Chadwick . . . still working some things out." And he'd wink and be on his way.

"Bastard," I'd mutter under my breath.

As time passed, Galileo and I felt like we had enough evidence to put Mr. Chadwick and Mr. Schuyler away for a long time, but we knew what kind of men these were and what they were capable of. Their power and connections would undoubtedly pose a problem, but we were in this together.

The long hours and late nights developed into a pleasant reminder of how soulmates meet. We connected on so many levels that oftentimes those long nights ended up with us struggling to fight off the spiritual and physical attraction we had for each other. We were both in a strange place; needing to needed, wanting to make a difference, and searching for something in the universe to fill the void.

My relationship with Kevin had settled down; I still had reservations about him wanting to be married, but he was cooperating and I was still moving forward with the arrangements. Sasha was growing like a weed, holding full conversations and doing new things every day. And I was getting the most out of life; what I thought I wanted, what I thought I needed.

I was drinking less, too, and focusing more. I think the relationship I developed with Galileo and the fact that Sasha was getting older contributed to my positive changes. I had had several run-ins with the woman in the mirror, but she was calling to me from a different place now and I was listening to her very carefully. I hadn't quite figured out what she wanted, but I had finally realized she was there to protect me. There was a difference in me. I was going to be someone's wife and the thought of that felt good.

But there was one thing left that I had to do. I had to tell Marcus I was getting married. I felt it was only fair that he heard it from me and not from someone off the street, or in the jail. But how would I do it? I didn't have time to drive up there to tell him in person, and writing him a letter seemed way too cold.

But he had to know. I decided if I did it right, I could tell him in a letter.

I sat at my desk, looking out the window, thinking about all the love I had felt for Marcus over the years. Was I over him, had I made the right steps to completely extricate myself from any remnant feelings swimming around my heart? Deep down in my spirit where no one else was allowed to enter, I felt like I hadn't; but the future I intended for my daughter and myself at the moment was more important. Not even what Kevin wanted or was feeling mattered to me right now. Marcus had been a major part of who I was and it was time to let him go. I had to let him go, get on with my life, my future.

I took out a piece of lined white paper and began to write. It took me a moment to put my words together, but as I thought of Marcus' eyes, as if they were there right in front of me; the words felt like they had been set free and began to flow. I wrote down everything I could think of that would explain to him how I was feeling—how much I was hurting for betraying him; how I knew he was innocent, but knowing him, how he felt guilty for playing blind to the obvious crimes he committed. I explained my forgiveness of the child he fathered that he had kept secret from me. I tried with all I had to let him know how much I still loved him and wanted to be with him, but couldn't. How our love was now tainted and irrevocably tarnished, and how I was going to marry Kevin, to have some semblance of a family life, some normalcy.

*Marcus, I still love you and I always will, but too much has happened, too much has changed. I have to say good-bye.*

And say good-bye I did.

# Chapter 90

I was finally home. I had mailed the final good-bye letter to Marcus and closed that chapter of my life. I snuggled up next to Kevin as close as I could when we went to bed every night, and smothered Sasha with all the love I could possibly muster—to a fault, maybe, to help fill any emptiness I was feeling inside. Kevin and I were to be married in a little over a month, and I sat in the bedroom contemplating my new life. I guessed since we had been living together for so long that not much would change, but I was happy that we were finally making it official. He was doing well at work, and my work with Galileo was progressing towards indictments for Mr. Chadwick and Mr. Schuyler.

I had decided to take the day off to tie up some loose ends for the wedding and all the madness we had ahead of us. I wanted things to go as smoothly as possible.

I leafed through magazines, books, and papers I had collected for the wedding, making sure I had everything the professional people said I should have, checking paid receipts and invoices yet to be paid. My parents and I were footing most of the bill, so I made it a point to keep track of all the things they paid for and all things I was paying for. I still hadn't gotten a ring but I figured Kevin and I would figure that out when we could.

I looked over the receipt for the ring I had bought for Kevin. It was a solitaire diamond, about a carat, with a wide gold polished band. I folded all the receipts and organized the invoices by order of importance.

I was ready and felt great about my decision to marry Kevin—well, my decision to force Kevin to marry me. Even though we were still living in Kevin's parents' house, I felt good. Everything was in place; Kevin and I would become husband and wife.

I would finally have the family I had always dreamed about—the love, the comfort, the security, all the things a good person and good woman deserved. I would make this union the most important transition of my life.

# Chapter 91

Then the bedroom door opened, and my bright shining aura dimmed. Kevin was standing in the doorway.

"Kevin, what are you doing home so early?"

He didn't say anything, just looked stricken.

"Kevin, *what happened*?"

"It wasn't my fault. You know the management at my job be trippin', they want to fire me over some bullshit."

"Tell me what happened!"

I stared at him, waiting for him to speak, but there was nothing even conceivable that could come out of his mouth to make me understand how he got fired from another job; even more ridiculous right before our wedding day. But I listened to the story, trying not to judge until I had heard what had happened.

He started. "A friend of mine sent me an e-mail, and in this e-mail was a bunch of Chinese characters arranged in rows. And if you looked at it straight on you really wouldn't recognize anything unless you read Chinese, but if you tilted your head to the side and read the script upwards the characters formed the words 'fuck you.'"

I thought to myself, I vaguely remember seeing that e-mail making the rounds at my office, and it really wasn't a big deal.

"OK, so what's wrong with that? Was someone around to see it, and deemed it inappropriate?"

"No, no one saw it on my computer in my area."

"OK. So what happened?"

"Well, I have two e-mail lists, my friends and family list, and my in-house business contact list, all the bigwigs from corporate."

"And?"

"Well, I was trying to forward the e-mail to my friends' list," he began, and when he said that I knew exactly what happened.

"Please tell me you didn't forward that e-mail to your corporate list."

He lowered his head. "Yes I did, and when everyone got it, there was a meeting and they called me in to let me go. I'm sorry, it was a mistake; I wasn't paying attention to what I was doing."

"Ah . . . you do know we're getting married in a couple of weeks don't you?"

"Yes, baby, I do."

"Then how could you do something so dumb?"

"It was a mistake, a simple mistake. I never intended for them to see that e-mail."

"Of course you didn't. Now what are we going to do? How are we going to pay my mom and dad back for this wedding, let alone the remaining balance on all the other things outstanding? And to top it all off, I haven't even got a ring yet."

"Look, baby, I know. I'm gonna fix this, I'm gonna make it up to you. I promise."

I left the room feeling dejected and afraid; Kevin knew we were not as stable as we should have been, considering all the money we had made over the years. The impulse buying, Sasha, this wedding—we were just barely getting along and now he loses another job.

I sat in the bathroom with the door locked, thinking about our future and wondering if maybe Kevin was right—maybe now wasn't was the right time to get married.

All the evidence pointed to postponing it or canceling it all together—but my rebuttal—pure pride—forced me into a false state of security. I'm going to do this. This is my day. I'll figure it out.

I leaned back against the toilet tank, breathing deeply, almost gasping for air, laboring to choke down this newly created obstacle. My thoughts turned to Marcus. If only things had not turned out the way they had. I couldn't help but think about how my life would have been different if Marcus had not been taken away from me.

As my breathing evened out, my head cleared. I'm getting married to Kevin, and he, Sasha, and I are going to have a wonderful life. It's set. We'll get through this; I know we can, together.

# Chapter 92

The day had finally arrived; I had made it through the planning and the preparation, the bachelorette party, and the sleepless night before the big day. I spent the night at my mother's house so that she could help Sasha and me get ready. There were so many things left to do, but I felt confident that everything would work out fine. But I was still very nervous.

I had taken my shower and put on the delicate pearl-white lace underwear we bought for this special day. My matching pearl-lace bra was sturdier than the panties, but I needed it because of the type of dress I had selected, off-white, fully laced and beaded bodice with a pleated satin full Cinderella skirt. My hair was spiral-curled and pinned up with long tendrils floating around my face. I decided I'd put my headpiece and nylons on in the dressing room, and while I contemplated my next life I got Sasha ready, packed up my bags, and headed for the car. We were headed to a new destiny—one I had envisioned all my life.

# Chapter 93

~~~~~~~~~~~~~~~

**W**E DIDN'T HAVE ANY MONEY left over for a ring for me, but Kevin told me not to worry, he was working on something.

But two nights before our big day, when Kevin's parents flew in from Tortola, he entered our room with several rings—rings I assumed were his mother's; she had an extensive collection of rings she had purchased in the islands because they were cheaper there.

When he walked towards me he handed me a one-carat diamond solitaire; I was stunned. How did he pull this off? He explained to me before I got too excited that this ring was cubic zirconia and that when he could he would buy me the real thing. I looked at the ring and placed it on my finger. Wow, it fit. I thanked him and kissed him gently on the lips. There was no reason to be upset, the wedding day was almost here and the time was now. I had no choice but to accept it.

And there were the other rings he brought from his mother's collection. The first ring he handed to me was a wide ring with a band filled with twenty small blue stones that he put on my finger next to the solitaire; I didn't like the way it looked next to the solitaire diamond.

The next ring he handed me was a ring that looked like a tree branch with several diamonds branching off the base, which the solitaire sat inside of; this one looked kind of cheap, and even though the solitaire was fake, no one would know unless I told them. The last set of rings he handed me were two rings shaped like mirror-image V's, each filled with three rows of rubies. The solitaire fit nicely as a third ring inside of the diamond shape the V made. I looked the combination over; I held my hand out in front of me and smiled. This was the one, my wedding ring and bands.

By this time I had gotten used to the fact that Kevin wasn't working; I knew he was doing the best he could to salvage the situation and get some kind of ring for me. I graciously accepted his efforts and thanked him again with a small kiss; he was trying. Kevin kept the rings to give them to Hassan, the best man.

When I arrived at the Calhoun Beach Club, everyone was there. My bridal party was in the dressing room getting ready and waiting for me to show up. Everyone was beautiful. They were semi-dressed in the plum satin bridal gowns I had picked out, their hair and make-up done; they looked stunning. I had seen the fellas as I walked in—they were fine as hell in their black tuxedos and plum-colored paisley vests and bowties. My aunt and two of my girlfriends were helping to pin all of the guys' boutonnieres on, and Kevin and his family were seated quietly in the dining area.

We had decided earlier to take the formal photos before the wedding to keep the flow going after the wedding had ended. We had a receiving line planned and added a special touch of hors d'oeuvres and champagne while the guests waited for the dining area to be set up. The planning was perfect and the vision I had longed for all these years was coming to fruition.

The music began. I watched from a spot on top of the spiral staircase as my mother and Kevin's mother and father were escorted in by the ushers, then my bridesmaids and the groomsmen sauntered in to the ceremony hall looking as happy as I was to be there. My little cousins, the flower girl, and ring bearer, came through the doors next, dressed to the hilt. Kevin and Hassan walked in soon after and took their places, standing tall side by side, looking at each other with admiration.

Kevin looked as fine as I had ever seen him, but I could tell he was a little nervous, even anxious. But he was here and he intended to marry me.

When the doors closed, I stood patiently waiting for the bridal music to begin; I looked down to see Sasha in her mini bride's dress and veil being rushed in. Apparently, amid all the excitement she had fallen asleep. My aunt walked her in and handed her to my mom. Then it was my turn.

# Chapter 94

Standing at the top of the staircase with my dad at my side, the butterflies I usually kept well tamed in my stomach revived themselves and began to flutter. I inhaled deeply, holding my breath for a moment to calm the stirring I felt deep down in my soul. I looked to my father and he smiled and winked, letting me know he was happy for me, and that all was right with the world. I kissed my father on the cheek and thanked him for being a great dad.

I interlocked my arm in his and we stepped together towards the first step. I smiled as all my friends and family turned to look at me. This was my day and I had finally received my just reward. I was poised and ready to become Mrs. Kevin Owens.

I walked with my father gingerly down the spiral staircase and down the aisle into my destiny, finally approaching Kevin, smiling and thanking God for allowing my dreams to come true. He took my hand, and our eyes met. He was so fine; I was making the right decision.

I turned to look for my mother in the front row and blew her a kiss to tell her how much I loved and appreciated her. As my grandfather opened his book of vows to begin my new life, I exhaled and released all I had been holding back, surrendering all to my commitment and the will of God.

I do.

# Chapter 95

Our flight for Las Vegas was the very next day. I had booked a four-day/three-night stay at the Riviera Hotel and Casino and planned to start the marriage off right with some rest and relaxation in the sunny warmth of Nevada. Kevin and I had packed everything the night of the wedding, so we didn't get any sleep; we would sleep on the flight. My mother, who was watching Sasha while we were gone, was taking us to the airport. So we stayed at her house and opened all the gift cards, looking for the gift money to take with us.

We'd gotten a good price on the flight and hotel, but spending and gambling money was another thing. We collected another three hundred dollars or so in gift cards and added that to the little bit we intended to take on the trip. We were set; or so I thought.

Traveling to Las Vegas with only five hundred dollars was like having only three dollars to gamble with. We were essentially broke, but we walked around like we had money to burn. We gambled and ate, walked around the city trying to find the right casino to make a quick come-up.

Needless to say we never found it, and we'd spent most of the money by the second night; we saved a hundred dollars for emergency purposes, but realized we were not going to be able to do much more while we were there. We spent the rest of the time in our hotel room discussing future plans and having sex, not necessarily in that order. Watching Kevin closely and listening to all the things he had to say about what he had planned for his new family made me feel like he was fully on board with my idea of happily ever after, but something in me stirred. Was he really being truthful?

We headed back home to start our life together as husband and wife.

The plane ride was uneventful. Both Kevin and I were exhausted and didn't talk much. And my thoughts were focused on getting back to Sasha. I missed her incredibly—it was the first time that I had been away from her for more than a night. She would spend the night with my mom from time to time, but I was sure to be there bright and early to pick her up.

The plane landed smoothly at Minneapolis/St. Paul International and we exited the plane feeling groggy and jet-lagged. We only had carry-on luggage, so we headed straight to the parking area to look for Mama; I had talked to her after we landed and she was just pulling up to the airport doors when we spoke.

Kevin had been silent all this time, but I had just chalked it up to exhaustion. But as I struggled with my bags, I watched as Kevin proceeded to the sliding doors looking for Mama's car. When he spotted her, he went directly to the car, leaving me to try to keep pace with his long strides.

I arrived at the car and lifted my bag into the trunk; Kevin had already let himself into the back seat. I followed and got in the front passenger side, trying to avoid my mother's eyes; I knew she'd have something to say about his behavior.

"Hey, Mom, how are you?" I said, reaching across the seat to give her a kiss on the cheek.

"Hey, sweetheart, hey Kevin. How was your honeymoon?"

"It was nice," Kevin replied.

His oh-so-casual tone seemed to seep effortlessly out of his pores, giving me an instant headache.

"Hey, Mom, where's Sasha?" I asked.

"Oh, I left her over at Denise's, she was playing with Montia and they seemed so content." Montia was my little cousin my aunt Denise had had right before I had Sasha; she was my forty-something aunt's surprise baby.

"Mom, you knew I would be missing my baby and you left her!" I laughed and turned to look at Kevin sitting in the back seat. "Do you want to ride with us to go get Sasha or do you want to go home first?"

"Man, take me home. I'm tired and want to get some sleep."

I looked over at mom and mouthed "Take his ass home." She looked at me with the "what's going on look" and I looked away, staring into the moving surroundings outside my window and waited for us to pull up in front of our house.

When we got to the driveway, I helped Kevin get the bags from the trunk and helped him carry them in. He set his down at the door and I carried mine partways into the living room.

"I'll be right back Kevin, OK?"

"Yeah, I'll be lying down, I'm exhausted.

I watched as he walked up to the bedroom without looking my way or saying another word. Shit, this is got to be the craziest emotional roller coaster I had ever been on. What the fuck had I done?

I got back in the car with my mother and the expression her face said more than a thousand words.

"Baby, what's going on?"

"Mama, I don't know, he's on something. I can't believe I'm going through this shit already."

I put my seatbelt on and lay my head against the headrest, thinking about all the times he would withdraw like this. I was dumbfounded by all the memories that flooded my mind, all the times; I disregarded my mantra by letting his actions dictate my reaction. I was his wife now, so things should have been different, but in the back of my mind I knew things were not going to change much. I had always heard that you couldn't change someone, even though with all my being I tried to do it. He was who he was and there was nothing I was going to be able to do to change that. Or was I right to just accept things the way they were?

My headache had developed into a full-blown migraine and I was aching to see my little girl. Just to lay my eyes on her would make everything all right. We pulled up in front of my aunt's house and I could see Sasha in the window waiting for me. I jumped out of the car and ran towards the house as she flung the screen door open and as fast as lightning jumped into my arms.

"Mommy!"

"Hey, my darling, how are you, I missed you so much."

"I missed-ed you too, Mommy," she said in her little-girl English.

I kissed her and held her as close as I could without squeezing the life out of her. Then I put her down, and we walked in hand-in-hand, smiling and laughing together on the inside and out.

I hugged my aunt and uncle, happy to see them.

"How was your honeymoon?" Uncle Felix asked, laughing that funny laugh of his.

Before I could stop myself, a torrent of obscenities and tears poured out from deep in my soul, in front of everyone in the room, even the children.

Tanisha, Denise's oldest daughter, rushed out of her room to see who was fighting; she stopped dead in her tracks to see me crying and screaming and out of control.

"That weak-ass motherfucker, how in the hell could you let me marry him? Are y'all crazy, there is no way in hell I should have married him. Shit, why didn't you stop me?" I yelled, tears streaming down my face.

My head spun, thinking about how I had just made the biggest mistake of my life. I ran to the bathroom mirror to search for the answers. I knew she would appear and give it to me straight.

From the other room, I heard the distant sounds of my family's voices, trying to understand and explain my tirade, but they were drowned out by the strong, clear voice I heard from inside as I stared insistently in the reflection of my soul.

*Jasmine, you know you still love Marcus. It's a crying shame how you sat up there and repeated those vows while secretly hoping he would walk into that ceremony to save you. How are you going to* go into a marriage with that kind of weight strapped to your chest? What kind of woman are you? You need to go to Kevin right now and tell him how you really feel and let that man get on with his life, let him find someone who truly loves him; a woman without baggage, a mate without character flaws. No, you're not perfect, but you're selfish and you need to recognize that before you ruin his life and yours.

I looked her dead in her eyes and screamed. "No, no you're wrong! I do love Kevin; and Marcus is history. I have a family now, I'm a wife and a mother first and foremost and I'm going to do my best to make this the best marriage ever. You'll see, I'm going to make it work; I'm going to make my fantasy work!"

I looked for a moment more and she was gone. Deserting me without explanation or retribution, she was the only one who knew the truth, and I hated her for it. But she was not going to get me to change my ways or be accountable.

I dried my tears and washed my face and returned to the family room where my aunt and uncle were sitting. My mother was in the kitchen fixing something to eat and the kids were down in the basement playing. My aunt and uncle looked at me strangely and laughed when I returned seemingly unscathed and normal.

"What the heck was that all about?"

"Never mind, auntie, I'm just tripping. What y'all got to eat?"

"There's all kind of food in there, go help yourself."

Uncle Felix stood and wrapped his long lanky arms around me and gave me a squeeze. I looked up at him, and he smiled this perfect, innocent smile, one I knew meant he totally understood where I was coming from, but wouldn't judge me for it.

"Thank you, uncle Felix."

"No problem, Jasmine Burrell—I mean Jasmine Owens."

I laughed. Uncle Felix always called me by full name. And with the correction from Burrell to Owens I felt he knew I would be OK. I had to forget the past and look towards the future. Make it what I wanted it to be regardless of how things may have seemed. Believe in what I chose and believe in God for the answers. Live for the moment and get out of life all it had to offer . . . until death do us part.

I smiled inside as I fixed Sasha and myself something to eat. I brought her plate down to her in the basement and returned to the kitchen table to eat. Food was definitely a comfort and I filled my plate a couple of times to ease my shattered soul.

# Chapter 96

For the next six months I submerged myself in my home life and my work. I had just about finished the case I was working on with Galileo, and our side meetings about the European Connection were going even better. Although it was hard, we were able to find tidbits of evidence that we compiled into a case to put Mr. Chadwick and Mr. Schuyler away for a long time, but we were trying to find the right time to bring everything we had gathered to the district attorney.

We figured we still had one major problem—getting people to testify. We had talked to several former clients, and a few disgruntled employees who gave us very detailed information, but refused to testify. There was one woman, a former girlfriend of Mr. Chadwick's, who reluctantly decided to help us. But we had to put her in a protection program, and promise her we'd win.

Galileo and I were sitting at a coffee shop up the street from my office, discussing strategy when he decided to confide in me how much he enjoyed spending time with me. The conversation and tone in his voice was so soothing, it felt like he and I were in a relationship. I listened closely to what he was saying, hoping to one day hear Kevin speak in those tones. As he spoke, my mind thought of Kevin and our relationship.

Kevin and I were doing just OK; the fact that we were married hadn't changed much. I believed Kevin settled into the idea of being a husband and father, but it was the complacency we experienced that kept things smooth. The role I played in the breakdown of our marriage was just that, a role. I always stayed in character, there were very few outbursts, and I rarely complained. I figured I had asked for this, so deal with it. My contentment in being a mother and being called a "wife" helped me keep my emotional balance. The ideal of being a legitimate family pacified me.

Galileo was penetrating my heart; I knew if there were not anything more important in my life, he and I would have definitely had more to talk about, so when the subject arose, which was quite often, I tried to divert our conversations.

But this day his words rippled through my psyche.

"Jasmine, are you happy?"

I looked at him as if he were crazy. "Of course I'm happy, why do you ask?"

"Well, you never talk about your husband; you're always talking about your daughter. And you spend more time with me than you spend at home. Tell me, Jasmine, what is your definition of happiness?"

I sat there stunned, wondering how he could have the audacity to even ask me such a thing.

"Look, Galileo, I know you think you're the shit, and women throw themselves at you every chance they get, but you got me fucked up if you think my spending time with you has anything to do with, more than getting these cases done. I'm here with you because I have to be, and believe me, as soon as this shit is all over, you won't have to worry about me ever again."

The rage in my voice shocked me more than it did him. Why was I so angry? I excused myself and headed straight for the restrooms. There had to be a good explanation for this outburst. I tried with everything in me to avoid the mirror but shrank when I saw my true self; tired, worn, unhappy. Was it that obvious to everyone? I had spent the last several months convincing myself my life was perfect, and in less than the time it takes to drink a cup of coffee, a man who had no clue who I truly was washed away everything I knew to be right, challenging me to find the true meaning of happiness, forcing me to find *me*.

This vicious cycle of me in constant transition was beginning to take its toll. I was tired of all the unsolicited comments from strange men forcing me into their corner of submission; I had had enough of their judgment and innuendo and was going to prove myself accountable to my own well-being. And I was going to start by telling Galileo to mind his own fucking business. I'm happy and I can prove it!

When I returned to the table Galileo was gone. Our paperwork was still sitting there so I knew he hadn't gone far. I sat down ran through the intellectual exchange I intended to have with Galileo when he returned.

As I waited, I nervously shuffled through some of the paperwork on his side of the table, looking through old e-mail print-outs and memos written on canary yellow Post-its, when I came across a page ripped out of a journal notebook.

The words were written in a beautiful, flowing script. As my eyes focused on the letters written across the worn, crumpled paper; I realized they came together in a poem obviously written for someone very special. I read through it, mesmerized by their intense tone; I had forgotten about him writing poetry. In all of the excitement of the cases, we never really got to discuss it any further than that first night. Wow, had he actually written these words? They were beautiful—eloquent, even.

The poem was to a beautiful woman who reminded him of Mother Earth. The words—their sounds, their meaning—seemed to reach deep into my soul and forced me to think about the forever love the writer felt for this woman. My eyes filled with tears as I reached the bottom of the page. Why was my name written there?

Just as the tears spilled over and started rolling down my face, I looked up to see Galileo standing over me stunned but concerned.

"Galileo, what is this?"

He slowly removed the paper from my hand and folded it neatly, then placed it in his inside jacket pocket.

"You shouldn't have seen that."

"What do you mean? It has my name on it."

"I'm not in a place where I can explain those words to you, maybe in the future when things aren't so hectic we can sit down somewhere private and discuss what I had on my mind when I wrote it."

He was clearly uncomfortable, but I honored his request to let it go. Besides, from the insistent look in his eyes I could tell he meant what he said; there would be no further discussion at this point and I would have to wait to find out what he was feeling when the pen poured out his heart and soul on that crumpled piece of journal paper.

We stopped talking about it. We spent the next twenty minutes discussing the case, mostly with straightforward questions and one-word answers.

During a silence, when we were both looking at the files, I looked up. The sweat that had developed on his brow was beckoning me to wipe it away, but I kept my napkin firmly in my lap.

Then I broke the silence. "Are you happy?" I asked him.

He looked up from what he was reading and looked in my direction—he didn't look directly at me but somehow he was looking through me.

"You know, Jasmine, I ask myself that question all the time, and honestly at this moment I can't give you an answer," he said slowly. "I believe true happiness comes from a place of absolute peace and contentment with one's present situation. A place where life may not be perfect, but you live perfectly in the moment. I'm always searching for a way to better myself, and the people around me. The relationships I choose to involve myself in and the positive connection I make with people tend to add to my happiness, but sometimes I feel darkened by things I see and feel each day, but can't have."

"What is it that you want?"

"I want it all, actually." He looked down at the lukewarm cup of coffee in front of him. He smiled.

"I want the freedom to be exactly who God created me to be, the freedom to live this life without prejudice or guilt. But most of all I want the courage to stand up and have all of that."

I looked at him, checking his eyes for cracks in his façade, but there were none. What he was saying came straight from his heart, and I didn't have to fight myself to believe it. There was empathy in his words, shattering my suspicious nature; I no longer needed to be an unbeliever of the possibilities of life with love.

He continued.

"That's something I feel when I'm with you."

Where was he going with this?

"When we're together, Jasmine, even for a short moment of time, I feel like I'm truly happy; you bring out a special energy in me, I never intentionally plan to hold on to it, but can't seem to let go. There's something about your spirit that resonates within me, like a sense of calm. But I feel tremendous guilt for wanting to harness and keep it to myself, as opposed to allowing you to use it for your betterment."

He paused and took a deep breath. "Forgive me for saying this, but I'm falling for you and it's killing me not being able to be there for you and to give you all you desire. And I hate to see you so unhappy all the time."

"Unhappy? Is that what you see when you look at me?" I was half angry, half sad.

"Let me tell you something: you're the master of blind deception," he said. "You walk around with this beautiful smile on your face, and the strength of an African nation on your shoulders, trying to convince the people around you that you have everything under control. But deep down you're hurting; you have none of the things you truly desire. Yes, your daughter and your family life are very important to you, but you have a special spirit that desires more. That's why you spend so much time alone listening to music and reading love stories. Your imagination is so powerful that you're making yourself crazy, sitting around dreaming up a magnificent universal scenario of true love."

"What are you talking about? How do you know that?"

He gently took my chin in one hand and looked deep into my eyes.

"Every time I look into your eyes I see your pain. You try hard to hide it, but because you have continued to resist how in-tune we are with each other, you don't realize that I see it. You don't have to say a word and I know how your night went. I hate to see you crying inside."

"You know what, Galileo, this meeting is over. I have to go." I pulled away from his touch, stood up, and rummaged through all my things, snatching all I could with one hand and shoving it into my briefcase.

"Jasmine, wait," he said and grabbed my arm. "I didn't mean to..."

"Galileo, please let me go." I stared at the table refusing to meet his gaze. He released my arm and I pulled together all I could and hurried out the door, breaking into a run once I got onto the sidewalk. I didn't look back.

"Who the hell does he think he is?" I slammed the car door, practically shattering the window. "He's got some nerve; motherfucker thinks he knows something about me. Fuck him, he don't know shit about me!"

I glanced in the rearview mirror, and of course she was there, staring back at me with that "I told you so" look I hated so much.

What? What do you want?

There was no response; she just stared.

"You know what, fuck you, too," I said out loud, and before I knew it, I had removed my block-heeled pump and shattered the mirror, sending the shards of reflective glass all over the console and floor. I sat there in a daze, trying to figure out how things went so terribly wrong?

I looked around to see the mess I had made. As I picked up the shards of glass from the floor, reality broke in. How would I explain to Kevin the missing mirror and the broken glass? It wasn't like I could say the entire mirror came off in my hand when I tried to adjust it.

There was no way I could go back to the office. I drove home, parked the car across the street from the town house, and called the Mercedes dealer; because I had had the same car for so long, the dealership was on speed dial. The guy in the parts department was great; he understood the urgency of my situation and said I could come in right away.

Whew—Kevin would never know I'm on the verge of a meltdown. I drove to a nearby gas station, threw away all the evidence in the big dumpster there and vacuumed out the little pieces I couldn't pick up by hand. Then I drove to the dealership. They took my car in right away and gave me a brand-new mirror and a carwash. I was so grateful.

As I pulled in front of the house, trying to compose myself so that Kevin wouldn't get suspicious took a few moments but I was able to get it together. I really wanted a glass of wine or some form of alcoholic beverage, but it was way too early. Usually I didn't care what time I had a drink, but Kevin was home and I didn't need him asking questions.

I walked to the bedroom figuring Kevin was still asleep (he never got out of bed before eleven when he wasn't working) and I would just jump in bed with him for a moment, and possibly get a little. Damn, the bed was made. I looked around the room and it was partially cleaned, more like straightened up. This was more than strange, because we were both get-up-and-go kind of people and neither of us usually took the time to make the bed. This for him was out of character and caused me to wonder.

I left my things in the bedroom and did a quick search of the house. The whole house was semi-clean, and he was nowhere to be found. What the hell was going on? Had this nigga had some chick up in here? He never cleaned like this.

I fished my cell phone out of my pocket and dialed his number. When his voicemail came on a twinge of jealousy hit the back of my neck.

"Kevin, it's me, call me as soon as you get this message. I'm at home."

Whatever, I didn't give a fuck how early it was, I was getting me something to drink. I went to the kitchen where we kept a stash of emergency liquor—the minis we got from one of Kevin's boys who worked for the airlines. I found them, all stuffed into a bag in the back of the cabinet and slowly pulled it out; it had a full bar in there, from vodka to Bailey's, whiskey, wine. Whatever I was feeling I could have.

With all I had just been through it was unquestionably a vodka day. I sifted through all the bottles, pulling out all the clear bottles and found three vodkas. I cracked open the first bottle, embracing the sound of the metal cap tearing away from the little metal ring that kept it sealed.

They were so easy to drink; just tilt your head back and swallow. Before I knew it I had finished all three and the rush of alcohol in my bloodstream brought on a hazy smile. Nothing but Sasha mattered now. I didn't care what Galileo had to say and I couldn't care less where Kevin was. This is where I wanted to be and I was glad to be there.

Since it was Friday and I couldn't go back to work now, I'd just start my weekend early. I had been so tied up in the day-to-day and Kevin and Sasha, I hadn't talked to the divas much since we got home from the honeymoon. I'm sure they were pissed at me for once again deserting them, but what could I do? I had a husband and a family now. I had responsibilities.

I decided that I would at least try and reach Sadie, though, just to see how she was doing. I dialed her number and listened to the answering machine message, saying she and the other divas had gone to Las Vegas for the weekend.

Damn, Vegas with the divas, now that would have been fun. I lay back on the couch thinking about a no-nonsense weekend with my girls, kicking up my heels and getting as grimy and dirty as I used to get. What am I doing? This marriage shit ain't for me. If it weren't for Sasha, I'd pack my shit and go find them.

# Chapter 97

I AWOKE SOMEWHAT RESTED AS Kevin came through the front door with four or five shopping bags hanging from his arms. I didn't know how long I had been asleep, but the crick in my neck let me know it had been quite a while.

"Hey, baby, what are you doing home so early?" he said.

"I decided to take the rest of the day off. I see you've been shopping," I added, eyeing him suspiciously.

"Yeah, I went and picked up a couple of things."

A *couple* of things? More like half the store. "So what did you buy?" I asked, really wondering where he got the money to buy all this shit.

"Oh, I bought a few shirts and a couple of pairs of pants. I'm trying to hook up some interviews for next week."

"Oh, that's good, baby."

He walked upstairs, obviously done explaining his whereabouts, and I lay back on the couch and channel-checked, looking for something interesting to watch.

Of course it was the middle of the afternoon, so there wasn't much. I stopped on "Divorce Court," a show where husbands and wives duke it out in front of a judge trying to convince her of their version about why the marriage had broken down.

I watched as the wife explained how her husband was more or less a waste of space. He couldn't keep a job, he was emotionally disconnected, and whenever she brought up their issues, he discounted them because as far as he was concerned, everything was fine. I sat there in a daze as the wife stood there crying, attempting to explain to the judge all she had done to try to keep the marriage together—cooking, cleaning, taking care of the kids, working two jobs in order to make ends meet. The judge listened quietly—you could tell she was sympathetic to the wife's cry for help. Then she turned to the husband, asking him why he thought the marriage should be dissolved. He launched into a barrage of excuses and lame explanations about how and why the woman he once loved and married was such a mess and unworthy.

"Look at her, your honor; look how big she is," he shouted. "She has gained over twenty pounds since we got married, what am I supposed to do with that?"

I looked down at myself, cringing at the twenty pounds or so I added since I'd had Sasha.

"Mr. Carter, calm down," the judge said. Then, without reprimanding the husband, she turned to the wife who was drenched in tears. "Mrs. Carter," the judge started, "you're a very beautiful woman, obviously loving and compassionate, but the problem here is you." I was stunned.

"You see, Mrs. Carter, all the things you've been telling me are truly wonderful and great things to do when you're in a loving and healthy relationship. But the relationship you're in is tainted. You have married a man who is uncaring, selfish, and couldn't care less if you vanished from the face of the earth tomorrow. Look at him. He's doing fine, because he is getting exactly what he wants out of the relationship—a wife, a lover, and a mother. He's not going to change—why would he? Mrs. Carter, listen to me carefully. You're enabling him and he is taking complete advantage of your overwhelmingly low self-esteem. If you were in a place where you were confident in yourself and in your abilities, there would be no way in hell you would do all these things for a man who clearly doesn't love or respect you.

"Mrs. Carter, you're a good woman, and I guarantee you there is a man out there who would fully appreciate you and what you have to offer. But you have to love yourself first before you can allow yourself to be loved. There's a man who will love, honor and respect you—all the things you said in your vows, all the things you deserve. And he's out there; I promise you he's out there. You just have to take some time to get to know yourself again, and most important, you have to forgive yourself. Let go of all the guilt you're feeling and live your life for *you*. No man can make you happy; you have to get your happiness from within. This man, while he may love you in his own way, doesn't love you the way you deserved to be loved. I suggest you take your children and move on. You can do it. Just have faith."

Then she turned to the husband.

"As for you Mr. Carter, you need to get a life. Coming up in here and berating and belittling your wife says a lot about you. You better heed what I say, because the next woman that comes along is going to give you a dose of your own medicine and I would love to be the fly on the wall to see that. You're a disgrace to all the good men out there trying to do right and I'm going to feel sorry for you fifteen or twenty years from now, when you're sitting alone in that one-room apartment with no one there to care for you. I suggest you reevaluate your priorities, sir; life is too short."

She slammed the gavel down, ending their marriage, and walked off the bench and back to her life.

I wiped the tears away and sat there thinking about what she had said.

Am I doing all these things because I have low self-esteem? I hadn't taken time to reflect on my life and my happiness, or lack thereof, for a long, long time. Now that I was a wife and mother, those titles—those jobs—came first. I was no longer Jasmine Burrell; she was long gone.

What am I going to do? I could feel the pangs of desperation rising up out of my belly and settling in my chest. All I knew was this ain't no way to live.

I sat for a moment longer, mulling over what seemed a hopeless situation. But there's got to be more to life than what I'm settling for. I deserve more. And I intended to get more, as that familiar spirit of defiance rose up in me again.

I'll go talk to Kevin, I thought. He can help me get through this, help me understand what's missing from my life. Get me back on track to finding and having true happiness.

I walked up the stairs, formulating in my mind how I wanted the conversation to go.

He would calm me and pacify me, giving me every reason he could think of to let me know what a great life we had together, and how he was going to make sure that all my needs and desires were met.

Mistake number one. I guess in my drunken state, my mind was playing tricks on me.

I slowly opened the bedroom door and watched as Kevin folded his new clothes and put them away. He turned and looked at me with a half-cocked smile.

"Hey, baby, what' up?"

"Oh, hey . . . I need to talk to you."

"Sure, what's on your mind?"

"Well, there are a few things that have been on my mind for a while now and I'd like to get your input on them."

He finished putting his things away and motioned for me to join him on the bed.

I looked at him earnestly. "Kevin, I'm tired, really tired; I need your help."

"What do you mean, my help?"

"I feel like I'm doing this all by myself. Taking care of you, Sasha, working, cooking, cleaning . . . do I need to continue?"

"No. No you don't, I understand. What is it that you want me to do?"

"I want you to help me! Take more initiative when it comes to Sasha and things around this house. You know this house needs a lot of work and you haven't even tried to look into that. Also, being more diligent in looking for a job. You've been off work for a while now and things around here are tight. I know this is your mom and dad's crib, but we should be better off than this. I'm unhappy and I want you to fix it."

"OK, hold up, Jasmine—you were the one who wanted all of this. Don't get me wrong, I love Sasha to death but *you* wanted her. And getting married, that was your plan. I told you we needed to wait on both those issues, but you had to have it. Now you're feeling unhappy and stuck. Look, Jasmine, I love you and Sasha and I want things to work out between us, but this is what you signed up for; why are you trying to change it now?"

My head fell to my chest. "OK, Kevin you're right."

I left the bedroom crying on the inside; I didn't want to let him see any more tears. I thought about his world and what he sees versus how I see things.

It was highly presumptuous of me to assume Kevin would understand my plight, since he had grown up with a confidence that seemed like a natural occurrence, like the rain and the sun, thanks to his intelligence and what he saw in the mirror.

He grew up using his looks and charm as a basis for progression. Not his fault, but we were raised in a time where those things were most important. From the pictures on magazine covers to the people we saw on the movie screens and in rap videos, the concept of beauty had taken a turn towards prettier and thinner are better. And with my so-so looks and the extra weight I had put on, coupled with my lack of self-love, my consciousness all at once plummeted into self-hatred and self-regret.

The picture I saw in the mirror did not reflect beauty as I understood it, it just intensified my need for acceptance and approval. It had been like a sword stuck between my ribs that I had been trying to extract all my life.

Yes, I was smart and successful, but every time I looked in the mirror, it was a gut-wrenching reminder of how truly weak I was, brains or no brains. It didn't matter that other people thought I was beautiful or saw me as attractive; all that mattered was what I saw. And that was: Nothing special.

# Chapter 98

THE NEXT COUPLE YEARS WERE filled with an alcohol-fueled haze that I hid behind my smile and the competent persona I presented to the world. No one ever knew how miserable I was, because I wouldn't let them. What everyone saw was what I wanted them to see. I took my old college view of "never let 'em see you sweat" to heart, multiplied ten times, and I walked through every day with my head held high and my self-worth in the toilet.

Sasha was my saving grace. She continued to grow into a beautiful little girl with a glorious spirit that shone right through mine and into the hearts of everyone she touched. My drinking and Kevin's disconnected feelings really didn't affect her because I showered her with as much attention as I could. I survived every day by living through her. She became my life, and I put everything I had into raising her to be a self-confident individual with her own ideas and her own personality. I allowed her to be who she was, no matter what others thought. There was no way in hell I was going to allow her to be subjected to the church's message of submission, society's view of what a woman should be for a man, and the idea that beauty was something you found in a magazine—all the things I had been force-fed as a child. She was going to be the legacy of what I had only dreamed of becoming—a strong, confident, vibrant, self-assured woman who was not only courageous but who made the right choices and controlled her own destiny. She was going to be a star, illuminated and illuminating, for the entire world to see.

# Chapter 99

There was so much going on in my life, the drinking, the busy days and fast-food nights, and it all increased my size another twenty pounds. Every morning was a struggle to find something to wear to work. I purchased a few larger size items, but really didn't have the money for a new wardrobe.

I stood in front of the mirror naked, staring at the bulges and rolls around my mid-section. "Oh my God, how did this happen?" I muttered. I lifted up my stomach; "this is crazy." The stretch marks from having Sasha looked terrible. I turned to the side. Wow—the dimply-looking skin on my thighs was too much. I have to do something about this. I thought about joining a gym, but the costs and signing a contract was something I didn't want to do. So I decided to just walk; hopefully it would help me lose some of the weight. It was free, I could go by myself, and it would give me time to think.

I started walking and over time it turned into a pilgrimage of self—reflection and personal growth. I didn't even realize it at first, but it had become a spiritual way to cope with my tumultuous reality. The birds singing, the leaves of the trees rustling in the wind, the bright effervescent green of the grass, and the morning sun shimmering off the lake were all reminders of how great God was. And I slowly began to realize that I had been letting every tiny thing in my life consume me so much that I had forgotten what was most important—life itself.

Walking seemed to be a way to release years of agonizing contempt for myself, so I would rise, dress, and drive five miles to Lake Nokomis. It was hard because I was still having my evening cocktail, but every day without fail, I would push through the two-and-a-half-mile walking path, complete with hills and valleys, talking to God about my situation, sometimes yelling on the inside, sometimes crying on the outside. And every day, by the end of my walk, the blood flow and extra oxygen to my system helped regenerate my being.

Kevin and I remained on different pages on a lot of issues. He was still unemployed, but he was actively looking, and I was still doing most of the work around the house, but the mood had changed. Because of the walking, my depressed moods were less frequent and the amount of liquor I was drinking went from an every-night occurrence to just drinking on the weekends. I had energy to burn and I was even starting to lose a little weight. The smiling face in the mirror didn't look so bad to me anymore. Even Kevin had become more communicative and responsive. I guess the change in my attitude affected his and he was willing to open up to a happier person rather than a miserable mess.

Even my work environment had improved. We went to trial on Galileo's case and after three weeks of intense examinations and cross-examinations, the jury came back with a not-guilty verdict on the conspiracy charges and a guilty verdict on tampering with evidence, which meant he would only have to do a year in a federal prison. But because he had helped me work so hard on the indictments of Mr. Chadwick and Mr. Schuyler, I put in a good word for him to the district attorney to see if he could get house arrest.

After the indictments of Mr. Chadwick and Mr. Schuyler were handed down, the pair mysteriously disappeared. No one knew where they were and we were a little frightened at the thought of that. But the federal government and the European authorities assured me that my family and I would be safe. I didn't know how they were going to make sure of this, but I had to trust them. All of the information we gathered on secret hideouts and property purchased under other person's names and aliases would hopefully lead them right to the "European Connection."

The next couple of months coasted by, and I was felling pretty good. I was looking forward to putting in my bid for a partnership with the firm. I hadn't heard anything lately about the selection committee's decision on when I could submit my application, but I wasn't worried about it. I had put in so many hours and had done so much extra work, I felt I was a good position to get the job. I called Wendy into my office and told her to get ready; we were about to make our bid for partner, which meant more money, bigger offices and happier lives.

## Chapter 100

I T HAD BEEN A LONG week. Galileo's house arrest was approved and I was relieved to see the weekend. My hair appointment was scheduled for eight a.m., but after my walk I was restless. I drove to Hair Freedom thirty minutes early just to sit and relax in the salon atmosphere. I picked up a couple of hair magazines and thumbed through the pages, looking for something special, something different. The receptionist called my name and I proceeded to walk towards Andrea's chair. I smiled, happy to see her, and she hugged me tightly and motioned for me to sit down. She caped me up and led me to the shampoo bowls. I lay back, eagerly anticipating her magical fingertips. As she massaged my head, the tension in my neck and shoulders flowed out of the top of my head and down the drain with the soapy water. We returned to her station and I picked up the magazine she had sitting on her station. All the styles were of women with natural hair—no chemicals and no relaxers. I carefully looked at all the beautiful women of color wearing their hair long, short, braided, but natural. I never knew there were so many different styles for natural hair. As I continued turning the pages, I came across a picture of a woman with a head full of gorgeous brown and gold dreadlocks hanging to her shoulders.

"Hey, Andrea," I said. "What do you think about me going natural?"

"Jasmine, you don't want to do that."

"Why not? Look at her locks, aren't they beautiful?"

"Yeah, they're nice on her, but not everyone can wear them."

"What, you don't think they would look nice on me?"

"No, I'm not saying that, you just don't want to do that. You'd have to cut all your hair off and I have worked too hard to grow it out. I'm not having that."

"Girl, you crazy! Can I have this picture?"

"Yeah, you can have it, but I'm not doing it, so whatever."

I smiled and carefully ripped the picture from the magazine, looking at it again before putting it in my purse. I'm going to do this, I said to myself; just watch.

I felt of rush of blood pulsing through my veins, confirming my decision. I sat there as Andrea worked on my hair, thinking about all the people I had met who were proudly wearing dreadlocks—Galileo, the man at the restaurant in New Orleans, people I had seen on the street. The only thing I hadn't seen was many women with them, but I wasn't sure why. Was there some stigma for women to wear them? But with my newfound self-esteem, I didn't care. I left the salon energized; I had formulated a plan for a major transformation that would undoubtedly shake things up a bit. There was freshness in my aura, and I relished the thought of sporting long, luxurious locks, maybe for the rest of my life.

When I returned home from the salon, I couldn't keep my excitement to myself; I shared the picture and my plans with Kevin.

He was not amused. He looked at the picture for a moment and then looked at me.

"This is what you want to do?"

"Yeah, Kevin, don't you think it would be cool?"

He shrugged. "Yeah, I guess—if that's what you want to do."

"What, you don't like it?"

"It's cool, Jaz, do what you want; it's your hair."

He had always liked the way I'd worn my hair, but me being me, I brushed aside his response. I put the picture away and went to check on Sasha.

She was watching TV in the bedroom. I lay down next to her and gave her a peck on the cheek.

"Hey, Mommy,"

"Hey, baby, how are you?"

"I'm fine;" she said, taking hold of my ear.

"What do you want for lunch, darling?"

"I want steak and salad."

"You want steak and salad?"

"Yes."

"OK, I'll go check to see what we got and I'll be right back." Sasha was a meat eater and loved Caesar salad. So at least twice a week we had some sort of steak and salad.

I walked back downstairs, thinking about my life. My husband was thankfully working again; my daughter was a perfect joy, and I was embarking on a new freedom that was going to be a big change, one I felt would make me whole, and give me the courage to be who I needed to be, and I thanked God.

I walked to the living room where Kevin was watching TV, hoping to snuggle a little before I started dinner, but he was gone. I hadn't heard him leave the house, so I figured he must be in the basement.

But what was he doing down there? There was nothing there but a bunch of junk his parents left and a bunch of junk we had added from our old condo. I crept to the top of the basement stairs, listening for anything, and heard him talking on the phone. I strained to hear better, staying stock still so he wouldn't know I was eavesdropping.

There was a strange undertone to it all—he would laugh quietly, then break into uninhibited banter; I could feel my heart speeding up and panic setting in. Who could he be talking to and why was he in the basement doing it?

I could feel the old me resurfacing, the scared, unsure panicky me. I raced down the stairs to confront him.

"Kevin! Who are you talking to?"

He paused and looked at me with his eyebrows drawn so tight against his forehead I thought his head would explode.

"What's up, Jasmine?"

"Who are you talking to?" I demanded

He covered the phone with his hand and scowled at me in such a way that I felt like I was violently reprimanded, without him even saying a word.

"Tell that bitch you got a wife and kids, see if she wanna fuck with that!" I shouted.

He put his mouth to the phone and told whoever he was talking to that he would call them later, closed his cell and stared at me with a look that dripped hate and disdain.

The argument to end all arguments began. I walked up to the top of the stairs and closed the door so Sasha wouldn't hear.

"Who the fuck you talking to down here in the basement? What you hiding for?" I shouted again.

"Look, you're trippin', you better get out of my face with this bullshit," Kevin shouted back.

"I better? I ain't got to 'better' do anything!"

We kept this up for who knows how long, until Sasha came bursting through the door, running down the stairs screaming, "Stop it, Mommy and Daddy, stop fighting!"

Snapping out my haze of anger, I looked down at Sasha. "Oh, baby," I said, putting my arms around her. "I'm so sorry you had to hear that. I'm so sorry, baby, everything's all right." She held me tightly, and my tears joined with hers. Even though she was getting to be a big girl, I picked her up and held her close, carrying her back upstairs and setting her up on a chair in the kitchen next to me to help me cook, as I tried to explain why Mommy and Daddy were fighting.

She wasn't buying it.

Sasha wasn't used to us yelling or screaming around the house; we tried to keep it from her most of the time. She didn't even understand heated, fun-loving discussions we had that took place at a louder volume. Conflict was just something she didn't like. Kevin had left the basement and headed upstairs to do whatever. But it wasn't over; it was just beginning.

# Chapter 101

Today was going to be the beginning of the rest of my life. All the shit with Kevin over the weekend, and everything else I had on my mind didn't mean a thing compared to the major changes that were about to take place. So what if my home life was in a shambles? I still had my career. And after all the hard work I put in getting the indictments of the two crooks from Europe, Tom and Steve decided to push the selection of partner up a few months and chose today as the day to make their announcement. I was a shoo-in for the position and I spared no expense in preparing for this day.

Dressed to a T in a midnight-blue Versace suit with a matching pinstriped button-down blouse and black suede pumps, I walked into my office as bright as the first day of spring. Wendy was already at work, God bless her soul, and she was as clean as the board of health herself.

"Good morning, Wendy, you looking pretty sharp there."

"Well, what can I say? I learned it from the best, and you don't look like you slacking in any way either, Jaz."

"Sho' you right!"

We laughed and I slapped her five as I entered my office. The big purple bag sitting on my desk threw me, but I was in too much of a zone to let it bother me. Nothing could muddle this day. I opened the card and read the words "Congratulations, baby. Kevin."

Oh, so he must have been feeling a little bad for the drama over the weekend. I opened the bag to discover a dozen vibrant red roses, each one nearly the size of my fist, effortlessly open, and smelling like garden. I almost caught a tear—but not today. I had too much going on to smear my perfectly applied makeup. I'd cry later, after my promotion.

I will call him, though, I thought, softening just a little towards him as the weekend's battle began to fade. I sat down to check my voicemail, but I couldn't believe the voice I on the first message. It was Marcus.

I sat stunned as Marcus said he was out of jail and living in a halfway house not far from where his parents used to live. He was hoping he could put me on his visitors list so that I could come and see him. There were so many things he needed to say to me, he said, and seeing me would surely make his day.

I hung up the phone without even erasing the call. I was trying not to panic but the goose bumps on my skin proved I was failing miserably.

Pull it together, girl, breathe, this don't mean anything, it's all good. Just get your promotion and keep it moving.

For once I listened to my own advice. This shit ain't about him or Kevin, this shit is about *me*.

I knew the selection committee meeting was supposed to convene at ten, but when I walked in I noticed there was already some movement in the conference room. I knew I'd seen Tom in there and I wasn't sure if Steve was here yet, but a few of the board members and some of the community leaders were strolling in as I sat behind my desk basking in the glory of my accomplishments.

I picked up the phone, this time to call Kevin.

"Hey, Kevin, thank you so much for the roses; they're beautiful."

"Ah, you welcome, it's nothing. You deserve it, and I'm sorry for the way this entire weekend went. Let's just move on and forget about all that happened. Just think, you're getting ready to be partner, and we need to be celebrating instead of fighting."

"You're right, baby, I'm sorry; and when I get this promotion we going to be doing a lot of celebrating. Starting tonight."

He laughed. "Oh, is that right?"

"Yeah, that's right. I got to go, see you tonight."

"All right, baby. I love you."

"I love you too, Mar . . . Kevin."

Oh God, I hope he didn't catch that. I hung up the phone and ran to the small mirror hanging by the front door of my office. Shit, I was sweating. I grabbed a Kleenex off my desk and blotted away the perspiration, careful not to smear my makeup.

The intercom buzzed. "Jasmine," Wendy said, "they're ready for you."

I took one last look at Jasmine the associate lawyer and stared into the eyes of Jasmine Owens, partner. The next time I walk into this building I'll be looking at the plaque reading Langdon, Marshall, and Owens. Hell, yeah, I got this.

It was all I could do not to run to the conference room as I wondered where my new office would be and how much more money I would be making. But when I opened the conference room doors, there was only Tom and Steve.

"Hey, Tom, hey, Steve," I smiled. "What's going on? I thought you were in here having a meeting with the board."

"Yes, Jasmine," they chimed in unison. "Why don't you have a seat?" Tom said.

A seat; I didn't need to take a seat, I was perfectly fine standing, easier for me to jump up and down if I was already standing.

"What's going on, guys?"

Their faces both stayed expressionless, but the energy level was so strange, so low. I was beginning to have doubts about my new position. I spun the plush leather chair around and sat down.

Tom started.

"Jasmine, first off, Steve and I would just like to tell you how very happy we've been with the work you've done for the firm. You're a smart and dynamic attorney and we're so proud of the way you've grown into such a promising addition to the company."

"Thank you, Tom. I have worked very hard to get to this point in my life and I owe a large degree of my success to you and Steve for teaching me everything you know." Smiles all around.

Tom continued.

"And we want you to know that the decisions we've made thus far, we haven't taken lightly."

Decisions? Lightly?

"I understand, Tom. What's this about?"

Steve spoke now, his coffee-brown hair slicked back like an Italian mob boss, his pale blue eyes staring at a spot past the top of my head.

"Jasmine, I'm afraid we're going to have to let you go."

I felt like someone had punched me in the gut. "What? Let me go, what do you mean?" I sat there, mouth agape and eyes fixed on the small sunburst design on Tom's tie.

"Jasmine, let us explain."

I sat motionless, refusing to look at either one. It was the same feeling I had had as a little girl, when my mom had to explain to me how Poochie, my black miniature poodle, had died; the same feeling as when Marcus left, but this time there was no coming back for me.

Steve and Tom tried to explain to me how the indictments of Mr. Chadwick and Mr. Schuyler really hurt the company. All of the investments Mr. Chadwick and Mr. Schuyler made and every single European investor involved with the buyout withdrew funding, leaving the company practically bankrupt. Even the money Tom and Steve had received was in jeopardy; the investors were trying to force an injunction to stop payments to them until their partners were found and their trials were over.

I couldn't believe what I was hearing; my thoughts swirled and seemed to muffle Steve's voice.

All the work I'd done, all the hours I spent trying to do the right thing. You've got to be shitting me.

"So Tom, Steve, what are you saying?" I still thought this couldn't be happening; there must be some kind of explanation.

"Were saying that there isn't going to be any partnership, there isn't going to be a future with you at this firm," Tom said quietly.

The sorrow in their eyes was almost enough to make me believe what they were saying. They looked genuinely distraught about the decision they had just made. But my pride kept me completely stone-faced, even though I was overwhelmed with grief and embarrassment. I rose and backed away from the table, turning to head for the big oak double doors.

"Jasmine—wait a minute," Steve said.

"Wait? Wait for what Steve? I've heard enough. I'm no longer needed here so I'm going to go."

"Go? Jasmine, where are you going?"

"You know what, gentlemen?" I paused, looked at my watch and took a moment to collect my thoughts. "There's something the saints in the church used to say when asked where they were going; you wanna know where I'm going? To hell if I don't pray."

I stormed out of the conference room, head held high. I didn't want to give Tom or Steve the opportunity to say another word. I rushed into my office, pulling stuff out of drawers, grabbing books off shelves, throwing everything I owned into the garbage bags I found in the supply closet. Wendy ran in flustered.

"What's going on, Jasmine?"

"Wendy, they fired me."

"What? What do you mean, they fired you? I thought you were up for a partnership."

"Yeah, that's what I thought. WRONG ANSWER!"

"Jasmine, what am I supposed to do?" she asked, choking back tears. "The reason I'm here is because of you."

I stopped dead and turned to Wendy; my anger had nothing to do with her so I wasn't going to take it out on her.

"Baby, I'm sorry. I'm not sure what I'm going to do so there is no way in hell I can tell you what to do. I guess you need to just follow your heart now—something I have been avoiding all my life. I'm going to do whatever it is my heart tells me and I suggest you do the same. Life is way too short to fuck around with dreams and future plans—live in the moment and figure everything else out as it comes."

I kissed her on the cheek and hugged her tight. She looked at me with tears in her eyes and watched as I carried everything I owned out of my old life and into my new. I didn't look back to see who was watching. I just followed my heart to where it wanted to go—and of course it led me to the liquor store.

# Chapter 102

By the time I pulled up in front of the liquor store, my craving for alcohol had subsided, but I forced myself out of the car and into the front door of Marty's Liquor and Spirits. I glanced around at all the different types of alcohol available to me and settled on a bottle of Rosemount Shiraz and bottle of Apothic Red. I took both bottles to the counter and paid; while I waited for my change I noticed a small travel-size corkscrew sitting in a bucket with all kinds of other liquor-store trinkets.

"Hey, can you add this for me?"

"Sure, it's two dollars and fifty cents."

I rummaged around in my purse for some change and gave the clerk two dollar-bills and fifty cents in dimes. I carried the bottles and the corkscrew to the car, thinking about going home, but knowing when I spotted that miniature corkscrew that home was the last place I wanted to be.

I started the car and drove it to the back parking lot. And then it hit me.

What a fucking failure I was. I was nothing; I had nothing and by the looks of things I wasn't ever going to be what God intended me to be. I had failed. I was unemployed, in the latest of a long string of loveless relationships, and living in a place—physically, mentally, and spiritually—that I despised and resented but wouldn't do anything about it. There was really nothing else to live for—except for Sasha. She was the only thing I had of any importance and now I was going to be a disappointment to her.

I cracked open the first bottle; it was a twist-off, so I didn't need the corkscrew. I tilted the bottle back and took two good swallows. The warmth of the fermented grapes expanded in my chest and coursed through my circulatory system. A couple more swigs; now things were a bit clearer. There's no reason to live like this.

I put the car in drive and headed for Lake Nokomis. I could be alone to freely drink and wallow in my own self-loathing without interruption. I would finally, once and for all, rid myself of the constant, excruciating pain in my chest and release the madness that invaded my thoughts.

My thoughts were only of the moment—what I was, and after my visit to the lake, what I was going to be. I drove as fast I could without attracting attention, sneaking swallows when there was no other traffic around. I reached the lake parking lot unscathed and prepared for battle. This was it; God and I were going to have one last confrontation. And if I won, He wouldn't ever have to worry about me asking Him for anything ever again.

I put the car in park, turned off my phone and listened to the radio for a moment, waiting for God to give me a sign, something to tell me what I was about to do was not the answer. Once again, He didn't respond.

I took another deep swig from the bottle, tears streaming down my face, and began apologizing to everyone I loved. I swallowed, the liquor had spoken; it was my time.

I finished the bottle and threw it into some nearby bushes. I got out of the car a little tipsy but walking down the hill toward the lake with confidence. When I reached the water's edge, I stood silently, praying to God in my head, yelling, screaming, and chastising Him—and begging Him to help me.

I kicked off my shoes and set each nylon-covered foot into the water. It was freezing. I looked to God—the least You could do is make the water warm. I walked further into the lake, water now covering the hem of my skirt. As the water rose to chest-level, I waded as fast as I could towards my new life, up to my neck in nasty moss-green lake water.

# I Surrender All

Then I began to think about my family. How would my mother feel? Mama—wow, my mom would be so hurt, this would kill her—and I know she would figure out a way to blame herself. I spoke quietly to her: Mom, it's not your fault; you were the best mother a child could have.

I thought about my brother. My baby brother Darnell, oh my God, Darnell, I love you, he was going to be crushed. I envisioned him at my funeral, head down, crying, so angry with me; so angry. But over time he'd be all right.

Then I realized I was far enough that my feet were no longer touching the murky bottom of the lake and treading water was something I really hadn't done since our water-fluency tests in high school. A sudden wave rose up and slapped me, covering my face and hair in fishy-smelling water. I gagged at the taste and tried to compose myself; I was now swimming—huffing and puffing a little because I was so out of shape.

This was it, I was done; there were literally no more reasons to fight. I lay back waiting for the water to close over me, when a picture of Sasha appeared from out of nowhere. I looked up towards the shore and . . . there she was, calling to me, telling me I had forgotten my shoes.

"Mommy, your shoes. You forgot your shoes." Oh my God, my baby. She was standing there waving, calling me back, looking at me trying to figure out what I was doing without my shoes. Oh God, she won't understand this, I won't get a chance to explain to her why I did this. I got to get to her and explain to her why Mommy is doing this. If I could just get to her to say good-bye I know she'd understand. I began swimming as hard as I could. Sasha, baby, Mommy's coming.

When I came to I was lying face down in the sandy mud of the shore. My clothes were soaked, my hair a wet, tangled mass. I had no idea how long I had been lying there but when I looked over to where I thought Sasha should be, she was gone. I looked around, through the trees and across to the bushes on the other side of the walkway, but she wasn't there either.

I stood up shivering and coughing up lake water. This is crazy; I know I saw her. I looked down at my feet and saw my shoes were there, standing on the soles as if someone had set them there that way. Did I leave my shoes sitting up like this? I thought. I looked around again to see if anyone was around, but there was no one—which was odd, because the lake path was usually full by now, with walkers, runners, and their dogs. I gathered my things and staggered back to the car; amazingly, I still had my keys. Then I got into the car and screamed "Thank you, God" at the top of my lungs for whatever had just happened. I didn't even question it.

I leaned back and rested my head against the headrest. I was exhausted. I was thinking about what I had just done, what had just happened, and shook at the thought of what could have been. The last thing I wanted to do was to look at myself in the mirror, but something summoned me to. "Look at me," someone commanded. I knew it was her.

I closed my eyes, trying to ignore her orders; there was no way I was ready to be to criticized by her again for being so pathetic. "Look at me!" she said again. And this time, something was stirring deep inside of me. I couldn't resist; it was a new feeling, a strong surge of energy I couldn't contain. I grabbed the rearview mirror, turned it toward me, stared as hard as I could, determined to finally come face to face with my true reality.

I couldn't believe what I saw.

There in the mirror, as vibrant as the sunrise, was the most beautiful woman I had ever seen. She looked back at me, smiling. I smiled too, studying her every feature, laughing at what had been there all along.

Her eyes sparkled in the sun's reflection, outshining its rays a hundred times over, giving light to all those with darkened vision. Her skin was caramel-smooth, flawlessly glowing and it blanketed the earth's surface, providing a place of protection and rebirth. Her radiant smile lit up the universe, illuminating all who dared embrace it. And her long, luxurious dreadlocks streamed down either side of her face like a mystical waterfall, washing away all impurities of the land. She was not a metaphor,

# I Surrender All

she was a divine strength raised from the dead and placed in a position to save and nurture the world. She was not a dream or a manifestation, she was real, and I embraced her wholly, smiling, laughing, and crying with her until all my tears were spent. There would be no more self-pity; all that I saw, I was to be and there was no turning back.

This person I had always seen whenever I needed her most was me, was God in me and she appeared whenever I was at my lowest, but I didn't know it. She was with me all along, and now I could finally take my place with her at the helm of my existence.

I looked over at the other bottle of wine on the passenger's seat, patiently waiting for me to open it. As quickly as I could, I uncorked it, and as the sweet aromas escaped from it, I kissed the bottle goodbye and poured the entire contents onto the asphalt next to my car. It didn't matter that the acid from wine was splashing and tattooing my car—material goods meant nothing to me anymore. I was on a new journey to find my true self, to live and love unconditionally, to forever be free of critical thinking, and to finally love myself with an intensity matched by no other.

This was life after death and I was finally here.

The drive home was free of drama, free of traffic and filled with the vibrant beauty of the world I had overlooked before. I noticed trees and flowers I had never seen before, heard birds and saw animals I never knew existed here. I was in heaven.

I got home, showered, washed my hair and changed my clothes; I looked at the mirror, smiling, happy to be alive. I studied my hair and could really see the new growth since it had gotten wet. I hadn't had it relaxed for a while, so the two inches of natural hair at the scalp was very noticeable against the rest of my bone-straight hair. My roots were so nappy and tight; I stood in the mirror contemplating my next move. I'm going to do it.

I walked to the bedroom and looked through the drawers until I found the large household scissors with the bright pink handles, the kind of scissors you use for everything but hair. Andrea is going to kill me, I laughed.

I grabbed a big handful of hair in the back of my head, took the home shears and began cutting. I cut off big chunks of hair and watched them fall lightly to the floor. Before I realized it, I had completely cut off all the hair at my nape, leaving a short, thick, coarse afro, strong and ready to shine. Although it was a bit overwhelming to see the remnants of my past lives lying on the floor like they were struggling for air, trying to survive, I looked down and smiled. Die, I commanded them, because we must begin again.

I had triumphed, releasing myself from my fear of change; my contractual commitment to self-destruction was cancelled and all there was now was the freedom of my energy to expand and explore all that this life had to offer.

I continued cutting; when I was done, the image in mirror of my misshapen afro and my radiant smile was all that mattered. I had shed what was left of my old life and walked into my new. I took a silk scarf from the closet and covered my head. I knew Sasha, Kevin, and my entire family would go crazy if I walked around looking like this. I figured I could get in to see Andrea the next day if I told her it was an emergency.

With the weight of the world off my head and shoulders, I decided to clean up the house, pick Sasha up early from school, have dinner ready when Kevin got home, then just sit and enjoy myself watching them watch the new me.

By the time Kevin got home, I had already gone to the preschool to pick up Sasha. I was in the kitchen cooking when he walked up to me gave me a kiss on the cheek and asked how my day was. He hadn't really noticed anything new about my hair yet because I always wrapped it up at night before I went to sleep. I turned to him and removed the scarf. The look in his eyes was exactly what I expected to see—shock and confusion.

"Jasmine, what did you do to your hair?" He spun me around.

"I cut it."

"I see that. Why?"

"Remember that picture I showed you? I'm going to grow dreadlocks."

"Oh really? And what are the people at your job going to say about that?"

"You know what, forget them and what they think. I'm doing this for me."

"OK, Jaz, what's going on?"

"Kevin, they fired me today."

I looked at him with sadness in my eyes. He pulled me close and hugged me.

"Baby, I'm so sorry. What happened?" he asked with genuine concern.

"I really don't want to talk about it right now, can we talk later? I just want to get this dinner done, feed Sasha, and relax."

"That's cool, baby, I won't bother you." He kissed me on the cheek and went to change for dinner.

I finished cooking, set the table and called for Sasha and Kevin to come and eat. As we sat at the dinner table, Sasha stared at me with a funny little grin on her face.

"Mommy, what happened to your hair?"

"I cut it, baby. I'm thinking about a new hairstyle. You wanna see it?"

"Yes." I reached over and grabbed my purse off the dining room chair and pulled the picture out. I handed it to Sasha and she looked at it curiously.

"Are those braids, mommy?"

"Well, something like that sweetie. They're called dreadlocks."

"Oh, they're long. I like them."

"Thank you, baby, I like them too." I took the picture from here and placed it back in my purse. I looked over to Kevin and he smiled. I wasn't sure if the smile was because of the decision I had made or if he was smiling because of the connection Sasha and I just made. It didn't matter either way. Sasha liked them and that was good enough for me.

## Chapter 103

THE NEXT COUPLE OF YEARS were like a whirlwind. Sasha was just beginning fifth grade, and Kevin and I were at a crossroads, trying to decide if we were better off staying together, unhappy, for the sake of Sasha, or divorcing and being separate for the sake of happiness.

Happiness won. Kevin moved out and into an apartment not far from his job. He told me a graphic arts company in Atlanta had contacted him about pursing a business venture there, and if it all worked out he would be moving. I asked him how he felt about moving so far away from Sasha and he remarked, "Sasha will be fine, she's got you and you have a stable family unit. She can come and visit me anytime she wants."

My reaction to his decision was whatever—I had pretty much been doing everything for Sasha anyway, so him moving to me wasn't a big deal. I knew that's what he always wanted to do, so I let it go. My main concern was Sasha; a child growing up without her father was hard, especially on, girls. I figured I'd just pray everything would be fine; and she could see him when she could.

I told Sasha what her father had in mind and that he would probably be moving to Atlanta sometime soon. She was sad, but very understanding. She had grown to be so mature that the things I would tell her and the things she wanted to talk about became second nature for us. So we talked about everything.

After Kevin moved into his apartment, my mother helped us purchase a townhouse in a suburb north of Minneapolis; it was a two-bedroom, three-level split with a deck and park nearby. Sasha loved it, and so did I. We moved at the end of her fifth grade year. We painted and decorated the house together and we grew together, sharing a friendship and a special mother-daughter bond. She was an amazing child, and I watched as she began to explore the world in a new light.

Me, on the other hand—my new dreadlocks were growing nicely and my life was starting to resemble the one I had always dreamt of.

I had recently taken a job as an attorney for a large nonprofit agency in a southern suburb. It was a long commute, but I had researched the company and it had a squeaky-clean reputation and a great group of employees. Every day at work was a good day; I no longer felt the pressure to perform for people who had never cared for the heart of man, only his money.

I grew especially close to one woman. We had a similar background, growing up in the church; she was the eldest daughter of a bishop and her life story was as crazy as mine.

Often during lunch and after work we would just sit and talk. Ten-, fifteen-minute conversations turned into hours and hours of smooth, easy exchange that represented mutual monumental stability and growth. Claudia Jameson became my confidant, my savior, and my friend.

She had a flawless dark complexion, and I hadn't ever remembered seeing a woman with such dark skin being so vibrant and expressive. Women with darker complexions were not deemed as beautiful as women with lighter complexions. Of course, slavery had a lot to do with this problem, but society and visual media perpetuated it and made it acceptable. It wasn't until supermodel Alek Wek started appearing on the cover of top fashion magazines did America start to notice the beauty in darker skin.

She was also what society had deemed overweight, but her perfect smile, sparkling eyes, and larger-than-life self-esteem were what everyone who worked with her noticed first. But her hair was what really stood out—she had that straight, jet-black silky hair that Asian women are known for. Every day when I entered the office I'd see her smile first, and then notice her hair. This particular day I had to ask—it looked exceptionally beautiful.

"Claudia, what is the deal with your hair?"
"Girl, what do you mean?"
"Your hair looks amazing."
"Thank you." She swung her head and flipped it at me. "I faithfully get it done weekly, and I wrap it up every night."

"Claudia, come on now, there has to be something else—the texture, the shine. Come on, what's up? You got some white folks running around in your blood, don't you?"

"OK, I'm going to let you in on a little secret. Yes, I have white and Hispanic people in my immediate family; in fact my maternal grandmother was half-Mexican."

I laughed. "Oh, that explains it."

I could understand now how her hair did what it did. I even contemplated going back to my old hairstyle to try and get it to look like hers. But when I mentioned it to her, she immediately talked me out of it. She explained to me the journey I was embarking on was just the beginning, and the locks were the key.

"They are beautiful—stay the course."

In the next few years, we settled into our new home; Sasha was busier than ever with friends and dance classes and growing into her teen years, and the world around me finally seemed at peace. I had come into my own.

My spirit blossomed, and as I began to explore music and poetry, my soul grew. I embraced my spirituality with emphasis on graciousness and acceptance; my love for life flowered, with gifts of long-lasting friendships and my locks grew exponentially, cascading down past my shoulders.

But there was still a part of me that was yearned for something I didn't have.

Of course I had met men and dated some, but I soon realized that none of them could offer me what I was seeking, could return what I wanted to give them. I was beginning to worry.

One Friday, Claudia and I sat at the Red Dragon sipping punches, eating curry chicken and teriyaki beef skewers. She could tell that night that when I opened my mouth I had something important I needed to talk to her about. I confided in her about my need for love and my urgency to have a boyfriend, a fiancé, a husband—someone.

"Claudia, tell me, what's your relationship with Anthony is like?"

Anthony was Claudia's long-time fiancé; they were planning to get married in the next year or so. I had met him and he was a nice man, but nothing special, I thought. So sometimes I wondered about their life together, with all the things I thought Anthony was lacking.

"Jasmine, Anthony and I have an understanding. I tell him what to do and he understands he better do it."

We burst into laughter.

"Nah—but for real, Anthony and I are working on our relationship just like everyone else. It's just easier when a man knows his place and stays there."

She took a deep swallow of her drink.

"Where is all this coming from, darling?" she asked me.

"I really don't know. It's like I'm at a standstill when it comes to meeting the right man for me. I feel like I'm cursed, and to be honest, I don't know if I'd know the right man if he were staring me dead in the face.

"Look, sweetie, don't worry about finding a man. God will find him for you, and when God sends a man, you'll know without a shadow of a doubt it's right. You deserve the best, and I will not allow you to settle for less than perfection when it comes to a man to spend the rest of your life with. God knows, I've already spoken to Him and He has shown me in a dream what he looks like and how good he's going to be to you. Oh, and by the way, be looking to have a son for me."

"What? You're trippin'—I ain't having any more kids, Sasha's twelve and I can't see myself starting over now. She's going into seventh grade this year, and I'll be damned if I bring another child into this world."

"Yeah. Yeah, I hear you." She smiled and put a forkful of curry chicken in her mouth.

"Claudia, don't start no shit; I mean it."

"I ain't starting anything. You're going to have a son and the man you have him with is going to be the bomb, you ain't even going to have to worry about the baby. He got it. You wait and see."

"Whatever, I ain't trying to hear you. You're crazy."

I took a swig of my drink, laughing, but actually toying with the possibilities.

There was something about what Claudia had said. I knew deep down inside that I deserved to be in a loving and fulfilling relationship, and I knew that the man of my dreams was out there somewhere waiting for me. But how would I find him? Even more, how would he find me?

There was no question in my mind that the odds were stacked against me. With women outnumbering men two to one, and men unavailable because of jail and/or sexual preference, coupled with those men who consciously and consistently dated outside their race, the number of beautiful black single women was staggering and just seemed to keep growing, year after year. Several friends had moved to states were there was a larger population of black men, and within a year they were in long-term solid relationships that eventually ended in marriage.

But in Minnesota, it was clear that the unfair and completely undeserved lonely plight of black women was rapidly becoming a way of life for most of us.

If I left Minnesota, would I find a loving, secure, confident man to spend the rest of my life with? Or am I single because of me? There was only one way to find out.

Lord, if it be Your will, send me a man who You have deemed proper and right in Your sight, I prayed silently. And allow me to accept him whole-heartedly for what he is through You. Amen.

I looked at Claudia. She knew exactly what had just transpired.

"Don't worry, baby, he's out there. Just be patient."

"I'm trying, I'm really trying."

We finished our dinner, said our goodbyes and headed in opposite directions towards home. I entered the house mulling over all the things Claudia had said, and submitted my search to God, giving it all to Him. Then I waited patiently for the outcome.

## Chapter 104

That fall, Claudia and Anthony were married. It was one of the most beautiful weddings I had attended, and to my surprise, they both looked truly happy. Claudia and I had had so many conversations about Anthony and some of his shortcomings, I guess sometimes I thought she wouldn't go through with it.

I walked through the receiving line, kissing everyone in the wedding party. When I reached Claudia I embraced her and we both shed a few happy tears. Weddings always made me sappy, and I didn't want to make her cry with my random "I love you speech" so I kissed her gently and moved on down the line.

I stood patiently waiting to talk to Anthony, thinking about what words of wisdom I could give him so he wouldn't fuck this up. I couldn't come up with anything on the spot, so I hugged him and just congratulated him, then stepped aside as more guests came down the line to share in the couple's joy and send them messages of happiness.

It was nice to see true love again, and it hit me how long it had been since I'd known anything like it. And how much I missed it.

After the reception, I went to Claudia to say my goodbyes and to wish her bon voyage. They were leaving the next day for Jamaica and I wanted to talk to her briefly before she was swamped with things to do.

"Hey, love, you look beautiful. You know I'm so happy for you," I told her.

"Thank you, baby, I am happy. This was a long road and I'm finally done traveling this path, it's time for a new direction."

It was cool. I fully trusted her intuition, and always followed her lead. She was so strong and so direct. I admired her for that; in fact I loved her for it. I silently thanked God for sending me such a special friend.

"Jasmine, wait—what are doing this weekend?" she asked me as I was turning to leave.

I looked at her, surprised. "Why, girl? You're going on your honeymoon—don't be worrying about me."

"Why don't you come with us?"

I laughed. "Are you crazy? I'm not going with you on your honeymoon."

"Why not? Sasha is in Atlanta with Kevin this weekend, isn't she? And I know you ain't got nothing else to do. Come go with us."

"I don't know, Claudia . . . that seems stupid. I don't want to be a third wheel, tagging along, hanging around you and your new husband. Y'all got some mating time to tend to, what I look like being a part of that?"

"Chick, don't worry about all that, just come with us, I promise you won't be disappointed."

"Claudia, you're crazy. When do you leave?"

"Our flight leaves at six-thirty a.m.—Northwest Airlines. Call and get your ticket and we'll take care of the hotel and resort stuff when we get there." I hesitated again. "Don't worry, girl, I got this all figured out. Just believe and have faith. I got you!"

I really needed a vacation, and the thought of getting down and dirty in Jamaica was an exciting idea, even though I still didn't see how I wasn't going to be in the way of the newlyweds. "All right, let me go home and get packed and try to get this ticket. I'll call you when I got everything straight."

I kissed her and gave her a huge hug. She grabbed my chin and looked at me so earnestly it spooked me a little. I stared back, although I felt a little strange; I knew she had my back, and I also knew there were things about her spirit that were so powerful I dared not question it. This was one of those times I felt I better do what she said.

I drove home wondering how in the world I could go to Jamaica on such short notice.

When I got home, I ran straight to the closet to find my suitcase. I started pulling out all the summer wear I could find, sundresses, skirts, tank tops, sandals, and swimsuits. I smiled at the thought of sunbathing in the Jamaican sun, sipping colorful cocktails poolside while a big, strong, handsome Rasta massaged my shoulders.

It all seemed too surreal, but I had actually known a few friends who had found true love on a beautiful island, so I couldn't help but feel optimistic.

It wasn't that I was naïve, and I knew it might not have been true love, but the stories they told of their wild sexual escapades led me into a euphoric dream-state of erotic fantasy that mimicked love; I was ready to experience for myself. I was in a good place and I welcomed the promise.

# Chapter 105

Arriving in Montego Bay was exhilarating. I was elated by the sheer beauty of all the darker-skinned men and women—shifting bags, directing traffic, basically taking care of business. I loved seeing the entire airport filled with my people working, managing, getting shit done.

As Claudia, Anthony, and I shuffled through the crowd towards customs, I noticed several Jamaican men looking my way. I knew by how feverishly they were working there was no time for conversation, but the thought of them noticing me made me smile inside. Maybe it was the locks, although I was surprised to see that a lot Jamaicans didn't have locks. I guess it was a little dumb of me to think that all the people in Jamaica wore dreadlocks like Bob Marley had.

The sweltering heat of the Jamaican sun hit us as we stepped out of the airport. It had been hot inside the airport, but nothing like this. But the excitement of seeing all these Jamaican people running around kept me awake. I was not going to miss a thing.

I looked around curiously as we waited for our shuttle to arrive, swelling with pride as I watched beautiful black men doing what they needed to do, keeping the tourist trade healthy to keep their economy going.

Jamaica was still considered a third-world country even though it had once been one of the primary agricultural exporters. It was the greed of other nations that forced them into the economic hole they hadn't yet recovered from. The forces of capitalism had ravaged this tiny nation, and judging by how hard people worked here, they were still trying hard just to survive.

## I Surrender All

In the distance, I saw a small line forming of tourists who must have been starving, since no flights served food anymore. The crowd lined up in front of the little wooden shack, smoke billowing out of every crack. I immediately recognized the smell of hickory, coupled with some kind of fruitwood. It was the intoxicating smell I remembered from working at Mr. Whitney's barbecue place; every night I would take that scent home with me in my clothes and in my hair. I hated it then, but it smelled delicious now.

The cook fit my image of a true Jamaican. He had locks like the Rastas' wore—a few big ones that hung practically to his waist, and a couple of wild short ones that sprouted out from under his wrap. His head wrap was, of course, green, gold and black, the colors of the Jamaican flag. And his skin was so black it was almost blue—it looked as if he stayed out in the sun just for the hell of it. I stepped closer to get a better look at him. His eyes were red, and the smoke in his establishment must be causing this, but I figured some of it was due to something totally herbal in nature. He was so efficient, putting together the orders and serving the endless line of customers, smiling and singing a little ditty in his Jamaican dialect; his customers walked away smiling, holding a handful of tinfoil full of meat, bread, and some sort of special sauce. I wanted to go over there myself, but I was on Claudia and Anthony's time so I kept to myself and soaked up the experience from where I was standing.

Meanwhile Claudia had found the man in the booth directing shuttles and was marching over there to see what was up and get our shuttle to the resort in Negril. Getting a van could sometimes be hectic, but it didn't take very long with Claudia at the helm. We had a shuttle pulling up within minutes.

A beautiful chocolate-colored man approached us and took our bags. He introduced himself as Wesley, asked where we were going, and motioned for us to sit wherever we liked. He placed our bags on the luggage rack and closed the door. Anthony had been very quiet since we arrived, maybe because he was trying to take it all in; or maybe Claudia told him up front not to embarrass her. Either way, he didn't say a word.

As we got out of the airport complex, the driver turned around and told us we would be on the road for about an hour and a half, which was totally fine with me—I really wanted to experience all I could since everything about this trip was about me.

I knew I was there because Claudia and her new husband invited me to be. But I had ulterior motives. I was going to find me a man and fall in love just like in all the books and movies where the lonely single woman traveled alone to a beautiful island and the perfect man comes out of the hills to find her and rescue her from her misery. This was my chance and I was going to take full advantage of the opportunity. Shit, first man to come to me right was going to get it. I laughed at myself, knowing damn well my chicken-ass was going to mess it up. But it was fun to fantasize anyway.

The drive to Negril was wild; there was only one highway that went in and out of the other cities, and we had to ride that road for a very long time. Without shame, I peered out the van windows looking for any and everything exciting I could find.

I found excitement, along with admiration, empathy, anger and fear. The real streets of Jamaica were nothing like what they show you on the "Come Back to Jamaica" commercial.

As we drove through the countryside and small towns the driver explained how poverty and economic genocide had left most of the people poor and hopeless. Seeing firsthand how they lived was proof enough that he was telling the truth.

We drove by crowds of men, women and children walking barefoot on dirt roads, sitting in front of small roofless shacks, looking aimlessly into oblivion. I saw the hustlers racing through the traffic-filled streets, towards carloads of tourists, trying to sell whatever they had to sell—fruit, sunhats, trinkets, even marijuana; everyone who needed something had a hustle and no one felt like there was any shame in it. Even the children worked, peddling trinkets on the corners, watching closely for any signals from potential customers that looked like profitable gain. I was stunned, but it was kind of invigorating. Kids in America were so spoiled they would probably die first before having to work as hard as these children were working, no doubt just for simple survival.

When we reached the halfway point the driver let us know that he would be stopping at a little corner store and we could get out and buy a Red Stripe or snacks. Red Stripe? What did he mean? We could buy a beer and drink it in the van on the way to the resort? Claudia and I looked at each other and without a second thought, yelled "Hell yeah, let's stop."

We got out of the van and headed for the small building sitting crookedly on a slope. When we entered, I was surprised to see that they carried a lot of the same products we had in the states. In my naivety, I somehow thought their corner stores would be different from ours.

I walked towards the glass coolers in the back of the store and browsed the selection of beer and wine, rum and soft drinks. He said we could have Red Stripe, so Red Stripe it was. I grabbed two, and Anthony grabbed something else. I handed one of the beers to Claudia and walked the aisles looking for something light to snack on. There were a few kinds of chips I recognized, but all in all the snacky foods were a bit out there—maybe this wasn't exactly like a U.S. corner store after all. I took a bag of U.S.-brand chips and proceeded to the counter to pay. The Jamaican woman standing there was a heavyset woman with a head full of micro braids. She had a Jamaican-print scarf wrapped around her hair and she wore an oversized flower-patterned dress cinched at the waist. She looked at all of our items and rang them up.

"That will be two hundred and forty dollars, please."

"What? Two hundred and forty dollars, are you sure?" I asked.

"Yes. That is in Jamaican money."

"Oh, I don't have any Jamaican money, how much in American?"

"Uh," she took her calculator and calculated the currency change. "It's five dollars and seventy cents."

"Oh, that's better," I gave her six dollars and told her to keep the change. I didn't want to be bothered with trying to figure out if she gave me the right currency in Jamaican money back. I grabbed my beer and chips and headed back to the van to wait for Claudia and Anthony.

The driver was in his seat; I handed my beer to him and he twisted off the top for me. I guess I could have done it myself, but why? I had a strong, handsome Jamaican sitting there waiting to be of assistance.

"Thank you. Are you sure we can drink while you drive?"

"Yeah, mon, no worries, the police don't care too much about it, we got too much other stuff going on for them to stop us for that."

I took my beer and sat back in my seat. A trickle of sweat dripped down the side of my face and I welcomed the cool beer I was now effortlessly slamming down. I was halfway finished when Claudia and Anthony got back in.

"Are we ready to go?" Wesley asked

"Yes, we are." I smiled, feeling a little buzzed.

The rest of the trip was more scenic than the first part. We traveled through exquisite mountainsides and lush, hilly areas full of all sorts of exotic plants and trees in brilliant colors. I was mesmerized by color, as if I were looking into a spinning kaleidoscope. As we neared the resort, a light rain started falling, and I thought how good it would feel if I could just run through it for a while, like a cleansing shower, and watched as people on the streets traipsed through the rain as if nothing had changed.

Where people in the states ran with umbrellas and hid their clothes, shoes and hair from rain showers, the people here welcomed this life-giving force. I felt their reverence too.

We drove through the rain and into a brilliant sunbeam. I turned to watch as the showers we left behind dissipated. As I gazed out the window, a huge rainbow shimmered into being.

Was this miracle for me? I couldn't help but to think that God was here leading me, showing me everything that I needed to see, pointing out what was truly important.

Arriving at the resort, we tipped Wesley and asked if he would be able to take us back to the airport on our date of return. He slipped me his card and told us to just call him when we were ready to go. Then we got out and went in to check in. I allowed Claudia to check in first seeing that they already had reservations. Once Claudia and Anthony were settled I approached the counter and asked the striking woman behind the counter if there were any vacant rooms near Claudia's suite. She smiled and asked me to wait a moment so she could check. I watched as she typed something into a small computer console and made a few phone calls. Her professionalism and grace was impressive. What a wonderful place to live, I thought—everyone is so nice and helpful, there's sun and beautiful scenery all the time, jerk chicken to eat. Shit, if these people don't be careful I might be moving here.

The woman returned and she smiled. She had a room for me. She handed me a key and told my room would be right next to Claudia and Anthony's. I laughed out loud.

"I don't want to be that close. They're on their honeymoon, I don't want to hear all that noise."

Claudia snickered and pinched me on my bare arm. I turned to her, smiling broadly, swung my arm around her neck, and whispered, "Just kidding." She pushed me away and motioned for Anthony to come.

The bellhop took our bags and told us they would all be in our rooms when we got there.

We were impressed with the service thus far, so we decided the first place that needed our attention was the bar. Of course, it was only to see if the bartenders were first-rate like the rest of the staff.

Claudia and I walked through the lobby to the outdoor bar and sat next to each other on the high stools that encircled the bar area. Anthony strolled down towards the clear blue water of the Caribbean. He seemed mesmerized, and neither Claudia nor I had anything to say. Shit, we were in our element and it was time to get it on.

The bartender, fine as hell, reached over the bar and proceeded to kiss my hand. After doing the same to Claudia, he asked us what we were having. My mind went completely blank, but Claudia spoke up and ordered whatever his specialty was.

I looked at him, then at Claudia, and then at him again. "Girl, I'm never leaving this place," I said, laughing. All she could do was shake her head in disappointment; she was married now and I knew at that moment she wished she could take some of them "I do's" back.

I grinned slyly, tapped her on the shoulder and whispered, "Don't worry, dog, I got your back; I'll handle your light work for you."

She was not smiling. I, on the other hand, was grinning from ear to ear.

The bartender returned with two amazing concoctions all fancied up with real flowers and cocktail umbrellas.

"What is this?" I asked.

"It's called Beautiful Black Woman."

We smiled.

"Oh, is it now? Did you just come up with that name?" I asked.

"Yeah, mon, I did," he said, grinning.

Claudia looked at me and decided this was her cue. She picked up her drink and stood up.

"Where you going?"

"I'm going down by the water ... *with my husband.*"

"Ah, damn, how you gonna leave me like that?"

She didn't answer, just sauntered down to the beach, where she slid underneath Anthony's arm. He smiled and kissed her on the forehead.

The bartender looked at me, still grinning. "Is there anything else I can get you?"

Looking him up and down I smirked, "No thank you, I'm fine."

I took my drink and headed for the pool. I wasn't dressed to swim but I wanted to lie out in the sun for a while, work on my Wesley Snipes tan. I turned the chair to face the water and sat there for a moment, mesmerized by my surroundings.

The sun was sparkling off the water, and I took in the whole scene—soft white sand, palm trees, and men, women, and children of all races frolicking happily. I was flooded with a wave of emotion. All the wonderment and glory of this magnificent place had made me think about Sasha and the love I had for her. She was the reason I was alive today and I wished she could have been there with me, sharing in this experience.

I started to cry. I took off my sunglasses and let the tears fall; it seemed so clear now. The presence of the Lord was around me, and I could feel Him shining gloriously down upon me.

"Thank you, God." I knew He knew my heart, but I just thought I had to say it once more, out loud.

I lay back, closed my eyes, and daydreamed. This had to have been the love I had been searching for. I was finally and completely at peace, a presence so strong in me that I vowed to never let leave. All my life I had used God and my religion as a crutch, as my own personal scapegoat—lying, blaming, and lashing out at God, when all along He was right there beside me, guiding me away from danger and leading me towards spiritual growth and clarity; carrying me when I needed Him the most, whether I believed it or not. Now, here on this island experiencing his unconditional love for me, I now knew I had a real chance at happiness. Everything in my life I had ever longed for was a part of me all along. God had given me the exact measure He had given everyone else; the capacity for love, forgiveness and exceeding joy. I had been the one to choose to bury my gifts in a sea of men, alcohol, and materialism.

All of the revelations were coming too fast for me to handle, and it became too much for me to contain; this day was the day of my rebirth. I stood up and ran full force across the gleaming sand and into the water, screaming, crying, laughing, professing my freedom, shedding all the demons and disappointments that held me captive for so long.

I was a wild woman, carrying on as if possessed; I didn't once stop to think about what the people around me would say or do. They looked at me at first as if I was crazy. But when they realized I was just happy, to my surprise many of them ran into the water after me, jumping, yelling and splashing. Feeling pure joy, just like me.

When I caught Claudia's eye, she just blew me a kiss, and mouthed, "I told you so." I ran over to where she was standing, my face drenched in tears, and hugged her with the strength of ten thousand men.

"Thank you, thank you, thank you, thank you," I kept repeating. We laughed and cried together as if there were no tomorrow. Anthony didn't say a word; he didn't know what had just happened, but he knew it was right.

You see, I *had* what I needed to survive; God with his infinite wisdom and grace had blessed and commissioned me to achieve the most important thing in life: self-love, self-acceptance, and the sheer joy of knowing I was loved—not just by my family and friends, but by the one true lover of all. Surrendering all to His will, letting go of the past, and waiting patiently for the future—living in the moment was what I needed to change my life forever.

My life . . . yes, my life was now in order and I was set to forge ahead into unbounded joy. I surrendered all to God, receiving His gifts of love and acceptance. I surrendered all to the universe, acquiring unlimited strength and perseverance. I surrendered all to my hopes and dreams of a future built on passion for life; and with arms raised, I waited to receive my true gift: Me.

# Epilogue

Looking back, I realize that all the drama and tribulations I encountered on this journey were of my own doing. Blaming my issues on men was not exactly true. Someone can only take advantage of you if you allow them to.

Most of my problems stemmed from my inability to separate the faults of the men in my life, from the emotions I felt for them. Of course the men who professed their love for me may not have recognized my insecurity and need for acceptance as an issue for them to resolve, but at the time I thought they should have known it. I took for granted what I had been taught as a child: Find a man to love you and make you happy. But no one can "make" you happy; you have to find happiness and love within yourself before you can ever have a chance of loving anyone else.

Because we as women are the caregivers, the nurturers, and the child-bearers of this world, evolution has deemed us an integral part of how this world should be run. But if women don't recognize their place in the universe, the paradigm shifts and creates a cycle of self-destruction that is hard to recover from. Lack of self-respect and self-worth causes the nurturing nature of a woman to spiral into a place of ultimate degradation, allowing her mind, body, and soul to be used for the pleasure of others, while she struggles with guilt, shame, and self-loathing.

During my suffering, it was never men who brought me to that distant and painful place. It was always me. I sabotaged my own life by being less than what God had created me to be. Blaming a man, or men, was always the easy part, and when I actually took a full-frontal look at myself, what I saw was never their fault at all. Looking in the mirror and seeing a shadowy, distorted image wreaked havoc on my conscious mind, so drugs, alcohol, and the attention of men were a way for me to see a different view of myself—or better yet, not to see myself at all, ever.

I was looking at myself through my own eyes and not through God's, and it almost cost me my life. I never wanted to accept God's perception of me, and thinking about God's view of me, and what I thought must be His disappointment in all of my failings, kept me from seeing the truth. The truth is that His love for me superseded my hate and disgust for myself. It took a life-altering encounter with Him—in fact it took a number of life-altering encounters—to finally realize that no man or liquor bottle could ever replace the feeling I got from wholly surrendering all to the most high. His love is a powerful and unyielding force, and if you can stand even a fraction of its glory, then life is surely worth taking a chance on. Happiness within was what I had been searching for; finally finding it when I looked in the mirror was the true satisfaction I craved. My own strength, my own destiny allowed me to experience true love, in love with myself for the very first time.

CPSIA information can be obtained
at www.ICGtesting.com
Printed in the USA
BVHW031813180321
602933BV00017B/59